AVENGERLAND REVISITED

The Definitive Guide to
The Avengers on film

edited by Rodney Marshall and JZ Ferguson

© Copyright 2015 Rodney Marshall, *Out There Publications*
(Essays are individually owned by specific writers as indicated in the text)

About the editors

Rodney Marshall is the son of *Avengers* script-writer Roger Marshall. He has written and/or edited eight books about this iconic 1960s television drama. He has also produced critical guides to the BBC's space opera *Blake's 7*, the ITC series *Man in a Suitcase* and the 1980s Granada TV drama *Travelling Man,* in addition to the first full-length study of Ian Rankin's *Inspector Rebus* novels, *Blurred Boundaries*. He lives in Suffolk and South West France.

JZ Ferguson is a long-time fan of *The Avengers* and *The New Avengers* in all of their various and sundry incarnations (comics, novels, radio, et al.). She has contributed chapters to the four previous volumes in *The Avengers on film* series: *Bright Horizons, Mrs. Peel, We're Needed, Anticlockwise* and *Avengerland Regained.* She is joint-editor of *The New Avengers* and Definitive Guide volumes, and contributed a guest essay to *Man in a Suitcase: A Critical Guide.* She has also written for the website *The Avengers Declassified*. She lives in Canada.

The Avengers on film collection:
Bright Horizons (Volume 1: Emma Peel monochrome)
Mrs. Peel, We're Needed (Volume 2: Emma Peel colour)
Anticlockwise (Volume 3: Tara King)
Avengerland Regained (Volume 4: *The New Avengers*)
Avengerland Revisited (Volume 5: The Definitive Guide)

In a year which has seen the passing of the series' defining on-screen presence, Patrick Macnee; the show's main writer, Brian Clemens; and one of the two men who provided the initial season with its innovative direction, Don Leaver, this book is dedicated to their artistic achievements.

My thanks – once again – to Jaz Wiseman for creating the book cover and to JZ Ferguson for her editing, proof-reading, inspiration, and positive spirit.

'*The Avengers* is at its best when it employs subtlety, rather than slapstick, where formula is played or toyed with, rather than simply adhered to in a predictably formulaic fashion. As viewers, we expect certain ingredients to be served up, but we also want to be surprised, challenged and taken out of our comfort zone.' (Rodney Marshall)

'Label *The Avengers* at your peril because the minute you do so, along comes a scene or episode which throws the category out of the window and illustrates the impossibility of neatly filing away the show in a one-dimensional dramatic drawer.' (Rodney Marshall)

'I've always preferred finding depth in shallow waters. *The Avengers* is happy to be read, and there is plenty to read. It leaves it up to us to take what we will from it.' (Sunday Swift)

FOREWORD: THE 'TIMELESS APPEAL' OF *THE AVENGERS*

Has *The Avengers* dated? As fans, our automatic response is 'no'. Many would say that one of the main reasons they love the series is because it is a truly timeless piece of television, one that the ensuing decades have treated kindly, even though half a century has passed since the series made the jump from videotape to film.

We're deluding ourselves somewhat, of course. *The Avengers has* aged, though it does possess one very important saving grace: it was filmed in the sixties, a decade almost universally adored for its iconic fashions, music, cars, hairstyles, cultural impact, social movements, and all-round ethos. It is certainly not subject to the same derision heaped upon other decades, including *The New Avengers*' natural environs, the seventies, although that era, too, has come in for well-deserved reassessment in recent years. But the sixties continue to be granted a free pass from disparagement; designers continue to be inspired by the decade, and musicians still draw upon it. *The Avengers* has undoubtedly benefited from this enduring love for the decade that played host to its original six seasons, as have many of its contemporaries. Those who grew up in the sixties often look back upon it fondly, and those that missed the entire phenomenon by an accident of birth sigh enviously and try to soak up as much of its legendary cool by proxy as they can.

However, nostalgia and ardour only extend so far; time has undoubtedly left its mark upon the series. Some of the science espoused by the characters is now woefully out-of-date (or was on shaky ground even at the time). The technology is primitive, with huge, room-filling computers or even Purdey and Gambit's consoles from *Angels of Death* now slow and unwieldly relics compared to today's sleek lap-tops and tablets. The politics have shifted, and the threats with them, with brand new concerns dominating international headlines. The fashions, while still coveted, would garner double-takes if worn on the streets today, even with the current penchant for retro chic. Some seasons were filmed/viewed in black and white, not as an artistic, avant-garde choice, but simply due to limits in funding or technology. The special effects are simpler and the use of stunt doubles often glaringly obvious. The casual treatment of smoking and drink-driving flies in the face of public health warnings. [1] And how many plotlines would have been wrapped up in a fraction of the time had Steed and co. been able to stay in touch via mobile phone? (Yes, Steed sometimes had a carphone, and Emma, Steed, Purdey, and Gambit all employed radios or walkie-talkies on occasion, but never quite so liberally, and certainly not with the same degree of success). I hasten to add that none of these observations is intended as a criticism of the series; indeed, part of the reason we love the show is precisely because it is a time capsule of a particular era, one we enjoy visiting vicariously because it is so different from our own. Others delight in the idiosyncrasies of this particular era of television history, or relish the opportunity it provides to recapture a significant period in their personal history. However, this begs the question: if *The Avengers* is a product of its time, can it still be timeless?

The answer, of course, is 'yes'. This is because every television series, regardless of its era or country of origin, must possess certain essentials if it is to be successful, both at the time and in the years to come. For example, a clever, witty script never goes out of fashion, nor does a fiendishly well-executed plot. *The Avengers* had both in spades, featuring crackling dialogue and *bon mots* aplenty, many of them remaining quote-worthy to this day. And a baffling, intriguing mystery or a tense thriller sequence will captivate regardless of whether the story is shot through with Cold War politics or revolves around an antiquated piece of technology. *The Avengers* proved this time and again, all while eschewing today's predilection for, and indeed reliance on, explicit sex and violence to persuade the audience to tune in. A modern audience still wants to see how their sixties and seventies heroes manage to escape their latest predicament, or unravel the mystery of the week, and the decades melt away in the process.

Speaking of the characters, *The Avengers* also owes an immeasurable debt to its leads, who breathed life into the words on the page and spun them into their remarkable performances as stylish spies and sophisticated 'talented amateurs'. No matter how strong the plot, an audience will be hard-pressed to follow the story if the leads do not prove to be interesting travel companions, and there can be no sense of peril if the viewers are ambivalent about whether the principals live or die. Nor can we delight in the sparkling, dynamic interplay between the stars if we are not invested in each of them as individuals. Many series have succeeded or failed over the years due to the audience's emotional investment (or lack of) in its main characters, but *The Avengers* was blessed with an ever-evolving cast, all of whom managed to strike a chord with at least part of the series' fanbase, ensuring that at least a few of its eight seasons lingered on in the collective consciousness long after the cameras stopped rolling.

In a testament to its prescience, *The Avengers* also 'future-proofed' itself to an extent. It did so most notably through its centuries-spanning format, which partnered a forward-looking, modern woman with a man infused with old-world charm, and then placed them on an equal footing in a world that was willing to hazard some fairly-accurate predictions about the direction everything from science and technology to gender roles would take in the next few decades. And then there was Diana

Rigg's pioneering status as the first actress on television to don a miniskirt!

While these factors all undoubtedly play a part in the series' enduring success, perhaps the best indicator of *The Avengers'* timelessness is that its influence is felt everywhere in the present media landscape. *The Avengers* may not have single-handedly invented the idea of the intelligent action heroine, but it certainly played a significant role in (re)defining it for the 20th century, especially on television, and in normalising it to the extent that such characters are now a familiar fixture in all types of media. The likes of Cathy Gale, Emma Peel, Tara King, and Purdey paved the way and set the standard for the portrayal of female television characters that were as mentally and physically capable as their male counterparts, one that has been replicated and built upon by everyone from Anne Francis in 1965's *Honey West* to 2015's Kiera Cameron in *Continuum.* And despite her comic book roots, every *Avengers* fan cannot help but look at the modern iteration of Black Widow from the Marvel *Avengers* franchise, a redhead in a black catsuit, and think of Emma Peel (for the record, the television series laid claim to the name two years before it was co-opted by Marvel).

On a related front, the show also made strides in the portrayal of male/female relationships, featuring truly equal dynamics between individuals that transcended gender and sex (in both senses of the word), and instead were founded on mutual respect, with liberal amounts of humour, affection, and the occasional clash of viewpoints mixed in for good measure. While a series focusing on a male/female pairing was hardly unprecedented, *The Avengers* set the tone for those relationships going forward, with similar two-handers becoming standard in series long after it ceased production. Eighties shows such as *Hart to Hart, Remington Steele,* and *Moonlighting* undoubtedly owed something to *The Avengers*, and fans of the nineties series *The X-Files* have often compared the Mulder/Scully relationship to that of Steed and Peel.

The Avengers has also left its mark on genre, ironically by refusing to be confined to one. What started out as a straight-forward crime drama with a touch of espionage on the side quickly evolved into a series encompassing everything from science-fiction to comedy. Other series, including *The Avengers'* own contemporaries, also dabbled in wildly different genres, but not with the same breadth and frequency. The late, great Douglas Adams, discussing his excellent novel *Dirk Gently's Holistic Detective Agency*, called it a 'thumping good detective-ghost-horror-whodunnit-time travel-romantic-musical-comedy-epic.' Similarly, *The Avengers* could be described as a thumping good spy-science fiction-drama-thriller-horror-comedy-parody-satire-crime-action/adventure-telefantasy- social commentary-mystery series, so varied and diverse are its plots, so difficult is it to classify without excluding one or more stories within its broad canon. Can we trace the current predilection for one-off musical, comedy, alternate universe, or fourth-wall breaking episodes in today's series to *The Avengers'* barrier-smashing genre legacy?

The series was also something of a trailblazer on the production side of the equation. The freedom afforded by the switch from videotape to film allowed the series to up the ambitiousness of its production values, and the series adopted its legendary credo to treat every episode like a mini-movie. The result was a consistently high standard in production design: eye-catching, beautifully-designed sets; superior direction; well-choreographed action sequences; a seemingly-endless parade of custom-made, trendsetting fashions modelled by the leads, often created by established (or on the cusp of the same) designers; high-profile guest stars; and an expansive library of music encompassing many cues written especially for particular episodes. Today, many high-budget series are typified by slick, glossy sets; star-casting from the world of cinema; eye-poppingly elaborate action sequences; Oscar-winning directors; and a wardrobe sourced directly from the most fashionable design houses, but *The Avengers* achieved the same long before it was in vogue, and with a comparatively small budget at its disposal.

Over the years, there have been multiple attempts to revive *The Avengers* for the big and small screens. While radio, novel, and comic book adaptations have met with modest (or significant) success, others, namely the 1971 stage production, the 1978 'American *Avengers*' pilot *Escapade,* and the notorious 1998 movie, floundered badly. Other projects stumbled at the start line, with the likes of *The First Avengers Movie*, *The Avenging Angel*, and *Avengers International* never making it past the concept/script stage. There are innumerable reasons for these failures, encompassing everything from insufficient financing, to poor scripting, to studios and production teams that singularly failed to understand the very essence of the property they were attempting to adapt. But perhaps there is another explanation for the absence of a 21st century *Avengers* series, which has failed to materialise despite undoubtedly crossing the minds of many a producer or scriptwriter influenced, directly or indirectly, by the series. The key word here is 'influenced'. *The Avengers* was a trailblazing series in every sense of the word, and has unquestionably left its mark on many shows. Leaving aside the (not insignificant) questions of who could adequately fill Patrick Macnee's Chelsea boots in the role of John Steed, not to mention the formidable task of casting a new *Avengers* girl, there is the question of what it would look like. So much of what made *The Avengers* unique is now fused into the DNA of countless series airing today, so creating a series that is indistinguishable from so many of its contemporaries would be redundant. Certainly, one could cast a John Steed and an Emma Peel, set them off on a series of bizarre adventures, and call it *The Avengers*, but would that be any more successful than a fresh series incorporating some of those same ingredients? And anyway, *The Avengers* was always about moving forward, about expanding its horizons; a straight remake would seem stultifying in comparison. At the same time, without the series' tenuous elements of continuity, provided by Macnee's Steed and the filmed episodes' creative team, any new development would be so much of a departure that it may as well be another show entirely, one free to grow and evolve as it sees fit, aided but not shackled by the kernel of *Avengers* magic it carries within. For that reason, the wisdom of creating an *Avengers* remake is questionable, but no matter. [2] The series will continue to be relevant and live on subtly, through its influence and its legacy, in a hundred different series. The showrunners of those series may or may not be cognizant of the debt that they owe for their latest success, but they will owe it just the same. And for that reason, *The Avengers* will remain timeless. See you in another fifty years.

© JZ Ferguson

1. I think that many modern day viewers enjoy the (now) non-political correctness of *The Avengers*, as demonstrated by the critical and popular appeal of a series such as *Life on Mars*.
2. The fact that the series was, paradoxically, both of its time and 'timeless' helps to explain why the idea of a re-make is highly questionable.

CONTENTS

Preface: *Avengerland Revisited* Rodney Marshall (pages 16-25)

Television, *The Avengers* & Cultural Revolution Rodney Marshall (26-31)

***The Avengers* and the Cold War** Dan O'Shea (32-38)

Subversive Champagne & The Art of Murder Rodney Marshall (39-46)

Graveyards Rodney Marshall (47-52)

The Country House Trap Rodney Marshall (53-62)

Main Title Sequences JZ Ferguson (63-74)

Teasers Rodney Marshall (75-82)

Tag scenes Piers Johnson (83-89)

Set Design and Locations Darren Burch (90-103)

***New Avengers* Set Design and Locations** Rodney Marshall (104-109)

Music JZ Ferguson (110-124)

Cars Piers Johnson (125-129)

Fashions Frank Hui (130-140)

Script-writers Rodney Marshall (141-150)

Directing *The Avengers* Darren Burch (151-165)

Silk and Steel: The Personalities of John Steed Lauren Humphries-Brooks (166-191)

And yet: 'Swinging self-invention', fetishisation, commodification, and aestheticism of Dandy Emma Peel by Sunday Swift (192-207)

Tara King Frank Hui (208-214)

Mother Piers Johnson (215-221)

Purdey JZ Ferguson (222-235)

Mike Gambit JZ Ferguson (236-252)

Eccentrics Margaret J Gordon (253-261)

Hand of the Wind: For Queen and Country - Martial Arts in *The Avengers* James Speirs (262-274)

Miss King, You're Needed! or Hedonism & Leather Boots: *The Avengers*' **success in France** Eric Cazalot (275-286)

An Insider's View Roger Marshall (287-290)

Avengers **Remembered** Raymond Austin (aka Ray Austin) (291-295)

Patrick Macnee: 'The World's Favourite English Gent' Alan Hayes (296-301)

Afterword: **Monochrome versus Colour; Emma versus Tara;** *New* **Avengers or New** *Avengers*: **eternal internet debates** Rodney Marshall (302-311)

Appendices:

The Avengers **and the Cold War** Rodney Marshall (312-320)

And Soon the Darkness/See No Evil: **Brian Clemens' post-*Avengerland*** Rodney Marshall (321-337)

Contributors (338-341)

Bibliography (342-344)

The 109: Filmed *Avengers* episode list (345-348)

AVENGERLAND REVISITED: A PREFACE

And now for something completely different.

In the previous four volumes of *The Avengers on film*, each and every one of the 109 filmed episodes of the original series and its reincarnation as *The New Avengers* is explored and analysed. These books offer a chronological examination of a television drama which continued to evolve unevenly from a mid-1960s film noir/Op Art fusion of realism/surrealism, through the candy-coloured, camp Pop Art of self-referential comic strip, to a psychedelic action adventure in the Tara King era. The latter recycled and reworked previous elements while adding its own unique stamp. Its rebirth in a mid-1970s context offered us a new blend of tradition and modernity which, in a sense, the original show had always tried to provide.

Just as *The Avengers* blurred the boundaries between existing genres – light entertainment and serious, subversive drama; sci-fi, spy-fi and spoof-fi, etc. – *Avengerland Revisited* seeks to blur the boundaries between the episodes themselves. The idea is to break away from the concept of 109 separate mini-films and, instead, explore the threads which help weave *The Avengers'* pattern or formula. What makes up the parallel universe of *Avengerland* is a fascinating mix of ingredients which are present – albeit in different measures – throughout the Peel/King/*New Avengers* eras. They are, of course, to be found in embryonic form in the videotape era as well. [1] The global popularity of the show reflects the unique blend which makes up *Avengerland*: the Avengers themselves, diabolical masterminds and other eccentric guest characters; the sets and locations; the fashions, cars and music; the innovative writing and direction. Naturally, there is plenty of cross-over between these ingredients. Part of the joy of this book is the ways in which we can draw out connections between different eras, episodes, characters and categories. Even if some ingredients are more important than others, the *Avengers* recipe relies on all the elements explored here. There is a fascinating 'otherness' about *Avengerland,* but it is also a product of its ever-changing social context: the emergence of television as a cultural hub or touchstone, a boom in consumerism, the 'white heat' of technology, the Cold War, etc. The series explores and interacts with these historical threads and they are examined in this book.

Avengerland is the beating heart of the series on film. It is a wonderfully weird world which I looked at in both *Subversive Champagne* and the earlier volumes of this *Avengers on film* book series:

'It is any physical space – location or set – which has one foot in the real world but one elsewhere. It might appear, from the outset, to offer a normal backdrop: a train station, churchyard, City bar or country pub. However, public spaces have been emptied of normality and the mundane. We have entered a parallel universe; a seemingly timeless, two dimensional never-never land.
Sometimes *Avengerland* promises a romanticised, green-and-pleasant land. This sense of arcadia is never allowed to establish itself, however. It is immediately cut through by unexpected or surreal acts of violence. The emptiness, and/or lack of ordinary people, simply adds to the sense of surrealism, providing an unsettling atmosphere. *Avengerland* becomes more a state of mind than a geographical location.
As the series moved on to film, unusual locations became the norm; the fantasy elements were taken to greater extremes. This heightened sense of *Avengerland* is carefully contrived and controlled by the writers and production team, ensuring that *The Avengers* offers us a wonderfully disconcerting, alternative Britain full of eerie locations peopled only by

extraordinary characters. Anything seems possible in this bizarre new land/cityscape. This *Avengerland* provides the audience with a disconcerting, constantly shifting, perverse world which appears to both reinforce *and* undermine the status quo, questioning our notions of capitalism, espionage, scientific progress, 'Englishness', gender and sexuality. It is, I would suggest, a world of 'subversive champagne' a phrase used by Emma Peel in *The Murder Market* (cut from the final filmed version).' (*Subversive Champagne*, pp. 17-19) [2]

Avengerland defamiliarises the viewer. It is a fictional world which, fifty years on, continues to fascinate, unsettle, delight and surprise, its unreality drawing us in for what, paradoxically, we are usually happy to accept as a 'genuine' dramatic experience. Playful or absurd displays of artificiality/self-referentiality do not deter us (as viewers) from immersing ourselves in the bizarre – at times nightmarish – surrealism of *Avengerland*.

I suggested, in my conclusion to *Subversive Champagne*, that *The Avengers* is capable of taking the banal and ordinary and transforming it into something extraordinary. All it takes is a spinning bicycle wheel, an overflowing petrol pump and the whine of an unseen milk float to turn a bleak RAF station into a magically surreal realm in which anything is possible. This is why I described *Avengerland* as more a state of mind than a geographical location. The setting is only part of the recipe. [3]

A 'classic' *Avengers* episode requires the fine blend of ingredients I referred to earlier. It might be described in culinary terms: a base created by a well-crafted script, seasoned by carefully-selected lead and guest actors, decorated with quirky sets, cooked up by an inspirational director, and served with a Laurie Johnson score to fit the mood. A mix of 'timeless' and fashion-conscious clothes and cars adds to the visual feast. When the ingredients are perfectly blended and stirred we get those 'four bowler' episodes examined in the previous *Avengers on film* books. By contrast, the following chapters explore the ingredients themselves which went into those 109 mini-films, those creative cocktails.

Some of the essays contained in this book centre on a specific character; others are more general chapters. Some contributors embrace *The New Avengers* within their writing; others have ignored it. This choice was left up to the individual. The endnotes which appear after each chapter are my own or those of JZ Ferguson as editors.

JZ Ferguson's **foreword** reminds us how important the 1960s context is: 'Those who grew up in the sixties often look back upon it fondly, and those that missed the entire phenomenon by an accident of birth sigh enviously and try to soak up as much of its legendary cool by proxy as they can.' She also stresses how the series' witty dialogue, clever plots and forward-thinking gender dynamics offer a 'timeless appeal'. Her exploration of the **main titles** examines the ways in which the show's revamping of its title sequences is 'in keeping with *The Avengers*' credo of constant reinvention.' I particularly like her suggestion that the main titles offer us 'the essence of *The Avengers*, distilled into a minute or so of footage.' She also invites us to consider the potentially surreal 'otherness' of the titles. **Purdey** is seen as a character who enables *The Avengers* superwoman to evolve once again, this time into a fascinatingly flawed but strong and believable female protagonist. Her relationships with Gambit and Steed are explored in depth. **Mike Gambit** is, arguably, the series' most complex and rounded character. The chapter dedicated to him explores his positive yet also somewhat melancholic character, as well as Gareth Hunt's dedication to making the part 'work'. I find it hard to believe that any critic or fan knows this character better. The chapter on **music** explores both the main themes and the incidental cues and scores. JZ Ferguson differentiates between themed and character scores, as well as examining the paradox that recycled material in Season 6 tends to have a negative effect on the viewer if written originally for an earlier episode, while recurring pieces are successful when employed as 'connective tissue'.

Piers Johnson's chapter on *Avengers* **cars** examines how the series' careful evocation of 'an air of archetypal Britishness, indeed a Britain that may only have existed on chocolate boxes and in story books...extended to the vehicles we see on screen.' He also explores how the leads' vehicles reflect a dandy chic/emancipated modernity polarity. His exploration of **tag scenes** examines the evolution of these 'add-ons' throughout the show's history. His essay on **Mother** looks at both the lighter and darker shades to his character. He asks us to wonder about the character's back story, while calling into question some viewers' desire to label Mother as being gay.

Darren Burch's chapter on **sets and locations** examines the ways in which these evolved throughout *The Avengers*' history, culminating in the wonderfully surreal Tara era sets. Regardless of the specific season, they always 'give the series a unique visual flavour.' As he suggests, the sets – as much as anything else – mark out the show as different from other 1960s series. Ultimately, they often make little sense in terms of realism, yet this fits perfectly with the increasingly fantastic nature of *Avengerland*. His chapter **Directing The Avengers** explores an area in which the show excelled even in the initial Dr. Keel season. He examines both the techniques employed and the evolutionary nature of the series' in-house style.

Alan Hayes' homage to **Patrick Macnee** explores his other roles, but he understandably centres on that which has made him a global icon: 'That one role, played to perfection week-to-week for a decade and then some, has caused him to be remembered, loved and admired for half a century.' As most critics and fans avow, no one could have played the part of John Steed better.

Frank Hui's essay on **Tara King** offers a wonderfully balanced exploration of 'the most polarising character to come out of the show and [one who] continues, even today, to be a source of heated debate amongst its ardent followers.' Frank explores the **fashions** of the show from Cathy Gale's leather through to the Purdey bob, examining how the outfits reflect the characters but also provide a cutting edge to *The Avengers*, adding 'depth and enjoyment' to the spectacle.

I met **Eric Cazalot** at an *Avengers* get-together in Paris in October. He is one of the leading European experts on the series. Here he explores the popularity of ***Bowler Hat and Leather Boots*** in France, examining the cultural history of the show – broadcasting, critical reception, popularity, video and DVD release – before asking why this British show continues to appeal to French viewers. His informative essay appears both in my translation and in its original form.

The 2015 passing of Brian Clemens left **Roger Marshall** as the only surviving multiple-episode writer from both the videotape and Peel eras. In **An Insider's View**, he responds to a number of questions I put to him about the series, including the show's unique qualities and Patrick Macnee's defining role.

In ***Avengers* Remembered**, **Raymond Austin** also offers an insider's view, with some of his recollections of different eras of the show, including *The New Avengers*. He praises Brian Clemens and Patrick Macnee as representing the heartbeat of the *Avengerland* universe.

In many respects, **Lauren Humphries-Brooks'** chapter on **John Steed** provides the centrepiece for this critical jigsaw. It offers us a close examination of a complex, contradictory character. She takes us back to the Cathy Gale seasons; after all, unlike Emma Peel, he did not appear from nowhere at the start of the filmed era. Cathy is viewed as a 'moral compass', helping to trim off his cynicism, which is seen as one of his many 'layers of concealment'. Steed and Mrs. Peel are a 'complimentary duo', their 'affinity' reinforcing Steed's character as 'the image of a traditional male with distinctly progressive views.' Tara King's arrival sees Steed forced into a more traditional role as a chivalric or 'heroic' knight. The need to protect those close to him manifests itself in an angrier, bitter character. Lauren suggests that 'the near-fatherly role he occupied with Tara comes to fruition in *The New Avengers*' where Steed is now a wise, mature man, but one who is tired out by espionage and for whom 'the past is a source of danger and of sorrow.' She argues that 'Steed's sexual love of women does not contradict his equally apparent feminism – rather, they become complementary aspects of his character.' In addition to exploring his relationships with each of his partners, aspects of his evolving personality are examined: his 'dualism', 'class fluidity', 'feminism' and attitude to violence. This chapter may well represent the definitive word on Steed.

Sunday Swift has tackled the most intellectual and challenging figure in *The Avengers*, **Emma Peel**, and her academic approach to the task mirrors the character. She explores how Peel is 'objectified' as a 'commodity', to be bought both by the gaze of male viewers and the money of female fashion shoppers. Sunday asks whether Emma Peel is in control of her 'surface image'. Drawing on the infamous *A Touch of Brimstone*, she argues that Peel is as emancipated a Dandy as Steed is.

Margaret J Gordon investigates the wild array of **eccentric guest characters** who pop up in *Avengerland*. She examines how these can be categorised and what they represent in terms of a typically English sense of humour. Her exploration brings out their heroic qualities, often hidden beneath the absurdity.

James Speirs places *The Avengers*' balletic display of **martial arts** within the historical context of the disciplines themselves and their use in literature, including *Sherlock Holmes* and *James Bond*. The fighting in each era of the series is explored and he argues that these costumed spectacles are a key element in the successful formula.

Dan O'Shea's exploration of the **Cold War** centres on the series' comic portrait of Russian characters and asks us to decide whether this gentle satire reflects a growing belief that politicians behind the Iron Curtain did not pose the threat that many had feared they did a decade earlier.

In my own chapters I have explored a range of topics: drawing on Dominic Sandbrook's ground-breaking social history books, I have contextualised *The Avengers* in terms of the 'white heat' of a technologically-driven, consumerist **cultural revolution**, particularly television's role; like Dan, I have looked at how the **Cold War** is explored in light-hearted, playful fashion throughout the series, but have suggested that perhaps this approach hides a cautionary message; **graveyards** are examined as a leitmotif; the **Country House trap** is a recurring theme in the filmed seasons and connects the series to a rich cultural history; **teasers** are an example of 'commercial serendipity', not unlike the financial need to film Season 4 in black and white, and they provide a fascinating spectacle and structural challenge; I have sought to re/define the term 'subversive champagne' and the ways in which the series both defies genre classification and aesthetically displays a

Hitchcock-esque '**art of murder**'. My chapter on **script-writers** explores their unique position in the series' food chain while also briefly exploring individuals. I have offered a brief chapter on *The New Avengers'* **sets and locations** to supplement Darren Burch's essay on those of the original series. In the Afterword I have explored and reviewed some of the most controversial internet **debates** among fans and critics. Finally, in an appendix, I have stepped out of *Avengerland* – in theory anyway – in order to examine two remarkable films which Brian Clemens created after the Tara King era ended and before his return to the small screen with *Thriller*, *The New Avengers* and *The Professionals*. Both ***And Soon the Darkness*** and ***See No Evil*** contain fascinating echoes of *Avengerland*.

There has been some questioning by readers of my use of 'season' rather than 'series' to define each era or run of *The Avengers*. After all, in the UK each vintage was originally called a 'series'. However, given that the show, in its entirety, is a television *series*, I prefer to use the more clear-cut or unambiguous term 'season', and it seems to naturally fit the idea of a programme which was constantly changing. Individual episode titles appear in italics – rather than in inverted commas – to highlight the film-like qualities of each one and its treatment in these five volumes.

It leaves me to thank the twenty-two writers who have contributed to these books: Raymond Austin, Darren Burch, Eric Cazalot, Denis Chauvet, Richard Cogzell, Sam Denham, Cindy Dye, JZ Ferguson, Bernard Ginez, Margaret Gordon, Alan Hayes, Frank Hui, Lauren Humphries-Brooks, Piers Johnson, Matthew Lee, Roger Marshall, Dan O'Shea, Mark Saunders, James Speirs, Frank Shailes, Sunday Swift, and Jaz Wiseman. *The Avengers on film*'s groundbreaking volumes only exist because of the individual and collective enthusiasm, not to mention the expertise, of our global band of writers.

Avengerland Revisited has provided the biggest challenge of them all, in attempting to offer a 'definitive' guide. In a year which has seen the passing of the series' defining on-screen presence, Patrick Macnee, the show's main writer, Brian Clemens, and one of the two men who provided the initial season with its innovative direction, Don Leaver, this book is dedicated to their artistic achievements. *Avengerland Revisited* can be enjoyed without reading the previous instalments. Just like any *Avengers* episode!

© Rodney Marshall, December 2015, Suffolk, UK

1. Cathy Gale is explored in a number of the essays, despite the emphasis in this book being on the filmed seasons. Her story is, after all, an integral part of the pre-history of *The Avengers* on film.
2. This citation has been cut in order to centre on the crucial aspects of *Avengerland* as a term.
3. *Avengerland* as a term suggests a physical space or place. However, if the setting is the key ingredient, it requires the writer, props, actors/characters, music score and director to weave the magic. *Avengerland* only comes alive when these are mixed and merged, shaken and stirred.

TELEVISION, *THE AVENGERS*, & CULTURAL REVOLUTION

[I'd like to place on record my thanks to Dominic Sandbrook, whose ground-breaking social history books *Never Had It So Good* and *White Heat* formed the inspiration and basis for this short essay on the cultural context of *The Avengers*.]

'Almost at once, affluence came hurrying on the heels of penury. Suddenly, the shops were piled high with all sorts of goods. Boom was in the air.' (Harry Hopkins, *The New Look*)

Harry Hopkins and Dominic Sandbrook are just two of the social historians who reflect upon the fact that 'the sixties' – in the sense of a material and cultural revolution – began in the mid-1950s. The austerity of war rationing had finally been lifted and for many people it meant a return to what Sandbrook describes as the 'dynamic forces' of pre-war British society: consumerism and advertising. The difference now was that it wasn't solely middle-class people buying new products such as radios, vacuum-cleaners, and cookers. With low unemployment, higher wages and the opportunity to buy luxury goods on Hire Purchase, an increasing number of working class families were able to enjoy aspects of this 'affluent society', as it came to be known. Washing-machines became a 'must have' item for any modern household and advertising campaigns heralded a new age in which the housewife could aspire to being a 'kitchen goddess', helped by the new labour-saving devices at her finger tips...if her husband could afford them. The pre-war trend of people moving out into an ever-expanding suburbia continued, and with this move came a desire to impress new neighbours with tangible proof that they were embracing both modern technology and cosmopolitan tastes, despite the negative connotations of suburbia. Sandbrook sees the emergence all over the country of coffee bars as symbolically representing these 'elusive' ideals. (The proliferation of coffee shops in 21st century British high streets reminds me that history can be cyclical as well as linear!) Millions of people began to holiday abroad for the first time, while television chefs and fashion designers looked to France and Italy for inspiration. Meanwhile, if the Suez Crisis had symbolised the death of *the* Empire, then a new one was being constructed with the emergence of the fore-runners of modern supermarkets.

This was a revolutionary age, with people abandoning the public railways for the private motor car; visiting large self-service stores instead of the smaller 'knowable' local shops; leaving damp urban Victorian terraced houses with outside/communal toilets for either Le Corbusier-inspired 'streets in the sky' tower blocks or new, sanitised suburban homes with a garden. Meanwhile, the arrival of Wimpy bars, American-style steakhouses and the popularity of Hollywood films demonstrated the growing fascination with trans-Atlantic cultural trends.

Television was at the heart of this Cultural Revolution. The beginning of the 1950s had been a boom time for the cinema, with British people visiting the picture houses on average twenty-eight times a year, representing a staggering 10% of the global audience (*Never Had It So Good*, p. 127). However, as the integral part of a new home-entertainment society, the 1950s saw television begin to take centre stage. Sandbrook notes that the number of households with a television went from 764,000 in 1951 to more than ten million by 1960:

'Within the space of a few years, television had been transformed from a minority interest, a mere novelty even, into the cornerstone of an evening's entertainment and the following morning's banter. It was no longer a luxury; it had become **a social necessity**.' (*Never Had It So Good*, p. 384)

This last observation is an important one. As the decade slipped by, pubs, cinemas and football grounds saw steady decline; the television was becoming king. In an evolutionary twist to this revolution, what Sandbrook describes as the 'cosy world' of the publically-owned BBC was rudely disrupted by the arrival of commercial ITV in 1955, promising 'a new kind of programming: modern, snappy, international and classless.' (*Never Had It So Good*, p. 384) This included American comedy series and US-inspired quiz shows, both still key parts of the diet two generations later. If television itself was seen by cultural commentators such as Raymond Williams as the epicentre of 'a synthetic culture, an anti-culture', then ITV was the demon himself, denounced by Lord Reith – among others – as the 'Black Death'. [1]

By the early 1960s, audiences were being attracted to both sides of the dial by new types of television shows: the 'slice-of-life' realism of *Coronation Street* and the new 'social realism' of *Z Cars*. Indeed, social realism played a part in the original season of *The Avengers,* too, but Sandbrook sees the Cathy Gale videotape era of Season 3 – and the arrival of *Doctor Who* – as representing both a thematic and stylistic alternative: a 'fantastic, elaborate and self-consciously modern approach.' (*Never Had It So Good*, p. 728) While Sandbrook acknowledges that *The Avengers* had an evolutionary base – by now it was *reflecting* the fascination in James Bond style espionage – he also sees it as revolutionary – *anticipating* cultural trends, particularly through Cathy Gale, a character who was 'bright, independent, sexy and self-confident.' Gale was no 'kitchen goddess' and her ability to outwit men – both physically and intellectually – was both ground-breaking and inspirational. For actress Honor Blackman it was an opportunity to break away from playing stereotypical 'English Rose' parts and instead portray a truly liberated, cerebral woman who would not simply put up with being patronised by her male counterpart. Revolutionary indeed.

If television itself was seen as a revolutionary medium, then up until now its programmes had rarely reflected this. Viewers swam in a lukewarm sea of slice-of-life soap operas, 'easy viewing' game shows, cooking and gardening programmes, realistic police drama, and American imports. (Much like today, I'm tempted to add.) *The Avengers* helped to change this, gradually evolving into a genuinely innovative series, demanding that viewers became active participants rather than passive consumers of an electric 'box' which had become the centre of their domestic world. Other 1960s television dramas, most notably those from the ITC 'production line', would attempt to offer a similar spectacle. However, *The Avengers* was a trailblazer and these other shows arguably failed to capture or rework its unique charm.

In embracing the modernity of 35mm film and then 'Glorious Technicolor', *The Avengers* reflects a London-based, mid-1960s cosmopolitan world of Op Art, Pop Art, coffee percolators, electric razors, toasters, breakfast bars, sports cars and cutting-edge fashion. Steed embraces French cuisine, uses foreign words, wears Pierre Cardin suits, drinks champagne and reads *Tintin* in its original language. Emma Peel and Tara King are fashionable, independent young women with their own apartments, ideals, fast cars and fighting techniques. However, in typically British fashion, *Avengerland* remains a world with one eye on the past, the traditions of Empire and Island, where the English eccentricities of the 'old school tie', bowler hat, umbrella and stiff upper lip are as important as kinky boots, leather outfits and continental culture. Sandbrook describes *The Avengers* as taking 'refuge in a careful blend of nostalgia and modernity', revelling in 'eccentric traditions' while also embracing 'the white heat...of technological revolution.' (*White Heat*, p. 401) However, as the author acknowledges, in *The Avengers* technology is feared as much as it is revered, reflecting the chill of the Cold War and the ever-present threat of nuclear weapons. [2] Like the 1960s period itself – which Sandbrook notes for its 'conservatism and conformity' as much as its 'radical transformation'– the series is an odd mix of modernity and tradition; it is, paradoxically, evolutionary, revolutionary and cautionary.

It is, arguably, this bizarre blend of ingredients which provides its appeal. *The Avengers* has one foot in the real world and one in a surreal, parallel universe; it is both a product of the evolving 1960s cultural revolution yet also reflects many people's desire for a timeless, picture-postcard 'never-never' England. *Avengerland* provided just that, but with a surreal twist. It looked back with (tongue-in-cheek) nostalgia but also celebrated a new modernity, albeit in typically British reserved fashion. It remains a delightful paradox.

The increasingly global popularity of *The Avengers* in the mid to late-1960s came at a time when imperial power was collapsing, definitively. As Sandbrook notes, a generation earlier Britain had been a major world power:

'By 1920 Britain had amassed two hundred colonies...British power held sway over more than one fifth of the world's entire land surface...One in four of the world's population lived and died under the Union Jack.' (*Never Had It So Good*, p. 278)

By the time *The Avengers* moved from videotape to film, less than fifteen million people overseas were under British rule. The Empire was over. [3] (Thankfully, some of us might add.) With the success of exports such as *The Saint, Danger Man, The Beatles, The Kinks* and *The Rolling Stones,* perhaps we can view the Swinging Sixties period as one in which a vibrant, new artistic British empire – of popular culture – was peacefully conquering large parts of the globe. *The Avengers* was at the very heart of this revolution, a (cultural) colonisation which this time we can feel justifiably proud about.

© Rodney Marshall

1. The idea of a BBC television monopoly from 1946-1955 can be exaggerated. After all, BBC coverage only reached Birmingham in 1949 and nationwide coverage arrived not long before ITV.
2. I explore both technology and hedonistic consumerism in my chapter on the Cold War.
3. Sandbrook suggests that public reaction to both the collapse of the British Empire and the Cold War threat was, generally speaking, one of indifference or apathy. The brave new world of washing machines, cars, supermarkets and television was far more important or real it would seem.

THE AVENGERS AND THE COLD WAR

The Cold War was still going strong during the *Avengers* years. The sense of dread that had been hanging over the world since its inception was still very real. World War 2 was a fairly recent memory and there was a seemingly legitimate fear that another world war could be necessary to curb an expansionist Soviet Union. In Dominic Sandbrook's comprehensive history of post-war Britain, *Never Had It So Good*, he quotes the historian Alan Bullock as saying:

'[The British public believed] there was a real danger of the Soviet Union and other Communists taking advantage of the weakness of Western Europe to extend their power. We know now that this did not follow, but nobody knew it at the time. This was a generation for whom war and occupation were not remote hypotheses but recent and terrible experiences.' [1]

Also, advancements in nuclear weaponry on both sides of the Iron Curtain produced perhaps the most fitting acronym of all time for what was called the doctrine of mutually assured destruction: MAD. This was a distinct possibility. The world had had a narrow escape in 1962 when Khrushchev finally blinked in his eyeball-to-eyeball confrontation with Kennedy during the Cuban Missile Crisis.

In the Western Bloc, the prevailing belief at the time in most government circles was that Communism was a monolithic threat that had to be contained wherever it tried to advance. This belief lead to bloody proxy wars, including the long and costly Vietnam War during the 1960s and 1970s, in which over 58,000 American servicemen were killed. Britain's government wisely refused the United States' request to send troops to this catastrophic war, but did provide covert assistance and publically supported it.

In *The Avengers* the Cold War was quite naturally the backdrop for many episodes. This potentially deadly conflict was certainly no laughing matter and that makes the series' approach to it quite interesting. Just who are the funniest characters (not played by the great Roy Kinnear) to appear in *The Avengers*? One could make a very strong argument for Brodny in *Two's a Crowd* and *The See-through Man*, 'General' Shaffer in *Mission...Highly Improbable*, and the trio of Olga, Nutski, and Ivan in *The Correct Way to Kill*. What these characters have in common, of course, is that they are Russians, Britain's Cold War enemies.

The character Brodny has his detractors – some fans find him a bit too buffoonish – but Warren Mitchell does a masterful job in making this character with all his foibles – pomposity, cowardice, lechery, servility – truly hilarious but also likeably human. He is really just a gentle soul. His masters in *The See-Through Man* knew he wouldn't have the heart to shoot Mrs. Peel when they ordered him to guard her. His scenes with Steed are especially good. Steed clearly has this clueless Russian Ambassador 'in his hip pocket' as the saying goes, but Brodny is blissfully unaware and considers Steed to be a friend and mentor in his quest to become an English gentleman and remain in England for as long as possible.

Ronald Radd, who went on to play Russian characters in films such as *The Seagull* and *The Kremlin Letters*, seems to be enjoying himself immensely as he hams it up in his role as Shaffer. The viewer can't help but like this pompous rascal a little as he good naturedly brushes off Steed's facetious compliment about the medal he supposedly won in the Crimean War. He's so darned convivial and good humoured that the viewer can be forgiven for feeling some affection for this head of Soviet Intelligence, despite his desire to kill Steed and provide the Soviet Union with a weapon that would ensure its world domination.

The amicable interactions between the British and Russian agents, and the send-up of the English Gentleman as epitomized by the S.N.O.B. organisation, make *The Correct Way to Kill* one of the funniest and most subversive *Avengers* episodes ever filmed. In true *Avengers* fashion, the impressive number of murders doesn't detract from its generally light-hearted tone. Michael Gough's Nutski, even though he turns out to be the diabolical mastermind in this one, is a downright charming fellow. The scene in which he reminisces with Steed about the good old days in Vienna when they were the "best of enemies" is one of the wittiest *Avengers* scenes of all time. The camaraderie and respect between these two seem to be genuine. Olga, wonderfully played by Anna Quayle, has a combination of naïve idealism and deadpan humour that makes her a very likeable character indeed. It doesn't take her long to size Steed up and start reacting to him with the same exasperation, amusement, and grudging admiration that his "decadent capitalist" partners do. Perhaps the most human of the Russians in this episode is Ivan. Phillip Madoc plays this character as a world weary Cold Warrior, a bit cynical but honourable in his own way. There is enough depth to Ivan that his murder is somewhat disturbing, perhaps – next to Mrs. Peel's childhood friend Paul's in *Murdersville* – the most disturbing death in the Peel era. A personal favourite scene in *The Correct Way to Kill* is the one in which Ivan barges into Steed's apartment with the intention of killing him, runs in to the back of a chair, flips over it, lands seated on the other side, and is handed a glass of wine by a smiling and gracious Steed. This scene seems to epitomise the *Avengers'* attitude towards the Russians; they are a bit of a joke, admittedly a potentially dangerous joke, but with a little proper handling very manageable.

The totalitarian system they represent certainly doesn't get a free pass from the series. It is mercilessly pilloried in *The Avengers* – witness the terror Brodny exhibits at the thought of having to return to The Motherland. There had been a time when international Communism was seen by idealistic Westerners as the glorious wave of the future, but by the sixties that view was held by only the most naïve. The brutal suppression of the Hungarian Revolution, the construction of the Berlin Wall and many other such incidents destroyed that illusion. Very few government activities could shout "we have failed!" louder than building a wall to prevent its citizens from escaping.

There just might be something a little subversive behind *The Avengers'* benign treatment of these individuals who represented this ideologically and, as it turned out, economically bankrupt enemy. The Soviet Union, although bristling with weaponry capable of destroying the world, was doomed to fail, and The *Avengers* team of writers, directors and actors was either consciously or unconsciously aware of it. They of course weren't the only ones. Students all over the world were in revolt against 'The Establishment' during this decade, but one place they did not look to as a revolutionary model was the Soviet Union. In their eyes international Communism had lost its moral legitimacy and was irrelevant. It was no longer seen as the wave of the future, and therefore no longer perceived as the threat it used to be by students and most other thinking people.

This hadn't been the case in the earlier stages of the Cold War. If *The Avengers* had been produced in the 1950s, it is extremely doubtful that Communist characters would have been portrayed so affectionately. British films such as *High Treason* (1951), about a potential Russian invasion, and *The Angry Silence* (1960), about Communist union sabotage, took a stern if not somewhat paranoid view of the Communist threat.

Even in the United States virulent anti-Communist films from the 1950s such as *Big Jim McLean, The Whip Hand,* and *The Red Danube* gave way to films in the 1960s like *The Russians are Coming, the Russians are Coming* and *Dr. Strangelove* that satirised the Cold War. Ironically, these films are probably the two funniest American films of the decade. The uncomfortable fact that American boys were fighting and dying in a war ostensibly against Communists at the same time these films were being made speaks to the deep divisions that were present in American (and for that matter Western) society during that era. It would be hard to imagine a comedy featuring likable Germans being produced in the US or Britain during WW2. [2]

Another type of Cold War character we see in *The Avengers* is the foreigner (presumably a 'Commie') posing as an English person as he or she infiltrates Britain in a scheme to take over the country. This would include such characters as Piggy Warren and his cohorts in *The Town of No Return*, Masgard in *The Living Dead,* and Basil and Lola in *Who's Who???* In contrast to the overtly Russian characters, none of these folks is particularly likeable. Not too many viewers felt sorry for Piggy when Steed set his moustache on fire, and that perennial villain Julian Glover plays Masgard so villainously that his own mother probably cheered when he met his demise. And who among us would quarrel with Steed's branding of Basil as a "fiend"? After all, he and his partner ruthlessly gunned down agent after agent. Let's write off the fact that Steed was actually upset about Basil's biting off the ends of cigars, rather than his murderous deeds, to *Avengers* quirkiness. But perhaps most unforgivable of all is the way Lola dances while she inhabits Mrs.

Peel's body. To dance that spasmodically while impersonating another is simply wrong.

Yet another character type seen in Cold War episodes is the British collaborator. Britain has a history of communist collaborators, the most famous of which were the Cambridge Five. It was fairly common in the early days of the Soviet Union for idealistic British intellectuals to sympathise with its cause. John Le Carré mined this subject to write some of the finest late 20th century novels. *The Avengers*, however, didn't really delve very deeply into the complex motivations that drove this phenomenon. It is never made clear what motivates Brandon Storey in *Too Many Christmas Trees* or George Burton in *The Forget-Me-Knot*, but we do know that for most of these collaborators, such as Sergeant Moran in *What the Butler Saw* and Dr. Chivers in *Mission...Highly Improbable*, it was simple greed.

The infiltrator and collaborator characters are really just boiler plate *Avengers* villains. There is nothing particularly interesting about them from a Cold War standpoint. The depictions of the Russian characters, on the other hand, say something about how the Cold War was playing out in the 1960s, and also how society was changing during that tumultuous decade. There is certainly nothing blatantly controversial about the way *The Avengers* allows Britain's enemies some humanity, but it is just a little subversive. In addition to being an indication that thinking people in the West no longer feared the Communist menace as an ideological inevitability, it was also one among many signs that the film industry was no longer in lock-step with government agendas.

© Dan O'Shea

1. Alan Bullock, *Ernest Bevin: Foreign Secretary 1945-1951* (London, 1983), pp. 844-845.
2. This is a key point, I feel, and the comic or humorous response to the Cold War tensions is explored in my own short essay, to be found in the appendices at the back of this book, pp. 313-320.

SUBVERSIVE CHAMPAGNE & THE ART OF MURDER

'Sometimes the best depths we can find are in the shallow waters, but Oscar Wilde does warn in *The Picture of Dorian Gray* that delving into the depths is perilous.' (Sunday Swift)

It was upon re-watching the monochrome filmed episode *The Murder Market* three years ago – alongside Tony Williamson's original script – that two things struck me: first, that the multi-layered *Avengers* was worth writing about in terms of analysis, as opposed to production history; second, that Emma Peel's phrase about 'subversive champagne' – cut from the final version – succinctly summed up what I felt makes the series not just important but also unique. The very best episodes combine the fashionable, 'shallow' or surface froth: witty dialogue, light humour, vintage and modern cars and clothes, balletic fights, etc.; *and* the darker, dramatic depths provided by atmospheric, deserted locations, black humour, tension and on/off-screen violence. Naturally, many *Avengers* elements provide cross-over ingredients: Laurie Johnson's music, the surreal sets, eccentric guest characters, and the increasingly self-referential qualities. These can be playful, perverse, terrifying, or a combination of all three.

My use of 'subversive champagne' is, on one level, a reaction to the ongoing attempts to pigeon-hole the show as simply 'light entertainment', despite the plentiful presence of disturbing scenes or entire episodes, such as *The House That Jack Built*. Most filmed episodes contain plenty of light fizz *and* darker, subversive aspects. Some *Avengers* 'films' veer almost uncontrollably between the light and the dark, such as *Quick-Quick Slow Death*, *How to Succeed...At Murder, A*

Sense of History and *Murdersville*. Even these can contain moments of subversive champagne, such as in the latter when the businessman/assassin goes into Little Storping to terminate a rival. As he wields a gun, in full view of the library readers, the librarian points to the 'silence' sign and the killer adds a ridiculous-looking silencer to his weapon before completing his task. The moment sees realism and surrealism merge, adding black humour while maintaining the drama, not least as we are viewing the event through the bewildered witness, Major Croft, who by now surely senses that he will be the next victim. 'Merge' is the key word here, as Brian Clemens successfully blends the subversion and the champagne, which is not always the case either in this episode or the series as a whole. It is testimony to the script-writers and directors that plots can maintain the dramatic undertones despite absurd avengerish elements. Equally, the wobbling or collapse of the fourth wall can be achieved without breaking our willing suspension of disbelief. Emma Peel's wedding/funeral scene in *Epic* is a perfect example of this. The camera reveals the large studio fan which is used to send confetti and then autumnal leaves across the set, yet the magical tension does not snap. This is equally true in *Requiem*, a powerfully psychological episode in which Tara King inspects the stripped-back-to-bare (polystyrene) brick walls of Steed's bombed flat, revealing it as a set while still conveying a sense of terrorist wreckage. *Something Nasty in the Nursery* is another colour episode where the subversive champagne mix is cleverly and playfully presented, not least when Steed encounters the noble nannies and he/we briefly think he is coming under attack in similar fashion to the deadly gentlemen killers of SNOB.

Characters such as Hickey the tramp, Quince the birdwatcher and Pongo the agent in Boy Scout attire are – on one level – absurd figures, yet they are also ones who can enter into the darker drama with consummate ease. Equally, diabolical masterminds and henchmen can create subversive champagne even without our Avengers being present, such as *The Rotters'* snobbish hit-men discussing the atmospheric advantages of moonlit murder as they stand in a churchyard:

Kenneth: It's a lovely old place, isn't it?
George: Mmm. Charming. Adore the countryside. Have you ever strangled anybody old chap?
Kenneth: Strangled? No, no, I can't say I have. Trees are awfully nice at this time of year, aren't they? Don't you think?
George: Mmm. Awfully nice. Just a hint of autumn in the leaves. I wonder what it's like.
Kenneth: What?
George: Strangling.
Kenneth: Oh. Rather unpleasant I should imagine. Not a method a gentleman would use.
George: Oh quite, quite. Awfully vulgar. Mmmm. Country air, jolly invigorating.
Kenneth: Yes – it makes one glad to be alive.
George: Mmmm. Shall we do it now?
Kenneth: I don't think so, no. Just get a good look at the geography and come back tonight. It's always better in the dark.
George: Much better. More sort of – dramatic.

The merging of the banal, the macabre and the self-referential within their conversation offers us both the (black) humour and the dramatic suspense which helps to make the series unique. It is a daringly playful blend which set *The Avengers* apart from the traditional kitchen-sink and slice-of-life television drama on offer. It was also far more innovative than most of the glamorous fantasy/espionage shows being churned out by the ITC 'factory'. Kenneth and George insist that the base act of murder is transformed into an aesthetically pleasing art form, to be admired as much as the autumnal beauty of the countryside. What they are discussing – like directors of a cleverly (and artificially) framed thriller movie – is the Art of Murder.

Other memorable examples of this art of murder include the aquarium assassination explored in my Teaser chapter and the urbane assassin groom of *A Funny Thing Happened on the Way to the Station,* who whistles or hums the Bridal Chorus (or Wedding March) as he sends people to their grave. [1] He is both a nightmarish figure yet also an example of pure style over substance.

Props can provide those unique avengerish moments which defy labelling or genre. The swaying ventriloquist dummies and dolls in the joke shop of *The £50,000 Breakfast* offer a spectacle which is surreal, terrifying and yet triumphantly, artfully stylish as the camera pans across their red faces and a creepy score breaks out, the murdered owner's kettle reaching the boil at the climactic moment of the killing. The fact that we share Mrs. Rhodes's viewpoint adds to the spectacle while the sight of the murderers hiding behind masks displays the scene's artificiality yet increases the dramatic tension. The mannequins and toys which surface in a number of episodes in each season are perfect examples of the bizarre blend which creates the perverse, parallel universe of *Avengerland*. Whisk in strange, experimental camera angles and pieces of music and these plastic figures take on irrationally disturbing qualities. They are particularly effective in Sir Lyle's glass-roofed plant room (*Man-Eater of Surrey Green*) and the factory workers' bus of *Killer*. How can a stuffed animal, nursery wallpaper, a bouncing ball or a nodding toy represent a sinister image? How can a tweed-capped robot/cybernaut maintain any level of dramatic tension? The answer lies in our desire to engage in the subversive champagne of this fascinating show.

The razor sharp wit of the dialogue, particularly in the monochrome filmed season, often provides an avengerish blend of humorous froth and menacing undercurrent. Steed's conversation with Omrod in *Silent Dust*, as they compare their guns, works on a number of levels:

Steed: Birds are getting scarcer minute by minute.
Omrod: I hadn't heard.
Steed: You better ask your gamekeeper.
Omrod: Mellors?
Steed: He mistook me for a partridge. Seriously ruffled my wing feathers.
Omrod: I must speak to him. I must tell him to be a little more...
Steed: Accurate?
Omrod: Careful!

Gambit and Trasker offer a similar spectacle as they compare their Smith & Wesson/Schmeisser guns – like boys with toys – in *The Eagle's Nest*. In both episodes, in addition to the intermingling of wit and dramatic threat, the two men are like stags preparing to lock horns, their weapons almost phallic extensions. At times, John Steed and Emma Peel provide this tension in their own 'banter', Steed threatening to undermine Emma's cover in *Dial A Deadly Number*, Mrs. Peel reversing the roles early on in *Castle De'ath*:

Emma: You don't have a Scots accent.
Steed: I was carried south by marauding Sassenachs when I was a bairn.

We almost have to reassure ourselves that they are on the same side.

In the truly classic episodes, this fine balance of style/substance and real/surreal is maintained throughout the hour. We struggle to deal with episodes like *Too Many Christmas Trees* and *The Hour That Never Was* where realism, surrealism and darker undercurrents swirl around, creating a dramatic fog through which we try to make sense of the events, particularly during spectacles such as the oneiric dream sequences in the former and the rattling chains/milk float scene in the latter. 'Subversive champagne' – like any label – is imperfect. However, I use it as a tool to explain why some scenes/episodes 'work' better than others. *The Avengers* is at its best when it employs subtlety, rather than slapstick, where formula is played or toyed with, rather than simply adhered to in a predictably formulaic fashion. As viewers, we expect certain ingredients to be served up, but we also want to be surprised, challenged and taken out of our comfort zone. Most television dramas can be 'contained' relatively easily within genre classifications such as crime, espionage, science-fiction, space opera, fantasy, action-adventure, light comedy, etc. Label *The Avengers* at your peril because the minute you do so, along comes a scene or episode which throws the category out of the window and illustrates the impossibility of neatly filing away the show in a one-dimensional dramatic drawer. Sunday Swift argues that the show relies on 'pure surface and style, pure and absolute aesthetic.' She goes on to explain her theory, one which connects with my idea of 'subversive champagne':

'Just because something is presented as pure surface doesn't mean there is not depth. We can read class and gender politics, and dozens of other topics. I've always preferred finding depth in shallow waters. *The Avengers* is happy to be read, and there is plenty to read. It leaves it up to us to take what we will from it. It presents itself as mindless distraction. Pretty people in pretty clothes surrounded by pretty colours...It wants to be seen as a 60s pop painting. It's not just pretty people, colours and clothes, of course, but it presents itself as such, as surface, refusing to signpost anything or acknowledge any depth. This doesn't mean depths aren't there, it just means the show pretends there are not. It's up to us to try to see something in the shadows. Whatever

The Avengers has to say will be on the surface, and we have to scratch the 60s pop painting away to see if there is any depth there. Sometimes it is hiding something. Sometimes scratching away just reveals nothing and we've left a hole in the painting. It's harder work digging without signposts. But isn't that what makes it worth it?' (Sunday Swift, private correspondence)

I love Sunday's idea of finding depth in shallow waters and looking in the shadows for subversion. As she suggests, isn't that what so many of us are enjoying doing while re-watching an episode, posting and interacting on an online forum, or writing a chapter such as this one? I also like the theory that the series presents itself as all froth and no substance, requiring hard work from us as viewers to discover hidden depths. As Sunday warns, sometimes the darker material won't be there at all, and we have simply scarred the surface for nothing. Sometimes the art and artifice will be covering a dramatic underbelly which engages – albeit playfully – with contemporary cultural concerns, including gender, creating those moments which challenge us. The 'surface' dazzles us, but we look beneath it at our peril, journeying through an *Avengerland* without 'signposts'.

Talk of surface and aesthetic display brings me back to the subject of 'the art of murder', discussed so diabolically and playfully by George and Kenneth in *The Rotters*. *The Avengers* shares with Alfred Hitchcock's films the thrilling ability to transform the banal act of murder into a true art form. In the best tradition of Ancient Greek drama, we are given a series of aesthetically shocking, macabre yet visually appealing and self-referential displays: Quince's face revealed in the midst of an 'apple cupboard'; a man drowning in a field, his mouth opening and closing like a fish; a store detective speared in a shop's camping display; a butler-trainer spinning around in a washing machine; a murdered agent displayed on a packing box on stilts; an exploded villain lodged in a tree, still clutching his steering wheel; a comedy writer buried in a paper mountain of scrunched-up jokes; a village local seen plunging to his death while the camera shoots through his abandoned glass lenses, his spectacles quite literally providing the spectacle; a racing driver's goggles filled with jigsaw pieces. Bodies can be displayed in rocking chairs, directors' chairs, Dickensian cobwebbed chairs; murder can even be meticulously rehearsed between victim and killer (*Honey for the Prince*), or discussed in terms of aesthetics by henchmen, as in *The Rotters*. Returning to Sunday's theory, sometimes these moments simply represent stylish veneer, lacking dramatic depth. To a certain extent it depends on the individual episode or character. The corpses displayed in the playground of *Game* don't affect us in the way in which the discovery of Smallwood, Hickey, Wade and Major Croft's bodies do. We have invested time and emotion in these men. However, as a generalisation, *The Avengers* disturbs, entertains and dazzles us with the art of murder. This usually digs deeper than surface style, and in doing so often represents pure subversive champagne.

© Rodney Marshall

1. Richard Wagner's piece is titled *The Bridal Chorus,* although it is often called the *Wedding March* in Britain, thus confusing it with Felix Mendelssohn's *Wedding March*.

GRAVEYARDS

'Ours was the marsh country, down by the river, within, as the river wound, twenty miles of the sea. My first most vivid and broad impression of the identity of things, seems to me to have been gained on a memorable raw afternoon towards evening. At such a time I found out for certain, that this bleak place overgrown with nettles was the churchyard.' (*Great Expectations*)

Like many Victorians, Charles Dickens had a fascination with graveyards and cemeteries. They feature in a number of his novels and shorter fiction, including *A Christmas Carol*. However, the most famous and captivating scene comes from the opening of *Great Expectations*, where the young, impressionable Pip encounters an escaped convict. On one level, the tombstones represent signs which the little boy cannot decode. On a practical and dramatic level, they create perfect cover for a stranger to hide behind, while the 'bleak' marshland setting and the time of day – dusk – create a dramatic, darkly disturbing atmosphere. Throughout the extraordinary novel, it is to this eerie location that both Pip and the reader's minds tend to return.

Fast-forward a century and, as the videotape era of *The Avengers* came to a close, Roger Marshall's ground-breaking *Mandrake* draws on the literary tradition of graveyards. As in *Great Expectations*, there is a sense of pathetic fallacy about the weather. The camera pans to a windswept graveside group as rain lashes down on the church of St. Alban in the parish of Treviathan. The Cornish churchyard – populated with London corpses – provides the principle setting. Twelve of the twenty-nine scenes take place here, and even when the action moves away from the village cemetery and church, we see Cathy Gale examining a skull in her apartment and the diabolical masterminds standing in a doctor's surgery in front of a skeleton. Reminders of mortality are everywhere. [1]

With the series moving on to film, there is an increasing fascination in coffins, graves, churches, hearses, vicars and funeral directors. More than a dozen episodes explore these interrelated locations, professions and objects. In terms of plot, it is not surprising to see the series frequently drawing on these, considering the show's interest in both unnatural, mysterious deaths and in people buried alive. Recalling Dickens, from an aesthetic perspective, graveyards provide brooding, atmospheric locations, most notably in the half-light of dusk. These settings also remind us that, in the midst of life, people are close to death, particularly in *Avengerland*. A number of action scenes take place in what, after all, is meant to be a place of eternal rest, adding black humour to the stories.

Season 4 begins with Emma Peel's introductory episode, *The Town of No Return*. The scenes in the graveyard and church at Little Bazeley set the tone and style for the monochrome run. We see a hostile-looking Saul, whose mad gaze is replaced by the 'PEACE' sign on a graveyard stone cross. The irony of the message is not lost on us, and we will be returned to it, twice. Later, as dusk settles, we are offered a series of noirish, chilling images. The camera moves directly onto a skull on a parish gravestone. As Smallwood approaches through the unkempt churchyard, passing the 'PEACE' sign, the hymn playing is *All Things Bright and Beautiful*, horribly at odds with the image of Saul following him. The sense of disquiet merges with surrealism as Smallwood opens the church door to find a deserted interior, despite the singing and music. The choir is no more authentic than the vicar who will later point a gun at Emma Peel while observing that the taped recording she is listening to is a requiem. There is a noirish, *avant garde* style to these scenes which are cinematic in their direction by Roy Ward Baker. It is like watching a mini-movie, not a television series.

The following episode, *The Murder Market*, is the first of many *Avengers* stories which play with the connections between marriages and funerals, a theme which reaches its climax in *Epic*. Here the images are daringly innovative. Emma Peel lying in her coffin, surrounded by giant candlesticks, is an iconic moment. Initially, she resembles a fairy tale princess or sleeping beauty. Steed joins in with the darkly playful nature of the scene – she is described as "resting peacefully" – later asking her if she is "comfortable". There is a dark humour at work, and Steed seems to be enjoying the whole experience. The champagne-related "hiccoughing in the coffin" quip makes way for the noirish graveyard cortege scene in which Laurie Johnson's funereal score draws on flute and violin before offering us the clichéd organ accompaniment. At this moment, we believe that Mrs. Peel has been buried alive, yet the levity of the flute contradicts our fears. The two scenes in hearses – the sombre ride with the baddies; the amusing tag scene drive with Emma as chauffeur – make full use of a morbidly stylish mode of transport which we will encounter a number of times in the series.

If *The Murder Market* draws on *Mandrake*'s black humour then *The Gravediggers* takes funereal imagery into a surreal realm. The same light-hearted Johnson funeral score is re-used, but now we have a series of strange images in which graves are associated with survival rather than burial. A hearse takes an exhumed man to a hospital where his coffin is carried into the operating theatre; Steed notes an undertaker booking funerals months in advance; and a funeral parlour equips coffins with holes to breathe through. We are being asked to question things we usually 'read' straight. In *Avengerland,* machinery can be operated on in a hospital, while florists' boxes can store radar-jamming equipment.

In Season 4, most of the cemetery scenes involved location filming, as directors attempted to create a sense of naturalism, in spite of the bizarre nature of the plots. However, the colour *Avengers* graveyard scenes are filmed on artificial sets rather than in real locations. [2] In candy-coloured *Avengerland*, artificiality is to be accentuated and forms part of the appeal. The headstones in *From Venus With Love* and *The Living Dead* are theatrical props, which is appropriate considering the surreal nature of the scenes which take place there.

This playful artificiality reaches its artistic peak in *Epic,* where Emma Peel's wedding and funeral take place on a set which is meant to be a set, in a studio which is meant to be a studio. Any pretence at realism has been removed, and yet it is somehow reinforced, the staged surrealism adding to the drama. In *Subversive Champagne* I described it as follows:

'*Avengers* leitmotifs — such as the interconnected wedding/funeral imagery — are literally flung at Mrs. Peel and these scenes are effectively subversive. A confetti-storm in a churchyard transforms seamlessly into an autumnal graveyard; wedding bells are replaced by funereal ones as illuminated headstones — 'R.I.P Emma Peel' — offer her the clear message that in the midst of life she is close to death. The ghostly-pale hearse driver provides a haunting image which is both playful and deeply disturbing. It is one of the defining scenes in *Avengers* filmic history.' (*Subversive Champagne*, p. 156).

Why does the twinned scene work so well dramatically and in terms of visual/aural spectacle? First, there is a dream-like quality to it, helped by the use of slow-motion as Emma runs up the path towards the vicar. He is a nightmare figure, beckoning her on, before violently pushing her away. The similarity between the wedding and funeral 'props' is highly effective: the vintage wedding car/hearse; the wedding invitation card/bronze funeral plaque; confetti/dead leaves, blown into storms by the same giant fan; the church bell ringing in celebration/as a death knell. There are also the contrasts: Wyngarde's character as smiling vicar/grim reaper; Emma's initial expression of light bemusement later transforming into a look of fear. The dark absurdity is topped off by the warning to the 'dead' Emma: "Mrs. Peel! We're waiting for you." It is a grotesque parody of Steed's "Mrs. Peel, We're Needed!" Our experience matches hers in a fascinatingly disturbing piece of pure art.

The Tara season is one of extremes as we veer between episodes with one foot in the real world and the other in the surreal. In *Killer*, agents' corpses are delivered to a graveyard "washed, sterilised, dry cleaned" or, as Steed sums it up succinctly, "packaged". If the presentation is oddly surreal, then so too is the forensic scientist:

Steed: How did he die?
Clarke: In alphabetical order: he was clubbed, poisoned, shot, spiked, stabbed, strangled and suffocated. And his ear drums are damaged.
Steed: His neck's broken as well.

In *Requiem*, we witness Mother's funeral, with a sedated Tara convinced that he is indeed dead. However, the floral wreath convinces us otherwise:

> In Loving Memory of Our Dear Mother...
> The Finest Chap We Ever Knew.
> Died Suddenly – Explosively. R.I.P.

The use of black humour descends – quite literally – into farce in *Bizarre*, where people who are very much alive are made to look dead. Once buried they go *down* into a *living* Paradise. The monochrome interest in challenging, noirish imagery has made way for a simpler comic strip fun. It is in *The Rotters* where we gain perhaps our best insight into why graveyards provide such a memorable recurring location or setting in *Avengerland*. As hit-men George and Kenneth admire the autumnal English countryside and discuss both the act and art of murder, they admit that the fresh air makes one feel fortunate to be alive, before moving on to decide when to kill:

Kenneth: It's always better in the dark.
George: Much better. More sort of – dramatic.

Spectacle is at the core of the project, in graveyards as elsewhere; in the midst of life one is close to death, and in the midst of death – in *Avengerland* – we feel very much alive.

© Rodney Marshall

1. Roger Marshall recalls exploring the various cemeteries in Northampton, looking out for any architectural detail or epitaph which could be used in the fictional graveyard.
2. According to Michael Richardson, *The Gravediggers* features New Southgate Cemetery (*Bowler Hat and Kinky Boots*, p. 139) and *The Murder Market* cortege scene is clearly filmed on location as well. *The Living Dead* reworked a cemetery set previously used on *From Venus With Love* (*Bowler Hat and Kinky Boots*, p. 205). In discussing *Killer*, Richardson refers to an 'exterior cemetery set that occupied the south-west corner' of the Elstree studio backlot, *Bowler Hat and Kinky Boots*, p. 316.

THE COUNTRY HOUSE TRAP

The isolated country house has played an important role in the English-speaking novel for centuries. In many 'classic' and popular works of fiction the rural mansion becomes a powerful force in its own right, offering both characters and readers a sense of claustrophobic stricture. It becomes a place of confinement, rather than refinement. Jane Eyre is locked up in the Red Room at Gateshead Hall as a child, and then later hears the 'madwoman' locked in the attic at Rochester's Thornfield Hall; the young, impressionable Pip is lured into the twin traps of unrequited love and capitalist greed at Miss Havisham's dilapidated Satis House, a cobwebbed mansion which remains frozen in time; Lady Dedlock suffers a spiritual death at the damp, dreary Chesney Wold. Young female protagonists, in particular, have felt the interrelated physical and mental torture of confinement in an almost endless number of novels: Catherine Earnshaw in the remote moorland farmhouse called Wuthering Heights, and the second Mrs. De Winter at Manderley on the Cornish coast, are just two famous examples.

In his 1991 essay *Murder in the Manor*, writer Peter Dickinson suggests that the 'myth' of the English country house is 'deeply rooted' in our national 'psyche'. [1] The country house isn't simply physically remote; it is also isolated in the sense of social exclusion. Its 'invisible' servants (and their carpetless staircase) are a key element in maintaining the myth, both on a real and symbolic level. Dickinson reads the 'unreality' of the country house as a microcosm of a particular world of wealth and leisure 'which in one sense was almost totally unreal yet really existed.' (This observation could almost be describing *Avengerland* itself!)

Dickinson suggests that economic and social reality 'broke in' at the beginning of the twentieth century. This meant that, for many, the time of the country house 'was over'. The outbreak of war in 1914 also meant that many of the wealthy owners' sons 'were called on to fight and die', as the real world rudely came knocking. This reminds me of Grenville and his troops arriving at the picture-postcard manor house in *Take-Over*. Dickinson draws a link between the Golden Age of the Murder Mystery (between the two World Wars) and the social context of war:

'The ideal setting for the mystery novel is the imaginary world of the country house. There, supposed **balance and harmony is broken by the act of violence,** just as in the real world it had been broken by the war.'

If this 'unreal, Golden England' of Edwardian country houses suited mystery tales and detective fiction, then it also offered a perfect setting for film makers who regularly picked up, recycled and reworked the theme of the country house as a literal or metaphorical trap. From silent comedy to Hitchcockian thriller and *Hammer* horror, the fascination has continued. *The Shining* – both in novel and film form – is, on one level, a modern American horror reworking of the English country house trap, with the isolated Overview hotel in the Colorado Rockies replacing the conventional house and Stephen King employing cabin fever as an equivalent to claustrophobic stricture.

What has all of this to do with *The Avengers*? The country house trap is a recurring *Avengerland* setting/theme. *The Avengers* had already explored this in its videotape era, most notably in *Don't Look Behind You*. However, film freed the writers, directors and set designers to explore their fascination in this sub-genre. Between Seasons 4-6 a number of episodes return to the remote country home: Brandon Storey's Gothic-revival Dickensian-themed house in *Too Many Christmas*

Trees; the torture-chamber dungeons and four-poster 'deathbed' of *Castle De'ath*; Professor Keller's fiendish trap in *The House That Jack Built*; Sir Cavalier's remote mansion shrouded in clichéd mist in *The Joker*; the Lasindall's Edwardian time-warp in *Pandora*; and the Bassett's country home in the disturbing episode *Take-Over*. In many of these, psychological drama threatens to over-ride the 'light entertainment' tag with which *The Avengers* is often labelled. Indeed, threat is at the core of these subversive stories.

The Avengers was drawing on a rich literary history. The Brontes – specifically Charlotte's madwoman in the attic – Dickens, Hitchcock, and Agatha Christie all influence the filmed *Avengers*, adding to the rich intertextual mix. In particular, *Avengerland* country houses draw on two traditions: the Gothic and the Murder Mystery. Eighteenth century novelist Ann Radcliffe's 'explained supernatural' – in which any supernatural intrusions turn out to have natural causes – is re-used by a host of *Avengers'* writers. Script-writers like Williamson and Clemens draw on the Gothic twinned interest in the thrill of fearfulness and the quest for atmosphere. In addition, there is a Gothic approach in terms of the architectural designs and settings. Christie's influence is most apparent in the murder mystery which is staged in and around the country house ruins on the island in *The Superlative Seven*. Returning to Dickinson's observations, *Avengerland* provides viewers with its own mythical Golden England, a parallel universe which is more fantasy than nostalgia. The harmony of *Avengerland* is routinely 'broken by the act of violence.' *The Avengers* responds to new realities and myths (the Cold War, the technological revolution, etc.) in addition to the timeless theme of revenge and the rich cultural heritage I have referred to.

The 1960s provided the perfect opportunity for writers to re-explore the private country house, at a time when many real ones were opening their doors to the public for the first time. Historian Dominic Sandbrook provides the context in *Never Had It So Good*. He suggests that agricultural decline, a collapse of land prices and increasing death duties and income tax meant that landed families often faced financial ruin, with three possible solutions: 'opening them as tourist attractions, selling them to wealthy businessmen, and simply demolishing them.' Sandbrook notes that 'the reinvention of the country house as a tourist attraction was an immediate success', and he points to 1965 as a boom time, with over five hundred grand homes open to the public. This financial dilemma is, of course, the one faced by the Scottish clan in *Castle De'ath*. In many ways we can see *The Avengers* as re-inventing the country house as an attraction, with both us and the Avengers themselves as the invited guests, shown around by a strange array of hosts and guides. In this *Avengerland* version of the country house, confinement, fear, physical/psychological danger and murder are at the heart of the plots, with a host of literary clichés explored and exploited. These clichés are, paradoxically, both reinforced and undermined. Unlike those paying guests at Woburn Abbey and other real-life country seats, leaving would be the greatest challenge facing Emma Peel, John Steed and Tara King.

Too Many Christmas Trees is the first filmed *Avengers* episode to explore the country house trap. In Season 4, Steed and Mrs. Peel become trapped in other types of buildings, such as a department store and robot/wine factories, but there the scenario is a very different one. After all, they are intruders and must expect trouble. Here they are invited guests, with a seemingly convivial, festive host. The trap begins before Steed even reaches Storey's country mansion. He has already (indirectly) visited it in a hypnotic dream. Throughout the episode the dream/reality polarity is constantly blurred. Storey's house is real, but is also a (Dickensian) fantasy. Steed's 'unreal' nightmares, meanwhile, are manufactured in the real world. Objects from Steed's dreams reappear in reality, while deaths are foreseen in dreams or are staged on Dickensian sets. What are we to make of an owner who tries to "recreate the atmosphere" of fiction in a real home? Steed describes Storey as "single-minded", Felix Teasel taking this a step further, calling him "obsessive". Storey becomes the first of many *Avengers* villains to trap Steed and/or Mrs. Peel in a confined country home. The obsequious butler, ornate staircase, roaring fire and antique furniture are all part of the stereotypical grand home, but here any sense of realism is constantly questioned. The fancy dress party sees actors already dressed to play fictional roles taking on secondary parts, such as Diana Rigg as Emma Peel as Oliver Twist and Barry Warren as Jeremy Wade as Marley's Ghost. Similarly, Storey's house – in reality a set in a film studio – is dressed up as secondary sets: the Hall of Great Expectations and the Mirror Room. The country house trap becomes artfully artificial, something which we acknowledge and yet which, paradoxically, reinforces the darker drama rather than undermining it. The creaking doors, cobwebs, secret passages, flickering candles, and ceremonial unmasking of the villain belong to the clichés of fiction and film, yet here seem appropriate, given the levels of fictionality on display. In sending up the country house trap of gothic romance and horror, *Too Many Christmas Trees* asks us to be wary of the artifice on display – the country house as Victorian myth or fiction – but still expects us to remain emotionally involved. The Mirror Room fight finale brings the layered, distorted artifice to its glorious climax. We are cheated on a number of levels in *Too Many Christmas Trees*. Not only are we asked to accept the late 'twist' that it is Mrs. Peel – not Steed – who is being 'got at', but also we are caught engaging in a country house tale in which even the fictional characters' names – Storey and Teasel – revel in their unreality. Ultimately it is us as real viewers, as much as Steed and Emma as fictional characters, who are trapped.

Castle De'ath also engages in (Scottish) Gothic stereotypes and clichés. The teaser sets these up with its images and sounds: a loch at dusk, the darkening turrets and moat, traditional bagpipes playing, suits of armour, the grand banqueting hall, coat of arms, tapestries, hunted stag heads... We are taken on a jerky, hand-held camera guide of the deserted castle, finally descending into a dungeon where a man is literally racked in pain and, as the bagpipes reach crescendo, the camera focuses in on an Iron Maiden. The main polarity or conflict is between tradition and modernity, a favourite *Avengers* theme. (This will be beautifully illustrated in the tag scene, as the Avengers drive across the surface of the 'timeless' loch in a modern amphibian car.) The country house – here a castle – appears to be the site of a struggle between a rich, dark history of clans, tribal warfare and English imperialism on the one hand, and modern day commercial tourism (or, rather, Cold War financial shenanigans) on the other. These two sides are, of course, inter-connected. The historical past consists of both facts and myths; the ghost of bag-piping Black Jamie is being re-used by Angus as an aural smokescreen, covering up his ultra-modern submarine missions. This is just one example of how the past/present divide is blurred in *Castle De'ath*. Steed has created a fake Scottish personal past and is pretending to be Jock McSteed, a historian; in reality he is a 1960s agent spying on a decidedly modern phenomenon. His traditional four-poster bed has been updated to include a deadly, downwardly mobile concrete roof; the medieval Iron Maiden provides the secret passage to the state-of-the-art control room; the Middle Ages torture rack (freshly oiled) is used to extract information from modern day agents. If Jamie – the black sheep/laird of the family – was "walled up 'til Doomsday" in the East Tower, as a traitor, five hundred years ago, then plenty of modern traps await Steed and Mrs. Peel. Just as commercial ventures such as the fictitious ABORCASHATA look to exploit Britain's cultural past, so *Castle De'ath* exploits our fascination for (the clichés of) Gothic Horror:

dungeons, torture chambers, deep moats, and ghosts. The cover story of modern-day tourism is a sham created by both Angus and Emma Peel. The only visitors who will be guided around the castle are us, as 'television tourists'. The plot – involving a crisis in the fishing industry – soon becomes unimportant as we are, once again, happily trapped in a fantasy world.

Brian Clemens' *The House That Jack Built* and *The Joker* explore the country house trap through both the theme of revenge and the cliché of the "tender young woman alone in old dark house", as the Strange Young Man puts it in the colour episode. Here every stereotype is exploited: dense fog; the dangerously eccentric, unreliable hostess/guide; the 'mysterious stranger'; the creaking rocking chair; cut telephone wires. We even have Dickinson's 'watcher lurking in the shrubbery'. [2] *The Joker* becomes a warped horror/mystery story with a darkly playful edge. The stranger is an actor playing an actor; the female guide is an actress pretending to be an actress; there is no one hiding behind the giant cards or suits of armour, despite the teasingly eerie score. We, like the diabolical mastermind looking through his peepholes, become voyeurs, fascinated by both the psychological horror and mock horror of the story. *The House That Jack Built* is, paradoxically, even more artificial and disturbing. 'Artificial' in that the country house is both trap and set. The clichéd Gothic mansion interior is stripped bare, to reveal an automated modern core which has been designed to drive Emma Peel mad. The old world charm is simply an outer theatrical layer, under which the dead owner – now stuffed in a glass box – has created a house that is literally deadly. The central 'hub', spiral staircase, Emma exhibition room and the suicide box offer a post-modern psychedelic reworking of the country house trap. It is a nightmarish labyrinth which removes the spectacle of *The Avengers'* usual wit and humour, its light froth. Unlike *Too Many Christmas Trees* and *Castle De'ath*, this monochrome mansion provides us with a genuinely disturbing experience which we are (almost unwillingly) trapped inside, forced to share Mrs. Peel's sense of frustration, fear, confinement and stricture. Intriguingly, it is the monochrome episode which seems more modern, revolutionary and daring. While the videotape remake *The Joker* effectively sends up the country house literary tradition, it also reinforces it as Emma requires her male knight in armoured bowler to rescue her. In *The House That Jack Built*, in addition to mirroring the series' fascination with self-referential sets-within-sets, the 'lone young female' fully undermines the damsel victim stereotype, able to defeat the professor and his deadly house trap through her physical and intellectual capabilities.

Towards the end of the Tara King run, Clemens returns to the country house trap on three occasions, in *Requiem* and in the stage play-paced episodes *Pandora* and *Take-Over*. (The latter may have Terry Nation's name on it, but the script was taken from a previous Clemens one and was reworked by him after Nation had submitted it.) All three are psychologically disturbing pieces which once again undermine the simplistic labelling of *The Avengers* as 'light entertainment'.

Requiem provides a radical twist on the country house literary tradition. Here, Steed's riverside home — potentially a trap — becomes a safe sanctuary in which he and his female guest can revert into a childhood world of games and toys, while it is Tara King who is trapped in a fake hospital where she is drugged and interrogated. The potential menace of the house is, playfully, never realised.

Take-Over also offers a fresh twist to the tradition in that it is Steed, rather than Tara, who is trapped. Nor is he alone. Nor is there much in the way of mystery concerning his captors. In fact, one could argue that any intrigue has been trimmed off, replaced by pure psychological fear. This stems from the eclectic nature of the villainous group: a female surgeon fascinated by her own beauty and the ugly operations she performs on others; a master chef whose wish to create the perfect dinner table *ambience* is matched by his desire to kill Steed on their hunt; a man so dedicated to the cause – exterminating members of a peace conference – that he won't stop to eat the gourmet food served up; a mastermind who enjoys party games as long as he wins them, but who will happily terminate Steed as payback for his classical music trivia victory. *The Avengers'* champagne froth of humour, light music and balletic fights are all removed, leaving us with a disorientating sense of loss.

Pandora shares much in common with *Take-Over*. It is not simply the fact that they are both slow-paced, studio-based and theatrical. In each, pure chance leads to the avenger's capture. Steed's annual visit to his friends for the weekend simply coincides with Grenville's take-over. Similarly, Tara happens to resemble Pandora and one of the Lasindall brothers 'luckily' works for the Ministry. The fact that these two traps revolve around coincidence rather than revenge somehow adds a cruel, fatalistic twist to the stories. *Pandora* continues the fascination with blurring the boundaries between past/present. The Lasindall's Edwardian country house is in a time-warp, the decoration, music, newspapers and mail stuck in 1915. Thrust into the teaser, we are disorientated, as we are by the late-Victoriana at the beginning of *Fog*. Has *The Avengers* time-travelled back to the Golden Age of the country house? Tara's shuttered and boarded windows effectively add a sense of physical confinement, while the mad uncle's mutterings in the 'attic' create a Bronte-esque intertextual twist or layer. The drug-created amnesia adds an atmospheric mental fog to the picture, not least when Tara/we see the skeleton in the rocking chair. Unlike the other *Avengers* house traps, we never get to see the outside of the Lasindall home, which effectively increases our sense of claustrophobic confinement. *Pandora* is arguably the series' most disturbing and innovative reworking of the country house trap.

The constant revival and reinterpretation of Gothic Horror and Romance, and the continuing popularity of stage plays like Agatha Christie's *The Mousetrap* – at the time of writing still enjoying a record-breaking run in the West End of London – demonstrate the insatiable fascination in the English country house as a murder/mystery trap. *The Avengers* engages with this throughout its film history, offering a modern, urban slant in *The New Avengers' Complex*. (Although Scapina is not a private house, like Stephen King's Overview Hotel it reworks the country house trap tradition, offering an urban skyscraper twist.)

In *Subversive Champagne*, I described *The Avengers'* history as one of terminal paradoxes. This certainly relates to its reworking of the country house literary tradition. It employs, exploits, playfully sends up and undermines, but ultimately reinforces our interest – bordering on obsession – with this 'timeless' tradition.

© Rodney Marshall

1. Peter Dickinson, 'Murder in the Manor', *The Armchair Detective*, Spring 1991.
2. 'Murder in the Manor'. In *The Joker* he is actually standing on the lawn, but it represents the same playful use of the cliché.

MAIN TITLE SEQUENCES

Many television shows are content to retain the same title sequence throughout their run. One or two variations will perhaps materialise when cast members join or depart, clips and stills require updating in grudging acknowledgement of the fact that the leads are not impervious to the ravages of time, or the theme tune is rearranged. But the basic structure of the sequence itself will often remain unchanged.

Not so in the case of *The Avengers*, though this is perhaps unsurprising. Notwithstanding the ever-evolving make-up of the principal cast, which never remained static for more than two consecutive seasons, the creative minds behind the series also had to contend with the switch from videotape to film and the transition from black and white to colour (not to mention the seven year gap between the original series and its 1970s 'sequel' *The New Avengers*). And yet, even when the status quo remained intact, the show would still voluntarily set itself the challenge of revamping its title sequences. This was in keeping with *The Avengers*' credo of constant reinvention, of always moving forward into pastures new, of refusing to become stagnant and set in its ways. The result is a multitude of *Avengers* title sequences. The videotape era opened with the Keel titles, the few examples still in existence presenting slight variations in their choice of photographs of Ian Hendry and Patrick Macnee. With Season 2, Steed's plethora of partners necessitated different title sequences for each, with Julie Stevens and Honor Blackman again represented by different photos in various versions, while the three Dr. Martin King stories feature Steed solo, Jon Rollason's brief tenure apparently not meriting any sort of formal acknowledgement until the closing credits. Honor Blackman's Cathy Gale would add to her repertoire with the Season 3 'running man' titles, featuring a fleeing silhouette being gradually entrapped by the words 'The Avengers' materialising around him. All of these sequences utilised a more primitive, blocky font, less-stylised than that adopted in the Peel era, and miles away from the colourful, chunky-yet-arty text proffered by *The New Avengers*. With the introduction of Diana Rigg, the series became more ambitious, offering different flavours for its domestic and international markets: the iconic photographic sequence featuring stills of Steed and Peel, sometimes shown in close succession to create a flipbook effect; and the live-action chessboard version, used to introduce the series to its new American audience. The switch to colour found Steed and Peel 'in action', striking various fighting poses (and exchanging knowing smiles) in a sequence that would be altered slightly for the first Tara King story *The Forget-Me-Knot*, before giving way to the orange target Tara title sequence and the summery armour titles. Add in *The New Avengers*' clips and animated titles, and we have a bevy of title sequences to choose from. And that fails to take into account mooted sequences that were planned or filmed but never used, or the countless modified versions created for the series' foreign language sales. A surfeit of titles, if you will!

And yet, in spite of the seemingly infinite number of titles produced for the series over the years, one notable characteristic ties virtually all of these various and myriad iterations together: a blank, featureless background. Whether it is Steed, Keel, and Cathy fleeing toward a solitary streetlamp, Steed and Emma clinking champagne glasses, Steed and Tara dodging a particularly persistent bullseye, or Steed, Purdey, and Gambit melding into a rampant lion, the void-like never-never-world is omnipresent. There are two possible exceptions to the rule: the Tara 'armour' titles and *The New Avengers*' clips sequence. However, in the case of the former, the background, while not completely featureless, consists of a landscape made up of grass, trees, and sky seemingly miles away from civilisation, an unoccupied green and pleasant land stretching out in all directions. This serves to isolate the characters from the real world in much the same way that the blank backdrops do in other sequences. And film clips aside, *The New Avengers'* sequence opens with the leads framed by a large circle, standing in front of a grey-tinged background every bit as featureless as its original series counterparts.

This repeated aesthetic choice to place the leads in empty space is meaningful on a number of levels. It serves to elevate the titles beyond a mere means through which to introduce the audience to the series' stars, and instead turns them into mini-films in their own right. In a series like *The Avengers*, which always accorded a significant amount of attention to its visuals, be it in its choice of fashions, sets, or locations, the decision to present an unadorned landscape is significant. Most notably, it differentiates the titles from the episodes they accompany, providing the inverse of the series' usual plethora of eye-catching flourishes. With nothing to distract from the stars and the few select props with which they share the screen, the titles create a carefully-curated summation of the series' ethos. It is probably no coincidence that so many of the images that instantly spring to mind when one thinks of *The Avengers* appear in at least one title sequence – the iconic rose in the barrel of a gun, clinking champagne glasses, the Union Jack rampant lion, red carnations, silhouettes in action poses, an artfully-arranged bowler and brolly, a pair of leather boots. These all serve to cultivate the image *The Avengers* is known for – a prototypically English world of style, class, and elegance, cut through with action, adventure, and a legendary reputation for subversiveness. To put it plainly, it is the essence of *The Avengers,* distilled into a minute or so of footage.

But there are further readings in the offing. Is this stark landscape a proxy for *Avengerland* itself, a blank canvas that can be modified at will to suit the needs of the story of the week? After all, this is a world that encompasses everything from diabolical masterminds to drug dealers, Cybernauts to skilled interrogators, man-eating plants from space to rogue military units, with a healthy dose of double agents and unorthodox scientists mixed in for good measure; a world where no extras were allowed on the streets, and the sets were practically devoid of anyone other than the leads and whoever they chose to interact with that week. Similarly, virtually no individuals other than the leads appear in the titles, and the few that do – the running man silhouette, the man with the target on his back in the chessboard sequence – are dehumanised, their faces obscured, reduced to the status of cardboard cut-outs. Whatever and whoever is brought into the void is there to service the leads in their current case, and then removed just as quickly to make way for the next story.

Or do the titles, in fact, represent another world outside *Avengerland*? Perhaps this is where Steed and co. retire after the screen goes dark, stepping through Tara King's red door to nowhere from the 'armour' titles and indulging in a glass of champagne until they are needed once again. Given that *The Avengers* is a series with a strong fantasy streak, one that spends less time on the personal lives of its leads than on the case of the week, it is not outside the realm of possibility to imagine that Steed and his respective partners go 'back in their box' between adventures, waiting until we are ready to watch them again. [1] Or does *Avengerland* simply cease to exist the moment its central players depart, Descartes-style? Does Steed fold up his picture-postcard version of England and pack it away until he is in the mood to foil another diabolical mastermind? Regardless of the interpretation, there is undoubtedly something of the 'other' in the titles. Their visual aesthetic places the leads in a world apart from that which they normally occupy, heightening the surreal nature of the series and its characters in the process. However, despite these unifying elements, each title sequence is also unique and reflects the season it accompanies, including the dynamics between the characters and the overall mood and feel of its stories.

Though strictly outside of this volume's remit, for comparison purposes it is useful to examine the title sequences of the videotape episodes. The Keel and Gale era titles are of a piece, utilising the same Johnny Dankworth theme tune and following the same format: a series of black and white still images. Steed and Keel/Cathy are shown running toward a streetlamp, Steed brandishing a gun, all three clad in long coats. This visually places the series within the crime thriller/noir/detective genre, with the leads dressed in classic gumshoe garb as they lurk in shady environs. Along with the brassy, jazzy nightclub-esque music, this jives with the series' more grounded, gritty tone, the filmed episodes' more fantastical bent still in the embryonic stages. The Season 3 titles have a similar feel, and feature the fleeing silhouette of a man, while the camera, playing the role of his relentless pursuer, closes in frame by frame. Similarly, Steed and Keel/Cathy are both on the run and on the alert, forever looking warily into the middle distance at some unseen foe with barely contained alarm. At no point do they meet one another's eyes, or even look at each other. Their attention is focussed outward, on the current threat – their watchword, as it is for the running man, is 'peril'. There is no time for witty banter and champagne here – our heroes are far too busy searching for a way out of their latest predicament to bother with the niceties. As a result, the characters come across as less a team than a pair of individuals thrown together and forced to fight for their mutual survival. This reflects the characterisation of the series in its early years, in which Steed's relationships with Keel and Gale were often fraught due to their clashing viewpoints and Steed's habit of drawing the 'talented amateurs' into his latest assignment, sometimes without their consent, requiring them to quickly adapt to the new threat. Though there were moments of friendship and mutual warmth to be found, they were sprinkled more sparingly throughout the stories than in later years, and the 'alienation' of the leads from one another in the title sequences is perfectly in keeping with this.

As the series made the transition from Gale to Peel and videotape to film, its identity also received an overhaul. While a handful of Season 4 stories could have fitted into Season 3 without too much difficulty, the series was actively moving away from the gritty, noirish environs that Gale and Keel had called home, and into *Avengerland* proper, a world of increasingly fantastical plots and, just as importantly, an enhanced emphasis placed on style and elegance. This is exemplified by the Season 4 titles. While still consisting of a series of black and white stills, as in the Gale/Keel era, the new, gracious age of *Avengerland* is reflected in the stylish shots of the elegantly attired Steed and Emma – Steed appears with bowler and brolly for the first time in a title sequence, while Emma dons both a leather fighting suit and a low-cut blouse, plus a sophisticated coat and gloves ensemble in the closing titles – and of iconic *Avengers* props that have become closely associated with the series, including the carnation Steed removes from his buttonhole and Emma's leather boots. While the leads still do not face one another when they share the frame, there is at least the suggestion of eye contact teased by Emma's brilliant over-the-shoulder smile in Steed's (off-screen) direction, while a close-up of Steed's sidelong glance insinuates that he is watching as Emma allows the trim on her blouse to fall away from her bosom. The sequence is slyly flirtatious, Emma's smile and Steed's stolen glances conveying (wicked) good humour as Laurie Johnson's sophisticated theme plays in the background. Even when the leads strike a series of action poses, their expressions are not as tense, their sense of danger not as immediate, as in the previous sequences. Interestingly, another set of titles was also produced for this season, though never used. It, too, consisted of a series of black and white stills, some in exaggerated close-up, and though Steed and Emma do manage to crack a smile and strike stylish poses, an action shot of Emma, hair flying and brandishing a gun, features the same sort of alert expression worn by Keel and Gale in their titles. Indeed, these titles feel, both in construction and content, very much like the next evolution of the Gale title sequences, and perhaps that is why they were never used – the thrilleresque vibe that had served the series so well through its first three seasons was no longer fitting for a series that had branched out well beyond its crime drama roots by this stage in its development.

As the series moved into colour, it took its cue from the chessboard title sequence developed late in Season 4 for the new American audience. Both the colour Season 5 titles and the chessboard sequence embrace the series' complete transition into a fantasy *Avengerland*. In the chessboard version, Steed and Emma casually ignore a dead body in favour of the much more palatable bottle of champagne in its hand. The colour titles eschew the unsavoury detail of a body altogether, instead using stylised action poses and Emma's crackshot corking of the champagne bottle in Steed's hand to represent the series' 'action' elements, rather than any genuine sense of danger. Both the chessboard and Season 5 titles also finally afford the leads the opportunity to look one another in the eye, and the result is mischievous glances alive with humour and private jokes, hinting at the nature of Steed and Peel's eternal 'are they?/aren't they?' relationship without providing any firm answers. Indeed, humour and style have become the order of the day on all fronts, with the post-title card image of Steed and Emma's (well-shod) feet propped up on the table the pinnacle of light-hearted irreverence – they could be recovering from a hangover acquired the night before or resting from the exertions of their latest adventure. All sense of the Keel/Gale era peril has finally been banished, the slight tension built with the crescendo of the opening percussion sequence swept aside in favour of class, elegance, and style, as well as the leads' mutual affection. This sequence perfectly encapsulates the sense that nothing terrible can befall them in the fantasy-based world of *Avengerland* – the stakes, no matter how high, will inevitably be resolved without consequence, leaving the leads with no more pressing problems than running out of champagne.

The Tara King title sequences move in a new direction once again, drawing on the youth, vitality, and sensuality of the new *Avengers* girl, Tara King. The bright colours of both the orange background and Tara's wardrobe in the target titles (the antithesis of the Peel titles' neutral palette), and the floral motif of Tara's blouse and the bevy of carnations in the suits of armour, tap into the swinging sixties 'flower power' ethos, a youthful movement coming to the fore in the summer of '68, just as Tara's adventures properly got underway. Tara's tender age makes her participation in that movement seem a natural fit, and her youthful enthusiasm is exemplified by the way she bounds and sprints across fields and over a bridge. [2] And just as the series portrayed Tara as being blatantly in love with Steed, the titles also emphasise the more sensual, overtly sexualised dynamic between the leads, with the target titles featuring her suggestively caressing Steed's lapel (an overt display compared to Emma gently resting her hand against the same the season before), while the armour titles close with Steed and Tara sharing a long, meaningful look. Tara herself is also more overtly sexy and feminine in the target titles, symbolised by curvy targets, pearls, and lipstick marks (and a queen playing card in the closing credits), and awarded an extra seductive trumpet solo in her version of the Laurie Johnson theme as she emerges from the grass in an evening gown in the 'armour' titles.

Finally, Steed's paternal, protective streak toward his partner is highlighted as he 'saves' Tara from the roving target, sacrificing his bowler in the process, and plays the gallant jouster to defeat the knights that would do her harm in the armour titles. [3] These proactive actions on Steed's part also serve to underscore Tara's naivety and inexperience as an agent, and her need for Steed's experienced 'guiding hand' in the course of their adventures. The watchwords for these titles, and indeed the season they accompanied, are youth, romance, protection, and inexperience, all of which are neatly incorporated into these brief films.

As it did in so many other areas, *The New Avengers* followed in the footsteps of its predecessor and once more used its title sequences to establish its key themes. By employing the familiar first few bars of the Laurie Johnson theme before striking off in another direction entirely, the theme tune highlighted the series' willingness to homage its past, but also its desire to strike off into fresh territory and to define its own identity. And yet, there is a bit of an oddity on the *New Avengers* title front. Despite creating an animated title sequence, featuring silhouettes of the three leads melding into a Union Jack-patterned rampant lion, another title sequence, consisting of clips of the first few episodes produced, was initially transmitted on the first seven episodes (as they appear on DVD releases) when they aired in certain markets. The mystery deepens as it has become apparent that other title sequences were also mooted and/or filmed. One version appears to have been shot and then used for scrap. Filmed through a white circle/tube, it opens with a shot of the trio standing side by side, the same shot used to open the clips titles. The shot of Macnee/Steed that features in both the clips and animated versions shares the same greyish background, and photographs reveal that this was shot through the same white tube, with corresponding shots of Hunt, brandishing a gun, and Lumley, reclining in her tube to allow her skirt to fall back and reveal her much-talked-about stockings and suspenders, also shot for the same purpose. Hunt and Lumley's head shots from the animated titles also feature the same grey background, suggesting that they, too, were filmed for this sequence, and brief clips of Lumley reclining in her tube and performing a high kick for the camera against a similar background appear in a short promotional film for the series. Why this title sequence was filmed, only to be cut up and used for various and myriad purposes, is a mystery as presumably it would have been more effective left intact.

Another, very early mooted title sequence, as outlined in Patrick Macnee's *The Avengers and Me*, featured Steed striding across a featureless landscape, with Gambit and Charly (the original name for the Purdey character) hurrying after him, Charly bringing up the rear and slowing down to lift her skirt and adjust her stockings and suspenders (earning a look from Gambit). She then joins Gambit and whistles to Steed, who waits for the pair to catch up before they continue on their merry way.

In contrast, the animated titles, which appear on the majority of the episodes, begin with the Union Jack rampant lion, which then morphs into various action silhouettes of Steed, Gambit, and Purdey respectively. With each character taking on one colour of the red, white, and blue motif, the three eventually blend together to form the lion once more. Though very different in format, each *New Avengers* sequence emphasises the themes of teamwork and togetherness – despite the characters being spotlighted individually, the sequences always begin and/or end with the trio being brought together in some way. The clips sequence opens with them shoulder-to-shoulder, as if they are their own mini-army, a front line standing between Britain and her enemies, then reinforces that image by closing with a clip from *The Eagle's Nest* featuring the trio marching and whistling in unison. Both images play on the coming together of the characters, emphasising that it is only when they are united that they will be able to march off into the featureless horizon to defeat the diabolical masterminds. The animated sequence communicates this even more forcefully by quite literally blending the characters together, subsuming their individual personalities to form a whole greater than the sum of its parts. All *Avengers* characters are portrayed as a team to a certain degree, but it was normally their differences that were foregrounded, rather than eschewing their identities in favour of a focus on the larger whole. Clemens and Fennell were effectively informing their audience that, more than any other iteration of the series that had come before, the team was all in this new series – they are stronger together, and must rely on one another to succeed. This was a theme that would echo throughout the series as the trio's enemies repeatedly tried to break the team apart in order to defeat them, only to fail as the lion, inevitably, reassembled itself. Meanwhile, the use of animation, a high-tech endeavour at the time, speaks to the new series' desire to be modern, while the dynamic poses struck by Gambit and Purdey's silhouettes and the use of 'high-octane' clips highlight the series' more action-oriented slant. As if to drive that point home, the animated titles close with the lion filling the screen with a vivid blood red, foreshadowing the series' decidedly more serious treatment of violence – symbolic blood hinting at real gore to follow, though, in true *Avengers* style, always used sparingly.

These various and myriad title sequences had many roles to play, not least of which was to provide a brief introduction of the leads and the characters they played to the audience. But they also served as a perfect encapsulation of the essence of the series as a whole, as well as the idiosyncrasies that made each era unique in its own right, all while positing some interesting questions about the show itself. As with everything else, *The Avengers* elevated the title sequence to an art form, creating mini-films whose images would linger on in its audience's imagination long after the episodes themselves had faded to black.

© JZ Ferguson

1. This reminds me of the musical box at the beginning of *Camberwick Green* which hid the 'protagonist of the week', and which was reworked in *Life on Mars*, a show which drew upon *The Avengers* for inspiration for its surreal elements.
2. The use of the iconic Tykes Water Lake bridge offers a connection to the *Avengers* past through this central image of the Peel era.
3. Both the knights and the theatrical door in the field reinforce how large a part both surrealism and artful artificiality were playing by Season 6.

TEASERS

Although production of *The Avengers* on film began in October 1964, the series was not bought by an American network until more than a year later. Nevertheless, the move from videotape to film – confirmed internally in March 1964 – was undoubtedly made with the lucrative American market in mind. Whether this influenced the modifications in terms of style and thematic content remains a controversial, disputed debate. Nevertheless, it certainly necessitated structural change, specifically the use of teasers and tags, allowing for extra commercial breaks. In one sense, these two additions to each *Avengers* episode provide the show with a frame into which the three acts are then placed. As with the decision to film initially in monochrome rather than colour, commercial serendipity shaped *The Avengers'* aesthetic evolution. The new structure/framing device becomes part of the winning formula on film: teaser, series of murders/strange events, investigation, fight finale, tag. While critics often accuse the film era of the show of suffering from formula fatigue or predictability, this was a key part of its global appeal. However, what precisely was the teaser, in an artistic rather than commercial sense?

One online dictionary defines a teaser as follows: 'an attention-grabbing opening presented at the start of a television show... establishing the basic theme.' Like all definitions, it is imperfect, partly because *The Avengers* tends to offer a unique take on things. However, it is a useful starting point. 'Attention-grabbing' and 'establishing the theme' represent two separate if inter-connected elements. Clearly, the teaser has to grab our attention by providing a 'hook', and in *Avengerland* that means offering us unusual or quirky images. While the series would occasionally provide us with a 'straight' scene, no teaser could be. It needed to be mysterious and intriguing. As for 'establishing' the theme, I have a number of problems with this. To begin with, 'establish' is too big or bold an enterprise for this brief encounter. In addition, the idea of teasing the viewer surely entails something more subtle. 'Hinting' at the theme might be more appropriate. An *Avengers* teaser offers a swift, stylish sketch which will require us to watch on in order for the theme to be established and the plot unravelled.

Teasers, like titles, come in different shades and styles. A title such as *The Murder Market* reveals quite a lot: the episode will almost certainly explore organised murders which are fuelled by a greed for money. On the other hand, *Silent Dust* is a mysteriously poetic title which, in itself, reveals nothing. This variety is also displayed in teasers. Examining the first two monochrome teasers illustrates this.

The Town of No Return sets the tone for many of the subsequent teasers. We find ourselves in a naturalistic setting as the camera pans across sand dunes and coastline, before fore-grounding a fisherman's powerful arm. Both the menacing score and the fact that he is holding a knife offer dramatic warnings. However, we soon establish that he is mending his nets and the score transforms itself into a lighter piece as the naturalism is threatened: first by a figure – covered by a waterproof tarpaulin – walking to the beach from the sea and then emerging as a dry, impeccably-clad man in a tweed suit, tie and umbrella. If the sight is a strange one then the required quirky surrealism derives more from the fisherman's lack of surprise. This type of arrival clearly isn't unusual at all. In this *Avengerland*, the unusual is usual, we are being told, and it is this which provides the hook. The subsequent comment about the weather – "looks like rain" – is both banal but also prophetic, working in tandem with Laurie Johnson's score which reaches a dramatic crescendo as the episode title arrives on screen. We have received a hint of things to come – expected strangers arriving in a coastal village – but nothing more concrete than that. The scene moves from real to surreal, before leaving us on a note somewhere between the two, blurring the boundaries as *The Avengers* often would. The opening offers both a mirror image of the title – mysteriously ominous – and **captures or bottles up the very essence or perfume of the story** we will experience. Perhaps this is a better definition for *The Avengers* teaser.

The Murder Market, in common with many of the Season 4, 5 and 6 teasers, provides the spectacle of a violent, unnatural death within the hook. The opening image offers us an avengerish frame-within-a-frame. The camera lens captures a smartly dressed man standing behind a glass fish tank, before his cleared image emerges into a deserted aquarium. While many *Avengers* teasers contain no dialogue at all, here much of the atmospheric drama derives from the fact that only one of the two characters speaks. The female assassin's silence is almost as ominous as her silencer, and the banal act of murder is transformed into art form by the three bullet holes in the tank, an oddly aesthetic sight as water emerges with the episode title superimposed. Apart from the initial image and the final one, there is nothing particularly quirky or innovative in the scene. Arguably the hook here is the gender reversal: a hit-woman sticking it to a man. We sense that what will emerge is a series of murders. What we cannot anticipate is the fact that the teaser will be playfully redeployed later, an effective technique used in a number of *Avengers* episodes such as *The Hour That Never Was*, *Stay Tuned* and *Pandora*. In these episodes, rather than being a self-contained scene, the teaser becomes something far more daring: a free-floating moment which can return to surprise us in the main body of the story. In one sense, these threaten to undermine the formulaic structure.

If, as I suggested, the teaser should somehow bottle up the essence or perfume of the episode, this is certainly reflected in the iconic *The Hour That Never Was*. A story which, perhaps more than any other, destabilises the show's formula requires a teaser to match. This is one of a rare breed, in that the Avengers themselves appear in the pre-title sequence. As in *The Town of No Return*, a naturalistic landscape and bucolic score are interrupted by a dog chasing ...nothing? As Steed recovers from the crash which this canine has caused, we have to ask ourselves what is unusual about this opening sequence. A surreal score emerges as the camera focuses in on the car's smashed clock and the title imposes itself. The original working title – *An Hour to Spare* – simply wouldn't have worked. The final one colours the teaser which preceded it, suggestive of an *Avengerland* in which we have to question everything we see. Maybe the dog wasn't chasing someone; what if it was running away from something? In an episode in which Steed and Mrs. Peel will be the only human figures we see for the majority of the 'hour', it seems – with hindsight – that they simply *had* to appear in the teaser. It is a remarkable episode which will continuously tease us, including returning us to the teaser itself – without explanation – half way through.

Some teasers, in the best tradition of the short story, contain a quirky twist in the tail/tale: a tediously sedate game of golf where a rifle is suddenly pulled out from a golf bag to shoot a man on the putting green; or a tropical jungle sequence – with drums, exotic animal noises and native calls – which ends when a man, with an arrow in his back, collapses by a roadside stone revealing that London is just 23 miles away. In both *The Thirteenth Hole* and *Small Game for Big Hunters*, the teasers provide a naturalistic narrative before shocking us with that final playful twist, almost daring us to turn off.

As *The Avengers* emerges into 'Glorious Technicolor', it becomes harder to continually surprise viewers, and some of the teasers either offer a scene which could just as easily have been contained within the main body of the story, or rely on cliché, such as an agent or civil servant escaping from an unseen pursuer. The stylish teasers for *You Have Just Been Murdered*, *Murdersville* and *Game* arguably give away too much, offering 'explanation' where a subtle hint might have worked better. However, the fact that these three openings are so memorable suggests that this 'establishing' approach can sometimes work equally well, allowing us to anticipate the plot and the pattern of crimes which will emerge to echo the teaser. Others continue the monochrome trend of lulling us into a false sense of security/realism only to shock us with the unexpected or surreal: the punch which knocks out Steed in *Stay Tuned* or the mummified mannequin in *Pandora*. *Bizarre*, appropriately, provides us with a forty second mini-teaser which reveals nothing at all, simply offering us the inexplicable image of a young woman in a nightdress crossing a snowy field before collapsing. Reworked from a *Danger Man* script, it is a minimalist scene in virtually every sense of the term. I said that it reveals nothing, yet by doing so it promises us an altogether different *Avengers* experience.

If teasers changed little between Seasons 4 and 6, then the re-emergence of the show in its re-created form – *The New Avengers* – also saw the teaser fine-tuned. In *The Eagle's Nest* we gain our first opportunity to see how the new series would rework a cult 1960s show in the harsher world of the mid-1970s. Like the series itself, the teaser immediately establishes its ability to 'make it new': structurally and stylistically.

The New Avengers places its teasers *before* the opening main titles sequence, meaning that we are immediately plunged into a bewildering

Avengerland without warning and without the chance to warm up/get into the mood through a familiar main theme score. Rather than opening with a realistic or naturalistic scenario which is then cut through with surrealism or a quirky twist, the teaser for *The Eagle's Nest* de-familiarises, thrusting us into a scene mid-action. The familiar image of a fleeing agent is warped by the sight of the pursuers and their weapons of choice: fishermen wielding rods. It is a disconcerting spectacle in which realism and surrealism merge. Neither the agent nor the viewer has time to drink in the glorious panoramic, cliff top view of the monastery coastline. Instead, as if spurred on by Laurie Johnson's vibrant, guitar-led score, he seeks "sanctuary" among the island's monks. The sight of him being reeled in by the grinning lead henchman during a religious service is bizarrely surreal and stays with us during the realistic interrogation in the dark, claustrophobic studio/cell. Back out in the natural light of the hillsides, the teaser returns us to the opening scenario. With the fishermen closing in, a desperate Stannard jumps off the cliff edge and the camera freeze-frames the image.

Despite the fact that there is a horrible inevitability about the agent's destiny, we are forced to wait while the main title sequences are played out, before re-joining the action: a literal tease. Once we are plunged back in, we are teased in the sense that Stannard appears to have escaped in a boat. However, Main's confident grin warns us that he is about to get his first catch of the day and the deadly rod hits home. The dead Stannard's boat gently drifts out to sea, the water dappled by late-afternoon sunshine. It is a beautifully poetic final image, cruelly at odds with the violence of the deadly chase. The teaser – which extends pre/post titles to an impressive three minutes twenty seconds – bottles up the episode's spirit without giving too much away. We realise that the fishing rods are lethal and that the island is not an ideal holiday destination but little else is revealed. With *The Eagle's Nest*, Clemens has immediately demonstrated *The New Avengers'* ability to rework the traditional teaser, in terms of structure, length and style. Its placing before the opening titles has a subtly unsettling effect on the viewer, while the freeze-frame device allows the teaser's climax to be held over. This split-teaser will not always be employed; some episodes (post-titles) simply move on to the following scene, thus undermining any sense of formulaic certainty or predictability. The teaser becomes almost a mini-film in itself, a series of scenes which reinvent and re-energise this key component in the *Avengers* structure.

Unlike the tag scene, which represents style over substance, providing a decorative flourish at the end of an *Avengers* episode – and often simply added on to the end of the final main scene in *The New Avengers* – the teaser has a crucial role to play in the filmed seasons. Offering a hint of things to come without giving the plot away, fusing realism with a surrealism or quirky twist, intriguing us, hooking us, plunging us into yet another bizarre *Avengerland* setting or location, the teaser can create the right ambience or atmosphere. It can surprise us, undermining our expectations, as in the silent, urbane hit-man of *You Have Just Been Murdered* who leaves his victim with a business card, rather than a bullet hole. It can take us on a psychedelic trip, as in the baby bouncer's spinning spirals which send us on a hallucinogenic journey into a child's nasty nursery.

Merging artistic and commercial concerns, the teaser – in the new American market – played a vital role. It needed to grip the viewer within a matter of seconds. If it failed to do so, then the consumer might well change channels during the subsequent commercial break. US ratings now represented 'make or break' for this British show. Like a potential reader looking through the blurb or first page of a new novel in a bookstore, the hook needed to be powerful enough to convince him/her to continue, to purchase the product. Thankfully, *Avengers* teasers normally provided that initial, instant magic.

As Frank Shailes suggested in *Bright Horizons*, part of the excitement stems from not knowing what strange realm we will be visiting this week. Experiencing an *Avengers* teaser is somewhat like walking into a restaurant for the first time: the welcome, the way in which the space has been used, the decorations, the lighting, and the 'aromas' all provide us with a sense of what is to come. Even before we digest the 'menu' and then the 'product', we have a *frisson* of anticipatory excitement, a wonderfully undefined sense of the visual feast which awaits us.

© Rodney Marshall

TAGS

Every James Bond film ends the same way; the hero gets to have his cake and eat it, as it were, as he is apparently set adrift (sometimes literally) with a pretty young woman and he quips about the adventure they have just come through. Similarly, nearly every episode of *The Avengers* ends with a whimsical reflection on the episode's themes. As with Bond, the tag scene can subvert a subtext or recurrent motif of the episode as a whole.

In the first season, there was no separate scene for the final exchange of banter; it was just a line or two of dialogue – Inspector Lewis saying he can finally go home and take a powder for his cold, or 'Mrs. Briggs' nudging Steed for payment of her acting fees. However, even in these formative episodes we see a tantalising glimpse of the future. *Please Don't Feed the Animals*, filmed in April 1961, is the first episode to finish with an outright joke as Steed defuses Keel's standard stiff-necked disapproval:

Steed: This is a very interesting book, you know, Doctor. Remarkably comprehensive. All sorts of snippets of information. Do you know how porcupines make love?
Keel: No.
Steed: Very, very carefully.

Nonetheless, it's not a new scene; it's the end of the rather long scene (number 150) which had twelve camera angle changes, the last five covering the joke. The sterner *Dance with Death*, next in the schedule, returned to a grim ending and the episodes that followed varied the light-heartedness. *Double Danger* and *The Springers* are upbeat while *Toy Trap* ends with Keel berating Steed for 'using' others. *Dead of*

Winter sees a joke pertinent to the plot with Steed warning Keel, as the doctor launches into another castigation of Steed, "If you're not careful you'll get a temperature."

The light ending as an end of scene persisted into the Dr. King episodes – Steed nearly answering the summons for a steward as Carla Berotti is led away, then realising he can relax and call one himself; Dr. King grimly joking that they're not going to fly back to London after leaving the convent hide-out of the plane wreckers. In *The Sell-Out*, there's nothing more than a close-up of One Twelve, smiling as Steed leads the thwarted assassin away, Dr. King bowing out quietly.

However, things changed almost immediately with the new scripts for the second season. In the very first of these episodes, filmed in June 1962, we suddenly have what may be considered a standalone tag scene. In *Death Dispatch*, Cathy and Steed return to the embassy where Travers maliciously tells them that the ambassador wants to see them, but ends up seeing Cathy and Steed feted while he ends up with Cathy's doll as consolation.

A month later – July 1962 – in *Propellant 23*, we have *two* tags: one where Curly turns up completely bald, a consequence of rubbing his head with rocket fuel disguised as hair restorer, and the other where Cathy tells Steed he's "forgotten his package" – he panics, thinking she is using code to mean the rocket fuel, but instead she hands him a bag of pastries. Both tags play on the different, interwoven themes from the episode and give the viewer a pleasant feeling as things wrap up neatly and happily.

Seasons 2 and 3 continued in this vein, with a short scene at the end of Act Three, the episodes still being expected to have two advertising breaks. These short scenes continued to vary between the serious and the funny, but most of them involved mild ribbing of one principal character by the other (in the case of Venus Smith, she was always the victim).

Over in James Bond's world, *Dr No* wrapped up filming in March 1962 and didn't hit cinemas until October, so it's hard to say if there was happenstance, coincidence or enemy action [1] in these cross-overs. Certainly, *The Avengers* had already started placing the tongue in the cheek in the supposedly hard-boiled first season, and it may have been an inspiration for Terence Young as he decided to inject humour into *Dr No*: 'a lot of things in this film, the sex and violence and so on, if played straight a) would be objectionable, and b) were never going to go past the censors, but the moment you take the mickey out, put the tongue out in the cheek, it seems to disarm.' [2]

The Avengers, certainly, was alone in doing this on television at the time, although it became a part of *The Saint* and other action series later in the sixties. This adoption of the concept by other series did not happen until after the next step in the evolution of the tag scene – probably the most important one.

When the series switched from videotape to film, a whole new world opened up for it, quite literally. Location work became essential to the series and the freedom offered by film meant the producers and directors could explore new possibilities. The most notable was also potentially a lucrative one: the creation of the new teaser and tag scenes, quite distinct from the rest of the episode, which allowed broadcasters, if they wished, to insert two extra advertising breaks into each episode's broadcast.

In Season 4, the producers decided on a formulaic structure for every episode: a teaser scene to hint at the plot yet to unfold, followed by a combination of red herrings and exposition. This would culminate in the Avengers solving the case, defeating the villains and then heading off in the tag scene, 'receding towards a bright horizon.' [3] To accentuate the tag scene even more, each week would feature a new, more *outré*, form of transport, from model train to hot air balloon; from helicopter to flying carpet. [4] These happy conclusions are always accompanied with upbeat dialogue and jokes, often at the expense of Steed. They serve to make the viewers contented and eager to tune in again the following week as they feel the rapport between the leads and, moreover, feel strongly for them as well. The technique worked and *The Avengers* became bigger than it had ever been before. The extra ad break must have worked as well, because Howard Thomas and Bob Norris were able to sell the series to the American Broadcasting Company in a $1,000,000 deal, estimated to be the biggest ever made in the States. [5]

It would be hard to pick the best tag scene of Season 4: the milk float in *The Hour That Never Was* comes close, but is marred by the speeded-up footage; the tiny bubble car is hilarious; the reversing ride-on model train is endearing; the apparent flying carpet is superbly framed and shot. But maybe your favourite is none of these.

Season 4 is often seen as the pinnacle of *The Avengers* but it was the colour episodes of Season 5 that were the real money earners, better remembered today, and still shown around the world nearly fifty years later. Foreign sales alone of Season 5 were in excess of £5,000,000, and the programme was screened in seventy countries. [6]

The tag scenes for Season 5 initially followed a similar path to Season 4, often centring around Steed taking Mrs. Peel somewhere in one of his vintage cars. To save time and cost, these scenes were filmed in a block at Lord Montague's Beaulieu motor museum, directed by Roy Rossotti, and often bear little or no relation to the episode that preceded it. Sensing that the vintage car vignettes were too disconnected, the producers dropped the device and the scripts changed to have little quips based on a theme of the episode's plot – a very light-hearted return to the ideas in the first three seasons, but as a separate vignette after an ad break. Not all of these are successful, but for the most part they are a joy to watch. [7]

A particularly brilliant tag scene takes place at the end of *Epic*, that most post-modern of episodes of *The Avengers*. Rather than reflect on the case, the Avengers are lounging in Emma's flat, deciding where to go that evening and are perusing the film listings. Steed wickedly suggests a revival of an old Stewart Kirby movie (Kirby being one of the villains they just defeated), and Emma raises an arch eyebrow in return. Electing to stay in instead, she kicks the wall of her flat and it falls down, revealing that they are still on the set – as of course they are every episode, and the illusion is at the same time dispelled and intensified. [8]

Tag scenes continued throughout Season 6 of *The Avengers* but not always with the same degree of success; something is lacking and the scenes often feel flat, although there are still moments of delight to be had. It may be simply that the chemistry and comic timing between Patrick and Linda was not as strong as he had enjoyed with Diana Rigg – although I feel that the scripts were often trying too hard to be humorous. If you have to spell out a joke, it isn't funny. [9]

This same malaise affects *The New Avengers* and some episodes are like Season 1 or 2 where they are not even a separate scene anymore, just a couple of lines of dialogue as a book-end to the episode. [10] The tags that are there will occasionally make you laugh but some, like the giant tomato at the end of *Gnaws*, are as unfunny as the giant mushroom scene was at the end of *The Rotters*. It seems strange that a more budget-driven decade should have seen the loss of the extra advertising opportunity, but it may well have been that the producers knew by then that the broadcasters were going to add as many breaks as they wanted anyway.

© Piers Johnson

1. PJ: To paraphrase *Goldfinger*.
2. PJ: Audio commentary, 2006 Ultimate Edition DVD.
3. PJ: Rodney Marshall, *Bright Horizons: The Monochrome World of Emma Peel*, p. 23.
4. PJ: The full list: A Vespa motor scooter; a model train which takes off in reverse; Steed sits in his veteran Humber while Emma departs in her Lotus; a pair of bicycles; an amphibious car; Steed's Bentley; hearse; Emma's Mini Moke; a milk float – which they realise no-one is driving so they leap off and chase after it; a taxi; in the back of a hay cart; a pair of horses; a horse-drawn surrey; a hot air balloon; a rickshaw; a Canadian canoe; a Messerschmitt bubble car; a golf cart; dancing a waltz; go-karts; a coach and four; a helicopter; a tandem bicycle; a motorcycle and enclosed sidecar; inside a moving caravan; on a flying carpet – on the back of a utility truck.
5. PJ: Anne Francis, *Julian Wintle: A Memoir*, 1986, p. 85.
6. PJ: Francis *op. cit.*, p. 86.
7. I wonder whether the 'Mrs. Peel, We're Needed' post-teaser scenes in the initial batch of Season 5 episodes constitute tags of sorts: post-teaser tags? In some ways they were closer to the simple style of the Season 4 endings.
8. Piers' choice is a great one; it is a rare example of a tag scene which genuinely adds to the episode which preceded it.

9. As I suggested in *Bright Horizons*, I feel that 'less is more' and that the colour tags increasingly seek to raise a 'cheesy' laugh. They can even be damaging. In the case of *Killer* – where Tara has been temporarily replaced – the postcard-popping tag pokes fun both at her absence in the episode and at her character, reinforcing the sense of her lack of independence.
10. JZF: For fans coming to *The New Avengers* from the original series, the lack of 'proper' tag scenes is sorely felt, wrong-footing the viewers and sending them abruptly and unceremoniously crashing into the closing credits where they expected another minute or two of footage. Occasionally the lack of a closing tag served *The New Avengers'* more serious tone – a light-hearted tag scene would have been grossly inappropriate at the end of *Obsession*, with Purdey's alienation from Gambit and Steed nixing the possibility of witty banter, or *Dead Men are Dangerous,* which closes with Steed's melancholy observation that Crayford was his friend. But the likes of the end of *To Catch a Rat*, with Purdey draping her arms cheerily over Steed and Gambit's shoulders, drives home how welcome the more frequent use of tags would have been, and how sorely they are missed. Their absence is a puzzling, and frustrating, artistic decision on Clemens' part.

SET DESIGN AND LOCATIONS

'If you could say it in words there would be no reason to paint.' (George Hopper)

Back in 1998, the term *'Avengerland'* was coined by the makers of *The Avengers* film starring Ralph Fiennes and Uma Thurman. [1] In common with action-adventure hero films, where Batman had his stylised fantasy world of Gotham City, *The Avengers* had their own fantasy landscape. The script and the design presented us with a world where the sixties had never ended and this they termed as *Avengerland*. Being a big budget feature film, they were free to create their own world to the smallest detail, embellished with effective special effect model work. Yet, to start with, they took their cue from the television series. The TV series didn't have to pretend the sixties had never ended to give it a distinctive look; they were making the show whilst it was swinging on around them. Without the big budget of an epic movie, they created their *Avengerland* by being selective in what they showed and where they went.

When the show was made on videotape, the sets were handled by an ever changing roster of talented up-and-coming designers, but with the advent of film it was up to the successive visions of first Harry Pottle, then Wilfred Shingleton and finally Robert Jones to become the 'architects of the small screen'. Series visionary and showrunner Brian Clemens had his own ideas about what he wanted the show to look and feel like. With his eyes on the American market, the show's budget and his own preferences, the Clemens version of *Avengerland* was created to play up to the overseas' perception of England, to embrace the clichés.

Set design is a very important part of any TV production. The production designer takes the scripts and seeks out the clues in the dialogue and stage directions as to what kind of world this story takes place in. To use an exaggerated example, it would be no good having a science fiction script set in a futuristic control room and then build a traditional sitting room. A good set for a home will clue the viewer into what kind of person lives there. The style of architecture would suggest if we were seeing a world that was progressive or stuck in the past. All kinds of inferences can be made from the details of a set. Writer/'media expert' Norman Hollyn:

'The look and feel of the worlds that the characters move through need to give a deeper look into their personalities and the script's meaning. In short, the design of the film must perform a storytelling function without using words. Otherwise, it's just radio.'

The set design creates the interior world (and sometimes the exterior one) of *The Avengers*. And the locations show us the physical world where these interiors reside. Together they build a picture; they give us a world, an arena for the games of espionage and adventure to play out in. Being a series that had a (limited) budget, some design decisions had to be based on cost rather than creativity; at times the budget fed the creativity. The most obvious budgetary solution involved the choices of location. It didn't really matter what the stories were about, and so in Season 4 a vast number of the settings involved a rural background. *A Touch of Brimstone* has Steed and Emma racing to the opening of the Hall of Friendship; we would expect such a place to be in the City as it has international ramifications, yet it is clearly in the countryside. The choice of road was budget related. With the show being made at Elstree Studios in the county of Hertfordshire, it was only a short drive away from the countryside, offering lots of fields, empty country lanes, quaint villages, manor houses, farm buildings and, on occasion, deserted airfields. At this time it was rare to have any significant urban locations, such as bustling streets of commuters and normal everyday people. *Quick-Quick Slow Death* features a very rare occurrence of physical interaction with a normal, busy suburban street full of shops – Borehamwood High Street. This was done for a visual gag showing what at the time must have been a rare sight – a lone man pushing a pram!

Emptiness is the order of the day with the majority of locations. Traffic on the roads is pretty much unheard of. These locations are isolated: a cut off village, an airbase, a country manor house, countless empty country roads for Steed and Mrs. Peel to race down. These secluded locations are all the better for getting away with some nefarious business. The evil doers and diabolical masterminds believe they are beyond the reach of those who could prevent them. But that didn't stop Season 4 wandering off the secluded track into locations where the everyday resided: stock footage of busy London traffic in *Dial A Deadly Number* as The Avengers sit in the back of a taxi; *Quick-Quick Slow Death* has the aforementioned Borehamwood high street opening scene, plus a later high shot of the cityscape from a partially demolished high rise. *A Touch of Brimstone* shows Steed and Mrs. Peel briefly driving home from a theatre down a high street of shops. *The Master Minds* has the rare appearance of the Houses of Parliament but, with Season 5, these forays became even rarer. When the series required an office block of high flying, corrupt businessmen in *The Winged Avenger*, the production crew chose what appears to be a barely-disguised, standard low-rise block of flats – a rather downmarket choice where an office block in the heart of the City of London makes more sense. The only significant location that interacts with the real world was stock footage for *A Funny Thing Happened On The Way To The Station* consisting of busy commuter trains travelling to and from the various stations of the narrative.

The show wasn't averse to having locations that were either studio sets representing an exterior street, or a graveyard, or using the Elstree studio backlot for locations, a practice followed by ITC shows such as *The Saint* or *The Baron*. *Escape In Time* features the memorable Mackiedockie Court, a very narrow, stylised street with an assortment of quaint shops, like a barbers and newsagents, for a sequence where men on the run could be spirited away; there is an element of 'toy town' about it. *Killer* has the metafictional idea of the Elstree studios backlot representing the backlot of an abandoned studio. The Emma Peel solo episode *Epic* uses the actual studio grounds, full of an abundance of props and set elements that would be found at an old forgotten film studio. The series had fun with some surreal and stylised graveyards in *From Venus With Love* and *The Living Dead*. [2] As there were night scenes to film, and the show rarely went out for night shoots, they were able to control the elements.

Creative ingenuity from the design department – due to budget restrictions – had already been a well-established part of the show from the first videotaped year, when they had often created sets to represent exterior locations. The film studio setup allowed the crew greater flexibility with the sets, such as having four walled sets as opposed to the figuratively speaking three walled sets of a TV studio (the fourth wall removed for the cameras). And as was common in many film series of the era, the sets would be re-painted, redressed and rearranged and used in consecutively-made episodes. Obvious examples include Shingleton's stately home, set with distinctive panels that appeared in the majority of his episodes, sometimes with the big fireplace. Tyson's ever transforming home in *Escape in Time* appeared as both Sir Lexius Cray's and Professor Poole's homes in *The Winged Avenger*, as wells as Jordan's school for birds in *The Bird Who Knew Too Much*. The pub set for *The Town of No Return* was reused in *Silent Dust* and *The Man-Eater of Surrey Green*.

There are quite a few episodes in the black and white Season 4 that have a setting steeped in history. *The Town of No Return*'s inhospitable Little Bazeley by the Sea seems untouched by the passing of time. The village pub liberally displays relics from the Second World War and there is no sign of anything vaguely sixties looking – at least until Mrs. Peel walks in with her contemporary accoutrements. This is a world that could easily be part of the early 1940s wartime period. It's a world that has been isolated from the rest of society and thus easy for the baddies to invade and conquer. In *Castle De'ath*, the De'ath cousins' home again shows little modernisation on the surface. Aside from light fittings and plug sockets, it is easy to see this as a period setting. It's for that very reason that it is ideal for adaptation as a tourist attraction. Ian, the Laird, wants to keep his home as a relic to the past, blissfully ignorant of what is taking place in the secret passages beneath the castle. *A Touch of Brimstone* features the home of Lord Cartney, which is very sparse and shows little sign of the passing centuries since the days of the original Hell Fire club. His home is an 18th century backdrop to the club's 1960s activities, albeit ones harkening back to that previous era. *Too Many Christmas Trees* presents us with a man obsessed with the works of Charles Dickens, so his home carries a stylised Victorian aesthetic.

Even when the episodes aren't giving us characters obsessed with the past or lost in years gone by, the homes of the villains always show that these are people of wealth and not petty criminals down on their luck. The variety of evildoers allows for some wonderful varieties of abode, even within the show's established aesthetic parameters. *The Man-Eater of Surrey Green* has a stately home owned by a hypnotised botanist. Steed enters to find a conservatory-like entrance hall with shop mannequins covered in ivy. This allows Steed to deliver the quip, "Come autumn I hope to see more of you." It is possible that this was scripted rather than an ad-lib and that the script refers to a statue, but designer Harry Pottle went with a mannequin for a more playful design element. The story concerns a plant monster who hypnotises humans and wants to consume them. The mannequins are almost symbolic of hypnotised human zombies being consumed by plants. [3]

The House that Jack Built has the celebrated, fantastic and iconic black and white trap designed by Harry Pottle. On the outside, it is a rather unremarkable, somewhat ugly manor house, yet inside a trap of endlessly repeating corridors with swirling shapes and archways. It's a beautiful stylised, almost Op-art design, albeit a simplified version. The house is designed to drive Mrs. Peel insane, distorting her perception. Op-art creates the impression of distortion for the viewer; Pottle's design hints at what is intended for Mrs. Peel's sense of perception.

Return of the Cybernauts gives us the home of villain Paul Beresford, played by Peter Cushing. From the outside this is an elegant white Regency abode, but the interior set design is that of a very modern, minimalist living space. Clean white walls, big square Perspex ceiling panels to light the room, and decorated with modern art, such as the deformed self-portrait sculpture that fascinates Mrs. Peel. The home is like Beresford himself. On the outside we have an elegant, classical man, yet inside he is deceptively different, hiding a very modern, technologically savvy man with twisted dimensions. [4]

Quite a few very modern interiors appeared in the second block of Season 5. The home of the banker Unwin in *You Have Just been Murdered* appears to be an apartment as part of a subdivided Manor House; we're given no sense of the rest of the house. The modern interior, just as with Beresford's home, contrasts with the old exterior of the chosen real location. It's rather fifties modernist in design. Even when creating more contemporary designs, the look was still influenced by an architectural style from the 1950s. The more contemporary 1960s looks were limited to accessories, like furnishings. *The Avengers* never presents us with any of the new architectural movements of the sixties, like Brutalism – which is just as well as it is not a very *Avengers* look, yet it is one that *The Avengers* film incorporates for the villain's secret base.

The Avengers often presents us with a neat and tidy world. Unless it is trying to suggest an abandoned locale or a character quality, mess wasn't a common occurrence. The homes and offices of this very English world are, on the whole, perfect. The residences are like that of clean, tidy, untainted show homes. The characters don't live in these homes, they merely float through. They rarely have any physical connection with them. On a practical production level, it's easier to maintain continuity between shots if there is less to dislodge, but in the fiction of the show it's a very ordered world. It delights in the surface details being perfect. There are, no doubt, busy servants who put lots of elbow grease into maintaining a high level of cleanliness for their employers. These practical people have no visible place in this world, only the effects of their labour. Should the staff appear, they certainly don't break into a sweat from hard work. This is a world for the rich to play out their games of murder, corruption, robbery, avarice and jealousy. The artificial show home quality of their abodes provide a backdrop to display their wealth. As long as their homes or offices display their wealth they don't have to do anything as vulgar as talk about how rich they are – that is unless they're bankers at a party talking to one another about how to make even more money.

In the stylised world of Seasons 4 and 5, the rich, upper class are the norm. But even with a wealth-centric bias, the lower classes rear their under-privileged heads. *A Surfeit of H₂0* gives us a rare glimpse into how the other half live. Simple wooden furnishings, damp wallpaper, wood rot. The humble dwelling creates a moment of humour as the kitchen roof is leaky, necessitating an assortment of pots and pans to catch the water.

With the original show entering its sixth and final season (third on film), the design work would see a shift in emphasis. As the storytelling reached into an arena beyond just the countryside-dwelling, wealthy criminal masterminds (diabolical or otherwise), the scenic backdrop shifted to more mundane, real world settings, whilst simultaneously becoming increasingly wild and, at times, quite surreal.

My Wildest Dream sees the use of central London streets for a car chase, as does *You'll Catch Your Death*. It is telling that they choose architecturally interesting roads like those of Regency houses near Regents Park. The unique and controversial episode *Homicide and Old Lace* sees what must surely be the only appearance in the show of such London landmarks as Tower Bridge, Buckingham Palace and Trafalgar Square. As one of the few surviving John Bryce-produced episodes, it's clear that his style reaches beyond the usual boundaries of *Avengerland*.

The new character of Mother is shown in a variety of locations representing his office of the week. The ever changing locations are the result of serendipity. As Mother's unique original office – with ceiling grid work of strap hangers, as seen on the London Underground trains of the day – had been dismantled by the time the character returned, a system of rolling offices was introduced. This meant that any existing set could be adapted for use for that one episode. In one episode, Mother could be seen travelling through the very real streets of a Borehamwood housing estate on a Routemaster bus. As with the opening to *Quick-Quick Slow Death*, it stands out as incongruous; it is a rare excursion into a domestic, suburban setting where the common man resides. A fantasy character, in a fantastically adapted mode of transport, traversing the mundane, un-Avengerish streets of Borehamwood. It is interesting to note that as the show in many ways became wilder, the locations became more realistic. [5] With other more static locations for his office, he would usually be ensconced in the safer, *Avengers* reality where he could not be reached – this would include a castle, a submarine, a field of buttercups, an underground cricket pitch and a subterranean garden nursery. All of these were adapted from previously used sets, achieved with simple set redressing (field of buttercups excluded). One of his most striking offices is featured in *The Rotters*; for a story about wood rot, he is safely enshrined in an entirely plastic chamber. This, like the Routemaster bus office, has been carefully scripted as Mother orders his assistant, Rhonda, to pump up his deflating, inflatable chair.

Whilst a fair few unremarkable designs are seen throughout the season, of the kind you'd expect to see in your average ITC action series, such as the simple ministry corridors in *Love All* and *The Interrogators*, the show could still have fun with playful and interesting designs. *Invasion of the Earthmen* shows us a kitsch attempt at a space-themed office, utilising Christmas baubles as planets and silver and blue crumpled wallpapering. *Split* gives us a modern, futuristic attempt at an operating theatre, featuring a pattern of square wall panels that would be recycled in further episodes, including the yellow research establishment in *All Done With Mirrors*. In that episode, the panels are built into central units and made to rotate, a simple means to imply experimentation and activity without the use of expensive mechanical equipment.

There is an increased use of strong prime colours to create this vivid *Avengers* world; although a part of the sixties, it had its own selective way of embracing it. Purples, blues, pinks, and reds appear frequently. Older spaces are given a contemporary makeover whilst retaining classical features. The home of stand-in Avenger Baron Von Kurt in *They Keep Killing Steed* has a room for the peace conference that is pure white with a modern table and chairs, over which a sculpture of flying doves of peace hangs. Smaller rooms are bright pink or blue with classical, styled gold plated furniture. Then there are the red office walls in the monastery in *Get-A-Way,* or the green and red office walls with gold details in *Look (stop me if you've heard this one) But There Were These Two Fellers...*

A standout episode that required virtually a whole world to be created inside the studio is *Fog*. Studio based street sets had been used previously, as with Mackiedockie Street in *Escape in Time*, but *Fog* needed an enclosed world to be bathed in special effect smoke. The streets are that of a nightmarish Victorian, Jack the Ripper fantasy: tight narrow spaces with random archways, doorways, windows and alleyways in all directions. This is a world to get hopelessly disorientated and lost in – and, if you happen to belong to a disarmament committee, murdered with a sword stick. The episode tells us that these streets surround Steed's apartment, yet they bear no relation to the mews streets a small walk from Oxford Street chosen as the location for the exterior views. This is a world that only existed for this one-off episode. It is a setting that displays little sign of the sixties. Only small details like Tara's flamboyant red coat and Steed's abode are contemporary. The clubhouse of the Gaslight Ghoul Club has its own highly atmospheric mock-up of fog-shrouded streets. It is only differentiated from the outside streets by being more artificial, with the kind of crudely painted backdrops normally reserved for hallucinogenic sequences in episodes like *Something Nasty in the Nursery*. *Fog* shows that even in a long season, the show would still experiment with highly individual and stand-alone settings. Visual continuity could be ignored every so often.

In the Season 5 episode *Death's Door*, the villains construct a fantasy set in which to play out their victims' nightmare scenarios. It is a large warehouse with undefined blue walls against which significant props are placed, yet come Season 6 similar spaces start to appear as creative alternatives to standardised rooms. These spaces have no definable boundaries and give the series an even more surreal look and feel. For the episode *My Wildest Dream*, designer Robert Jones, no doubt encouraged by debuting director and former *Avengers* designer himself, Robert Fuest, created the impressive observation room. This was probably presented in the script as simply a hospital bedroom, but the designer presents us with a large white space containing only a bed in the centre, surrounded by opaque screens. The screens serve no useful function; they don't protect the patient in any way. Along the back wall are huge letters spelling out OBSERVATION. The first letter 'O' forms the doorway. As a therapy room in which to be psychoanalysed, the patient couldn't be more exposed. With the bleached-out look due to the white walls and floor, the space could almost be like something from a dream. It clearly demonstrates the fun that imaginative directors could have with the *Avengers* format.

Further undefinable spaces appear in the season, such as Mother's briefly seen office from *Super Secret Cypher Snatch*. It presents us with no clues as to where it could be. Steed and Tara are seen descending into the strange chamber via individual ladders. Mother sits in his parked Rolls Royce. The only decoration comes in the form of some large model oil tankers. It makes no sense as an office as it isn't practical. In reality, the setting is probably a blue screen, part of the studio for projecting moving footage to simulate cars travelling. As a budget saving device it harkens back to the early days of the show, when designers like Robert Fuest, aided by innovative director Peter Hammond, would invent interesting minimalist spaces to save on set building. Just as back then, they give the series a unique visual flavour.

Another possible budget saving space, again involving psychiatry, is Dr. Meitner's consulting room from the episode *Stay Tuned*. The actors are shown in extreme close-up. The only identifiable elements are a bed, a chair and a powerful operating theatre light. A wider angle of the space is seen by a high shot looking down over the area. The floor is mostly black but the bed, chair and light are on a blue carpet. The black floor seems infinite, with no clear boundary. To the uninitiated it could look as if the centre is surrounded by large columns made from material; in reality the camera is looking down through the lighting gallery, yet the visual is freely open to whatever interpretation the viewer wants to give it. Could it actually be representative of Steed's internal thought processes, an imagined scenario or actual dream of the real event?

Game and *Legacy of Death* feature more subtle variations on the undefined walls. With *Game*, a huge cyclorama surrounds the space filled with games like Snakes and Ladders. For the killings that lead Steed and Tara to the villain, the spaces are often black walled with the lighting covering the centre, thus giving us no view of the walls. By the time that Steed arrives for the big showdown, the walls are illuminated in blue light and show a lower border. Considering the beautiful gothic house owned by 'Games King' Monty Bristow, are we to assume this fantasy arena is a basement? (We are given no reason to think that.) As with a dream, the spaces that these adventures play out in don't always make logical sense. [6]

Steed's apartment for the colour episodes certainly doesn't always conform to any continuity. In some of the early Season 5 episodes, the lounge is shown to have a very high ceiling, almost the height of an additional floor, yet later on it has a much lower one. There is a door off the lounge, usually out of camera sight, but like the ceiling it tends to move around. In the Season 5 episode *Who's Who???*, it is shown on the fourth wall (the one usually behind the standard camera position), yet come Season 6 it is just a wall. However, elsewhere in Season 6 the door has moved to the right of the window. We see it in a few episodes but the tag scene to *Wish You Were Here* proclaims it to be a bedroom. This in itself is not a problem, except that the geography as previously established through the location footage of Steed's apartment suggests that this door clearly must only lead out on to the mews. The marrying of an exterior location to studio interior is never very accurate. The location footage view from Steed's apartment varies from week to week and no one exterior is definitively pinpointed as the exterior to Steed's home – certainly none along that row match what we know from the interior. The real explanation is that the interior design came first and a location was only chosen later as a rough establishing of the location.

However, *The Avengers* is a fantasy. It is a dream world, and settings in dreams rarely make sense to our conscious mind. Even when they are logical spaces – isolated locations, country manor houses, research establishments, farms – they most definitely represent a fantastic, individualistic playground for our heroes to put things to rights. *Avengerland* is very much its own world.

© Darren Burch

1. *Incue Productions* created the mini-documentary entitled *Welcome to Avengersland*, sanctioned by Warner Brothers as

part of the film's promotion. In these books we call it *Avengerland*.
2. In a strange, surreal way, the more stylised the set – the less realistic it is – the more effective the scene becomes as a spectacle. A number of writers suggested using sets rather than locations, in order to enhance the disturbingly strange mood of a scene. In *Silent Dust*, Roger Marshall offers the director the following note: 'Shots of Manderley and other areas laid waste would be more effective **in the studio**. An air of artificiality would **heighten** the atmosphere.' (*Silent Dust*, shooting script, May 1965)
3. This is a good example of a set both establishing and reinforcing themes.
4. We should mention the two-way mirror as well, enabling Beresford to spy on his guests, allowing him to see people off their guard.
5. This is yet another wonderful *Avengers* paradox.
6. This is part of their surreal charm, as Darren's essay demonstrates.

NEW AVENGERS SETS AND LOCATIONS

Darren Burch understandably refers to *Avengerland* as a fantasy. However, *The New Avengers* is often seen as being made from 'thicker cardboard', and one might expect the sets and locations to reflect the shift from a sixties surrealism towards something closer to seventies realism. This expectation seems to be reinforced by two of the three homes of the new Avengers. Steed's country mansion is impressive in terms of scale, location and façade, yet its interior/set is (disappointingly) banal and ordinary, lacking the quirky flourishes of his 1960s Stable Mews apartment. While Purdey's London basement flat mirrors her personality and the mid-1970s social context, it isn't *outré* in the way that Emma Peel's monochrome flat is – with its cyclops eye in the front door and circular, central fireplace. Nor does it offer the action-adventure playground of Tara King's split-level pad, with its endless assortment of eccentric props and potential hiding places. Both Steed and Purdey's homes seem more 'real' and sober. [1] (Interestingly, it is left to Gambit's high rise apartment to add the quirky touches, explored in minute detail in the chapter dedicated to him by JZ Ferguson.)

Yet a brief survey of the memorable locations and sets in *The New Avengers*' twenty-six episodes soon reinforces the sense of a re-emergence of a deserted, surreal *Avengerland*: for example, the frequent use of atmospheric, echoing factory shells and redundant glass-roofed buildings. A former gas works employed in Season 1 was used by more realistic, rival shows such as *The Sweeney* and *The Professionals*, but it also found use in the sci-fi worlds of *Doctor Who* and *Blake's 7*. *The New Avengers* lies somewhere between these two dramatic extremes, and the multiple use of the same location reminds us that it is what you do with the setting which is more important than the place itself.

Bleak, menacing quarries – a favourite location in the candy-coloured *Avengers* of Seasons 5 and 6 – reappear, as do picture-postcard villages, unfriendly pubs, laboratories, and empty streets or military bases. Certainly, when the series headed abroad we see busy Parisian boulevards and populated Canadian roads, but for much of the two mini-season run the fantasy world of a depopulated *Avengerland* is re-established.

As a generalisation, *The New Avengers* is memorable for its location settings, rather than its clever set designs. The former include the Highlands and Isle of Skye shooting for the opening episode, *The Eagle's Nest*, which immediately recalls similarly deserted – though less spectacular – coastal shots of Norfolk in *A Town of No Return*. In both Clemens episodes, a disturbing, brooding atmosphere is created as neither we nor the Avengers have time to admire the natural beauty. Equally surreal are the events in the sloping field in *The Tale of the Big Why*, where we witness the strange, savage spectacle of both the dead Brandon and his car being stripped almost bare. There is a visceral quality to the scene which is absent in the original series, but the irrationally disturbing, deserted rural location echoes the 1960s settings. Equally Avengerish is the primeval, misty woodland with its demonic-looking scarecrow (*Cat Amongst the Pigeons*), Zarcardi's Sactuary of Wings façade, and Crayford's mock-gothic, theatrical folly (*Dead Men Are Dangerous*). Perhaps the most memorable nod to the show's glorious past comes in the form of Base 47 (*Faces*). The real life Pinewood Sanatorium's dilapidated buildings recall *The Hour That Never Was* and *The Town of No Return*'s use of abandoned, mothballed or rundown airbases. Grey and beige dominate, in a salute to the monochrome era. Purdey's echoing calls to Gambit bounce off colonnades of peeling paint and clumps of neglected grass. It is a wonderfully atmospheric location.

Pinewood Sanatorium also features in *Target!*, where the exterior location becomes what Michael Richardson describes as a 'standing set'. [2] This is classic *Avengerland*, Robert Bell working wonders with an assortment of working props and mannequins. It is this set/location that fans of the new series often remember most fondly. It offers a delightful spectacle and – like the best *Avengerland* settings – is almost a character in its own right. At the other end of the scale, the clever use of emptied London streets provides an eerie atmosphere in *Sleeper*, arguably the series' most ambitious and successful project. As in *The Hour That Never Was*, it is the little details such as a spinning bicycle wheel which create the surreal mood. The repeated use of Peace Road in Black Park as a Cold War borderland – in *Dead Men Are Dangerous* and *Angels of Death* – recalls similar use by ITC shows in the 1960s, including *Man in a Suitcase*, where McGill is attacked by armed guards on the East/West German border (*Somebody Loses, Somebody...Wins?*). The location is darkly sinister and brooding, but in *The New Avengers* it also offers us a playful, intertextual nod to the sixties' heyday of espionage drama.

One of the redeeming features of the overseas episodes is the extensive use of fascinating *New Avengerland* locations, such as the Parisian and Toronto cityscapes, Chantilly Forest and the Toronto islands of Lake Ontario. The episodes filmed in France and Canada need these spectacular locations as sets were – understandably – sparsely used.

In general, *The New Avengers* lacks the creative sets of the Emma Peel and Tara King eras; instead, we are often provided with the greys and browns of bureaucratic corridors of public power or colourless private dwellings. Memorable exceptions include the deserted, time-capsule Parisian storage warehouse in *K is for Kill* with its enormous kegs and beams of sunlight accentuating a generation of dust, and Felix Kane's artfully artificial headquarters in *The Last of the Cybernauts...??* Photographed faces of Steed, Purdey and Gambit are mounted on a white backdrop, while smaller versions are displayed on the contrasting black floor. Cardboard cut-out figures provide a three-dimensional aspect to this self-consciously theatrical display, one which reminds me of Mother's set in *Wish You Were Here*, although it also offers a nostalgic nod to the monochrome era. The abandoned Old Picture Palace (*To Catch A Rat*), General Gaspard's mannequin museum (*K is for Kill*), and Spelman's 'fun palace' (*Hostage*) also cleverly recreate the surreal atmosphere and menace of the original show. Another highlight is the diabolical maze in *Angels of Death*. It works on both a real and metaphorical level, as James Speirs notes in *Avengerland Regained*:

'The Impossible Maze of dazzling snow-blind whiteness, consisting of a grid network of small cells with two doors and internal and external shifting walls, which are fortified on top by rows of inward curving spikes. The walls and cells of the maze are computerised and can be electronically, remotely re-configured to make an escape route impossible. The maze is, in effect, a 'chessboard' of inter-connecting cells where chess pieces double as 'patients' or moving walls. The individual cells or chess pieces within the maze are perhaps a metaphor for an espionage intelligence network of secret compartmentalised cells of high security.' [3]

Enhanced by a teasing Laurie Johnson score, the maze's spikes recall a prison, while the confused rodent running around the miniaturised version offers a clever, cruel mirror image. It is a rare jewel in *The New Avengers* and recalls sadistic, diabolical devices in a number of Emma

Peel outings, most notably in *The House That Jack Built*. As James Speirs acknowledges, it is almost asking to be read.

There is little doubt that the far higher budget of *The New Avengers* encouraged the production team to seek out spectacular, scenic locations which offer panoramic backdrops, and both urban and rural empty roads with the potential for spectacular car chases. Cleverly created sets were the exception, rather than the rule, in this *New Avengerland*. This, arguably, makes it all the more pleasurable when we do finally encounter one.

© Rodney Marshall

1. JZF: Purdey's flat is less-'out-there' but is, arguably, dressed and used in a way that is in keeping with the series' focus on character. The barre is the focal point, and not only ties in with her past as a dancer, but cements that part of her backstory by showing her practising with it onscreen, indicating that dance is still very much a part of her life, and giving a glimpse into her daily routine and workout. The other most significant feature is undoubtedly the beaded curtains that serve as her bedroom door, which not only hint at Purdey's femininity, but are also used to both explore character dynamics – despite being an insubstantial barrier, only Gambit and Steed are ever permitted to breach it, which speaks to the level of trust within the team – and occasionally serve as a plot point (*Hostage*). Purdey's flat is also often deconstructed, whether by accident (*The Last of the Cybernauts…??, Hostage*) or design (like Emma Peel before her, she undertakes a renovation in *Medium Rare*), allowing for a level of engagement with it as a setting. The fact that it is in a basement "21 steps down" is a nod to Purdey's unorthodoxy, but also a source of humour, both verbal ("To be just passing by, you'd have to be on your way to a coalmine."), and physical (Gambit trips on his way up in *The Last of the Cybernauts…??*).

The set itself is therefore designed to be 'used' to service both plot and character, rather than simply looked at, in keeping with *The New Avengers* credo.

Steed's house is far less innovative in comparison to his previous abodes, and lacking the idiosyncratic touches that made those spaces so special (a lamppost lashed to the bannister, etc.). Ostensibly designed to reinforce Steed's seniority and ability to indulge in country pursuits since he now has two in-town colleagues to do the legwork, its best quality is the sheer amount of *space* it affords the leads, both inside and out. All three leads move throughout the house and grounds for both work and leisure (cricket and horse riding outside; parties, reading, and cooking inside). Purdey and Gambit treat the house as both headquarters and a second home, moving in and out at will, and therefore the space again serves to establish the team dynamic. However, it undoubtedly could have done with some added visual touches to make it more aesthetically appealing in its own right.

2. *Bowler Hats and Kinky Boots*, p. 380.
3. I have edited/shortened James Speirs' description.

MUSIC

Received wisdom often dictates that, if the viewer is consciously aware of a television series or film's background music, the composer has done something wrong. The reasoning behind this assumption is that, while music should set the scene, encapsulate the broader tone of the production, and influence the perceptions of the audience, it should always do so subtly. The viewers' emotions must be unconsciously manipulated to serve the story, while they remain completely unaware that they have been 'played' like an instrument in one of the compositions. But such a viewpoint does a disservice to the musical tenure of Laurie Johnson, the man who took over composition duties for *The Avengers* upon its switch to film. Many of Johnson's creations actively, and consciously, insinuate themselves into the minds of viewers, even as they serve to imbue the series with energy, suspense, and whimsy.

Following the tenure of previous *Avengers* composer Johnny Dankworth, Johnson quickly established a new sound for the series, drawing upon a suite of instruments made up of his perennial favourites. That suite included a heavy emphasis on brass – trumpets, trombones, French horns – and percussion, from drums and cymbals to cabasas and the vibraslap, and was augmented by a robust woodwind section, a touch of strings, and keyboards (sometimes manned by the legendary Rick Wakeman, the piano player on David Bowie's *Life on Mars?* and the man behind T. Rex's *Get it On* piano glissando, a gig famously awarded to him by Marc Bolan to help Wakeman make that week's rent). After Dankworth's jazzy theme and pounding fight scene cues, Johnson's Peel music was marked by a new, sophisticated sound for an increasingly sophisticated series, and his cues incorporated elegance, humour, suspense, and adrenaline in equal measure. At the same time, Johnson instinctively knew when corny was the order of the day, and composed believably generic pieces to fit an episode's needs – a slightly silly Foxtrot or Waltz for dance school lessons in *Quick-Quick Slow Death*, or some over-the-top cinematic music and saloon piano in *Epic*.

While the filmed *Avengers* seasons are widely considered to be Johnson's domain, he shared his duties in the series' sixth season. A casualty of the ousting of Clemens and Fennell after the completion of Season 5, Johnson subsequently committed to the stage musical *The Four Musketeers*, and was unable to return to the full-time job of scoring *The Avengers* upon the producers' reinstatement. [1] Composer Howard Blake was Johnson's choice of substitute. Blake came highly recommended and had previously played the piano in Johnson's *Avengers* recording sessions, including that for the Peel era theme tune, and so had a sense of the series' house style. Blake would ultimately score ten episodes of the season, his contributions augmented by previously recorded Johnson cues.

In retrospect, Blake's task was a difficult one. Well aware that his tenure was limited from the outset, Blake undoubtedly understood that he could only go so far in tinkering with the series' sound. *The Avengers* had always embraced innovation, but a modicum of consistency was required lest the music begin to seem less innovative than disjointed. Had Blake gone in a radically different direction with the series' music, it would have proved jarring for the audience when the season segued from Johnson's style to Blake's and back again. Blake's task was further complicated by the fact that Johnson's musical cues were often recycled in the episodes he scored, leading to Blake's and Johnson's pieces sitting side-by-side within individual stories as well as the season as a whole. This was not the time for ambitious experimentation. And yet, Blake undoubtedly would have wanted to leave some sort of mark on the series. Ten episodes of simply churning out straight Johnson sound-alikes would have been tedious for any creative personality.

Despite the restraints in place, Blake performed admirably. His scores blend seamlessly with Johnson's house style, with Blake maintaining Johnson's predilection for brass, percussion, and woodwinds. For example, *My Wildest Dream*'s *Action Sequence* cue features frantic percussion elements and a dominant brass section, augmented with bursts of woodwinds, and can comfortably sit in the same category as the *Fisticuffs* cue played over Emma Peel's dramatic fight sequence in *Death at Bargain Prices*. The same can be said for the opening portion of Blake's *Main Title* from *My Wildest Dream*, with its muted-yet-slow-building brass and barely-there cymbal, two Johnson favourites, which come together to form a prototypically *Avengers*esque atmosphere of suspense. This replication of the classic *Avengers* sound allows the viewer to watch Blake's episodes without any sense that some dramatic musical shift has taken place behind the scenes. At the same time, Blake made room for some idiosyncratic flourishes of his own. Most notable is the inclusion of the guitar in his compositions, an instrument that is noticeably absent from Johnson's Peel and King work. Blake recruited bass guitarist Herbie Flowers for *My Wildest Dream*, and brought in Vic Flick, late of the James Bond theme, as a session musician. The guitars make themselves known in episodes including *Take Me to Your Leader* and *Noon Doomsday*, and while the result is still undeniably *The Avengers*, it is **Blake's** *Avengers*. It is interesting to note that guitars later went on to feature heavily in Johnson's work for *The New Avengers*, in particularly the classic seventies 'wah-wah' variety, which briefly cameo in *Leader*. Was Johnson solely influenced by the sounds of the new decade when he chose to add the guitar to his repertoire, or did Blake's pieces provide some inspiration?

In keeping with the filmed seasons' credo of treating each episode as its own mini-film, individual episodes often received their own, unique musical cues, with particular pieces penned to accommodate certain storylines. Johnson, originally leery of the idea of writing for television, cited this production choice as a major factor in his decision to join the series:

'Julian [Wintle] assured me that he planned to produce each episode as though it were a feature film, with great care...[and] the financial budget to guarantee high quality'.

These pieces not only lent their respective episodes a unique identity, separate and apart from the series as a whole, but also served to convey the atmosphere and mood viewers could expect of that week's instalment, a valuable shorthand for a series like *The Avengers* that could be sinister and suspenseful one week, and light-hearted and silly the next. One of the most famous of these is undoubtedly the ominous, suspenseful piece from *Return of the Cybernauts*, which echoes the steady, mechanical rhythm of the robots' gait, and the pounding of their victims' heartbeats, as the robots slowly but surely advance upon their targets, before annihilating them with the swish of one whip-cracking blow. At the opposite end of the spectrum is the earworm composed for *Dead Man's Treasure,* a lighthearted, vaguely goofy, looping piece that backgrounds the episode's seemingly-jolly car rally, capturing the spirit of the competitors speeding through the countryside without a care in the world (despite the top secret nature of the prize and the blood that has already been spilled to acquire it). The underlying repetitive percussion suggests the turning of a car's wheels, while blasts of brass emulate car horns, and the occasional breaks in the rhythm signify the characters' frequent pit-stops to puzzle out the contest's clues. *Escape in Time* earns high-pitched squeals to convey the characters' journey through time, along with period music to announce their arrival in new eras. *What the Butler Saw* taps into the episode's rich vein of humour with its *March of the Butlers* theme, following Steed as he is schooled in the ways of butling in typical over-the-top *Avengers* fashion. And *Castle De'ath* sets both the episode's mood and location with its haunting Scottish bagpipes refrain, always seemingly played off in the distance, as though by a particularly mobile ghost. Howard Blake gets in on the action in *Game*, with a specially-written theme – part-spy movie pastiche, part game show – to accompany both characters and audience through round after round of the deadly Super Secret Agent. *My Wildest Dream*'s theme contrasts the woozy, dreamlike quality of the victims' conditioning, complete with tinkling piano and floating harp, with bursts of sharp, sobering brass to emphasise the gravity of the actions they took while 'under the influence'. *Noon Doomsday*'s take on the Western genre is sealed with a rollicking score that would make Clint Eastwood proud. And there was always room for an episode to debut a new, inventive spin on the series' theme tune – *From Venus with Love* features a catchy string version, given an energetic percussion upgrade.

Johnson repeated this trick in *The New Avengers*. In some cases, he made use of distinct leitmotifs to link recurring story elements together. Examples include the rattlesnake-like sound effect that accompanies the appearance of the death warrant half-playing cards in *House of Cards,* or the escalating chords that correspond with the rapid back-and-forth cuts between horrified individuals and their smiling doubles in *Faces*. Other episodes merited their own signature themes, as in the original series. Purdey's scenes with Larry Doomer feature a soft, schmaltzy, pseudo-weepy romantic theme to signify their doomed relationship, while *Tale of the Big Why* earns a signature jazzy tune to reflect the languid, slightly seedy quality Roach and Poole lend to the pursuit of Burt Brandon. Many of *To Catch a Rat*'s pieces feature echoing strings and guitar with a vaguely European quality, mirroring Gunner's distant, hazy memories of his time in the Eastern Bloc. And *Cat Amongst the Pigeons* sets viewers on edge with a relentless, pounding build that gives way to an unnerving silence, punctuated by ghostly birdlike calls that leave their ears straining for the fluttering of wings, before bringing a crashing cacophony down upon their heads.

However, *The New Avengers'* oeuvre was sonically distinct from the original series. Johnson created a militaristic sound, established in the theme tune (on which more later), that focused heavily on snare drums and would not be out of place on a parade ground, with marching rhythms and up-tempo brass to match. This gives the majority of *The New Avengers'* music an upbeat, energetic tempo, in keeping with the more action-oriented bent of the series, one in which the two younger leads were more often than not running around open environs, fighting, or driving fast cars. There is far less of the original series' more drawn out, slow-burning suspense, the sort that would accompany Steed and Peel's clandestine investigations – in *New Avengerland*, events unfold at double-time. The introduction of the guitar to the mix, meanwhile, lends a funkier, swaggery edge where previous compositions had been subtler and understated – consider the pieces that accompany Gambit's pursuit of, and fight with, Ivan in *Three Handed Game,* and the guitar-heavy cues of *Dirtier by the Dozen,* featured during Gambit's scuffle in the early airport scene and Purdey and Gambit's run through the army base grounds, topped off with the sexy wah-wah that accompanies Gambit using Purdey's tight-clad leg as a distraction. Elsewhere, *Sleeper* features a heavy guitar base when Hardy makes a break for it, and a slower burn, investigative guitar cue as Purdey strips the belt from one of her unfortunate opponents. Occasionally, the guitar is allowed to be languid and whimsical, punctuating moments of humour (Purdey witnessing the hand-kissing in *The Midas Touch,* for example, or her drilling of her loyal army of pop star fans in *House of Cards*) or indicating that the characters are at their ease ('Purdey's theme'). But regardless of the tempo, the new, guitar-heavy sound signified the series' entry into a new decade, one influenced by the likes of glam rock and disco.

Perhaps the greatest example of the series' willingness to customise its music, however, is *Mein Liebling, Mein Rose*, a piece composed for *The Joker* by Johnson, with lyrics by Brian Clemens (translated to German from the original English), and recorded as a single by the pseudonymous Carl Schmidt. A key plot point, the record is played repeatedly by Max Prendergast in order to torment Emma Peel, a reminder of Emma's own use of the record as a delay tactic to prevent Prendergast from catching his flight, ultimately resulting in his arrest. Ostensibly romantic (Prendergast at one point recites the chorus: "My love, my rose, my tender, beautiful rose") and suitably authentic-sounding as a piece of 1950s/1960s German crooner music, it stands easily on its own as a single released within the confines of the *Avengers* universe, but takes on sinister overtones as Prendergast's obsession with Emma and her 'betrayal' are revealed. A worthy candidate for radio play, it is a testament to the series' attention to detail and the dedication of its behind-the-scenes personnel.

However, this musical idiosyncrasy could occasionally backfire, particularly when the series' makers chose to reuse iconic cues. Perhaps the most egregious case of recycling occurs in *Never Never Say Die*, with the reuse of the iconic Cybernauts theme to accompany Christopher Lee's character Professor Stone's sinister walkabouts through the countryside, but other examples include the use of the Mackiedockie Court music from *Escape in Time* in *The Curious Case of the Countless Clues*. [2] Perhaps when the episodes were broadcast this was less of a problem, as viewers might easily not have seen the episode that originally featured the music in years (if ever), but in the age of DVDs and streaming, where episodes can be watched at will, the repetition is sometimes painfully obvious, and the music prompts the viewer to recall the scenes the cue originally accompanied, distracting from the current story rather than enhancing it. Johnson's absence led to this type of recycling, and this sometimes hinders the experience of watching the King episodes by imposing comparisons with the Peel years, something that both Tara King as a character, and her season as a whole, have been subjected to (and suffered from) all-too-often as it is. Ironically, the Blake scores, despite sometimes breaking new ground sonically for the series, were often more in keeping with the series' spirit and better at establishing Season 6's identity than the recycled Johnson originals.

Despite the emphasis on originality, Johnson also composed a number of cues that were reused throughout the series, most notably for action sequences. While *The Avengers* had made an early commitment to avoid serialisation in favour of standalone stories, these recurring pieces serve as important 'connective tissue' to link the various and myriad episodes together into a coherent whole, both by creating a consistent overall feel, and to signify important story beats and elements that every *Avengers* episode reliably contains, regardless of the plot of the week. A piece written for *The See-Through Man* became an action staple, as did the cue accompanying the climactic fencing fight scene in *The Correct Way to Kill,* and that played during Steed's encounter with the machine-gun toting nanny in *Something Nasty in the Nursery.* The piece that prefaces Purdey's first major fight in *The Eagle's Nest* recurs in the lead up to Bilston's murder in *Faces,* and the composition used during Purdey and Gambit's running chase in *The Midas Touch* accompanies Purdey's fight in *Faces.* One brassy, exciting Peel era action piece was so iconic, it accompanied the clips compilation created to celebrate the special BAFTA award bestowed on the four *Avengers* women, which included countless examples of the series' female leads demonstrating their fighting skills. Action aside, most episodes would also reliably feature some sort of investigative scene, in which the characters broke into/snooped around the premises of the baddie of the week, with Johnson's understated, steady percussion-based music, punctuated by occasional bursts of sound to signify our heroes narrowly avoiding being caught in the act, accompanying the search. Examples of this include the jaunty cue accompanying Emma's reinfiltration of Castle De'ath after her unceremonious ousting, the percussion-laden cue played during Emma's discovery of the hidden lab in *Death at Bargain Prices*, *The Superlative Seven*'s quiet, xylophone-driven creep, and the *Purdey's flat* cue from *House of Cards*. A chase (often featuring some unfortunate victim) was another familiar plot element, so the frantic, charging piece from *A Funny Thing Happened on the Way to the Station* received numerous outings, as did the pursuit piece from *Something Nasty in the Nursery*. And, perhaps most famously, every Season 4 episode ended with Steed and Emma departing in some unusual mode of transportation, set to the same jaunty piano tune. [3]

Johnson also created some recurring signature pieces for the *Avengers* women who appeared during his tenure. A testament to Johnson's attention to detail, each piece encapsulated the character's essential qualities. The most famous of the three is undoubtedly the piece written for the infamous 'Mrs. Peel, We're Needed' opening tag scenes, in which Steed would contact Emma for that week's assignment by some unusual means. Despite the flourish at the end signalling Steed's unceremonious arrival, it is undoubtedly Emma's piece. Sometimes rearranged in different orchestrations to suit a particular episode, it captures Emma's playful, kittenish quality, lively sense of humour, quicksilver intelligence, and sprightly physicality, as well as her warm, affectionate relationship with Steed. It is also undoubtedly the most energetic of the three women's pieces, in tune with Rigg's own vivacious performance. Tara's piece is at the complete opposite end of the spectrum, a slow, languid, sexy number that would often accompany Steed and Tara's post-assignment tag scenes. The piece plays upon the sensuality Thorson brought to both her role and her relationship with Steed, an altogether more overtly romantic dynamic than the subtleness of the Macnee/Rigg coupling. Tara's piece hints heavily at the possibility that Steed and Tara will go to bed together after the screen goes dark. Compared to these two pieces, Purdey's theme was used most sparingly, and thus is not as deeply connected to her time on the show, but nonetheless does the character justice. A soft, floaty, romantic number, it draws on Purdey's femininity, a perfect piece for a woman with a past career as a dancer, wrapped in satin and reams of tulle. The use of the piece when Purdey is at leisure in her flat is no doubt due to its mellow quality – it reflects a Purdey at ease, vulnerable, her guard down as she relaxes in her own domain, not a tough, no-nonsense action woman out in the field.

Though *The Avengers* obviously possesses an extensive cue catalogue, a brief detour outside *Avengerland* is warranted, namely to the 1971 ITC series *Jason King*. Just as *The New Avengers* served as a sequel to the original series, *Jason King* was the sequel series to *Department S*, the original *Avengers*' one-time stablemate at Elstree studios, and a show that was undoubtedly influenced by *The Avengers*' outrageous, sci-fi-tinged plots. With both series finished by 1971, Johnson took on the composing duties for the new, Peter Wyngarde-starring vehicle. The result could arguably be termed the missing link between Johnson's work on *The Avengers* and *The New Avengers*. For instance, the episode *Nadine*'s second act features slow-burning but sinister horns and slightly-eerie woodwinds, and eventually introduces a solitary cymbal as it builds toward its conclusion, elements that typify the opening scene of many a Peel or King story. *A Thin Band of Air*'s pre-credits sequence features many of the same elements, but adds an oscillating trumpet to ramp up the tension as sinister happenings unfold, and later utilises harp, vibraslap, and brass to create a suspenseful backdrop that would serve an Avenger's investigations just as well. *Nadine* also features a pleasingly pastoral piece that would suit the original series' rurally set stories to a tee, as well as a piece reminiscent of the Arabian Nights music from *Honey for the Prince*. A brief, untitled piece from *A Deadly Line in Digits* features a fluttering, melancholy harp that segues into a building brass chorus, which would have provided the perfect conclusion to a Tara King story. The same episode also includes a frantic piece that would have made an excellent accompaniment to an *Avengers* chase scene, and indeed all of the aforementioned pieces could easily be substituted into an original *Avengers* story without anyone noticing the joins. Similarly, the first act of *A Thin Band of Air* features splashes of jaunty acoustic guitar that predict the investigative music of early *New Avengers* stories, and hints of the jazzy motif from *Tale of the Big Why*. *A Deadly Line in Digits* features a 'groovy' guitar number that the doomed guests at Midas' party of death could have easily jived to. *An Author in Search of Two Characters* contains a deep, drawn-out cello that sounds as if it has been lifted directly from the *New Avengers* catalogue. *Nadine* features subtle bass guitar and a swaggery *New Avengers* rhythm in an otherwise traditionally-*Avengers*ish cue, and an up-tempo, stridingly rhythmic piece that calls to mind Purdey or Gambit sprinting across one of many disused, outdoor locales. And *Toki* has hints of the romantic sentimentality that would be laid on heavily in *Obsession*. Johnson's transition to a more guitar-heavy, seventies sound, the trademark of his *New Avengers* work, is made here, sitting side-by-side with his original *Avengers* oeuvre, along with a host of other pieces that are idiosyncratic to *Jason King*.

Along with the myriad in-episode cues, Johnson was also tasked with creating a new theme tune for the series, to replace the jazzy Dankworth original. Though the Peel era theme was not an original Johnson composition, but a revamp of an original piece by Johnson entitled *The Shake*, it highlighted the series' clean break from what had come before, leaving viewers who had tuned in to previous seasons in no doubt that the series had undergone a sea change. [4] After the heavy, nightclub-esque jazz of the previous Johnny Dankworth theme, the opening burst of percussion and brass promises high drama, the skittering piano and leisurely strings speak to a new age of elegance, style, and whimsy, and the up-tempo harp closes things out by assuring the audience that there are still action and thrills to be had. All remnants of murderous gangs, drug cartels, and chain-smoking spies have finally been swept away. Sophistication and the fantastic are the order of the day, and Johnson's theme ushers viewers into this new, gracious *Avengerland*. With the introduction of colour, Johnson augmented his theme with a tense percussion intro that added a shot of adrenaline to the mix, highlighting the series' gradual drift into a more action-adventure heavy format, though the consistency of the rest of the theme assured viewers that the series' new focus on style would remain.

Like Dankworth before him, Johnson elected not to write a completely new theme when Steed changed partners. Unlike Dankworth, however, Johnson chose to record a new version in keeping with the character of Tara King and the series' new ethos. The result is playful rather than sophisticated, drawing upon Tara's youth and vitality and the bright, summery vibe of 1968 through the introduction of a quicker, upbeat rhythm picked out on the xylophone; however, it retains an abbreviated version of the previous season's percussive intro to ensure that all sense of drama and substance is not lost. The new trumpet solo that accompanies Tara's introduction, meanwhile, is a nod to the character's sensuality and overt sexiness, accompanying as it does the visual of Tara rising from the field in a slinky black evening gown. By remixing the theme rather than composing a completely new piece, Johnson allowed the Peel and King eras to retain their own unique identities, while at the same time bringing them together under the same umbrella as a block of stories distinct from the three previous videotaped seasons.

Later, in addition to his new role as producer on *The New Avengers,* Johnson was tasked with creating a unique theme for the series. Luckily for him, Johnson's infamous 'noises in the head' were working at full capacity, and the theme came to him quickly:

'One day, leaving my office at Pinewood, heading downstairs to the restaurant, I "heard" the theme almost complete, instantly returned to my office, wrote it down at my desk and arrived at the restaurant fifteen minutes later.'

The result was a theme that opens with a cheeky, speeded-up snippet of the original *Avengers* theme, signifying the series' strong ties to its predecessor, before launching into something very different, thus emphasising the 'new' in *New Avengers*. A true mix of old and new, the result was a military-influenced, fast-paced, percussion-laden number, punctuated by dramatic bursts of the Johnson staple, brass, but with a new starring role for the guitar in the bass line, as well as part of the background mix. The theme's punchy brass sections and fast tempo also played into the series' heavy emphasis on action, with the athletic Purdey and Gambit performing ambitious stunts and engaging in car chases. The implication is that the series, like the music, will hardly slow down for a minute to let the audience catch its breath. Sadly, where the Peel and King themes garnered extended versions of their themes that were played over the episodes' closing credits, the same, abbreviated *New Avengers* theme was played over both the opening and closing credits. More recent recordings by Johnson feature a longer version of the theme, in keeping with earlier seasons, but the very fact that they are re-recordings means that they differ greatly from the arrangement of the original version, and it is regrettable that we have never been able to hear the whole of Johnson's *New Avengers* theme as it would have sounded circa 1976.

And yet, the fact that Johnson has re-recorded his *Avengers* themes at all, and compiled numerous *Avengers* releases of his music over the years, suggests that he has always known that the received wisdom had it wrong – if the audience notices a series' background music, it is not because the composer has done something wrong. It is because he has done something spectacularly *right*. [5]

© JZ Ferguson

1. Even if one can partially understand ABC's desire to change the direction of the show, from fantasy to something with one foot in the 'real' world, the decision not to keep Laurie Johnson on-board seems baffling.
2. Occasionally, as in the re-use of the joke shop murder score from *The £50,000 Breakfast* in *Killer* – when we encounter the dummies on the factory bus – this can offer a clever intertextual echo or nod to an earlier episode with shared themes. One could argue that the re-use of the Cybernauts theme hints that Frank N Stone is as dangerous and deranged a scientist as Dr. Armstrong was. However, these are the exceptions and – all too often – the recycling of a score from a previous episode simply grates, such as the jarring re-use of the *Murdersville* score in *Noon Doomsday*.
3. This is a key point. Recycled material in Season 6 does not work – generally speaking – if it was originally written for a specific

episode or scene, while recurring (thematic or character) pieces are successful when employed as 'connective tissue'.
4. The track *The Shake* came from Johnson's recently recorded album *The Big New Sound Strikes Again* (released in February 1965).
5. *The Avengers* on film without Laurie Johnson's music simply wouldn't work nearly as well. It is an integral part of the recipe, not simply a welcome addition.

CARS

To most people, *The Avengers* is about two people – John Steed and Emma Peel – and about two cars: the light, modern Lotus Elan for her, and the stately, lumbering Bentley for him.

These two marques encapsulate the dichotomy of the most famous years of *The Avengers*, where the apparently conservative figure of Steed is paired with the 'positively emancipated' modern woman in Mrs. Peel. That Steed is not actually conservative is the crux of the pairing. He may seem to be an old-fashioned establishment figure, but he is progressive, open, and egalitarian. The seeds were laid in an earlier time, when he was paired with Honor Blackman's similarly emancipated Cathy, and it is this equality that makes the show such a stand-out, having few rivals in a display of sexual equality in the sixties.

The series was carefully produced to evoke an air of archetypal Britishness, indeed a Britain that may only have existed on chocolate boxes and in story books. This national identity extended to the vehicles we see on screen. At first sight, one might decide that this was for purely budgetary reasons; it would clearly be cheaper to obtain or hire domestic vehicles, but when you look at the bigger picture, it's obvious that this was a deliberate policy. While other series have the heroes driving Volvos, Ferraris or Mercedes, our avenging heroes would only be seen behind the wheel of a locally built car.

Naturally, there is little use of motor cars in the studio-bound videotape era, but even in those episodes there is an unwavering dedication to the locally produced marques in preference to imported prestige. Cathy, in the few instances we see her driving, has an MGA roadster, and Steed has an AC Greyhound, an Alvis Speed 20 open tourer or a dowdier Triumph Herald. The supporting players have local cars of varying prestige – a Ford Consul, a Sunbeam Alpine, a Rolls Royce, an Austin. The third season sees Cathy experiment with a Triumph Speed Twin motorbike and Steed with a Lagonda open tourer of a similar vintage to his future Bentleys, while the supporting cast, in their rare moments behind the wheel, continue to support the local motor industry.

The defining moment for *The Avengers* and motor cars is the beginning of Season 4, when the move to film from videotape freed them from the studio and the show transformed into a series of hour-long feature films, offering a great deal of location work and many cars. Clemens knew what he wanted – sleek, sporty but character-driven (in every sense!) vehicles. He wanted the elegance and stateliness of vintage cars for Steed, as foreshadowed by the Alvis and Lagonda, but something fast and powerful for his action girl, Emma Peel. As the story goes, he wanted a Jaguar. [1]

Jaguar declined the request for two cars for filming and when Clemens turned to Lotus, Colin Chapman leapt at the chance for the best free marketing in the world and delivered a car immediately. History was made. Brian Clemens once stated in an interview that "Lotus were pretty pleased with the result, they told me the publicity was worth £5 million to them, a helluva lot of money then." (Giles Chapman, *TV Cars: Star Cars from the World of Television*). The association with *The Avengers* was so important to Lotus that they had Diana Rigg appear at their stand in the 1965 London Motor Show, dressed in outfits from the show and draping herself across the car while the photographers snapped up as much as they could. The official brochure for the Elan featured a model similar in appearance to Diana Rigg in a conscious echo of the association. [2]

From this point on, the choice of car for the leads was crucial. Steed with his Edwardian dandy chic was normally paired with vintage cars; mostly enormous green Bentleys and, on one early outing, a Vauxhall Prince Henry. When he went off-road, it was of course in a Land Rover. The mantle slipped a bit when John Bryce put him in an AC 428, but when the original producers returned they put him in a pair of Rolls Royces – still at odds with the previous two seasons, but Steed was increasingly being scripted as more upper class so the cars followed suit.

His companions, meanwhile, had sleek, low, speedy sports cars to underline their emancipated modernity. Importantly, the cars were not brutes; the lines of these sports cars had to emulate their occupants, so Lotus, AC and MG were more natural partners than Ford or Jaguar.

Again, the defiantly artificial world of *The Avengers* was similarly populated – the backdrop is wall to wall with British marques, notably Jaguar, Rolls Royce, and Daimler alongside more pedestrian marques such as Austin, Ford, Humber, Morris, Triumph, and Wolseley. Exceptions from this rule are rare: only two Mercedes spring to mind (although there are a few more in the background), a few Citroëns, a single Renault, and an NSU – employed by a foreign agent of course.

By the time of *The New Avengers*, different forces were in play. The British automotive landscape had changed irrevocably with the formation of British Leyland, and so it was to this company that the producers turned for a partnership to deliver the cars, including Purdey's ugly, rubber-bumpered MG sports car. The boys fared somewhat better than Purdey, being supplied with more prestigious marques and ending up behind the wheel of huge, ostentatious Jaguars and matching Range Rovers.

Unfortunately, the quality of cars produced by Leyland was inconsistent and there were frequent issues with the vehicles. Purdey's MG, when delivered, had the wrong gear lever on the shift and it took the crew ages to work out how to get it into gear. This is a typical tale of Leyland's woes and set the tone for many of the cars supplied, which had to be repaired, often with the wrong spare parts being delivered. Steed was given a Rover SD1 in a marketing move for the car named European Car of the Year in 1977 – a remarkable feat for a car beset with poor construction quality such as loose door seals and vibration in the steering. [3]

With *The New Avengers* receiving the injection of money from Europe and, later, Canada it ceased to be the British vehicle cavalcade that *The Avengers* had been. This is probably just as well, as there was little to celebrate in touting Leyland's marques. The episodes filmed in France and Canada, naturally, had vehicles in keeping with the locations; the Canadian episodes are drenched in the oversized saloons peculiar to the American market of the time – dreadful Lincolns, ugly Plymouth police cruisers, gargantuan Pontiacs, juxtaposed with incongruous little Toyotas. [4]

The Avengers was never about reality. It does not have the harsh bitterness of *Callan* or the earthiness of *The Sweeney*. It is a fantasy, and the cars chosen to represent this have a touch of glamour and expense in keeping with the elegance of the rest of the series. However, despite this it is never ostentatious; you would never see a Ferrari centre stage in *The Avengers*. While this careful crafting of the visual slips a bit in Season 6, when Steed starts driving a Rolls Royce, it is, on the whole, judiciously played. A rare diversion is von Curt's gleaming Mercedes roadster in *They Keep Killing Steed* but, after all, he wasn't an *Avenger*.

© Piers Johnson

1. Brian Clemens himself was known for his love of fast, sporty cars and *Avengers* writer Colin Finbow happily recalls that Clemens "owned the only E Type Jaguar I have ever ridden in." (*Bright Horizons*, p. 365)
2. *The Avengers*-related marketing once again reminds us how iconic and culturally powerful the series had become.
3. It is tempting to see the car issues in *The New Avengers* as a microcosm of the production problems which beset the show throughout its short life.
   JZF: *The Avengers* had a long history of car troubles, with Steed's Bentley being notoriously difficult to start, to the point that it was often pushed into shot by the crew. (This was still the case in 1984, as seen in the introduction to Patrick Macnee's episode of *This is Your Life*, in which Gareth Hunt struggles to get the Bentley to start.) The pop-up headlights on Emma Peel's Lotus were often unreliable, with one stubbornly remaining open/closed. *The New Avengers* undoubtedly had the worst track record, though, with two XJS models acting as substitutes for one another due to their faulty electrics. Steed's 'Big Cat' Jaguar was much-coveted by the audience, but loathed by the crew due to its bulky tyres and wheel-arches, which made it cumbersome to drive. Purdey's MG often required a crew member to lie in the footwell and fiddle with the wiring/mechanism in order to keep it moving. It was for this reason that the MG gradually dropped out of use as the series wore on, and Purdey increasingly hitched rides with Gambit or Steed. Lumley recalled that, in scenes where all three leads were required to share a vehicle, Purdey was often relegated to the back seat, "like a nodding dog."
4. Presumably the number of French cars which pop up in the UK-based *New Avengers* episodes are a nod to the French funding.

FASHIONS

Costuming can play a powerful part in a film or television show. Good costuming can help to shape a world, enhance the cinematic atmosphere, support the subtext of a scene, and even influence culture. The landscape of *The Fifth Element* (1997) would be dull without the fun costumes of renowned French fashion designer Jean-Paul Gaultier. The late Eiko Ishioka won an Academy Award for bringing her own Japanese sensibility and arch theatricality to the Victorian finery of *Bram Stoker's Dracula* (1992). Janie Bryant received great acclaim for her sublime and thoughtful use of wardrobe on *Mad Men* (2007-2015) to underscore plot conflict and character development. Charles Knode and Michael Kaplan's chic, retro-influenced designs for *Blade Runner* (1982) not only added to the film's neo-noir tone, but would go on to affect contemporary fashion.

The Avengers was a show where wardrobe and costuming played a distinctive role, highlighting the way the series redefined gender. The programme broke ground with the fashions it introduced, reflecting and influencing the changes in the cultural climate throughout the decade. The main characters' clothing became just as memorable as the characters themselves.

The most notable sartorial elements to come out of the series – an umbrella and bowler (and charm) – are at the heart of the show. *The Avengers*, along with actor Patrick Macnee, would develop an iconic image of an otherworldly dandy, pairing these distinct accessories to go with a series of elegant, bespoke suits. Steed's hat and brolly would become representative of the fanciful, fictitious version of Britain the show would come to create. These vintage remnants of English culture would become so indelible, they would even occasionally pop up modelled by other characters in various episodes, such as *The Charmers* and *The Bird Who Knew Too Much*. By the latter part of the 1960s and the advent of colour, designer Pierre Cardin would expand and elevate Steed's look. It still embraced the mystique of the Edwardian gentleman, but many of his suits were now styled in a unified way that extended to his shoes, brolly and chapeau – all perfectly matching. It still referenced a bygone era but in the context of a singularly integrated palette creating clean lines for a modern touch. Thus we have a look that is, on the one hand, temporally anachronistic, yet on the other hand, chic and stylish. How 'fashion forward' was the Steed look? So much so that Macnee was photographed by Terry O'Neill in a spread with fashion icon Twiggy. That same manner of dress then transitioned successfully into the 1970s with *The New Avengers,* and even into the 1990s when the movie adaptation came about. Such highly synchronised attire is not uncommon even in the major fashion runways today.

However, it is with Steed's partners that the series became best known for blazing a trail and achieving some truly *avant garde* moments.

First there is Mrs. Cathy Gale. Initially Cathy's wardrobe appears very much in keeping with what was expected of a woman of the early 1960s period. Her wardrobe reflects an affluent status with its mix of smart apparel for the daytime and elegant formal attire for the evening. What is different is the inclusion of leather. The sight of Mrs. Gale fully decked out in a leather suit could be argued as having as potent an impact on women and twentieth century fashion as the arrival of sportswear or the incorporation of the jersey. On the surface, her use of leather seems very practical. Mrs. Gale rides a motorcycle and she often helps Steed to investigate cases under dangerous circumstances. It provides ideal coverage for work at night, and leather jackets function as a source of protection while riding. Like sportswear did in the 1920s, it is accommodating to the changing lifestyle of the new, liberated woman that Cathy represents. Black leather ensembles are functional and would support Cathy's active lifestyle. They also give off an aura of strength, a clean, visible armour to reflect her empowerment. Cathy isn't just educated and capable. She is a tough, heroic woman – independent of Steed or any other man. Dressing her in such an atypical way not only highlights all of that, it gives Cathy a dominant edge and an aura of danger that make her all the more appealing. It even resonates with the more kink-inclined, as can be attested by the illicit requests in some of the fan mail that actress Honor Blackman received.

With Mrs. Emma Peel, Cathy's successor, this new style of attire would continue to evolve while reflecting further changes to come in the decade. Emma's wardrobe initially appears very much in keeping with Cathy's. In her earliest episodes, she wears nearly identical outfits, raising the question of whether she simply received Cathy's hand-me-downs. Soon the wardrobe would evolve and diverge as Emma's persona became better defined. While there would be touches of typical early '60s fashions, Mrs. Peel's style becomes sleeker and more adventurous, with a futuristic bent. She gains a softer look than Mrs. Gale, mixing more fitted leather pieces with contrasting blouses or shells. The independent tone is still there, but in a more feminine, relaxed context. By the end of her first year, she would pretty much abandon leather. That change, while partly due to Diana Rigg's discomfort with the material, is in keeping with how Mrs. Peel would be distinguished from Mrs. Gale. While both women are strong, emancipated and highly educated, Cathy comes across as more earthy and appeared to have no problem being in tune with the rougher classes, such as bikers and rockers. [1] Emma exudes a more sophisticated bearing and is more akin to a free-wheeling socialite.

Leather didn't seem to suit Emma as naturally and her character leans more towards the growing Mod culture. There is a shift to more leisurely suits, with hip hugging pants and blocked, finishing details. Ironically, Emma's signature outfit during that time is a sporty leather jumpsuit with seductively placed metal zippers. Her other main look during filming is a formfitting catsuit made from different textures of black fabric strategically blocked to highlight her figure. These garments are effective in conveying that more futuristic feel, with Emma looking ready to partake in an Italian adventure movie.

The onset of her second season brought the popularity of Emma's character to a stratospheric level, and her style of dress comes to full fruition. Emma embraces Mod fashions and the rising hemline. As overseen by designer Alan Hughes, we see the occasional miniskirt, shift dress or A-line cocktail number, as well as big caps or velvet hip boots. Her street attire is now composed of outerwear perfectly coordinated with her pants and offset by assorted turtlenecks – allowing for ensembles that are clean, functional but flattering. We are less likely to see her in gowns now. Instead, there is an ensemble consisting of wide-legged evening pyjamas made in a soft print that permitted full movement.

Furthermore, this persona, which was more in keeping with the Carnaby Street vibe, results in one of the most iconic looks in television costuming, the 'Emmapeeler'. For while Cathy may have been the new woman, Emma was the new superhero. Alan Hughes cemented that image with a series of colourful jumpsuits that accentuated Emma's slender and slinky attributes, evoking a lean, feline mystique. Made primarily from Crimplene [2] and designed in variations of the same general template, the Emmapeelers dominate her wardrobe throughout the colour series. They generally tended to be constructed in darker or more muted shades of blue, green or purple, often with some colour blocking to add that sixties mod-style element. At times there would also be matching booties with the more form-fitting suits that would give off a comic book effect. The Emmapeeler would come to be her signature style. It's striking, memorable and manages to balance femininity and independence. As costuming, they still hold our attention, even today. From a fashion perspective, the effect is more mixed. From a creative standpoint, a number of them do hold up well. One of the more effective designs was a jumpsuit either in green or blue with a normal pant width. White ties positioned at the sleeves and/or neckline added an interesting visual detail that works even in a contemporary timeframe. An additional accessory that could appear with it was a matching belt with an oversized metal buckle. Another interesting outfit that was used in a number of publicity shots was a sleeveless, navy cat-suit with a pair of keyholes set above the hips and adorned with a pocket watch. The look was finished off with a matching mini-jacket. Other pieces, however, are more dubious and have not aged well. Emmapeelers such as her orange number from *The Superlative Seven,* or the green one with white blocking and tall boots from *Return of the Cybernauts*, come across as rather 'costumey', looking more appropriate as attire for *Star Trek* or hitting the slopes during Olympic competition.

After Emma Peel, we have Miss Tara King. Tara was the youngest of Steed's partners and the one who underwent the rockiest development. In keeping with that, the show never quite managed an indelible look that persisted for her. On the positive side, her outfits undergo the most varied and interesting of evolutions, with continual changes taking place. The show even switched designers during the course of her run.

In the early episodes, the emphasis with Tara's attire would be on her sexuality. Model-tall with stunning eyes, Tara is seen early on in outfits that accentuate a brash youth and curvaceous figure. There is a full blown representation of the vibrant fashions of the swinging sixties that were overtly alluring. Interestingly, the costuming choices made for her wardrobe downplay the strong Indian influences that cropped up at that time. They include tailored mini-suits, rompers with open backs and lots of tops in sharp prints. We see a palette that utilised soft pastels much more than with Tara's predecessors, but also embraced bold colours. The sexiness was amped up and set off with skin-tight boots, metal accessories and plenty of fur coats and stoles. This is a girl who stands out and turns heads when she enters a room. The silhouettes observed in these early episodes, courtesy of designers Harvey Gould and Alan Hughes, are full-on feminine: usually short on the hemline, emphasis on the curves and unafraid to incorporate the occasional *décolletage*. Although Tara's clothes may not have been as ground-breaking, it can be argued that they were the most fashionable. One of the most memorable designs is a mini-dress that she wears in *Have Guns, Will Haggle*, a feminised take on the Highland kilt. Youthful and bold, the well-tailored formal tartan flatters her figure while the pleated ruffles of the chemise highlight her cleavage without exposing it. The youthful aspect can be seen in the ensemble she dons in *My Wildest Dream* – a motorcycle jacket paired with a miniskirt and boots. It is unlikely that such a look would have been worn by either Emma or Cathy. The increased softness can be observed in the cocktail dress Tara wears in *Split*, a hooded outfit done in pale pink chiffon with an empire waistline that gives off a gentle, sweet air. Perhaps the one dress, though, that shows off Tara's sexual confidence is the party piece she wears in the tag scene of *Two Fellers*: a gold number that incorporates Georgian period elements in the neckline, sleeves and in the gathering of a very short skirt. It is a striking dress that requires an exuberant woman who is truly assured in herself to pull off.

It is in these early stories where the show comes closest to developing a signature look for Tara. It can be speculated that Alan Hughes attempted to create for her the equivalent of the Emmapeeler. This came in the form of suits consisting of culottes, usually paired with a matching vest or bolero jacket, and designed in a variety of colours and tones. These ensembles afford her the necessary freedom of movement in a fight while being much more suited to her figure than a catsuit. Although flattering and more in keeping with her softer, more feminine personality, these would later be abandoned as her character changed.

As the season progresses, Tara's persona becomes much more physical and action-oriented. Her wardrobe shifts to reflect a ferocious yet fashionable 'tomboy'. The outfit most representative of this is the mustard denim leisure suit worn in *All Done With Mirrors*. Another feminised take on menswear, the outfit creates an athletic feel while flattering her figure. It is a strong look that is still considered one of Tara's best. [3] It would be repeated in a red version that was topped off with a tie. As Tara's feminine tomboy grows in strength and conviction, her style becomes more and more dominated by varying combinations of pantsuits to enhance that mystique. Often it is form-fitting slacks paired with a matching vest or a sporty jacket. They would, however, still reference the earlier, brash version of Tara by incorporating tops in bold, graphic prints. This fiercer sartorial reflection peaks in the episode *Requiem,* where Tara is seen in a potent ensemble inspired by the uniform of Cossacks.

As *The Avengers* returned in the mid-1970s, the colourful Mod fashions of the 1960s would give way to a more sober – even more traditional –

style. Steed would still be Steed, successfully so with such an inherently individual look; but with his two young partners, Purdey and Gambit, the show would come full circle. The world of *The New Avengers* is more grounded in reality, with all the ugly deceits and heartaches that come with it. The clothes for this generation of spies are in sync with that tone.

Mike Gambit is presented on the show as something of an enigma. The series would only ever give away fragments of his personal background which hint at a working class upbringing and being educated in the 'school of hard knocks'. Gambit can be charming and personable, but out in the field he exudes an air of subtle power and body language that reads 'warrior'. It is the kind of presence that one would associate today with a high security detail. In keeping with that, Gambit is dressed in a style that could be best described as presentable but utilitarian. He often keeps to dark suits, the kind one expects to be worn by bodyguards in today's world. He is a modern man who maintains a level of anonymity and a minimalist style. This would be the sartorial antithesis of Steed: without the presence of any frills, fanciful touches or noteworthy accessories. Steed is a noble gentleman who commands the room; Mike Gambit is a ninja who can blend into the background. Such a crisp, but low-key, manner of dress is a perfect way to underscore this aspect of him, especially in a fight. A barrage of blows has more impact when it's sprung from a source that is unobtrusive.

Then we have Purdey, just Purdey. It would be with her that the show's play with fashion would finalise its development. The *avant garde* styles initiated with Mrs. Gale come to an end and are replaced by a broad wardrobe that can accommodate a woman who is more akin to our mundane world. In many regards, Purdey represents the natural evolution the series' portrayal of women had undergone and the fashions that accompanied it. She is an intelligent and charismatic person, in tune with the offbeat environment Steed occupies, but without any need to be a specialised dilettante to excel at the job. There is no need for any surface armour to mark her agency. There is no room nor desire for kinky leather gear or assorted space-age jumpsuits. Her choices in attire reflect a person who is comfortable with who she is: a woman who enjoys wearing a flowy dress and high heels as much as a t-shirt and dungarees. Purdey's wardrobe includes upscale sportswear as well as simple, down-to-earth pieces with styling that reference her time as a professional ballerina. Many of her dresses exhibit a delicacy and refinement owing to a lower hemline and soft, subtle prints. They tease sensually, but tastefully, via sheer fabrics, strategically placed slits at the skirt and seductive necklines, sometimes strapless to expose her bare shoulders. A definitive example is her soft blue print dress with a halter neckline that is paired with a sheer matching cape. The look could be inspired by the Wilis from the ballet *Giselle*. [4] There are also blue pyjamas that are as smooth and satiny as one would expect from someone who performed with the Royal Ballet. They even come with matching slippers. However, dancers aren't fragile creatures. They are athletic, resilient and practical about their bodies. It is often reflected in their style of dress. On many occasions, Purdey intermingles her outfits with various leotards, tights or stockings to underscore that mindset. And for every frilly dress there is a garment that is more about functionality than fashion. While Purdey can be lovely and stylish, there is a sense that she has plenty of grubby work clothes in her closet as well. [5]

While the show doesn't establish a signature outfit for Purdey, there is a signature look nonetheless. That is her coiffure. Purdey is the only one of the Avenging ladies whose hairstyle caught the audience's attention. She sports a short, mushroom bob that feels as modern and practical as the woman herself. The style is clean and distinctive and looks easy to manage. The Purdey bob elicited a moment that was, in its own way, as fashion forward as Cathy Gale's leathers were. It resulted in a notable number of female viewers who not only embraced the look but would go on to mimic it. [6]

As stated, *The New Avengers* is set in a much less fantastical world than the original. The new show used its costuming to powerfully underscore this. While the clothes of the original series' characters are fashionable and striking, they are the kind of wardrobes that only exist in the landscape of television. The very suits and pieces worn on the original programme read 'luxurious', and television often distorts the means and disposable income of the people who populate it. Only the rich can afford to assimilate the latest collection off the runway. Steed may be from a genteel family, but how does a government employee manage to be a steady customer on Saville Row? How can Tara afford such high-end couture? At least it was established that Emma is wealthy. Because the original *Avengers* was pretty much a fantasy, the audience can easily ignore this discrepancy. Yet compare them with Purdey and Gambit. Both of them have a nice array of clothes and they look good, even fashionable. However, their wardrobe comes across as being much more accessible and, in theory, affordable. [7] There are no decadent affectations; Gambit and Purdey's clothes do not overindulge in expensive accessories. There is a reality to their clothes that reflects the reality of their world. The viewers don't need to suspend disbelief. Even the discrepancy with Steed is resolved. This version of Steed is clearly moneyed with a respectable estate and staff in his employ. He now has the gentry trappings to match his gentry manner.

Dandy, Biker, Superhero, Tomboy, Ninja, Dancer. Television shows often get to play with character archetypes to create great entertainment.

Part of the way such creative development is successfully achieved is through effective costuming. It is fortunate that *The Avengers* was the type of programme whose elastic format allowed it to tackle a variety of these character types. And it is to the benefit of its fans that that the series was able to craft fashions that skilfully underscored the personas and personalities of these heroes, thus adding to the show's depth and enjoyment.

© Frank Hui

1. JZF: This is in keeping with Cathy's written backstory, which emphasised that she was sophisticated, but not upper class.
2. Wikipedia describes Crimplene (polyester) as a thick yarn used to make a fabric of the same name. The resulting material is heavy, wrinkle-resistant and retains its shape. ICI developed the fibre in the early 1950s. 'Crimplene was often used to make the typical A-line dress of 1960s fashion. Likewise, it was popular amongst men in British Mod culture for use in garish button-down shirts.'
3. For me this outfit seems to suit her personality and looks perfectly, allowing her the freedom to take on her action-girl scenes while displaying her tomboyishly pretty figure.
4. A French romantic ballet of the 1840s.
5. JZF: And indeed she does. *Medium Rare* has her in a long, baggy mannish shirt and oversized overalls as she renovates her flat.
6. The Purdey bob demonstrated that *The New Avengers* was as able as the original series to have a powerful effect on popular culture.
7. JZF: *The New Avengers* also saw a fair amount of recycling of its leads' wardrobes, in whole or in part. This adds to the realism by implying that Purdey and Gambit do not have unlimited time or money to keep adding to their closets, and instead rotate through their outfits like the majority of the population.

SCRIPT-WRITERS

With *The Avengers* being a series in an almost constant state of evolution – mirroring the decade – the working conditions of its set designers, directors and actors changed dramatically during the 1960s.

In the early videotape era, set designers like Robert Fuest attempted to make the unreal appear real, on limited resources. By the end of the filmed era, designers – inspired by new fashions and larger budgets – created sets which had become wildly, colourfully stylised, stylish and surreal. The wonderful Op Art-inspired tie shop *(The £50,000 Breakfast)*, the cat corridor *(The Hidden Tiger)* and the various *Game* sets spring immediately to mind. Rather than offering the illusion of realism, these now displayed and flaunted their unreality.

Inspirational directors such as Don Leaver and Peter Hammond – shooting through mirrors to provide an in-house *avant garde* style, as well as providing the illusion of space – worked wonders within the stricture of a cramped studio. Shoot across some loaves of bread and there you have a (minimalist) bakery, as Brian Clemens observed. Later, the freedom and flexibility of film allowed directors to shoot mini-movies rather than record stage plays. For the actors, the pressure and the (excitingly) tense nature of a 'live' videotape recording – where fluffed lines, wobbling sets and sound issues remained, uncut – had made way for the relative ease of film.

Despite film allowing the script-writers to create plots which involved location shooting, little else changed for them. They were still writing what was, effectively, a three act play and most of the stories would remain 'studio-heavy'. A graveyard or country house will require a studio set, in both the videotape age and film era. More importantly, their role is far harder to analyse. The work of set designer, director and actor is visually evident throughout *The Avengers'* history. What we see is what they gave, as it were. With the writers it is a very different story, no pun intended. We need to look at their role in general, before turning our attention to individuals. Director Roy Ward Baker acknowledged the cornerstone role of the *Avengers* script-writer on the DVD commentary to *The Town of No Return* in 2010:

'The director is basing everything he does on the writer. It's the writer that's the fundamental genius at the bottom of the enterprise and everybody starts to build on that foundation.'

To appreciate fully what the writer brings to the visual feast, we have to begin with the paper trail: original treatment, draft script, and shooting script. An examination of the 'dialogue sheets' for an *Avengers* episode barely scratches the surface in terms of what a script-writer provides. Of course dialogue – witty, diabolical or otherwise – plays a significant role in each episode, but a writer's 'draft' and 'shooting' scripts also include extended pieces of descriptive writing and wide ranging advice/ suggestions in terms of everything from actors' facial expressions, reactions, movements and style, to the story's general mood and atmosphere, etc. The writer also uses his script to express his opinions or desires in terms of wardrobe, set dressing, props, sound effects and camera work: point-of-view angles, panning, close ups, reveals, etc. Arguably the most vital ingredient in the *Avengers* recipe is the director's ability to *interpret* the writer's script, to read between the lines and turn the theory into a practical reality, where this is possible.

We can take the iconic *The Hour That Never Was* as an example. Roger Marshall clearly felt that the moment Steed and Emma encounter the overflowing petrol tank – in the final scene before a USA commercial break – is the key dramatic moment when the strange spectacle transforms from 'amusing' to 'serious': 'The sound of gushing petrol grows steadily louder and more menacing.' The creative baton is passed on from writer to director at this point, but the latter is usually grateful to receive an exhaustive, 'visual' script, as was the case here. (Gerry O'Hara modestly claimed that the episode was a 'cinch' to direct because of the script.) It is often the attention to detail which makes all the difference. When Steed finds himself back in his car, immediately after another commercial break, Marshall warns that 'every attitude in this sequence should be exactly the same as in Scene 3 [the car crash].' However, it is the detail of Steed reaching for Emma's high heels, only to encounter an empty rear seat, which will allow us to see that, rather than being in a strange dream, something is horribly wrong. Marshall's advice to O'Hara in one dramatic scene – 'Inanimate objects suddenly assume a sinister air', stressing the importance of 'empty silence' – is at the very core of *Avengerland*. A classic *Avengers* episode requires a script which is not simply a starting point but is a complex work of art.

Sometimes, of course, the absence of paperwork and/or the episode itself makes our job as critics impossible. The Dr. Keel era is one remembered for talk of the main actors ripping up scripts – another *Avengers* myth? – before taking the initial ideas and reworking them, rewriting dialogue, etc. With most of the Season 1 episodes lost or wiped, and some of the scripts missing, we will probably never know in most cases how much was altered between the initial treatment being accepted and the stories being recorded. There are two episodes – *Hot Snow* and *Brought to Book* – where more than one version of script survives, and these give an idea of the sort of revisions that were made between draft or rehearsal and camera scripts. However, the telesnaps that survive for later Season 1 episodes reveal that some details were changed even from the camera script to production, so to gain the most accurate picture of the episodes as screened a degree of detective work is necessary. [1] Even in the filmed seasons, a large number of the original scripts have disappeared. How can we be sure who exactly created the episode we are watching? The short answer is that we can't. A perfect example is the quirky monochrome story *A Surfeit of H2O*. It carries the name of Colin Finbow as script-writer and he has stated that he was 'chuffed' with the final, filmed version. [2] However, years later Brian Clemens claimed that Finbow 'didn't write a word of *A Surfeit of H2O*' and that it had been re-written by him. [3] While I find it hard to believe that Finbow would have been 'chuffed' by this situation, the lack of firm evidence leaves us unable to verify the real author. At the other end of the scale, the existence of Roger Marshall's original treatment – *Overkill* – and the shooting script for *A Funny Thing Happened on the Way to the Station,* allows us to see exactly what was taken out, left in, added and changed once Brian Clemens took hold of it. Officially penned by a man who never existed – Brian Sheriff – it is the creative fusion or result of two writers in conflict with each other. While this is an extreme case, a study of many of the Season 4-6 scripts reveals major changes and re-writes from the script editor. This isn't unusual for a television drama series, but *The Avengers* had a unique script editor in its initial filmed era. In Season 3, Richard Bates had been a neutral observer/editor, someone who never contributed a script himself. Now the shadow of Brian Clemens loomed large. A prolific writer himself, he was determined to govern the creativity of others:

'A writer would come into the office with an idea and we'd talk it through, and as we went I would be typing a rough outline. By the end I would have three or four pages...and I would give the writer a copy. I worked on the principle that if he got knocked down by a bus I could always write it myself.' [4]

Clemens might have added that he also worked on the principle that he could always substantially alter the story if the subsequently submitted script did not match his own vision of the 'weird' world of *Avengerland*. [5] While praising him for being both 'fecund and indefatigable', Roger Marshall has questioned his fellow writer's ability to perform the triadic roles he took on in the filmed era:

'No exaggeration to say his influence pervades almost every scene. Lead writer, associate producer and story editor. In my book that was at least one job too many...No longer was a writer able to write what he wanted and in the way he wanted. Wit and style were being squeezed out.' (*The Avengers Forever!* November 2007)

Marshall's comments raise interesting questions about creative freedom and objectivity. After all, who edited Clemens' contributions? When he returned to the show weeks into Season 6's production, he installed Terry Nation as story editor but still pulled rank when ordering and/or undertaking substantial re-writes for a number of Nation scripts. It is hard to generalise about Clemens' editing of the other script-writers. At times he injects a necessary quirkiness into scripts which were arguably too dry. This certainly refers to *Too Many Christmas Trees,* which he helped to transform into an *Avengers* classic. However, sometimes he simply runs roughshod over an existing script, turning *The Girl From Auntie* into a light-hearted romp around town, as opposed to the darker original idea. He can justifiably be accused of making petty, unnecessary, and unhelpful changes when he chose to, such as cutting Emma Peel's wonderful 'subversive champagne' quip in *The Murder Market* and adding a speeded-up milk float/rickshaw in the tag scenes to *The Hour That Never Was/A Room Without A View*. As Marshall acknowledges,

Clemens' 'fecund' imagination was a key element in the evolution of *Avengerland*. However, his censorship of other's ideas and the rules he imposed dictated the creative direction of the series, making it increasingly one man's vision and narrowing the possibilities for others, including the viewers. [6]

The first and third filmed seasons of the original show saw a large number of writers pen one or two episodes, including Finbow, Robert Banks Stewart, Malcolm Hulke, John Lucarotti, Martin Woodhouse, Donald James, Leigh Vance and Dave Freeman. Most of their scripts offer refreshingly different stories and this variety is at odds with Season 5 and *The New Avengers*' runs, where the lack of writers arguably shows.

Jeremy Burnham's arrival as a new script writer in Season 6 offered a particularly welcome injection of new creative blood. Having appeared as an actor in episodes such as *The Town of No Return* and *The Forget-Me-Knot*, he seems to instinctively understand the *Avengers*' unique style, in stark contrast to Terry Nation's strange, erratic assortment of stories. Burnham's scripts are memorable for their odd guest characters, such as deadly cleaning lady Martha Roberts, and some wonderfully surreal, comic-strip scenes involving a giant nose, a piano-computer which writes romantic fiction, and a deadly butter machine, among others. He also provides us with Mother's best HQ, the Routemaster London bus; it is a mobile masterstroke. It is Burnham's *You'll Catch Your Death*, *False Witness* and *Love All* which, for me, encapsulate the essence of the Tara King era, even if one could argue that they cover too much common ground, both thematically and visually.

Tony Williamson – under-used in Season 5 and rejected in *The New Avengers* era – offers up two of the very best monochrome episodes, *The Murder Market* and *Too Many Christmas Trees*. Both combine stylish wit and genuine menace, with a claustrophobic atmosphere to these studio-bound stories. The visual spectacle of the aquarium, Lovejoy's 'love seats', Emma Peel in her coffin, the Santa Claus nightmares and the Dickensian sets-within-a-set offer us classic *Avengers* scenes. Later, his *Stay Tuned* challenges the *Avengers* formula, and *Super Secret Cypher Snatch* reflects his ability to create surreal darker and lighter notes within the same script, ones which complement each other perfectly.

Philip Levene has been unfairly labelled as the series' science-fiction writer, partly because of his iconic creation, the Cybernauts. The original episode is remembered for the visual and aural impact of the robots, yet it offers us a fiendishly subtle plot and structure. While a number of his colour episodes are possibly too similar in terms of theme and plot formula, *Something Nasty in the Nursery*, *Who's Who??*, *Death's Door* and *Get-A-Way!* illustrate his ability to provide us with a rich variety of odd spectacles and playful, ingenious story-telling devices. Without his *outré* creative ideas we would never have had baby bouncers, a machine-gunning nanny, Nightmare Alley's dream factory, witnessed Emma turned into a 'living' cybernaut, seen Steed and Mrs. Peel reduced in size or taken for a thoroughly confusing and enthralling out-of-body experience. The Peel colour era is, largely speaking, one of his making. (He wrote precisely half the episodes.)

Roger Marshall was one of the few *Avengers* writers to crossover from videotape to film. He is renowned for creating scripts which crackle with an almost Wildean wit. [7] Many of the best Avenger/villain and Steed/Peel verbal exchanges occur in his stories as the masterminds and our heroes verbally joust. Typical examples include Diana Rigg's witty confrontation with Nigel Davenport's Major Robertson in *The Danger Makers* and the post-teaser boating scene in *Silent Dust,* where the camera slowly reveals that it is Emma punting, while Steed relaxes:

Steed: Tired?
Emma: Exhausted.
Steed: No stamina.
Emma: No comment.

His scripts tend to have one foot in the real world and one in *Avengerland*, [8] with 'baddies' often being flawed characters – such as Major Robertson – rather than comic-strip caricatures, and where masterminds are more likely to be running merchant banks or hotels rather than being deranged ex-government scientists. He also provides us with something which was usually sadly lacking: female villains. Both Ruth Boardman and Miss Pegram are darkly cerebral, memorable characters. The bank cellar wine duel, the champagne cork knock-out and the 'fox' hunt for Emma Peel reflect Marshall's preference for scenarios where realism and a gentle surrealism merge. (This may well partly explain why Clemens and he had conflicting visions for the future of *Avengerland*.) It is ironic, perhaps, that the episode he is best remembered for – the iconic *The Hour That Never Was* – is one which contains less verbal wit and realism than almost all his other scripts. It does, however, reflect his interest in the Steed/Peel relationship and the sense of 'two against the underworld'.

Brian Clemens is the sole writer who is inextricably associated with *The Avengers*. There is no doubt that *Avengerland*'s evolution is mainly and increasingly one of his making. Unlike Marshall, he had little interest in creating rounded characters. His villains are, frequently, twisted caricatures, hell-bent on revenge, money-making or world domination. There is an undeniably dark, sadistic streak running through some of his best-known episodes – *The House That Jack Built*, *Epic*, *The Joker*, *Murdersville*, *Pandora*, *Dead Men Are Dangerous*, etc. – but, equally, it is Clemens' scripts which often provide us with the most chilling, disturbingly atmospheric scenes: the country house traps discussed elsewhere, the 'badger hunting' on the Norfolk sand dunes, Lord Cartney's Hell Fire club orgy, Emma's staged wedding/funeral, her ducking stool ordeal, Crayford's folly countdown. At his worst, he mistakes overtly stylised self-referentiality for artistic innovation, or slapstick comedy for subtle humour; at his best, he merges the show's unique dramatic subversion with its champagne style. In *The Town of No Return,* he creates the nearest the series comes to a 'perfect' episode. *Death at Bargain Prices* is not far behind. At other times – as in *How to Succeed...at Murder* – he is out of control and in need of a script editor himself.

Without Brian Clemens, the exhilarating opening season of *The New Avengers* would never have been made; paradoxically, he is, ultimately, responsible for the creative failings of its second season, though clearly not the financial ones. Clemens and Spooner's mid-story swapping of scripts smacks of a creative paralysis which might have been solved by welcoming in other writers. [9] Without his substantial ego, *The Avengers* might have been even better. However, without that ego *Avengerland* would probably never have become the fantastic – in all senses of the word – place which we still enjoy setting off to half a century on. Whether you agree with Clemens' version and vision of *Avengerland* is, ultimately, a matter of personal taste and choice. The same applies to his labelling as the show's best story-teller. What is unquestionable is his position as the series' most prolific script-writer and his unique role in the show's daring evolution on film.

Ultimately, we should be grateful for all the script-writers who worked on the show. *The Avengers* had wonderfully dynamic lead and guest actors, dazzling sets, innovative directors, creative fashion designers, and an inspired composer, but – as my father reminded me only today –

it is the writer who has to begin each episode with the daunting sight of a blank piece of paper.

© Rodney Marshall

1. My thanks to Alan Hayes for his input here.
2. *Bright Horizons*, p. 364.
3. Cited in *Bowler Hats and Kinky Boots*, p. 141.
4. Cited in *Bowler Hats and Kinky Boots*, p. 134.
5. Clemens' own wording.
6. These rules included: no killing of women, no blood, no police officers, no black characters, and no extras in background shots. Cited by Michael Richardson in *Bowler Hats and Kinky Boots*, p. 134, and who observes that all of these rules could be, and were, broken.
7. David K Smith suggests that 'it was Marshall who arguably gave *The Avengers* some of its sharpest wit.' (*The Avengers Forever!*)
8. This comment is echoed in *The Avengers Dossier*.
9. JZF: The Clemens/Spooner monopoly on scripting during *The New Avengers* was also undoubtedly responsible for its high level of character continuity, unprecedented in the film era. The resulting character notes and recurring exchanges are one of the highlights of the series and the source of its internal richness and sense of history. However, the small writing pool also undoubtedly led to repetitive plots and a certain amount of stagnation that could have been rectified with some fresh voices. Roger Marshall's comment that Clemens took on too many roles is particularly apt; Clemens would have been better suited to the role of showrunner, overseeing the series' overall feel and character beats, rather than churning out a critical mass of stories.

DIRECTING *THE AVENGERS*

A television director's job is chiefly one of communication. They take the words from the script and bring them to life with the aid of the actors, cameramen, designers, lighting and general technical crews. They have to translate the dialogue and descriptions into a physical reality, bringing emphasis to certain moments. The audience has to be able to engage with the story, not just through the words but through the visuals. American painter Edward Hopper said, 'If you can say it with words there's no reason to paint'; transferring this to television, it may as well be a radio play.

Right from the first *Avengers* episode, *Hot Snow*, the series was incredibly visual. Even when contemporary reviewers were critical of the episodes' storylines, they were complimentary of the show's 'look', thanks to its innovative directors Don Leaver and Peter Hammond. These directors would embellish scenarios with interesting locations, albeit within the limitations of a videotape studio set up. So, even before the show was made at Elstree Studios on film, it had already established itself as a stylish and visual series.

Whatever the scenario in an episode, the *Avengers* director would have to make it stand out from the norm and add a degree of heightened reality, to make it distinctive from other shows of its ilk, such as the contemporaneous ITC action adventure shows (*Danger Man*, *The Saint*, *The Baron,* etc.). Whereas the makers of those ITC shows often pursued stories with an international flavour to encourage sales aboard, *The Avengers* was unashamedly English and embraced the clichés. In the filmed era, the directors weren't called upon to fake some foreign location using the studio backlots and stock footage. The *Avengers* directors could enjoy the countryside and villages within easy reach of the studios.

John Hough, who started as a second unit director on Season 6, before being given full episodes to direct, said that the directors were encouraged and given licence by the producers Brian Clemens and Albert Fennell to make the show look distinctive, to give it a stylish aesthetic. The look was important to the show's identity:

'Albert and Brian weren't just interested in how quickly you shot something, they were just as interested in *how* you shot something. All the conversations I had with them were about artistry. They schooled the directors, challenging us to come up with something that surprised and interested them. *The Avengers* was the only television series I worked on at that time where this happened.' (*The Avengers: A Celebration*, p. 128)

The shift to film saw only a few of those from the videotape creative teams remain on-board, albeit just for the one season. As he recounted on a DVD commentary, producer Brian Clemens originally tried to secure the talents of Peter Hammond, but he declined the offer. It is a tragedy that the man who did the most to set the style template for the show and whom Patrick Macnee credits for shaping Steed's style didn't expand his style with the freedom that film offered. In the end, it was only Don Leaver and Bill Bain, handling three episodes and one respectively, who would make a temporary transfer to the film studios. Many of the new directors to the series were film veterans like Charles Crichton (famed for his work on the Ealing comedies), Roy Ward Baker (celebrated for the Titanic film, *A Night to Remember*) and James Hill (*Born Free*), amongst others, many with a background in editing as well as direction. Brian Clemens stated that he wanted each episode to be like a 'mini-movie'.

Don Leaver's initial episode for the show could – with few changes – have been made under the previous system. *Dial a Deadly Number* is entirely studio-bound, based in interior settings like offices, apartments and wine cellars. He flies with the new benefits of filming; there are wonderful little touches sprinkled throughout the episode that add flair and style. As Steed has a meeting with a stockbroker he says, "It was quite a killing", and the shot moves to close-up jump cuts of a large mounted fish with a small fish in its mouth. During the wine tasting duel, there is a marvellous 'two-shot' [1] of Steed and Mrs. Peel: Steed is foregrounded holding up a glass to the camera and Mrs. Peel is seen through the glass. There's a stylishly shot dinner party scene where the room is virtually dark, aside from the table lighting; Leaver starts the scene with an aerial shot of the table. Later, when Mrs. Boardman arrives home to find Steed spinning his primed-to-explode pocket watch, which she earlier planted in his apartment, the shot is on her but the watch is foregrounded as that's what her attention is on. It's a great way to build tension.

Leaver later handled the iconic episode *The House That Jack Built*. He takes inspiration from the stylised black and white set that aims to drive Mrs. Peel to madness. A wonderful moment sees Mrs. Peel descend the spiral staircase at the end of the maze; the camera tracks in the same directions as her descent and travels around the concentric circles surrounding the stairs until it alights on a pair of dirty feet (we assumed she was alone). Abstract shapes intermittently line the walls of the corridors and Leaver at one point has the camera outside of the set, tracking alongside Mrs. Peel as she runs – viewing her through a black gauze material that when lit correctly appears solid – the shapes along the walls creating depth and motion. These things add visual interest and dynamism. The directors new to the show were just building on the groundwork that Leaver and his contemporaries had laid over four years on videotape. [2]

The Avengers formula carried a set pattern of ingredients that the audience could expect to see in any given episode. There would be a teaser used as a hook for the audience, to tell them that something bizarre or suspicious or corrupt or murderous was taking place. There would be moments of investigation, maybe creepy locations, surprises, or moments to make the audience jump. At some point there might be some car action, either a dialogue scene or a car chase. Usually there was a physical fight scene to add pace and energy. There would be a confrontation with the master minds. And it would be finished off with a fun little tag scene. It generally conformed to the stock adventure thriller clichés whilst having fun with them.

The teaser is the set up for the episode, the establishing scene. How did *The Avengers* directors set the scene, how did they hook the audience to keep watching? The 'fan favourite' *The Cybernauts* starts with an establishing shot of a desk with a pen resting on top. The pen will, of course, be significant to the episode as a means to guide the titular assassins. We hear a thwacking sound and the camera quickly pans and tracks to look at the door. We see a man enter and move a sofa in front of the locked door. The camera tightens on his sweaty, fearful face. The door is ripped apart by something powerful and unseen. The camera becomes the Cybernaut's point of view and tracks into the intended victim. He fires fruitlessly and is finally felled with a killing blow. The scene sets up that someone with superhuman strength, who can shatter whole doors, is out to commit murder. Director Sidney Hayers creates an atmosphere of tension, intrigue and horror through what is seen and what is unseen – keeping the Cybernaut obscured. The lighting is perfect with excellent use of shadows. He leaves the audience hooked.

Veteran film maker Charles Crichton handles *Death At Bargain Prices.* He uses silence and a measured pace to show us the slow reveal of an empty department store. A lone agent wanders the floors before descending in the store's cage lift. His point of view shows the various floors passing vertically before us. Something is going to happen, we just don't know what or when. It's a waiting game that Crichton builds until a murderer appears from behind Yogi Bear and shoots the agent. Through the economic use of silence, punctured only by the drone of the descending lift, the audience is given no clues as to what is approaching. We're kept guessing until Yogi Bear starts to wobble, then the music comes in and the tension is punctured.

The controversial episode *A Touch of Brimstone* takes the very simple scene of a man watching television and makes it into something distinctive. James Hill's direction starts with a high contrast shot of an elegant high-backed chair reversing in silhouette and casting a long shadow through a well-lit archway. The chair turns and an unseen man sits on it. We see him place some expensive chocolates in a row on the arm rest. He's watching a man speak about peace talks. We finally see the occupier of the chair. A man who is clearly very rich and distinguished (brilliantly played by Peter Wyngarde). The cigar of the man on the screen explodes and humiliates him, the camera resting tightly on the villain's evil, smiling face as the title comes up. Hill takes a perfunctory scene and makes it unique and visually interesting.

Into Season 5 and colour (or 'color', as the screen titles would have it). *The Living Dead* opens with location footage of a derelict mine workings. It zooms into a dark area of the image and goes to black. We're then taken to the wonderful horror film cliché of the creaking pub sign moving in the breeze (clearly implied to be in the vicinity of the mine workings). The camera tracks down to look inside this public house.

Something is building as director John Krish establishes the setting. It's very much a mood piece. We're kept guessing as to where it could be leading. A drunkard named Kermit collects a bottle and leaves. He is viewed through the window of the door. The location shifts to an overgrown graveyard. The camera tracks along with the drunkard as he tumbles through the long grass. He falls to the ground. Now that the mood and atmosphere has been established, it's time for the significant hook. The drunkard sees a grave open and a tall man dressed in white rises from within. There is a close-up on the drunkard as he looks on in horror. The 'ghost' goes up to the church and starts to ring the bell, causing alarm to the villagers seen in the pub. They race up through the stylised graveyard and come to the church. The ghostly figure has now gone, but the bell pull continues to move. Krish establishes a pace and atmosphere through the measured movements of the camera, gliding through the setting, revealing these new characters going about their lives.

Murdersville sets the scene of an idyllic country village, a beautiful central pond surrounded by small houses. Robert Asher lulls us into a false sense of security: the warm summer weather and the 'yokels'. The innocence is destroyed by a man being pushed from the public house doorway. Asher shows us the lack of reaction from the two men; this is significant for the episode. The man is shot. It is handled like a western in an English postcard setting. Then the title is established over a wide shot of the village, now with a dead body lying beside the pond.

In Season 6 the series gets arguably wilder and more playful. *They Keep Killing Steed* opens with a long shot of a desolate quarry. At its centre is an old taxi with a solitary figure some distance from it. The passenger door of the taxi opens and a man appears, calling out to the solitary figure. Director Robert Fuest uses fast cutting for an intense close-up on the solitary figure's face. It's the face of an evil mastermind. This man is not a goodie. He races towards the taxi, seen in the reflection of the taxi door. He and the other man enter, only to then be seen descending into an underground chamber. The camera tracks in reverse in front of them and settles as they join another man with a bulbous silver mask over his face. The three faces surround one another in close-up. As the villain, Arcos, removes the mask, and the camera sweeps around his back, suggesting that we (the audience) are moving in for a closer look, the face of Steed is revealed. This man is not Steed, though, and panics. A handheld camera follows his panicked dash for the exit. He is shot dead and falls; the camera then spins around and views his dispassionate killer. The episode title is a shot of the dead Steed look-a-like, surrounded by photos of Steed seen through the eyehole of the mask. Fuest uses different shooting methods to create a visually appealing sequence.

The final episode, *Bizarre*, is handled by Leslie Norman, father of film critic Barry Norman. He presents us with the Hitchcock-esque images of a beautiful statuesque blonde woman dressed in a nightgown gliding barefoot through a snowy landscape. Norman shows her blank expression. She falls to the cold ground. Her facial expression is frozen and a tear freezes on her cheek. The mystery is visually set up – it's clear what questions need to be asked of our heroes. Where did this woman come from? Why was she in the middle of a snowy nowhere dressed only in her nightwear? Bizarre indeed (in big red letters).

Steed, Emma and Tara have to visit various organisations, offices or manor houses in the course of their investigations. We're never in any doubt that those they question have something to hide, even if they aren't actually the guilty party; there are usually lots of lurking henchmen up to no good. In *Man-Eater of Surrey Green*, Steed arrives at

Botanist Sir Lyle Peterson's home. We see the villain's henchman up to no good in the side mirror of Steed's car. Steed is unaware. In reality, Steed would have seen him, but it's a stylish visual to show the audience that something has been done to Steed's car without just seeing the assailant lurking behind a tree. A similar thing happens in *A Funny Thing Happened on the Way to the Station* when an agent is tricked into alighting at an abandoned station. As he investigates he passes a lit gas lamp. Director John Krish shows the ceiling lamp and a hand reach up to turn it off. We see the agent turn to see the lamp now extinguished. In reality he would have seen the person who turned it off but, like the audience, all he sees is the lamp now unlit. The style of the show is such that the visual grammar of the scene is more important than the realism. The scene finishes with the agent being killed by a smiling assassin. Instead of us seeing him killed, he goes out of shot and a train thunders past. We see the light from the carriages illuminate the assassin's face; the noise and visual chaos tells us all we need to know. Sometimes the drama is more powerful when left to the audience's imagination. [3]

Quite often there will be someone around spying on our heroes. The director will use a point-of-view shot, looking through a window, peering around a corner. In a car, we might see their eyes in the windscreen mirror. This last example would reach epidemic levels in Season 6, as we see many a spy sat in their car with their face revealed in the side or windscreen mirror (*My Wildest Dream, The Curious Case of The Countless Clues, Love All,* etc.).

Avengers directors are often called upon to realise deserted, isolated, creepy and atmospheric locations for our heroes to investigate. Cult favourite *The Hour That Never Was* is a perfect example. Gerry O'Hara places Steed and Mrs. Peel in a seemingly abandoned military airbase. The opening act is dedicated to watching them wander this expansive location. O'Hara often employs the use of a tracking camera (where the camera physically moves along a track, as opposed to a panning shot where it turns on its axis) to suggest the leads' perspective as they view the various buildings and abandoned vehicles. We get zoomed close-ups on open windows, spilled petrol and other confusing clues as to this situation. O'Hara often draws our attention to important narrative points. He uses wide shots to suggest the emptiness where Steed and Emma are the only moving aspects of a large screen image. There are a number of handheld camera shots which can sometimes make us feel like we are with the characters, exploring with them. All these visual techniques unnerve us, keep us guessing and draw us into the mystery.

Another significant abandoned location features in *The Morning After*. John Hough shows Steed and guest character Merlin walking through a deserted urban landscape. We see a child's baby pram, broken or uncollected milk bottles, a discarded policeman's helmet, coal dumped in the middle of the road, curtains blowing out through open windows. All these details add atmosphere as well as telling the story.

A few episodes would require the directors to create dream or hallucinogenic sequences. Roy Ward Baker would be the first with *Too Many Christmas Trees*. Steed has dreams induced by the villains. Baker presents the dream in a very artificial manner. We see cardboard cut-out Christmas trees, with no attempt made at realism. [4] Fades are used as Steed runs amongst the fake trees; he runs in slow motion with the panning shot of the trees faded over him. It is simply achieved but the audience is given enough to suggest that this is not reality.

In *Silent Dust* a surreal hallucinatory sequence is presented with an emphasis on comedy. Steed has been shot on a derelict farm and Mrs. Peel arrives to remove the bullet. Baker, again, uses Dutch angles where the camera is tilted so that the horizontal lines are not parallel, thus suggesting Steed's distorted, delirious perspective. The fact that Mrs. Peel appears in the scene in full cowboy outfit, with a ludicrous moustache, removing farcically oversized bullets, is a large clue as to the reality, or rather lack thereof.

When the show moves into colour, *Something Nasty in the Nursery* is the next time we see the programme featuring dreams. Characters are given hallucinations when they touch a toddler's toy ball. James Hill oversees the translation to screen. He chooses to do quite simple shooting and leave the work to the set design. The hallucinating characters find themselves in crudely painted, almost cartoon-like locations. One character sees himself inside a baby's cot, which is achieved in a non-linear fashion, i.e., the set design is presenting the distortion rather than the camerawork. Sidney Hayers is the next to find a dream sequence in his script.

In *Death's Door*, we see the victims of this week's master minds experience premonition dreams where various props are used to induce fear when they see them in their waking life. Hayers uses both the set and camera to construct the dreams. The scenic aspects are distorted by being tilted or enlarged, etc. The camera footage is speeded up to suggest a dream state. Of course, later Steed and Mrs. Peel discover that the dreams were faked inside a warehouse where the victim was drugged and placed into the faked scenarios; just as the victims are tricked, Hayers tricks us.

The next time a dream features, in *My Wildest Dream*, the victims (used as murderers by the villains) aren't sure what is reality and what is dream, and neither are we. Robert Fuest, in his directing debut for the series, employs various visual tricks to play with our audience perspective. There is an overlap between the dreams and reality. A psychiatrist uses a drug to induce a dream state where the client can imagine killing a person they hate with a passion – with supposed therapeutic benefits. He uses a dummy mock-up of the person with a photo for a face for his client to stab. The drugged state is then used as a means to actually kill. During one murder, the photo face from the dummy appears on the victim. The murderer's perspective is distorted; we see this through Fuest's use of a point-of-view shot. A few times we are tricked into believing we've just witnessed a real murder, only to find it was dreamt. There is little attempt to clearly define dream from reality. From making it clear what was a dream, the show went in a direction where the audience could no longer be certain of anything.

In Season 6, car chases become an increased addition to the action. One of the most elaborate car chases that the show ever attempted in its sixties run is during *Super Secret Cypher Snatch*. The bad guys are a firm of window cleaners. When Steed gets too close for comfort they chase him and try to put him out of action. It's a wonderfully dynamic sequence as they attempt to injure him with the use of their ladder – attacking him from their vehicle while tailing Steed's Rolls. Director John Hough shoots from a vehicle that is viewing the action from the front at one point, yet gets full dynamic coverage of the action by shooting from all around. With the directors encouraged to 'go for it', there are some ambitious moments in other Season 6 episodes. *Have Guns – Will Haggle* has Tara chased by the bad guys. The cars race parallel to one another at great speed, before zig zagging past one another and narrowly missing the camera in the middle of the road. [5]

It wouldn't be *The Avengers* without a fight at some point in the episode, with either Steed, Emma or Tara facing opponents. A wide shot would establish the fighting space. This was usually done to allow the stuntmen (and sometimes woman) free reign to play out the fighting scenario without trying to obscure their faces. In Season 5, a number of directors favoured a low wide shot to allow us to look up at the action, and sometimes a high shot to look down on it unfolding below the camera. Punctuating shots would be thrown in with the actors providing the reactions. In *From Venus With Love*, director Robert Day as good as has Diana Rigg have a fight with the camera as it represents her attacker's point of view and she karate chops it. Later in Season 5, in *The £50,000 Breakfast*, Day shoots a fight between Mrs. Peel and her female attacker with chaotic handheld camera moves. It is as if the audience is a third person involved in the tumbling. Some directors were more suited to the action shooting than others, yet by Season 6 most of the directors knew how to make a dynamic and stylish sequence; they'd honed their craft and discovered how to give the show its own fighting style. Opening episode *The Forget-Me-Knot* begins with a fight in a glass store. The low hanging lights of the room are swaying violently back and forth as the two men tumble around the room. James Hill shoots it through the shelves of glass bottles to add depth and interest. [6] Stuntman turned director Ray Austin gives Linda Thorson one of her best fights in *All Done With Mirrors*. He shoots high angles of Tara leaping through the air to dropkick her burly attacker. He shoots angles through the attacker's legs, incorporates low shots, and creates an exciting and dynamic action sequence. In *The Curious Case of the Countless Clues,* an invalided Tara has to fight off her potential murderers. Don Sharp uses a low dynamic shot of her flat for the general tangling, and then punctuation action shots are thrown in to build the pace. In *Who Was That Man I Saw You With?,* the fight takes place in a boxing ring. Don Chaffey shoots the wide shot as though we are spectators paying to view a boxing match. Sometimes the fights will play to a certain genre. In *Castle De'ath*, James Hill plays the fight scene like a swashbuckler, Steed dancing on the table of the banqueting hall whilst sword fighting his attacker, all the time avoiding the candlesticks. In *The Gravediggers,* director Quentin Lawrence plays with *The Perils of Pauline* clichés but instead of a full-size train, they have a miniature railway. [7] Steed and his attacker struggle to remain on the train carriage as they pirouette around one another. They speed the footage up as Steed races to save Mrs. Peel, who is tied to the railway lines, providing the image with a jerky quality that mimics the rhythm of the silent movies. *The Winged Avenger* entertains the conventions of the *Batman* television series of the '60s. Mrs. Peel wrestles with the titular villain on the ceiling, both of them wearing gravity-defying boots. Steed enters and attacks the murderer with large boards declaring comic strip terms like POW! SPLAT! and BAM! Unfortunately, the director on that sequence didn't use the exaggerated Dutch camera angles of *Batman* to really sell the point. The directors can really have fun with the fight scenes. No scene exemplifies that more than *Look...* A 'quick change artiste' confronts Steed and proceeds to change outfit with every passing punch. Steed is left dumbfounded by each new costume and persona that Merrie Maxie Martin adopts. Of course, in reality the changes aren't possible, but director James Hill simply runs with the conceit of it, cutting in each new outfit with lightning speed and enjoying the silliness.

The tag scenes were originally created for the American market to keep them watching until the credits. Roy Ward Baker seems to have handled the majority of the vehicle-based tags of the black and white Season 4. Steed and Mrs. Peel engage in banter, sometimes relevant to the episode and sometimes just a simple vignette of its own. There is a close-up on the pair and the final shot consists of the vehicle/method of transport zooming off into the horizon. Simple, but effective and unique. When the show went into colour, the scenes became more dialogue based. The set-up would usually still be quite simple. It allowed the actors to have fun and shine. There are quite a few 'two-shots', as in

Return of the Cybernauts when Steed and Emma are seated at a table as he fixes her toaster, or *The Correct Way To Kill* when the pair are in Steed's kitchen at his dining table. Early on in Season 5, they dabble with more vehicle-based tags. These fun scenes were shot at Lord Montague's Beaulieu motor museum, all by Roy Rossetti.

Once into Season 6, the bulk of the tags are situated in Steed's apartment and, later on, more in Tara's split-level apartment. Two episodes deviate from this formula by stepping outside of our heroes' homes. *All Done With Mirrors* takes us out to a wonderful field of buttercups as Steed wines and dines Tara. It celebrates the summer of '68. Ray Austin chooses a more elaborate set-up, with multiple camera angles instead of just the standard 'two-shot'. Then later, *Homicide and Old Lace* breaks with the formula by omitting Tara and including Mother and assistant Rhonda. The whole scene is set in Mother's office and John Hough shoots it in one take/one shot, as well as including what appears to be a 'blooper' as the actors erupt into laughter.

The *Avengers'* directors found an evolving visual identity for the series. With each new season, they took advantage of a bigger canvas, from black and white film to colour, responding to the increasing eccentricities and dynamism of the programme. It is pleasing to note that those who honed their skill on *The Avengers* – like Ray Austin, Robert Fuest, and John Hough – and veterans like James Hill and Sidney Hayers, returned when the show moved to its next evolutionary stage, *The New Avengers*. They brought with them all the skills, knowledge and craft that they had learnt in the intervening years, for the benefit of this new series.

© Darren Burch

1. A two-shot is one in which the frame encompasses a view of two people, sometimes with one figure foregrounded and the other in the background.
2. Interestingly, Leaver states on the DVD commentary to *The House That Jack Built* that – as a videotape era *Avengers* director – he was made to feel unwelcome in the new filmed era.
3. This fits in with Hitchcock's "There is no terror in the bang, only in the anticipation of it."
4. Indeed, it is the lack of realism which creates the (artificial) atmosphere.
5. John Hough was also responsible for one of the most experimentally-directed episodes of *The New Avengers*, *Cat Amongst the Pigeons*.
6. There is almost a homage to Peter Hammond here.
7. *The Perils of Pauline* is a 1914 American melodrama film serial.

SILK AND STEEL: THE PERSONALITIES OF JOHN STEED

John Steed is the only character whose arc spans the entirety of *The Avengers*, from the videotaped seasons of the early '60s, through the Emma Peel heyday, and into the grittier world of *The New Avengers*. Following the departure of Ian Hendry, ostensibly the original star of the series, Patrick Macnee's gentleman secret agent became the solid, sustainable anchor of the show, a hero in more than name, whose always breezy, occasionally ruthless, often idiosyncratic charm and dashing good looks formed a complementary counterpoint to his brilliant female partners. But John Steed was far from a static or uncomplicated character – over the course of eight seasons and two television shows, Steed would evolve while never losing the fundamental aspects of his character.

Steed's origins can be found in Patrick Macnee, the actor tasked with taking a barely delineated character and making him into a fully-fledged human being. Macnee gave Steed his trademark bowler and brolly, but more than that, he gave him his background, his old Etonian tie, and his insouciant attitude. Macnee stated that Steed was an 'exaggerated version of myself', a compendium of Macnee's own background and attitudes along with elements of his father, a racetrack tout, and his personal boyhood heroes. Macnee would make various claims for Steed's background over the years, but certain things never changed: he was a lover of racetracks, fine wines, gorgeous cars, and strong women. He was also a far cry from his fellow spy, James Bond, to whom he is often (unfairly) compared. After reading *Casino Royale* at the suggestion of Don Leaver, Macnee chose to play Steed as the opposite of Bond, whom he regarded as a brute and a bully (later referring to the character as 'reprehensible'), a man who didn't like women: 'Bond used women like battering rams, and seemed intent on drinking and smoking himself to death.' [1] Steed would not be like that; Steed would be better than that, a sort of antidote to the womanising roughneck with only a veneer of heroism. Steed reverses the trend: 'Underneath he was steel. Outwardly he was charming and vain and representative, I suppose, of the kind of Englishman who is more valued abroad...The point about Steed was that he led a fantasy life.' [2]

Steed occupies a dualistic role, concealing his abilities as a secret agent behind a man-about-town façade. One of Macnee's major reference points for Steed was the Scarlet Pimpernel, an 18th Century hero who was never quite what he seemed: 'It seemed to me that if Steed was this shadowy person who was helping to rescue other people, he was something like the Pimpernel – somebody extremely well-dressed who gave the impression of being a fop, so nobody thought he was a threat.' [3] Just as his bowler is lined with steel and his umbrella conceals a sword, Steed the man is also all about concealment. During the Season 3 episode *Concerto*, a villain remarks that "that bloke in the bowler hat, the English one: he's not as harmless as he looks." Steed's apparent harmlessness means that his adversaries (and, occasionally, his allies) are apt to underestimate him. His underlying steel thus remains concealed: just as Sir Percy Blakeney hid the hero the Scarlet Pimpernel beneath a veneer of foppery, so does John Steed conceal the hero John Steed. But like Sir Percy, Steed is not only acting a part: he is a real dandy, enjoying his wine, his cars, and his Savile Row suits. He appreciates the lifestyle afforded him by his chosen profession, allowing him to indulge what Cathy Gale will refer to as his 'indolence' while maintaining a useful cover for his professional work.

Steed's concealment stretches beyond the Gentleman of Leisure and Secret Agent personas. He plays roles within those two: he attended Eton, and often wears his school tie; he holds the rank of Major in the British Army, and was attached to the I-Corps during World War II, where he had his own personal batman. He plays cricket and polo as well as rugby, and lives in a Westminster flat, itself decorated with sports trophies, military paintings, and, during Season 3, a portrait of his grandfather. Through the series, Steed takes on the personas of various eccentric and upper class figures, each representing an exaggeration of Steed's own traits. The wine merchant of *Steed, Steed, Steed, Steed, and Jacques* in *A Surfeit of H$_2$O* mirrors Steed's role as a wine connoisseur. Steed's portrayal of three armed forces caricatures in *What the Butler Saw* exaggerates his military experience. The various playboys whose personas Steed makes his own in episodes like *Death of a Batman*, *Lobster Quadrille*, and *A Touch of Brimstone* reflect the relaxed gentleman of leisure whom Steed makes a large part of his non-agent personality. Steed's upper-class background gains him entrance to various clubs, and his position within the British hierarchy gives him access to the upper and aristocratic classes.

Steed's dualism is further reflected in his ability to shed those trappings of the upper classes. In the Season 1 episode *Brought to Book*, Steed poses as a member of a murderous gang; in *The Frighteners*, he's an underworld figure who threatens to cut a man's ear off with a razor; in *The Girl from Auntie*, he is a criminal looking to purchase Emma Peel. He slides into these roles as occasion demands it, shifting between personas, and fantasy lives, with apparent ease. His flat likewise reflects this dualism: he reads both Proust and Tintin, and seems to have as much interest in erotic photographs purchased from the newsagent as he does in fine art prints. Especially in the early eras of the show, Steed traverses social classes, oozing into London jazz clubs, wrestling rings, and charming shop girls with the same ease with which he speaks to Cabinet ministers and walks the corridors of Parliament.

The series develops these elements of class fluidity in Steed's lack of respect for authority, and refusal to walk the company line – another element that sets him off from contemporaries like James Bond. Although he is a member of a shadowy spy organisation (sometimes referred to as the Ministry), Steed nevertheless moves outside of that organisation on a regular basis, often to the horror of his superiors. He employs amateurs as partners for five out of six seasons, relying on the intellects and abilities of those outside the secret service. While not a rogue agent by any means, he is also not a company man, evincing a strong disdain for paperwork, protocol, and even his fellow agents, and placing far more faith in himself and in those he chooses to work with than he does in official authority.

With each passing era, aspects of Steed's personality are revealed and then concealed again, making his character complex and difficult to define. Each of Steed's partners brings out new elements of his personality, shaping him and exposing the man that he is as much as the man he pretends to be. Cathy Gale draws out his fundamental decency, his concern for humanity; Emma Peel reveals a calmer, content, more playful man; Tara King draws out his protectiveness, his heroism, and his anger. *The New Avengers* exposes an older, wiser, but more sorrowful man, a man who has experienced loss. Yet, all of these aspects have always been a part of Steed's personality, and all of them evolve throughout the eras.

While it is difficult to analyse the John Steed of Season 1, given the paucity of available evidence, Season 2 introduces us to a more morally grey figure than Steed's later incarnations. Cathy Gale's influence cannot be underestimated in the development of Steed's character. Cathy acts as Steed's moral compass, forcing him to either justify or change his behaviour, or risk losing her. The Steed of this period often conceals his needs and wishes, to the degree of manipulating Cathy into a desired position without confiding in her. Cathy challenges him in this, as in all things. In *The Golden Fleece*, Cathy admonishes her partner for refusing to openly tell her what he wants:

Cathy: This ridiculous charade you always have to play!
Steed: What ridiculous charade?
Cathy: You can't just tell me in plain, straightforward language that you're after a gold smuggler. We have to go through this ridiculous rigmarole.

The tendency towards concealment transfers to Steed's personal relationships, as he guards his intentions rather than explaining what he needs or wants from Cathy. At the same time, however, this concealment reflects more than a secret agent's habit: it indicates a lack of confidence underlying Steed's brash behaviour. He believes that he has to manipulate Cathy to keep her with him, drawing her into his world without having to confess his reliance on her; yet, this manipulation also distances her from him. Because she can never know what his real intentions are, he can avoid further blame or emotional entanglement, relying first on himself and then on another human being.

This erodes throughout Seasons 2 and 3, however. Steed becomes ever more reliant on Cathy, her strength and intellect, and her personal relationship with him. While we have occasional instances of Steed manipulating Cathy, he never forces her to assist him; usually he couches what he does in her terms: as a humanitarian action for the good of the world. Cathy regularly challenges Steed's perceived cynicism with her humanitarianism, declining to play by his rules. In the early Season 2 episode *Propellant 23,* Cathy meets Steed at a French airport, where she complains that he's interrupting her work. She shows him images of starving African children, whom she says she's helping.

Steed: I see.
Cathy: Do you?
Steed: Yeah, of course I do. Now, the plane'll be here in twenty minutes...

Steed's apparent dismissal of Cathy's humanitarian efforts for his own work does not erode their relationship; rather, it becomes a source of character development for Steed, who begins to understand that what she does is just as important to the running of the world as his work. The fact that Cathy continues to assist him, despite his occasional carelessness, speaks volumes about what sort of man he is: a man who does good, even if it is not exactly the same kind of good she does. Cathy's continued faith will become Steed's greatest asset, as she challenges what is cynical in him and uncovers his inherent decency.

In *Conspiracy of Silence,* Steed and Cathy clash on a moral and ethical level, as Steed believes that he should try to draw out Carlo, an assassin, by threatening him. Cathy believes that offering Carlo amnesty would be more likely to result in his cooperation:

Steed: You're an idealist.
Cathy: And you're a cynic.
Steed: Oh, I can't have this conversation again. There's no time for it now!

The argument repeats throughout their relationship; while neither is correct, Cathy's optimism and faith in humanity prompts Steed to develop his own. His moments of tenderness towards her, as in the end of *Six Hands Across a Table*, exhibit a man capable of emotional depth and gentleness. Following the arrest of Oliver, a suspect with whom Cathy has become emotionally involved, Steed asks that Cathy drive him home. His gesture is multi-faceted: he's already told Cathy that Oliver is dangerous and that she should not trust him, but he does not seize the opportunity to use his earlier warnings against her. He places her in a position of power in asking *her* to drive *him*, literally allowing her to 'take the wheel' with him and offering her support without invading her emotional space.

As Cathy Gale reveals, Steed's cynicism is another layer of concealment. Steed in action is less cynical than Steed in speech – while he might pay lip service to his man-of-the-world persona, Steed's behaviour tends far more to the heroic. Cathy brings out Steed's decency by her faith in him: when he's accused of treachery in *The Wringer*, she stands by him, confident that, of all things Steed might do, he would not betray his profession or the people he's meant to protect. While it has often been stated that Cathy leaves Steed in the end because of his cynicism and willingness to use people, this interpretation does not seem to be supported by the events of the episodes. [4] Cathy has shown herself to be fiercely loyal to Steed specifically, willing to take his word over those of his superiors in episodes such as *The Wringer*, *The Nutshell*, and *The Outside-In Man*. Though she at times objects to the means he uses, she fully recognises that the end is always for the betterment of humanity, and if he sometimes strays into morally grey territory it is not because of any inherent disregard for human feelings or lives. What is more, the affection demonstrated between Steed and Cathy throughout their episodes together is difficult to explain away: they consistently spend their leisure time together throughout both Seasons 2 and 3.

Cathy's presence further influences Steed's dawning respect for, and enjoyment of, strong women. In *Mr. Teddy Bear*, one of the earliest Cathy Gale episodes, Steed and Cathy grapple on the floor together. After she succeeds in pinning him, Steed attempts to kiss her, resulting in her slamming him back to the mat. He's certainly annoyed by this, but it's Cathy's physical domination of him that inspires this amorous display: he remains beneath her, physically subordinate to her, as she remains in a position of power above him. While his attempted kiss could be seen as an effort to re-establish dominance, his continued submission to her indicates his willingness to remain subordinated, an acknowledgement of her position of power in their relationship that nevertheless makes plain his desire for her. In this subtle play of power, Steed does not become a sexual aggressor, taking the physical 'no' without responding with greater violence. What is more, being dominated by a woman does not insult or demean Steed: it excites him.

Even as early as Season 2, Steed exhibits no fear of strong or powerful women; in fact, he enjoys being surrounded by them, spending more time with Cathy than with anyone else. As later episodes show, Cathy's physical and moral strength is a major source of her attraction. Though Steed enjoys baiting her, he always accedes to her intelligence and physical prowess. He's impressed by her knowledge in *The Little Wonders*, reassures the owner of a boxing gym that she's more than capable of managing a boxer in *Killer Whale*, utilises her occult knowledge in *Warlock*, and gets her to become a German sniper in *Intercrime*. His faith in Cathy sometimes even exceeds her abilities, as when he believes that she can pose as a 'budding eye surgeon' in *Second Sight*, despite her lack of medical knowledge. His respect for her will prefigure the more harmonious relationship he shares with Emma Peel. Steed believes that these women are capable of anything and is unthreatened by their power.

Cathy's departure represents the first real loss in Steed's life. While Ian Hendry's David Keel left the show, he was never given a final episode in the sense of *Lobster Quadrille*, after which Cathy goes to sunnier shores. Every change in partner signals a transitional period in Steed's character. Going into the Emma Peel era, Steed underwent a subtle shift. Less prone to bouts of cynicism and violence, Steed's rougher edges, while still present, were honed and directed. Unnecessary bloodshed and, particularly, the harming of innocents became anathema, as did the more manipulative aspects of Steed's personality. Cathy Gale's influence shaped a Steed with a stronger faith in humanity and an understanding of his place in the moral universe; a Steed that was complementary to his new partner.

Steed and Emma Peel are arguably the most complementary duo in the history of *The Avengers,* down to their social and sexual attitudes, their humour, and their choices of outfits. Visually they reinforce one another, dressing in complementary colours that often match the décor of each other's apartments. Steed wears a green shirt that matches Emma Peel's newly painted walls in *Return of the Cybernauts*; Mrs. Peel wears a blue coat matching Steed's tie and pocket square early in *The Correct Way to Kill*. They are often filmed in balanced two-shots, emphasising their compatibility and two halves of a single worldview. The world of *The Avengers* only becomes imbalanced when they are not together, prompting one to seek the other out. [5] They are partners, not antagonists, and their coordination reflects the inner emotional and personal correlation of their characters.

The Steed of the early seasons was a dandy, but still solidly modern; during Season 4, Steed affects a more Edwardian appearance, reinforcing his apparent role as a traditional form of masculinity. His sports cars are exchanged for a vintage Bentley; pin stripes give way to three-piece suits, often offset by coloured cravats and neckties. Steed more fully embodies the role of traditional gentleman during these seasons, but his complementary relationship with Emma Peel presents a complete worldview, revealing the fluidity of his masculine persona in concert with the feminine.

The affinity with Emma Peel reinforces Steed's character as the image of a traditional male with distinctly progressive views – as with Cathy Gale, he does not treat her strength as a threat to his masculinity. But while he and Cathy are occasional antagonists, challenging one another at a physical and moral level, Steed and Mrs. Peel seldom clash. When they do, it's quickly forgotten, often not lasting more than a few scenes. [6] The manipulative techniques Steed employed with Cathy Gale simply don't work with Emma Peel, their inherent harmony becoming more important than conflict. [7] This culminates in *Two's a Crowd*, where he fools Mrs. Peel into believing he has a doppelganger who is trying to kill him (a semi-repetition of the Gale episode *Man with Two Shadows*, in which Steed as doppelganger becomes a central crisis of confidence for the pair). Steed's persistence in keeping his partner in the dark nearly results in his death when Mrs. Peel threatens to kill him under the impression that he has murdered the real Steed. This is a watershed moment for his character: here he discards the remaining cynicism and tendency to keep his own counsel that had been so detrimental to his relationship with Cathy Gale. Like Cathy, Mrs. Peel is willing to kill or harm those who threaten Steed; Steed comes to accept this, his self-worth reflected in the value his partners place upon him.

Steed's willingness to trust in the abilities of his female partners, occasionally more so than himself, develops consistently from one season to the next. In *The Girl from Auntie*, Steed explains that Mrs. Peel is desirable for her mental powers, not her physical ones:

Georgie Price-Jones: What's so special about this Mrs. Emma Peel? You'd think she was Madame Curie and half a dozen others all rolled into one.
Steed: Her vital statistics...of the IQ variety.

In *Room Without a View*, when Ministry lackey Varnals refuses to answer Mrs. Peel's questions, Steed pushes him on it, subtly indicating that he has greater faith in Mrs. Peel's ability to deal with a disturbed person than Varnals':

Varnals: Perhaps I should warn you: it's not a pretty sight.
Steed: Oh, well, if it worries you, you stay outside. After you, Mrs. Peel.

There are numerous instances of Steed standing up for his female partners. In the Season 6 episode *The Interrogators*, Steed reprimands a fellow agent for underestimating Tara:

Steed: She is different from you and Casper.
Charles: She's a woman.
Steed: Hm. She's also sharper, brighter, and more intelligent.

Steed here responds to the masculine prerogative that Tara will be treated differently because "she's a woman", by reinforcing other positive, and non-gendered, aspects of her personality. To Steed, Tara's femininity goes hand in hand with her intelligence – an intelligence that far exceeds those of her fellow male agents.

Steed's unwillingness to participate in the patriarchal superstructure comes to the fore with *A Touch of Brimstone*, unfortunately an episode overshadowed by the few minutes of Diana Rigg in a corset. The episode draws out the conflict of masculinities in which the progressive Steed, by outward appearance an entrenched example of traditional masculinity, comes up against a group of aristocrats. Steed's contempt for John Cartney's brand of masculinity is established through his sarcastic remarks ("Feather dusters at four hundred yards?") as he succeeds in besting the poseurs on their own ground. Cartney and his friends in the Hellfire Club enact their prerogative through exercising power over others, especially women. Cartney refers to women as "mere vessels of pleasure", and then later forces Emma Peel, an example of defiant femininity, into a dominatrix outfit. Steed, however, has no need to enforce his power over others: he demonstrates his masculinity through the typical hallmarks of a gentleman, by being kind to others (his gentleness with Lord Darcy), his verbal contempt for Cartney and the Hellfire Club, and his respectful treatment of women. Steed is the true gentleman, declining to participate in the prerogatives of aristocratic masculinity by instead fulfilling the gentlemanly rules of conduct. Regardless of his place in the social hierarchy, Steed maintains the behaviour and fundamental aspects of a gentleman.

Steed's sexual love of women does not contradict his equally apparent feminism – rather, they become complementary aspects of his character. In *Death Dispatch*, Steed flirts with an attractive young woman by the pool, later telling Cathy that she was "very round". However, the attraction was quite obviously mutual: Steed's relationships with women are exclusively reciprocal. In *Mandrake*, Steed strikes up a rapport with shop girl Judy, a flirtatious and entertaining exchange that is one of the most enjoyable extraneous sequences between Steed and a woman not his partner. Another shop girl in *Death at Bargain Prices* is subject to Steed's charm: in flirting with her, he rattles off a recipe for beef, and subsequently offers to cook it for her. Steed's offer might simply be flirtatious, but it highlights his sense of fair play: he offers to cook for a woman, establishing his essential independence (he does not expect a woman to cook for him), and his willingness to provide exchange within a relationship. His further one-off episodes with new female partners (Georgie in *The Girl from Auntie*, Lady Diana in *Killer*) have Steed quickly stepping into a comfortable rapport with women, while the Venus Smith episodes of Season 2 show Steed taking on an older brother role with the younger and more naïve Venus. Steed's most important relationships are with his partners and, from Season 2 onward, his partners are almost exclusively women.

The issue of Steed's sexual or non-sexual relationships with his female partners raises some questions, many of them never answered. Patrick Macnee would claim that Steed and Emma Peel were having sex 'four times a week', while he was far cagier about Steed's romantic attachments to either Cathy Gale or Tara King. Given Steed's apparent emotional attachment to these women, however, in concert with his evident sexual attraction to them (and, it must be remarked, theirs to him), it is certainly not extreme to assume that there was a serious and likely non-chaste relationship between Steed and each of his female partners.

Sexuality and the fluidity of Steed's relationship to the opposite sex is a major point of departure in comparing Steed to his swinging spy counterparts. James Bond's well-documented misogyny and apparent dislike of women (except as sexual partners) is in direct contradiction to Steed's apparent appreciation of women. Steed comes to rely on female interaction of both a sexual and non-sexual nature as a driving force in his character: his flirtations with his partners form a playful and fundamental basis for their relationships, while the tacit respect he gives to their individual abilities reinforces his view of them as his equals. Most importantly, none of the women have to fight Steed to be given their due; rather, he consistently indicates that his faith in them exceeds his faith in anyone else, and that he will trust them with his life long before he will trust anyone else. Steed is no womaniser – women are not just disposable bedmates, but a necessary part of his emotional, social, and sexual life. If James Bond is essentially a conservative, misogynistic male fantasy, John Steed is a progressive and feminist one, one who enjoys equal exchange with women and will not use his masculinity as a weapon to harm others.

Steed's experience of violence and violation may be key to his lack of patience with aggressive masculinity. In *Room Without A View*, we learn that he was tortured in the Ni San prison camp in Manchuria. Ministry man Varnals posits that Dr. Wadkin has been held at Ni San because of certain behaviours that he's read about in the Ministry manuals. Steed responds with his own sensory memory:

Steed: Rice husks, gruel, shavings of bad pork, and water. Brackish water, tasting of dust. Unfriendly sort of place, Ni San. Nothing to do all day but lie in the cell, listening to the world go by. Marching feet, foghorns of the ships going up-river, and the chiming of the clock. Only there's no sense of time, because whatever the hour in Ni San, the clock always strikes three.

Steed's memory comes as a surprise to both Varnals and to Mrs. Peel, who go silent as he recounts his experience. It is also an indication of the darker aspects of Steed's character, and a part of the violent side he must increasingly keep at bay. *Room Without A View* is not the first time that the series provides a glimpse into the less palatable aspects of Steed's background. In *Man with Two Shadows*, Steed reveals that he underwent psychological torture while being held for three days by the villains:

Steed: They'd use me too, if they could get to me again.

Cathy: Again?
Steed: That's a long story.

This revelation surprises even Cathy Gale, obviously unaware of her partner's experience, and one which Steed does not elucidate. His reticence to discuss his experience of interrogation forms a contrast to his later memories of Ni San in *Room Without A View*, but the audience (and Cathy) will later see first-hand Steed's ability to withstand physical violence. In *The Nutshell*, Steed is subjected to violent interrogation by his own organisation: suspected of treason, he's beaten, deprived of food and rest, and forced to spend time in an electrified cell. He undergoes all of this voluntarily, as a way of forcing the real traitors into the open – an example of his self-control and willingness to suffer through severe deprivation for his work.

The Ministry again tortures Steed in *The Wringer*, as Cathy Gale rescues him from a camp in the Scottish Highlands where he's held after being convicted of treachery. As with *The Nutshell*, he's sleep-deprived and mentally tortured by sadistic agents that the Ministry has all but forgotten about. While we are never directly told that Steed's experience of torture influenced his character development, it forms a part of his background: he has undergone great privations, has suffered mental and physical violation, and has survived with mind and body intact. What's more, his loyalty to the Ministry cannot be questioned: he's tortured twice by the people he works for, and remains loyal to them.

This experience of torture further complicates Steed's relationship to physical and psychological violence. Prior to the revelation of his imprisonment in *Man with Two Shadows*, Steed beats a fellow agent Borowski, a victim of the same villains, who has gone insane. Steed's violence even surprises his superior, Charles, who turns away as Steed kicks Borowski. Yet, Steed places a limit on his willingness to harm and to kill, as he explains in the Season 6 episode *Get-A-Way*:

Ezdorf: You have killed, I have killed!
Steed: There is a difference. I kill when I have to. You because you like it.

The major difference between Steed and the villains he faces is not in loyalty or even ability to kill, but rather the motivation behind violence. Steed will only kill when he has to, whether it becomes necessary in the line of duty, in the defence of the innocent, or in the protection of those he cares for. Steed's most prevalent moments of true violence and ruthlessness come to the fore when his partner is in danger. In *Concerto*, he bashes a man in the head with a telephone while searching for Cathy Gale; in *The Girl from Auntie*, Steed tortures a Russian agent to get the name of the villains who have kidnapped Mrs. Peel. He lights Piggy Warren's moustache on fire in *The Town of No Return*; the possibility of Tara King being in danger provokes him to almost smash a man's head in with a car bonnet in *The Curious Case of the Countless Clues*. Steed's violence and ruthlessness is most prevalent when the life of his partner has been threatened: rather than official torture or interrogation, it becomes centred on protection, to defend those for whom he has special affection and responsibility.

Steed often occupies the position of chivalric hero for his partners, acting as their protector. In *Escape in Time*, he charges into a 16th Century dungeon armed with a lance to liberate Mrs. Peel from the stocks; in *The Joker*, an injured Steed appears to rescue Mrs. Peel from Prendergast, the man who has imprisoned her. This element of 'damselling' the leading lady is a feature of *The Avengers*; however,

Steed's role as the 'knight' is also consistently punctured. Emma Peel quips about it in *The House that Jack Built* when Steed comes to her rescue bearing a lance:

Mrs. Peel: What happened to the shining armour?
Steed: It's still at the laundry.

Emma Peel does not really need a knight with a lance – she's already managed to save herself. What she does need is Steed as a friend and supporter: taking her hand, he provides her with emotional support following her ordeal. The same occurs in *The Joker*. Steed is barely present in the episode, and it is Emma who faces a demon from her past in the shape of villain Prendergast. Steed arrives to hit Prendergast and lead Emma back into the light, but he does not ask for acknowledgement or reward for his heroism. Instead, he offers his hand in a show of solidarity. It is a modern twist on the knight motif: rather than simply providing physical rescue for which he is rewarded, the knight is there to provide emotional support, his reward being the continued and equal partnership of a woman capable of taking care of herself.

In the opening sequences for the Tara King season, Steed continues to be associated with knight imagery, posing with a shield and suit of armour until Tara (unarmed) runs up to him. He pushes the armour over, turning to take his place in its position vis a vis Tara, visually forming himself as Tara's knight in shining armour. Tara forms an immediate emotional and physical dependence on him within the episodes proper. In *Invasion of the Earthmen*, their first full episode together, Tara consistently hides behind Steed as they break into a booby-trapped camp. She ends one section of the episode by embracing him, an action which will be repeated across the series and one which none of his former partners ever makes, establishing Tara's need for his physical and emotional support. This dependence places Steed's character into a new and more traditional mould, as he becomes the protector of a weaker, less experienced counterpart. Just as Tara is explicitly referred to as a 'damsel in distress', Steed becomes more typified as her rescuer.

Tara is less experienced than her predecessors, and consequently less capable: a young agent, she looks at Steed as an idol, and it is this idolatry that Steed himself must navigate. Early in the Tara King season, Steed takes on responsibility for Tara's professional education: he teaches her judo in *Invasion of the Earthmen* and *The Curious Case of the Countless Clues*; he lectures her on Ministry protocol, excuses her occasional lack of knowledge, and often explains events to her rather than converses with her. Though he has always defended his partners, they have often not needed defending: Tara becomes Steed's pupil and his ward. He performs more as the chivalric hero during the Tara era than he does in any other period. No longer able to depend upon the strength of his partner, Steed must become infallible, even to the degree that he overestimates his own capacity to protect others.

Throughout Season 6, Steed grows accustomed to taking on a traditionally heroic role, willingly placing himself in positions of danger rather than risk failing in his responsibility to Tara. This comes to a head with *Noon Doomsday*, where Steed is incapacitated with a broken leg and confined to a wheelchair. This forces Tara to do most of the episode's heavy lifting, fighting villains and protecting Steed when even his fellow agents decline to assist him. Nearing the end of the episode, however, Steed has realised that Kafka, an old nemesis, is specifically targeting him:

Steed: I'm at the root of this little problem and I think that I should deal with it. Alone.
Tara: Kafka won't be alone, will he?
Steed: All the same, I'd prefer for you to be out of the way. I really would prefer it.
Tara: You won't stand a chance. Now please sit down ...

Steed's common sense takes a backseat to his protective instincts, even in terms of his awareness of physical limitation. He would rather face the danger alone than face it with Tara and run the risk of her loss. Now used to being the hero, Steed cannot allow himself to be saved:

Steed: Now Tara, I hate to do this to you, but I'm going to lock you away until it's all over. What was it? A valuable property to be protected?
Tara: But that's ridiculous, Steed, I can help you!
Steed: You'd be a hindrance. Now I'd be worrying about you, get us both killed.

In *Noon Doomsday*, Steed's heroic mentality, fostered throughout the season, becomes his greatest detriment. He becomes unable to show weakness because of Tara's dependence on him. He's not allowed to reveal his own vulnerability, as he often did in earlier seasons, least of all to the person who depends on him. He's reached a point where he's almost entirely incapacitated but he still tries to keep Tara from going into danger; he believes that both the danger and Tara are his responsibility – to the extent that she has to bash him on the head to keep him from leaving the room. While the episode might have been a watershed moment for the character, an acknowledgement of his fallibility and need for her support, neither Steed nor Tara credit that fallibility beyond the episode itself. They fall back into the same patterns, with Steed as the irreproachable idol (in Tara's eyes at least) and Tara as the adoring *ingénue*.

Steed's overprotectiveness here becomes a dominant feature of his character, recalling that the loss of those he loves has taken a toll on him. Both Cathy Gale and Emma Peel leave him, their losses as final as if they had been killed. Several episodes during Season 6 feature the death or endangerment of old friends, men and women that Steed knew and loved, as in *Get-A-Way* and *Take-Over*. Concurrently, Steed loses much of his sense of humour, more readily giving way to anger and violence. He becomes violent with fellow agents in *The Interrogators* and even physically dominates Tara in *False Witness*. His harshness with villains, hitherto curbed, becomes more ruthless as he kills, crushes, and beats those who stand in his way. The awareness of his physical limitations, necessity for him to play the hero in front of Tara, and the desire to protect others all combine to produce an angrier, more bitter John Steed, one acutely aware of his responsibilities in the lives and safety of other people.

The theme of loss runs throughout *The New Avengers*. The divide between Steed and his much younger partners grows as the show emphasises Steed's exhaustion with his work and his equal inability to leave it behind. In *The New Avengers,* Steed begins to default to his lone wolf status – a role that he's previously disowned through increased interaction with, and trust in, his partners. But the near-fatherly role he occupied with Tara comes to fruition in *The New Avengers*. In *The Last of the Cybernauts...??*, Steed refuses to confide his suspicions about the Cybernauts to his partners, instead choosing to face the danger alone – and, consequently, to nearly get everyone involved killed. The past is a source of danger and of sorrow for Steed, a place that he lives in but in which his much younger partners cannot participate.

The New Avengers relies heavily on references to previous episodes, yet Steed is curiously resistant to active discussion of his past. Mention of

Emma Peel is confined to a minimum – except for her brief cameo in *K is for Kill*, her name is only brought up once, and then in a conversation between Gambit and Purdey. Mention of either Cathy Gale or Tara King is virtually non-existent, and Steed rarely discusses his past partners with his current ones. This does not seem to point to a lack of feeling on Steed's part, but rather an unwillingness to elucidate the past for those who did not participate in it. His home is a virtual museum to his personal history: he keeps old school trophies and medals, and retains pictures of his partners in favoured places. The décor echoes his earlier apartments, emphasising military history and an English country elegance. He painstakingly attempts to reconstruct his Bentley after it's blown up in *Dead Men are Dangerous*. The Bentley is a marker of Steed himself, a connection to a past that he retains but no longer utilises (he drives a luxurious Jaguar instead). Steed further faces multiple villains who are figures from his past: from the new Cybernauts in *Last of the Cybernauts...??* to the more diabolical Mark in *Dead Men are Dangerous*, the past has become a combined source of comfort and of pain. Old friends are killed with surprising regularity:

Steed: One's friends, cut down, decimated. It makes you feel like Adam: lonely.
Gambit: You don't have to be; I'm still here.

Steed's partners are his main source of community and comfort, but they still remain at a distance. Where the partnerships of *The Avengers* tended to progress over a single or double season arc, the partnerships in *The New Avengers* remain relatively static throughout its two season run. Purdey's infatuation with Steed is a call back to the potential romantic relationships that Steed shared with his other partners, and it is with her that he's most emotionally open. He resists overtures of a more romantic nature, but confesses on more than one occasion how very much she matters to him, even to the degree that a threat to her will provoke him to give away state secrets in *Hostage*:

Steed: It's only paper. You're Purdey.

It is with Purdey that Steed most clearly delineates his fears of losing those that matter most to him, as in *Dead Men Are Dangerous*:

Steed: Everything I care about. You said it, remember?
Purdey: Steed...
Steed: You said it.
Purdey: But Steed...
Steed: My pictures. My porcelain. The Bentley. You.

Steed rightly predicts that Mark, an old friend he believed was dead, intends to harm Purdey, believing that in harming her he can take his revenge on Steed. Steed's awareness of this highlights his reasons for resisting greater emotional or romantic entanglement with the younger agent: his involvement with her would not only place them both in danger, but also means that he'd have to acknowledge the potentiality of her loss. Steed's past stops him from engaging too emotionally with his partners, aware as he is that they may die or leave him. [8]

Steed's romantic relationships in *The New Avengers* are both more explicit and less intimate than in *The Avengers*, as he moves through a number of girlfriends over the course of the two seasons. The speed with which he goes through romantic relationships implies that he does not become emotionally involved with any of them. Even his happier moments are tinged with melancholy: in presenting a horse as a gift for his girlfriend Laura, he tells her that the horse makes her happy and "I like people to have what they like." When another girlfriend betrays him in *House of Cards*, he explains that he cannot save her:

Steed: I never did tell you about my marriage, my one and only marriage. I married a job, I married a profession. I've been very faithful.

Steed's statement is complex: it's true that he has remained loyal to the Ministry, and loyal to his country, but he has always been willing to bend, and even break, the rules of his profession in order to protect those he cares for. And he continues to do so, all the way through *The New Avengers*, belying his own statements about 'playing by the rules'.

In some ways, Steed has become the benevolent patriarch of *The Avengers*, occasionally lecturing his younger partners on their professions. His attitudes and behaviour have grown more conservative over the years: he continues to wear his Edwardian suits and bowler hat into his middle age, no longer a younger man driving fashion but an older one comfortable in it. His attitude towards women has not shifted, but he certainly behaves with greater paternalism towards both Gambit and Purdey. Steed of *The New Avengers* is Steed as an icon, a larger-than-life figure whose underlying emotional experience appears less accessible than in earlier incarnations.

While *The New Avengers* obliquely hints at a potential future during the brief conversation with Emma Peel (who is "not Mrs. Peel any more") in *K is for Kill*, Steed's sense of loss and increased isolation has become the major feature of his character. His activity (partially due to his age and Patrick Macnee's fluctuating weight and nascent arthritis) has been curbed to a degree, yet he is still energetic, if not nearly so violent as in previous series. He has curbed his anger – which is still present, but directed – and, if he is showing his age, he is also showing his maturity. Steed does not go out with a bang in the final *New Avengers* episode,

Emily. He goes out with a carnation in his buttonhole, an echo across the seasons to the dashing dandy who first stepped onto the screen in 1961. Steed began life as a hero, and would remain a hero until the last. He was Sir Percy Blakeney and the Scarlet Pimpernel, Beau Brummel without the costumes, James Bond without the brutality. Traversing generations, he was a voice of male feminism long before those words were ever put to it, quietly and tenaciously championing his female partners simply by letting them be the women they were. He was the charming, solid anchor of *The Avengers*, content to let his partners stand in the limelight, to support them and to give them the credit they so richly deserved. He might have been another British superspy, his traditionalism ingrained rather than a façade. Rather, he was a contradiction, a hero on his terms, a man in his own right. He never became a caricature – no man has ever worn a bowler half so well, or so naturally. Despite changes in partners, in time period, and even in visual medium, he remained the same man that Cathy Gale grappled with in *Mr. Teddy Bear*, that Emma Peel crossed swords with in *The Town of No Return*, that Tara King tossed over her shoulder in *Invasion of the Earthmen*: a knight in tarnished armour, a steel glove wrapped in silk, a sword concealed in an umbrella. A true and unconventional hero. In his own words – and I think his partners would agree – John Steed was irreplaceable.

© Lauren Humphries-Brooks

1. *The Avengers: the Inside Story*, p. 22.
2. *The Ultimate Avengers*, p.18.
3. *The Avengers: the Inside Story*, p. 23.
4. Ultimately, Cathy Gale leaves Steed because Honor Blackman decided to quit the show; there was nothing personal, either from the character or actress' perspective.

JZF: While Cathy is loyal to Steed, and cares about him, there are fundamental aspects of their personalities and *modus operandi* that prove to be recurring sticking points in their relationship. Cathy's departure suggests that she is not angry with Steed, but weary of the recurring cycle of their sometimes conflict-habituated dynamic and debates, and feels the need to move on.

5. This explains why ('holiday') episodes largely dominated by one or the other always leave us with a sense of missing a key ingredient.
6. JZF: This shift in dynamic between Steed and his partner is perhaps never better illustrated than by Steed and Emma's brief fight in *The Murder Market.* The entire sequence, from Emma knocking over Steed's toy soldiers to the pair's raised voices, is anathema to the Steed/Emma dynamic the audience knows and loves. While Steed and Cathy were often at loggerheads, the relationship between Steed and Emma is characterised by its warmth and synchronicity, and the fight is the more disturbing and upsetting for it. Undoubtedly a scripting hangover from the Gale years – of which there were many in the early Peel episodes – it is notable that Steed and Peel would (rightly) never participate in such a visceral onscreen disagreement again.
7. Steed's manipulation of the 'seaside' trip in her introductory episode seems to merely amuse her, although she warns him that she won't carry his bucket and spade.

JZF: Steed's treatment of Emma is also undoubtedly correlated with his affinity for her. While Steed may have enjoyed Cathy's company, there is no question that he is more deeply in simpatico with Emma. He does not dare push Emma too far for fear of alienating her and causing her to abandon him completely, something a strong personality such as Emma would do without a second thought if she felt she was being mistreated. Steed's unwillingness to gamble with his relationship with Emma, as he did with his previous partners, is perhaps the best indicator of how much she means to him. This makes it all

the more tragic when she leaves him, not because of his own actions, but due to circumstances beyond his control.
8. There is a sadness, almost an elegiac edge, to Steed in *The New Avengers*.

AND YET: 'SWINGING SELF-INVENTION', FETISHISATION, COMMODIFICATION, AND AESTHETICISM OF DANDY EMMA PEEL

Z.Z. Von Schnerk: I needed a woman like you, Mrs. Peel, a woman of courage, of beauty, of action, a woman who could become desperate and yet remain strong; a woman who could become confused and yet remain intelligent, who could fight back and yet remain feminine. You, and only you, Emma Peel, have all these qualifications. (*Epic*)

Critics examining the gender dynamics within *The Avengers* have long argued over whether the programme presents women who are exploited and fetishised for their appearance and sexual allure. James Chapman, for example, suggests that '*The Avengers* heroines do still function as the fetishised objects of the male gaze.' [1] Emma Peel, in particular, is very often the focus of the objectification of women within academic criticism: despite clear attempts to show that Peel is an independent woman capable of physically defending herself, as well as being an intellectual in both the arts and sciences, it could be argued that it is Peel's visual identity that often takes priority within the programme. [2] The plotlines, dialogue of the characters, and the camera framing often linger on Peel's body, clothes and face: there is no doubt that, through actress Diana Rigg, Peel presents an inviting and even intimidating image. Of course, *The Avengers* is a programme that prioritises surface and image – Steed, as a Dandy, for example, is arguably just as visually objectified and fetishised as his female counterparts – and, in some cases, even more so. Dandyism is, at the core, the willing and controlled objectification of a surface identity – and

Steed, as a Dandy, maintains control over this image despite (or, indeed, perhaps because of) the constant prioritising of surface and objectification of his own identity. As such, whilst debate on whether *The Avengers* presents an objectified image of Peel is necessary, it is equally important to investigate whether Peel, like Steed, maintains control over that image. Accepting that Peel is, in fact, objectified and commodified through the prioritisation of aesthetics and surface, this article investigates whether Peel, like Steed, successfully manages to maintain control over that surface image or not.

Gazing into *Avengerland*

Brian Clemens positions *Avengerland* as a 'Never-Never Land', populated only with dashing heroes and villains, beautiful colours, and high society. [3] Clemens suggests that it is the aesthetics and imagery that made *The Avengers* special: 'the women looked beautiful, and all the men were stylish and charming, even the villains were charming.' [4] The house-rules of *Avengerland* rest entirely upon an idealised surface: it is the epitome of style over substance. In *The Critics* on *BBC Radio* in 1963, Harry Craig referred to the programme as 'excited surface. What is it about? Search me! It has the usual vocabulary of a thriller, gun play, and judo throws, with a hero who goes through an imminent deadly ambush with a bowler hat and rolled umbrella.' [5]

Similarly, when American executives were purchasing the programme in 1965, Macnee was asked to sum it up, but all he could 'splutter' in response was '*The Avengers* is about a man in a bowler hat and a woman who flings men over her shoulders.' [6] That both the critics and actors define the programme not by the events or dialogue within the show, but with the aesthetics of a man (Steed's bowler and rolled umbrella, primarily) and the actions of a woman (Peel's martial arts and physical power) suggest that the objectification through aesthetics is not limited to women but, in fact, might even prioritise objectification of men. Where Emma Peel is consistently shown to have many talents and hobbies both in the arts and sciences (sewing, chemistry, anthropology, sculpting, etc.), the defining characteristic of Steed rests solely on his style. Careful attention is constantly paid to recognising his perfected aesthetics: characters within the programme dressed almost as well as Steed himself constantly declare astonishment at his style, meaning that Steed is constantly recognised not for his personality or skill, but for his debonair flair. In fact, Piers D Britton and Simon J Barker suggest that 'the bowler and brolly have become as much a signifier for Macnee as for Steed', so much so that 'it would have been virtually impossible for Steed to appear without these accoutrements: they had become his "trademark".' [7]

Of course, for Steed, it is a very specific form of objectification. I mentioned previously that Steed, as a Dandy, is, by nature, objectified. Dandyism is, above all, 'an exercise in perfecting the externals and giving the impression that anything beneath the surface was incidental.' [8] But this exercise is one that must be maintained – as Catherine Spooner suggests, it is the 'managing of surface' that is crucial. [9] Steed, presenting an Edwardian-inspired external, maintains absolute control over not just his external image, but also absolute control over his persona: he rarely loses control of his emotions. Even when a criminal mastermind has him held captive and is threatening him, for example, Steed tends to act as though he is having a friendly chat over tea. Arguably, Steed is 'feminised' by maintaining an identity that is almost entirely based on his appearance. Steed's inactivity provides him (and his female partners Gale and Peel) with a certain androgyny and play with gender, as Barbey insists a Dandy must have, but also complies with Baudelaire's assertion that 'A dandy does nothing.' [10] Macnee himself sums this up, stating 'I did as little of the action as I possibly could.' [11]

The gender dualism that several critics have commented upon for both Steed and Peel proves only to reinforce the Dandy's power. Ellen Moers argues that

'it was no accident that Barbey d'Aurevilly...had written of George Brummel as the ideal *androgyne* – and of the dandies as double and multiple natures, an indecisive intellectual gender. The Androgyne is the ultimate artistic gender; it confuses the two principles, the feminine and the masculine, and balances the one by the other. Any exclusively male figure lacks grace, any exclusively feminine one lacks force.' [12]

Thus, with Steed, in the role of masculine but emphasising the grace, and Peel, in the role of the female, emphasising force, both Steed and Peel attain exactly what Dandies like Brummell were attempting to achieve: liminality. [13]

Whilst Cathy Gale undoubtedly maintained control over herself, she lacks the knowing wink of a Dandy that suggests nothing could be taken too seriously. Gale is positioned as something of a modern revision of the New Women of the late nineteenth century, whilst Peel embraces a modern twist on the female aesthete:

'The line between female aesthetes and New Women was so thin as to seem, sometimes, almost imperceptible...both invented new fashions, and both mingled in the world of academia and journalism. But the difference is that the female aesthete chose to participate in high-art tradition rather than a political movement. Thus the female aesthetes used their publishers, stories, articles, friends, clothes, and education for a very different reason – not to bear witness to the desperate need to expand women's lives but to precisely question the value end of limits about the expansion of female identity. Where New Women novelists protested against existing laws, female aesthetes imagined an ideal woman, placing her in a romantic past or casting her as the witty *mondaine*, to use Ouida's term, whose speech dominates her social milieu. Where New Women agitated for real reforms, female aesthetes described spaces where no reform would be necessary.' [14]

Essentially, Cathy Gale, as the (modernised) New Woman, constantly attempts to reassert her equality with Steed on a regular basis. Peel, as the aesthete, automatically assumes that she already has it, declaring, 'I'm thoroughly emancipated' (*Escape in Time*). Gale demands reform, but Peel just assumes that the reform has already occurred. It is a subtle difference, but an important one. Where Gale and Steed were constantly at loggerheads due to Steed's occasional sexist tendencies and inability to take events seriously, in Peel, Steed finds a partner who refuses to ask for respect and just takes it. Further, Peel, as a female Dandy (often referred to as a Dandizette), understands that nothing in *Avengerland* should be taken seriously – Steed's knowing smirks, met with disapproval from Gale, are only returned with Peel's knowing smirk of her own. [15]

As such, whilst there is no doubt that women (in particular the character designed to gain the Male (M-) Appeal, Emma Peel) are visually positioned, as objects of the gaze, so, too, are the men (in particular, John Steed). In *The Town of No Return*, Steed approaches Peel's door, which famously holds a giant eye capable of blinking and moving, adorned with eyelashes for Peel to see her visitors. As Britton and Barker suggest, 'it could equally well be said that she was returning and reversing the male gaze.' [16] Steed may very well, like the viewer, be gazing at Emma Peel – but there is every indication that Peel is gazing back.

High-Street A-Peel

'A dress is a prop, no more – it's the way that she wears it that counts.' [17]

Initially, Emma Peel is not strikingly different from her predecessor Cathy Gale. Gale is an anthropologist who was widowed after the death of a post-colonial British farmer who died in Africa. She is replaced by sybarite Peel, who is (seemingly) widowed after the death of her husband, a post-colonial British test pilot lost in South America. Each is highly intelligent, and particularly adept at physical force against her opponents, expert in karate and judo. Both women are clearly intellectual, professional women and 'amateurs' (not professional) spies who aid Steed in his investigations. Each found noticeable fame due to her aesthetics – Gale, for her 'kinky boots' and fetishised leather catsuits, and Peel for her miniskirts and Emmapeelers. [18] Wesley Britton even suggests that

'In a sense, Emma Peel out-Galed Gale. Peel was proficient in the art of combat, knowledgeable on any number of subjects, irreverent, charming, and graceful. Like Steed, she enjoyed the life of danger and, like Cathy Gale, she kept Steed's amorous attentions at bay, although the two clearly enjoyed each other's company during and between bouts with evil.' [19]

Fashion designer Frederick Starke, who designed Gale's outfits, stated:

'I thought of [Gale] as a female James Bond, alias Secret Agent 007. She does a great deal of fighting so the clothes had to be practical. Cathy is meant to be a fashionable woman. There are occasions when she will need simpler clothes. She has two basic suits and a pinafore dress. She can wear anything so long as it isn't fluffy.' [20]

This suggests that the design concepts first considered utilitarian, *action-*orientated needs (i.e., martial arts and fighting sequences), while their aesthetically pleasing display was a secondary concern.

The fashions for Peel, on the other hand, were far more varied than Gale. Far more Mod in style, Peel initially used leather catsuits similar to Blackman's, but quickly found her own style. Maria Alvarez suggests that, through aesthetics,

'Mrs Peel evoked the pitiless dominatrix, the machine age's version of Venus in Furs – Venus in Leathers. Her smooth, dark, helmet-shaped hair and sleek outlines feed back through the likes of Louise Brooks, star of silent screen, to archetypes of female warriors such as Joan of Arc. These types suggest women who become erotic through "masculinisation".' [21]

Crepe flouncy blouses, for example, often accentuated the leather suits, a hard 'masculinised' action-orientated image contradicted by the feminine cravat-like ruffles on her chest. Chiffon maxi dresses, bright '60s shift dresses and pea-coats, and fur-trimmed black and white coats were highly visible. Tweed Jackie Onassis-inspired suits appeared throughout the monochrome Peel/Steed era. The Gale-esque leather catsuits were eventually abandoned in favour of her famous jumpsuits for action sequences, the 'Emmapeelers'. Bates designed Peel's aesthetics based specifically upon Rigg's shape and personality. In fact, these designs were ahead of the times, with the invention of the 'smallest dress in the World' just in time for Peel to make her screen presence. [22]

Whilst action sequences and practicality were issues for fashion designer John Bates of the Jean Varon label, who designed Peel's wardrobe for the monochrome series, Bates was concerned less with the practicality of the costumes (Bates even designed outfits with patterned tights so Peel could fight in her mini-skirts, though these were ultimately declined) and more with allowing clothes to be used as part of the personality of Diana Rigg's character:

'Cathy Gale was not at all my type of girl. The clothes I have designed for Diana, anyone can wear – and short skirts as well. A girl must never rely entirely on a dress to make her pretty, or fragile, or alluring. She looks the way she feels, no matter what she wears – and it shows. If she is sexy, you see it in her face and body. If she is demure, you see it in her eyes, in the way she moves her hands. A dress can't do that for her. It can help. But it is for the woman to be expressive.' [23]

In arguing that one must never rely completely on clothes to create an identity, and that anyone could wear his designs, Bates's comments could initially seem contradictory to Dandyism. He argues, essentially, the opposite of the famous Carlyle quote, 'the clothes make the man', or, in this case, woman. In his treatise on Dandyism, Honoré de Balzac argues that, *'Clothing does not consist so much in clothes as in a certain manner of wearing them*. Consequently it is not [so much] the rags in themselves as it is the spirit of the rags that one must grasp.' [24] Bates's approach to Rigg/Peel's attire is the same, arguing that a 'dress is a prop, no more – it's the way that she wears it that counts.' [25] In suggesting that what is special is not just the design of the clothes, but how that design is worn, essentially he argues that it is the [wo]man that makes the clothes. Bates declares that '[a] dress is a prop, no more – it's the way that she wears it that counts.' [26] It is Peel's personality, attitude and humour that make the clothes more interesting. The clothes allow an expression of her visual identity, but the clothes are special because Peel wears them, not the other way around.

Bates's designs (and later designs by Alun Hughes), though, were not just designed to be visually striking on Diana Rigg, but also to be replicated:

'Like Gale, Emma Peel's tight-fitting leather fighting outfit became a sensation, as did her cat suit, dubbed by the press as the "Emma Peeler" [sic] which was created for the color [sic] season. Knowing the power of merchandising, John Bates designed a speciality line of clothes for Rigg to wear on screen and to be sold in retail stores, the first time fashions were designed for this purpose.' [27]

In fact, articles began appearing as early as September 1965 outlining Peel's wardrobe going on sale, promising the public that '[y]ou can do an Emma down to the last detail – gloves, shoes and all':

'And the clothes themselves, designed by John Bates at Jean Varon, are the sort which demand a second look: one little number, a bra top, plus hipster trousers, plus an acre or so of midriff, is guaranteed to cause a riot at any party, anywhere. What with sensational outfits and television's hypnotic effect on the buying public, the *Avengers* clothes can't but be the success of the season. [...] Even if the leather fanciers regret Cathy Gale's departure, I feel that there are going to be a lot of men who feel cheered up by the thought of the Emma Peelers.' [28]

In suggesting that 'a lot of men' will be 'cheered up by the thought of the Emma Peelers', Peel is, therefore, already commodified by the time she appears on screen, designed to be visually consumed by the audiences who would find her attractive. Moreover, the article promises a 'hypnotic' power over women, encouraging the purchasing of Emma herself because, as Felicity Green in the *Daily Mirror* argues, '[t]he question, the morning after, will undoubtedly be: Did you see what Emma wore – and where can I buy it?' [29] In promising that '[y]ou can do an Emma down to the last detail - gloves, shoes and all', Peel's persona – aesthetics, intellectualism, personality and all – is designed to be consumed by the audiences who would want to replicate her. Peel is, from inception, objectified completely.

And yet, when critics discuss the objectification of Peel, the debate tends to centre around one episode (*A Touch of Brimstone*) due to the more overt example of the objectification and fetishisation of Peel, focusing specifically on the infamous 'Queen of Sin' scene and her attire. Steed and Peel go undercover to investigate The Hellfire Club, and Peel is eventually forced into a costume that raises even the unflappable Steed's eyebrows. Peel steps onto the stage specifically to give those men (and women!) in the Hellfire Club the opportunity to gaze upon her. Dressed in stiletto knee-length boots, a reverse bouffant, severely dark cat eyes that stretch extremely high up her face and accentuate her natural cheekbones, and gems on her forehead, the rest of her attire is hidden below a cape. She is then physically unwrapped for all to see: an Edwardian boned corset with a three inches of a very fine mesh modesty wrap that serves to both hide and reveal her body to the onlookers; gloves that crawl three-quarters of the way up to her arms; a black collar with three-inch long spikes with a chain attached to a cuff on her wrist; and a snake in her arms. Moving beyond arrant objectification, the aesthetics project a highly fetishised and commodified identity. The camera starts at her boots and works the way up her body. The drunken audience goes silent, and we receive the occasional flash onto a male audience member: Steed goes wide-eyed; a man licks his lips. A close-up of Peel's face shows a cold, non-responsive expression – she could be a mannequin at a fashion shoot. The snake slithers, and she makes no reaction. Everyone is frozen in the room: all eyes are upon Peel. This changes instantly when the audience is told by the Hellfire leader, Cartney, 'she is yours to do with what you will.' The fashion shoot turns to savagery as men and women both crowd toward the stage. As one, the mob picks Peel up and carries her out, throwing flower petals everywhere. Just as she refused to move when the snake slithers on her arms, Peel lies in their arms, giving no reaction. Steed attempts to follow, but is stopped by the crowd.

Of course, this is only one of the reasons the episode is so iconic: as several critics like Chapman have noted, the episode was heavily censored for a later scene involving Emma Peel, in this same 'Queen of Sin' outfit, being first attacked by a smaller man in a silly ballet step, but, more importantly, having Cartney attack her several times with a leather whip. In fact, Emma holds her own quite well: she may have the chain running from a spiked dog collar to her wrist, but no-one else holds control over it. When the small ballet man attacks her, she stands, legs apart – immoveable. Her chain is pulled – but only ever by herself – to the point where it breaks in the fight. She clearly belongs to no-one, chain or not.

The Hellfire Club leader (Cartney, played by Peter Wyngarde) is more imposing. Where Peel quickly disposes of the unarmed ballet dancer, Carney is armed with a whip. The sequence is fairly long – he snaps the whip and Peel actively avoids being hit. Fetishist sado-masochism implications aside, it is this attack in her corseted outfit that causes Chapman to argue that this visual – the dominant female constantly trying to avoid being whipped by a man – suggests that Peel is

'therefore made to play the roles of both dominatrix and victimised woman: *The Avengers* heroine embodies aspects of both dominant and passive femininity, a characteristic that runs throughout the series and represents its strategy for coming to terms with the rise of the women's movement.' [30]

Undoubtedly, Peel's aesthetics do position her as fetishised and visually dominant – yet the scene does appear to show a menacing male with a weapon confronting an unarmed female.

Where Chapman argues that Peel presents a 'passive' image, however, I would argue that Peel, thus far unrecognised as a Dandy, only maintains her Dandy coldness. Just as Steed will quietly nod or half-smile to a villain who holds him captive, at no point throughout this episode does Peel lose control of herself. As the crowd envelops her during her initial reveal, she is like a statue, unmoving, barely blinking. Rather than being victimised, thus placed in a position to lose her identity, Peel's very immobility – crucial to the Dandy (and, by extension, the Dandizette) – is the very thing that proves she is far from passive. She does not run from the merging crowd, nor does she crouch in a corner to avoid the cracking whip: she shows her strength and control through that immobility. Further, as Chapman also points out in *Saints and Avengers*, 'Emma successfully avoids the lashes so that not once is she actually touched by the whip.' [31] Cartney is killed not because Peel takes action against him, but because his whip accidentally catches the lever on the wall (disguised as a torch) that released the trap door in the floor and falls into a pit. In truly Freudian *Avengers* fashion, Peel wins because her overly enthusiastic and aggressive opponent doesn't know how to handle his own whip.

Conclusion
In *Epic*, Von Schnerk, a criminal mastermind 'casts' (kidnaps) Peel to 'star' in his film, declaring that she was cast because of her courage, beauty, strength, intellect, and gender ambivalence, that '[y]ou, and only you, Emma Peel, have all these qualifications.' And yet, it is these very these qualities that Von Schnerk wishes to destroy: the denouement of his 'film' involves Peel bound to a table trying to avoid being cut in half with a buzz-saw. Peel looks behind her at the circular

saw as she moves closer to it. She does not cry, she does not panic, and does not desperately try to shift herself free from the ropes: she merely offers a cold, snarky pun ('I think I'm in danger of becoming a split personality'). Peel is far more concerned about what this buzz-saw might do to her beautiful suit than whether it might kill her or not. Her inactivity here – just like in *A Touch of Brimstone* – can be mistaken for passivity. But, in fact, for a Dandy like Peel, inactivity often suggests control and surface rather than victimisation or powerlessness.

Undoubtedly, as scholars have argued, *The Avengers* presents an objectified (and even fetishised), 'contradictory image of modern womanhood that both celebrates female empowerment and yet at the same time attempts to establish control mechanisms whereby women can be kept in their place.' [32] And as important as it is to explore this, it is also crucial to understand that absolutely everything and everyone within the programme is fetishised, commodified and contradictory. Further, as these discussions of gender representation very often centre upon Emma Peel, it is crucial to recognise that she is, like Steed, a Dandy. Because Dandyism is, at the core, an intentional commodification of self through aesthetics, Peel's objectification takes on a different tone than one might first anticipate. That Peel is often fetishised and commodified is not in question: the most interesting thing about Peel is not, then, how well she fits into that corset, but how she negotiates and retains control over not only her aesthetics and gender representation, but also how she utilises and controls them just as effectively as Patrick Macnee's Dandy Steed might ever have done.

© Sunday Swift

1. James, Chapman, 'The Avengers: Television and Popular Culture During the "High Sixties"' in *Windows on the Sixties*, eds.

Anthony Aldgate, James Chapman and Arthur Marwick (London: I.B. Tauris Publishers, 2000), p. 57.
2. SS: In the majority of critical analysis on Emma Peel, she is referred to as 'Emma', and John Steed is referred to as 'Steed'. I refer to her as 'Peel' (and, by extension, Cathy Gale as 'Gale') for two reasons: firstly, within the programme itself, she is rarely referred to as 'Emma', but by her surname; no more often, in fact, than Steed is referred to as 'John'. Secondly, I find some of the critical analysis emphasising 'Emma' as diminutive, particularly as it is usually used in regards to her appearance or aesthetics. Chapman is prone to this when discussing both Cathy Gale and Emma Peel (James Chapman, *Saints and the Avengers: British Adventure series of the 1960s* (London: I.B. Tauris & Co.) 2002, see page 81 for an example) In referring to Peel as 'Emma', it emphasises the more *feminine*, and as my argument is that Peel, like Steed, represent a queered double gender, I find referring to her as 'Emma' in terms of aesthetics and costume somewhat contrary to both her character as well as her gender representation.
3. [Interview with Brian Clemens] in *Avengers Revisited [Documentary]*, 10 Nov 2005, Sara Tiefenbrun, BBC, UK.
4. *Avenging the Avengers*, dir. Paul Madden, Dean Stockton, StudioCanal, 5 June, 2000.
5. Transcript from Harry Craig BBC Radio 1963 *The Critics*, cited in Patrick Macnee and Dave Rogers, *Avengers, the Inside Story*, London: Titan Books, 2008), p. 39. Lord Peter a fictional detective created by Dorothy L. Sawyers, also presented Dandy tendencies.
6. Patrick Macnee and Marie Cameron, *Blind in One Ear* (Bath: Harrap Ltd/Chivers Press Ltd, 1988), p. 286.
7. Piers D Britton, Simon J. Barker, *Reading Between the Designs: Visual Imagery and Generation of Meaning in The Avengers, The Prisoner and Doctor Who* (Austin, TX: University of Texas Press, 2003), pp. 52-53.

8. Michael Bronski, *Culture Class: The Making of Gay Sensibility* (Brooklyn: South End Press, 1984), p. 54.
9. Catherine Spooner, *Fashioning Gothic Bodies* (Manchester University Press, 2005), p. 101.
10. Jules Barbey d'Aurevilly, *Du Dandysme et de Georges Brummell* [*Dandyism*], trans. by Douglas Ainslie (New York: PAJ Publications, 1988 (1897)), p. 74; Charles Baudelaire, *Journaux Intimes* [*Intimate Journals*], trans. by Christopher Isherwood (Mineola: Dover Publications, 2006 (1947), p. 74.
11. Macnee and Rogers, p. 69. SS: This changes dramatically in the Tara King era, as American executives were concerned about him appearing too feminine. RM: Androgynes have a gender which is simultaneously masculine and feminine, though not necessarily in equal amounts.
12. Moers, p. 309. The original French read: 'natures doubles et multiples, d'une sexe intellectuel indécis...L'Androgne est le sexe artistique par excellence, il confond les deux principes, le féminin et le masculin, et les équilibre l'un par l'autre. Toute figure exclusivement masculine manqué de grâce, toute autre exclusivement féminine manqué ce force.'
13. RM: Liminality literally means 'threshold'. It is a transitional period or phase of a rites of passage, marked by its ambiguity and disorientation.
14. Talia Schaffer, *The Forgotten Female Aesthetes: literary culture in late-Victorian England*, University of Virginia Press: 2000, p. 25.
15. RM: Of course one could observe that *Avengerland* itself – and therefore the rules – had changed too!
16. Piers D Britton and Simon J Barker, p. 69.
17. Quoted in Richard Lester, *John Bates: Fashion Designer*, AAC Editions (Suffolk: Antique Collectors' Club Ltd, 2008), p. 79.
18. Patrick Macnee even argues that Emma Peel was the first woman on television to wear the miniskirt in the documentary *Avenging the Avengers*.

19. Wesley Britton, *Spy Television* (Westport: Praeger Publishing, 2004), p. 67.
20. Diana Lancaster, "The Immaculate *Avengers*, A look at The *Avengers* fashions of Patrick Macnee and Honor Blackman (Fredrick Starke period), *TV Times*, issue 418, pages 4,5, and 7, 1 Nov, 1963.
21. Maria Alvarez, "Feminist icon in a catsuit", *New Statesman;* Aug 14, 1998; 11, 517, p. 16.
22. SS: Arguments persist over who invented the miniskirt, but Bates does suggest that it was his invention in refusing to allow ABC to lower the hemline of his short skirts. See Lester, p. 43 for more on this.
23. *TV Times*, 15th-21st January 1966
24. Honoré de Balzac, *Treatise on Elegant Living*, trans. Napoleon Jeffries (Cambridge: Wakefield Press, 2010 (1830)), p. 71, italics original.
25. Quoted in Lester, 79.
26. Ibid, 79.
27. Wesley Britton, *Spy Television*, p.67.
28. Judy Innes, 'From Now On Girls You can be Your Own Avenger,' in *The Daily Mail*, 27 September, 1965, p. 6. Text available online at http://deadline.theavengers.tv/mail001.htm
29. Felicity Green quoted in Lester, 43
30. Chapman, *Windows on the Sixties*, 57
31. Chapman, *Saints and the Avengers,* p. 354, footnote 46.
32. Chapman, *Windows on the Sixties*, p. 57.

TARA KING

"Excellent. Great action. But liked her oats too much. I sold her to an Arab prince. I think he eventually had to shoot her." (*House of Cards*)

Tara King. Fans of *The Avengers* have diverse opinions of her. Charming, vivacious beauty. Dynamic, ferocious combatant. Fawning, dim-witted heroine. Disappointing pretender. She is the most polarising character to come out of the show and continues, even today, to be a source of heated debate amongst its ardent followers.

Tara was a doomed character from the beginning. She had one of the most difficult acts to follow in British television. She was the successor to Mrs. Emma Peel, who was regarded as the best of John Steed's partners. Mrs. Peel was crafted as the ultimate female: mentally and physically gifted to a near impossible degree. A sophisticated fantasy figure who still retains an enormous impact on popular culture. So while there were people who embraced Tara, many fans felt let down and resoundingly rejected her.

It is understandable why a number of viewers would react so negatively to Miss King. Despite whatever charms actress Linda Thorson may have brought to the role, Tara is a character in flux for a good part of her era and underwent an extended period of development by those involved in the series. She is no superwoman. She isn't a lady of letters. She has no doctorate. She doesn't own her own company. She isn't an expert in cyphers or cybernetics. Tara is flawed. She is impetuous and can make mistakes. She can even show fear and weakness. However, perhaps in those foibles lie her strengths. She is relatable, human and very real. That in itself could be considered ground-breaking for the time. She displays a great exuberance and verve. If Tara were around today, television audiences would less likely have an issue with her.

Tara was established as a professional agent and not a specialised recruit, nor a fabulous dilettante indulging in a love of adventure. Like her predecessors, she reflected a turning point in the role of women in the real world and how it would eventually evolve to the modern day. Tara chose a career in a field still heavily dominated by men. Yet the world was changing and much more so in the land of *The Avengers*. While we would not see many professional female agents in the King episodes, they at least had a presence and were acknowledged. And their duties drifted away from that of the *femme fatale* whose sole role was to seduce an enemy. (Even Mrs. Peel and Mrs. Gale had engaged in that sort of mission). Tara works as an official – red security pass holding – member of the Ministry. It was a small but important stride to further the idea that women were inherently just as capable as men but didn't need to be (to quote Georgie Price-Jones) "Madame Curie and half a dozen others all rolled into one" to be taken seriously. As a professional spy, she would not be expected or needed to be an expert in anthropology, physics, medicine or chemistry. Espionage would be her main specialty. After all, was Steed or any of the other men in the Department masters in those areas? [1] It is noteworthy that Tara seems to have the respect of her male colleagues (aside from the overly protecting attitude from Steed in the earlier episodes). While Tara is often written into the trope of damsel in distress, her co-workers at least do not appear bigoted or patronising towards her. It's a far cry in attitude from a few years prior, when *Danger Man*'s John Drake openly sneered at the employ of women in the business.

Adjustment of Tara's rank to that of an official agent is part of the above mentioned flux and ongoing evolution. When observing the first two completed episodes, Tara is as much an amateur recruit as her predecessors. This is quickly changed to her being a professional after 'The Powers That Be' switched the reigns of the show from John Bryce back to Brian Clemens and Albert Fennell. Her change in status was a wise move to justify why Steed was working with a woman who lacked any of the specialised expertise observed in those who came before her.

Closer examination of Tara's character shows a persona that reflects and embraces late 1960s mod culture. The lens through which that influence would operate changes as well. In the early episodes, Tara is bold, colourful, sexually open and assertive. The sets and costuming underscore this. Tara's flat is a spectacular, almost garishly eclectic explosion of imagery. Her early wardrobe, mainly designed by Harvey Gould, highlights that boldness with rompers with open backs, hip boots and sexy mini-dresses. With the change in career status comes a shift away from the flirtatious Tara and gradually towards someone who is more action oriented. Tara is still feminine but she exudes a vibrant physicality that would have categorised her back then as a 'tomboy'. Her costumes, now by Alan Hughes, reflect that change accordingly. First there is a transitionary period where her clothes are composed of bolero jackets and vests with matching culottes. Later the programme settles on an array of fitted pantsuits that often incorporate tops made from bright prints. It is an athletic but fashionable look, ideally exemplified by her mustard or red ensembles in *All Done With Mirrors* and *You'll Catch Your Death*.

The tomboy aspect is evident when observing Tara in action, most notably with her speed. On several occasions she can be seen convincingly engaging two or more opponents at the same time. She is never afraid to throw a cross right or a haymaker. Further, though trained in judo and other martial arts, Tara uses a combat method that has its best parallel with Sammo Hung's character from the US series *Martial Law*. Like Sammo, Tara uses a mix of formalised fighting moves while adapting the surrounding environment to her advantage. She is never above making use of the nearest available object to aid her in combat: a magazine, a vase, a frying pan, her handbag. If it is within arm's reach, she can turn it into a weapon. It can best be summed up as a 'make it work' type of approach to beating up bad guys. Such battle tactics can come across as less sophisticated, creating a rougher, edgier feel. This along with her quickness results in some intense brawls.

Some of the most vivid fights choreographed for the show occur during the Tara King era. *Noon Doomsday* perfectly showcases her adaptive style during her showdown with the assassins hired by Gerald Kafka to kill Steed. We see her hurtling about, overwhelming the killers with whatever is at hand, be it a ladder, rope or hay bales. In *The Rotters*, Tara deftly fends off the 'gentlemanly' adversaries, Kenneth and George, faring even better against them than Steed did. In *My Wildest Dream*, the violence is at its most brutal with Tara's fight with the assailant Dyson. It's a furious encounter as they wrestle manically around the room, punches and kicks freely flying, with the scene punctuated by Tara ramming his head through a stain glass window. In perhaps the most action packed episode of the series, *All Done With Mirrors*, Linda Thorson and stunt double Cyd Child are put through the most demanding of paces. Tara's fight with the gargantuan thug Gazzo boasts some of the most impressive martial arts moves the show has ever incorporated into a fight. The final showdown at the lighthouse is equally impressive as Tara systematically and singlehandedly takes out five enemy agents.

Furthermore, her abilities extend beyond fisticuffs. As stated, Tara was not conceived as someone scientifically educated but who functions by her instincts and wits. This seems to serve her just as well as a right cross. She might not have been a formal academic but she manages to be resourceful, often getting out of tough situations with great ingenuity. In *You'll Catch Your Death*, she is able to jury-rig an explosive. In *The Rotters* she escapes capture using some acid and a bottle of wine. The accumulation of all her guile can be observed in the episode *Wish You Were Here,* where she is able to overtake a diabolical prison in the guise of a hotel, outsmarting its entire staff. She accomplishes all of this by sheer cunning, without throwing a punch or firing a gun.

All this begs the question, if Tara is so formidable and capable, wherein lies the rub? The main problem is that these marvellous traits are not presented consistently. For every moment of brilliant cunning, there is one of doe-eyed denseness or sheer stupidity, particularly in the early episodes. Although there are many examples of Tara being every bit as dangerous as Steed's partners, there are many times that demonstrate the opposite. It is particularly frustrating when these contradictions happen in the same episode or, worse, within the same scene. The above-mentioned fight with Gozzo from *All Done with Mirrors* exemplifies this perfectly. In the beginning of her encounter, she panics and is running for her life in fear. Then suddenly she turns into a ferocious wildcat, and gives the audience a fight they would not forget for some time. And in both *The Rotters* and *You'll Catch Your Death* she pulls off an impressive escape, only to be recaptured minutes later. And captured she was, in many, many episodes. [2]

Why the inconsistency? One explanation could be tied to the edict that prevailed for several episodes of writing Tara as an impetuous novice. Then there was her relationship with Steed, which was far more blatant in romantic terms and, at certain points, annoyingly fawning. Even though the former was phased out and the latter aspect was eventually downplayed, they would not have necessarily been evident to the British audience. Unlike in the US, the episodes of this era were not aired in the UK in a manner that aligned with the production order. Further, there appeared to be a policy that Tara had to be regularly captured, put in danger and rescued by Steed. She also seemed to have to be portrayed at times as dense or slow, not only in accordance with this rule, but also for a given script to fill out the timeslot. A prime example is *Pandora*. During most of the episode, Tara is kept in a drugged state. Barring a couple of moments of lucidity, she is essentially passive, gullible and brainwashed for the bulk of the story. Drugging her is necessary to the villains' plan, but keeping her sedate is required to stretch out the hour. Any sustained or proactive action on her part would have ended the plot almost immediately. A sober Tara would have easily overpowered her kidnappers and settled the matter in one act. But instead we get a heroine who offers us – over and over again – a stupefied daze. Can you imagine a script with this happening to Cathy Gale or Emma Peel?

Who was ultimately responsible for this? After more than 45 years, a lot of ambiguity remains. It is difficult to assign blame to any individual source, and likely several were accountable. It has also been discussed that there was a desire to bring the show back to a more realistic level and to strengthen Steed's character. Certainly, having a more vulnerable and fallible heroine would accomplish this, and balance out Steed. However, while Tara started out relatively weak, she progressively got stronger throughout the production of the series. And with it came a gradual change in Steed's attitude towards her. In their early adventures he regarded Tara as a reckless young woman who treated their business like a game. By two thirds of the episodes in, he speaks respectfully of her as a proficient partner and an equal.

Had Tara been more consistently written, her character would have been better actualised. A much more effective statement could have been advocated about the inherent capability of women and how they are not required to be a fantastical wonder woman before they are even worth considering. Not until the advent of Purdey in *The New Avengers* would such a subtext be effectively delivered. Still Tara can be perceived as the forerunner to Purdey, as Cathy Gale is to Emma Peel. Both are professionally trained agents, possessing a very feminine allure yet not afraid to get tough and physical. While Purdey is considered a superlative agent, she never demonstrates any intellectual specialties. They exist in a world where women were equal to men, separate, but equal. It is an assertion that a generation later would become the norm in the general television landscape. A good case can be made that many of the current TV heroines are much in the vein of Tara King. Women like Elizabeth Keane of the *Blacklist* or Kensi Blye of the *NCIS* franchise have far more in common with her than her predecessors.

© Frank Hui

1. In some respects this makes Tara King more realistic than the 'impossibly' talented Emma Peel.
2. Captured and *chloroformed*, I'm tempted to add.

MOTHER

The Mother character is problematic on many levels. He is at times the comic relief, the establishment figure, the caring Mother-figure and the irascible departmental head. Some of this is due to the shifting sands of the production, the changing scripts and the broadcast schedule, but we may find all these conflicting characters and characteristics within a single episode.

Whenever I think of Mother, I think of an irate man in a wheelchair, barking orders at his subordinates and behaving in a gruffly sarcastic manner. However, a closer inspection of Patrick Newell's portrayal of the character reveals that this is not always the case. In fact, Mother starts off as a generally friendly boss, a benevolent father figure (or is that a mother figure? Freud would have a field day). As the season progressed, he became more prone to angry outbursts, and from *The Interrogators* onwards he is the figure I remember, the sarcastic disdain for others and irascibility taking centre stage. [1]

Mother represents the establishment and therefore has to be subverted because the establishment is always worthy of derision. He first appears in the Emma Peel farewell episode *The Forget-Me-Knot* as the blustering head of the unnamed Ministry. He is presented as an irate paraplegic, bridling at everyone and trusting no-one. The episode was filmed in January 1968 and featured Patrick Newell as Steed's newly-revealed boss. Mother, it is said, was initially introduced as a throw-away guest part but the American producers loved him and demanded he appear in every episode.

He is a tongue-in-cheek jibe at James Bond's M (itself a play on the head of MI6, who is always named C after the initial of the first head of the department). Naturally, in order to fool the enemy, the male head of the unnamed Ministry has a female title, and when his second-in-command stands in, she is called Father. Another episode has Mother off-handedly mention contacting "Grandma", who we must suppose is his superior.

While Mother doesn't reappear for some time, this is not unprecedented in *Avengers* history and I suspect that Clemens planned to reuse the Mother character or at least keep him up his sleeve. Steed's superiors had appeared sparingly in the previous two seasons (indeed, Mother is the first truly regular boss for Steed since One-Ten; all the others appeared only a couple of times at most). I'm sure, having invented the character for the Diana Rigg farewell, Clemens would have been struck by the potential of such a character – he would deliver both humour and exposition without compromising the narrative, a handy device for an hour-long series. We see this stretched to an almost illogical extreme in *Homicide and Old Lace* where Clemens, true to form, subverts the exposition and turns it into a farcical parody of a tall story, elevating the narrator's task, taken on by Mother, to that of a joker's lampooning of the genre. Here, Clemens uses Mother as a vehicle not just to ridicule the inept Colonel Corf and his warehouse of national treasures, but also to ridicule the material he had been given when he resumed as producer of *The Avengers*. This early episode of a season that never was, hopelessly overambitious and misguided, was so lost in its own tortured attempts at reinvention that it had forgotten what *The Avengers* was.

In *The Forget-Me-Knot*, Mother resides in a secluded country house, the central office of which has handles attached to the ceiling so that he may swing himself around the room and free himself from his wheelchair. This is a truly impressive set. On screen, its stark black outlines against the bright red ceiling and walls capture the eye and imagination of the viewer. Its high contrast reflects the cantankerous nature of the mother character – brusque and dogmatic, gruff yet polite. Indeed, it's not until Steed is considered a defection risk that he loses his cool. It is claimed that after the episode was finished it was dismantled, but when the American producers saw the episode they demanded that it, and Mother, appear in every episode. In response, the local producers decided it would be too expensive to reconstruct and would instead have Mother in a new, even more unlikely location for each episode. Another *Avengers* myth? The only real cost involved in the set would be in the rubber handles. The rest of it is simply wooden beams that would be used for a multitude of other sets anyway, affixed to a lighting gantry.

There may well have been a directive to have the Mother character feature again, but he doesn't appear in every episode from that point on. It seems likely that Clemens himself devised the visual device of having him turning up in outlandish locations that were his office-of-the-week. Thus we have him turning up in a cobweb-draped crypt, in an office made of inflatable plastic furniture, in a submarine lair, Steed's flat on two occasions, his country house a couple of times and, most iconically of all, on the top deck of a red London double decker bus. It was this last location that was reused in the 1998 feature film version of *The Avengers*, as well as being misappropriated for *The Spice Girls Movie*. Other locations worthy of note are in the middle of a swimming pool; driving around in a Mini Moke equipped with radar; in the middle of a field several times; at the bottom of an empty reservoir; in a purple room, reachable only by ladder; in his Rolls Royce, surrounded by models of tanker trucks (the model tankers were props from *The Billion Dollar Brain*); and on one episode he grumbles about being made to come down from his hot air balloon (never seen, to spare the cost). [2]

Mother's demeanour whenever he is installed at Steed's flat is that of a cheeky, excited boy. He relishes the opportunity to sample every single bottle in Steed's liquor cabinet while his stoic aide and bodyguard, Rhonda, looks on impassively and mixes him the drinks. Except for *The Forget-Me-Knot*, when Mother was still in a nascent phase, he is rarely seen without Rhonda nearby. She steers him through the episodes and, on one occasion, is instrumental in bringing the enemy to heel, defeating them with a flurry of martial arts. Rhonda is a blonde Amazon; tall and muscular and completely silent. In the only episode in which she appears to speak, *Homicide and Old Lace*, it transpires that it was in fact Mother, practising his ventriloquism. However, she is not mute as we hear her laugh loudly when Mother cheekily adds, "Gottle of Geer".

In examining the Mother character, I have discovered a cultural divide across the Atlantic. Not only do many Americans think that Steed's department is literally called 'The Ministry' rather than just not being named outright, many of them also seem to think that Mother is gay. The confusion about The Ministry I can understand, and it infects the 1998 feature film; viewers unfamiliar with the British habit of never quite naming a department but referring to someone as being 'from the ministry' would easily make the mistake. Indeed, in previous seasons Steed has posed as being from the Ministry of Trade. Britain doesn't bandy its abbreviated departments around like the CIA; MI6 was not acknowledged to exist until 1994 despite the whole world knowing it did. But how do we explain questions about Mother's ambiguous sexuality? After all, in *All Done with Mirrors* he has surrounded himself with bathing beauties in swimming costumes, Rhonda chief among them, which certainly raises Steed's eyebrows. [3] Mother seems to relish female company and it's clear that he has a better relationship with women than with men. He is frequently curt with his male agents and less so with his female agents. Is this the basis then? Do some people think that a man who is not misogynistic must therefore be homosexual? Is a man only 'manly' if he is macho and chauvinistic? I would hope not but it seems to be an opinion currently gaining popularity in Russia as well as America. However, despite his apparent progressiveness, he is occasionally written as being paternalistic (or is that maternalistic?) and condescending to Tara, presumably whenever the scriptwriters decide he needs to be concerned about her safety and degree of expertise. (In *All Done with Mirrors* it is Steed who is made to question Tara's ability). Again, these vagaries may be due to reordering of the broadcast and production schedules.

One aspect of Mother that intrigues us, but to which we never learn the answer, is the origin of his paralysis. Has he always been confined to a wheelchair? Was he wounded going over the Wall? Is it something that happened during the war? We can only guess, but it's sad that there was never any development of the back story behind Mother – another consequence of *The Avengers* being a series rather than a serial, as the producers were at pains to ensure each episode could stand alone and would not be dependent upon one another for exposition. [4]

Patrick Newell claimed many years ago that, struggling for bit parts, he decided to go for the 'fat' parts, thereby typecasting himself into secondary, often comedic, roles. [5] This was clearly a wise career move as he was seldom out of work, a rare thing for a character actor even in a country with as large a television industry as Britain. He provided comic relief in shows from *Danger Man* to *Doctor Who*; enjoyed a stint as the perennial butt of jokes, Inspector Lestrade, in a production curtailed by Reaganite sanctions; and even had a couple of parts in the anarchic New Wave comedy *The Young Ones*.

Accordingly, Mother is often used to defuse tension in the plot by injecting some comic relief, taking advantage of Patrick Newell's comedic skills. His appearance and pompous depiction of Mother make him an obvious figure of fun, a risky tactic to take with a character who has a disability but here it is successful. So much so that I often forget that Mother is in a wheelchair. Sometimes the script fails to live up to Newell's skill, as in the torturous sequence in *Wish You Were Here,* when he and Steed bandy single words of dialogue when discussing a banal plot point.

As with all spymasters, Mother has his share of professional rivalries. There are other arms of the secret service with which he competes, as well as his subordinates whom he is determined to keep subordinated. In *Super Secret Cypher Snatch*, it's MI12 he's up against, as the Minister has decided the junior department needs to be 'blooded'. Mother relishes the fact that the rival department is unable to handle the job and loses agents left, right and centre. This is one of the rare episodes that actually mentions the Ministry of Defence by name. In *Take Me To Your Leader* he is competing against Colonel Stonehouse, who turns out to be the villain behind the courier chain. This theme is an undercurrent of Season 6, with Mother feeling threatened by other agencies and relishing their failures as it offers him the opportunity to show his department's worth.

Ultimately, the central aspect of Mother that endears him so much to the viewer is his relationship with Steed. They work well together and are close friends, and this camaraderie with our elegant hero engenders an affection for Mother in the viewer that might have been lost had their rapport not been so apparent.

© Piers Johnson

1. Does that suggest that he gradually becomes more of a caricature?
2. Many of these sets are thematically linked to the story/plot itself, as in the plastic furniture which cannot fall victim to *The Rotters*. This adds a clever extra layer to the headquarters.
3. Are these bikini-clad women there for Mother's enjoyment? Perhaps they are simply brought in to keep Steed occupied and side-track him from Tara's quest.
4. Would this also have made him too real a character in a comic strip world?
5. *TV Times* interview, 1968.

PURDEY

When Brian Clemens set about revamping *The Avengers* for its 1970s comeback, he made a conscious choice to increase the attention paid to the characters in their own right, beyond their role in solving the case of the week. Describing previous *Avengers* leads as 'cardboard' characters, Clemens resolved to construct his new creations from 'thicker cardboard', imbuing them with a certain weight and substance in order to bring them a step closer to multi-faceted human beings, rather than ciphers. This approach to *Avengers* characterisation was not entirely novel. The series had, after all, begun life with Dr. David Keel cradling his dead fiancée scant hours after their engagement, and the first season was peppered with references to the good doctor's sometimes-fraught attempts to balance his day job at a busy surgery with his adventures with Steed, the death of Peggy never far from his mind. This emphasis on character continued throughout the videotape era, with Cathy Gale and Venus Smith receiving fairly detailed backstory write-ups. But when the series made the leap to film, the emphasis shifted to envelope-pushing plots, witty dialogue, and stylish visuals, and the personal lives of the leads outside of their adventures receded into the background. While the fate of Cathy Gale's late husband, a Kenyan farmer murdered in the Mau Mau uprising, was well-documented by the production team, Emma Peel's marriage was barely acknowledged until her final episode, *The Forget-Me-Knot*, when the suddenly very much alive Peter Peel was summoned into existence as a convenient means by which to write her character out of the series. It is probably not coincidental that this shift in focus coincided with Clemens' increased role behind-the-scenes, and in his quest for revitalisation, he seemed to be looking back to the series' early years, before he assumed the producer mantle. As a result, Purdey arguably had the most attention paid to her character of any *Avengers* woman in the film era, and the final product was a proficient agent who was also complex, flawed, multi-faceted, and undeniably human; a creation who contributed to the series' internal richness while also affording Clemens the opportunity to deconstruct the concept of the '*Avengers* woman'.

Of course, any character is the joint creation of writer and actor, and Purdey was no exception. Though Joanna Lumley claimed to have limited input into the series' scripts, she influenced Purdey's portrayal in other ways, from changing her name (from Charly), to selecting some of her fashions, to getting the infamous Purdey cut. [1] Lumley also had a strong vision for the character's persona, a 'keen, no-nonsense head girl of a secret agent, with easy-to-keep hair and no real boyfriends. I wanted her to be tough and reliable, competent in scrapes but in bed alone by eleven.' However, the scripts did not always jive with Lumley's plan, something she acknowledged and took with good grace. While these differing approaches could have undermined Purdey's characterisation, between them they cultivated a more realistic character, a somewhat eccentric woman full of contradictions and surprises, not quite as she first appeared, and endlessly intriguing as a result.

On the surface, at least, Purdey is very feminine. Initially a characteristic bequeathed to her by predecessor Tara King, Purdey quickly put her own spin on it. A trained ballet dancer, she emerged from a world characterised by grace, poise, intricately beaded costumes, and reams of tulle. Purdey retains that dancer's style and aesthetic in her new career, favouring long, flowing skirts, sometimes made of diaphanous material or featuring a high slit for ease of movement, and never shied away from the dancer's aesthetic of bright colours and patterns. Even her undergarments are frilly rather than practical, consisting of gauzy stockings and lace-up patterned corsets, plus ample amounts of lace. Her footwear, consisting largely of sky-high heels and boots, while at first blush highly unsuitable for her current profession, was a natural choice for a woman who had spent years punishing her feet and wrapping bleeding toes, and whose own innate sense of balance and tolerance for discomfort would compensate for any impracticality. She also wears jewellery, ranging from earrings and gold chains to rings, sometimes several per hand. Her flat, originally painted in exceptionally feminine shades of purple, and containing a baby blue piano, sparkly beaded curtains, and romantic furnishings, retains several feminine flourishes even after a remodelling resulted in a neutral motif. Beyond aesthetics, Purdey is also vulnerable, her emotions bubbling to the surface in extreme circumstances. She weeps openly when she fears her partners have been killed (*Faces* and *K is for Kill*) – shedding more tears than all of her predecessors combined – and was visibly moved by the deaths of fellow agents George Myers, Marty Brine, and Terry, amongst others. And she is quick to remind the men in her life that she is a member of the female of the species, whether by bestowing kisses (*Sleeper*), pointedly asserting that she is a "girl" (*K is for Kill*), offering knowing commentaries about her own sex ("It has all the vindictiveness of a woman...Inside every woman there's a degree of pure cat."), framing her actions in terms of female 'idiosyncrasies', or relishing the monopoly of male attention that having two partners affords her. And she has a robust case of the green-eyed monster, the traditionally 'feminine' trait of jealousy, particularly where Gambit was concerned, on which more later.

In contrast, Purdey also bears all the hallmarks of a tough, no-nonsense *Avengers* woman and professional agent. With no qualms about being in the thick of the action, her high-kicking panache-inspired fighting skills are often punctuated by a mean right hook, and Lumley's insistence on doing the lion's share of her stuntwork lent her action sequences an extra measure of grit. She cut her hair short and occasionally forwent dresses in favour of trouser suits, pseudo-combat gear, and jumpsuits. She is completely unafraid of taking risks, be they shimmying up a drainpipe or dangling from a helicopter. She drives fast and expertly, whether in one of her sports cars or on her motorcycle. She drinks like a sailor, and could probably swear like one, too, in the right circumstances (and if censors permitted). She has a healthy appetite, evidenced by her near-constant obsession with food, partaking in everything from marshmallows to omelettes, and even a roadside sandwich in a pinch, and fantasises about a good *steak au poivre*. Despite her sometimes romantic sense in dress and décor, her actual views on romance and the male of the species' ability to commit are cynical and jaded, and she often assumes the dominant role in her male friendships. At the same time, she functions well in an all-male department and successfully blends in as 'one of the boys', to the point that Steed and Gambit at times forget they have a woman in their ranks.

Sandwiched between these seemingly-irreconcilable aspects of Purdey's personality is a streak of strangeness and eccentricity. Steed was traditionally the most eccentric of *The Avengers'* leads, due to his in-born ability to switch on his Wodehousian 'dotty English aristocrat' persona at will, a role he played with a little too much ease for it to be entirely a performance. This necessitated that his co-stars be more grounded, particularly as the series took on ever-greater flights of fancy and required at least a modicum of an anchor lest it float away entirely. With Gambit assigned that particular role in *The New Avengers'* triumvirate, Purdey often manages to out-Steed Steed, leading the Avenger-in-chief to arch an eyebrow at her in much the same way he caused many an eyebrow to be arched over the years. Purdey's particular brand of impenetrability consists of often-unfathomable leaps in logic, mostly accompanied by impatience when her fellow conversant fails to follow her tangential trains of thought. Examples include her response to Steed's muttered utterance of "It doesn't balance" (an explanation of Scotland's cartographical precariousness); her insistence on Gambit proving his identity on the off-chance that he has been replaced by a robot (that may or may not have been able to play the bassoon); and her random resurrection of an argument from last Tuesday. This lateral thinking is often invaluable to her work, as it leads her to uncover new lines of inquiry, such as her method of identifying the location of David Miller's cottage based on the church in the background. In other cases, it helps her to disarm the enemy, whether by deflating their threats, encouraging them to underestimate her, or simply throwing them off balance; see her quirky ripostes to 'Mad Jack' Miller ("I'm afraid we have no facilities for the imprisonment of young women." "You mean you haven't got a hairdryer?") and Professor Turner ("I'll bet she [the golden figure] can't cook an omelette. French style. With *fines herbes*."). While she comes by her eccentricities honestly – her uncle has a particular aversion to ice as fervent as her addiction to marshmallows – in some cases it might also be a front, a way of keeping her feelings at a distance when they become too overwhelming. In this way, it can be a double-edged sword and negatively affect her relationships, whether by inciting frustration (usually in Gambit, often by pressing him for answers to questions that he can't possibly hope to provide, as in *Forward Base*) or slipping into callousness when utilised inappropriately (such as her flippant comments about the funereal atmosphere at Steed's before she realises that his friend Clifford has just died, and at the expense of the brain-drained Larry).

There is also a certain recklessness to Purdey, accompanied by an ambivalence about where life takes her. She often makes snap decisions that put her in danger, even when other, less-risky options are available. This can be a good quality for a secret agent, as taking calculated risks is part of the job description. And Purdey's gambles do pay off, such as her choice to swallow the fake poison capsule in *House of Cards*, which allows her to unravel Perov's scheme. On other occasions, however, they jeopardise her own life, as well as those of her colleagues, and the success of their current assignment; for example, her executive decision to draw the 13th Special Commando's fire in order to give Gambit the opportunity to capture the unit's leader, 'Mad Jack' Miller. This only serves to maroon Purdey in a minefield, where she is used as leverage to force Gambit to let Miller go, effectively enabling their recapture had Steed not arrived in the nick of time.

These decisions may partly stem from overconfidence and inexperience on Purdey's part. She is naïve regarding certain aspects of the Ministry's inner workings – consider her surprise and indignation at being labelled not 'above suspicion' due to her one month absence while lost in the Amazon, her unfamiliarity with the department's back catalogue of enemy agents, or her outrage at the use of a sniper on the target range – which suggests that she is a less-seasoned agent than Steed or even Gambit. Indeed, Purdey appears to be even younger than Lumley herself, who was on the cusp of turning thirty when she won the role, arguably the only one of the series' leads for whom a noticeable discrepancy exists between the age of character and actor. (Given the seeming lack of maturity and judgment she brings to her relationship with Larry Doomer, Purdey's age circa 1970 could be estimated at around 21, meaning by 1976 she would be 27, three years Lumley's junior.) As she grew in experience, Purdey's judgment would no doubt improve and she would be better able to assess whether a risk was calculated or simply reckless. However, her actions may stem from more than inexperience. It is notable that Purdey's father – with whom she was close, if her close relationships with her mother and her uncle are any indication – was shot as a spy, and yet Purdey chose to enter the same profession. Perhaps it was a way for her to feel close to her late father, or to understand why he felt the job was worth such a sacrifice. Perhaps she simply wanted to honour his memory. But there may also be a measure of ambivalence at work. Somewhere in the period between the conclusion of her relationship with Doomer and the start of the series, Purdey's career as a dancer ended when she was ejected from the Royal Ballet for being too tall. That loss, coupled with the loss of her father around 1966, and the implosion of her dream family life with Doomer, may have culminated in a personal crisis as all of Purdey's plans were swept aside in the space of a few years, and something 'broke' within her as a result. Believing that hoped-for life was out of reach, she turned to a new one of danger and intrigue, slamming the door on those dead dreams. After having lost so much already, the risk of losing her life on the job would not seem to be much of a deterrent.

Of course, Purdey's personal contradictions and history of loss inevitably affect her relationships. While Lumley's comment about Purdey having 'no real boyfriends' is not a completely inaccurate summation of Purdey's relationship status, it is also an incomplete one. Throughout the series, Purdey cheerfully flirts with many of her fellow Ministry agents. She playfully rebuffs some advances (George Myers in *Target!*), but also agrees to dinner dates (with American agent Marty Brine, George Stannard, Spence, et al.). She is also not averse to waxing lyrical about the attractiveness of men that catch her eye, including the unfortunate Larry, victim of the brain-draining machine in *Three Handed Game*, and the aforementioned Brine. And yet, unlike her male counterparts, Gambit and Steed, Purdey never appears to take those relationships any further. This is not due to any prurience on Purdey's part, as she shared a bed with her ex-fiancé, Larry Doomer, but that failed engagement has undoubtedly affected her perception of, and approach to, relationships. In 1970, Purdey was openly and unguardedly in love and affectionate with her fiancé. Her transition to holding prospective suitors at arm's length is almost certainly attributable to the slap that ended that engagement. As a result, Purdey became wary of romance, having opened herself up once before with disastrous results. She subsequently holds cynical views about relationships, and plays her cards very close to her chest, unwilling to divulge her deeper feelings lest they open her up to more hurt – unless circumstances push her outside of her comfort zone and lead her to say more, such as when she believes Gambit had been murdered by 'Terry Walton' in *Faces*.

It follows, then, that Purdey's disastrous engagement also influences her relationships with her two partners. Her professional relationship with Gambit is imbued with a high level of trust, as they frequently save each other from certain death (Purdey prevents Gambit from being shot in *The Midas Touch*, while Gambit returns the favour in *K is for Kill*), and they operate as a seamless unit when the situation calls for it, whether by executing their 'party trick' manoeuvre (*The Last of the Cybernauts...??*) or tackling multiple opponents in a fight (*Dirtier by the Dozen*). They also socialise off-hours, going out for dinner and dancing, and playing board games. They pepper both on- and off-duty conversations with a multitude of tangential debates on everything from the differences between the sexes to their perennial favourite, old movies, and share several running in-jokes. However, their relationship fails to develop further, with Gambit's romantic pursuit of Purdey repeatedly foiled by her determination to keep him at arm's length. The result is a playful to-ing and fro-ing that is more complicated than it first appears, and conveys Purdey's contradictory desires. While Purdey mostly spurns Gambit's verbal advances with tart rejoinders, avoids his attempts at physical contact (*Faces*, *Last of the Cybernauts...??*), and deliberately broadcasts her interest in other Ministry colleagues (often with the seemingly sole purpose of getting a rise out of Gambit), she is not as disinterested in Gambit as she may wish others (particularly Gambit) to believe. She periodically hints at deeper feelings, whether by teasing Gambit by revving her car so that he cannot hear the most pertinent word in "but I do love you" (*Target!*), kissing him on the lips (*Sleeper*), subconsciously initiating physical contact (*Dirtier by the Dozen*), or taking great interest in every slip of the towel covering his naked body (*Three Handed Game*)! Even more telling is her attitude toward Gambit's romances, which often tip over from disapproval to outright jealousy. She reveals that she has been following the rumours about his love life at the Ministry (*To Catch a Rat*), volunteers to run interference when he meets Olga (*House of Cards*), drags him bodily away from his date with Dr. LeParge (*K is for Kill*), playfully threatens to immobilise him when he admits to having a date that evening (*Dead Men Are Dangerous*), and is repeatedly outraged at the existence of his 'little black book' of telephone numbers (*Faces, Sleeper*). If Purdey truly had no interest in Gambit, she would perhaps poke fun at, or disapprove of, his trysts, but there would be no reason for her to be upset about, or attempt to sabotage, them. Most tellingly, she tips her hand when she thinks she is talking to Terry Walton, rather than the man himself, by openly expressing her interest in Gambit under the guise of Lolita, and comes very close to confessing to 'Terry' what she would do if the supposedly murdered Gambit were still alive. This sets up an interesting push-pull dynamic in which Purdey refuses to let Gambit get too close, but also wants him to forgo a relationship with anyone else – her ideal state of affairs is a sort of limbo in which Gambit remains unattached, neither hers nor anyone else's.

This reluctance to act on her attraction may partly stem from Purdey's desire to be considered a talented agent in her own right, which could easily be jeopardised by a romance with one of her partners and lead to salacious rumours about how she 'earned' her stripes. But if that were her only motivation, she would have spurned the advances of other agents, rather than joined them for dinner. Her fear of being 'burned' again romantically plays a much larger role, and while she undoubtedly has too much trust in Gambit to believe he would treat her as badly as Larry did, she may doubt her ability to pick up the pieces once more should some other disaster befall them. Complicating matters would be the risk of spoiling both a deep friendship and a successful professional partnership should things turn sour. Plus there is always the very real possibility that Gambit could be killed in action, the prospect of which Purdey confronted once before (albeit briefly) in *Faces*. Keeping Gambit from getting too close is a way for Purdey to protect herself should neither of them be so lucky the next time.

Similar factors shape her relationship with Steed, though the result is somewhat different. Where Gambit's willingness to initiate a relationship combined with his lurking mortality leaves Purdey chary of taking things further, Steed's legendary status as a seemingly-invincible superspy engenders a crush and a case of hero-worship in Purdey, much as it did in Tara King before her. Purdey's awe for her superior makes him a safe candidate for her ardour: given his exceptional record and long career, her fears for his life are not as strong as they are for Gambit. The fact that Steed also makes a point of gently rebuffing her advances – note his refusal to let her climb in his window (*The Eagle's Nest*), his offer to call her a taxi to take her home rather than reciprocate her advances in *Dead Men Are Dangerous*, and his failure to follow-up on her imminent confession in *Angels of Death* – allows her to be more forward with Steed without worrying about it developing into something more (and even if it did, it would not be serious and long-lasting, the way it could potentially be with Gambit). Steed, in essence, is 'safe ground' for Purdey, and she can indulge in her hero-worship and flirtations risk-free. At the same time, Purdey's singular lack of jealousy regarding Steed's love interests, about whom she is complimentary rather than snide – note her lack of animosity toward both Laura and Tricia at Steed's birthday parties, her good-natured amusement at his reply to Chinese agent Sing's "many sons" comment, and her willingness to smooth over Steed's difficulties with girlfriend Suzy (*Hostage*) – demonstrate that her affection for Steed, while genuine, does not run to the deeply romantic. Purdey simply has no desire to sabotage Steed's love life or lay claim to him. [2] This allows for the evolution in the Purdey/Steed relationship over the course of the series, with Steed's two near-misses in Paris (*K is for Kill*) leading Purdey to treat him less like an untouchable legend and more like a flesh-and-blood human being. The result is a warm friendship marked by deep mutual affection and equality, rather than awe or flirtation, in the series' final episodes.

Having established the aforementioned ins and outs of Purdey's character throughout the series, Clemens was finally in a position to deconstruct her as both an *Avengers* woman and a human being in her own right, and thereby imbue her with the final facet that would make her the ultimate in the new *Avengerland* line of 'thicker cardboard'. The episode *Obsession* was the perfect vehicle to complete this task, depicting as it did the doomed relationship between Purdey and the (appropriately-named) Larry Doomer, her fiancé circa 1970. Doomer's obsessive quest for revenge drives a wedge between Purdey and himself, and her foiling of his assassination attempt against the man he believes responsible for his father's death ends with Larry slapping Purdey across the cheek. While all of the *Avengers* women, Purdey included, were often violently attacked by their enemies, Purdey's slap is arguably the most shocking physical blow endured by any one of them over the entire course of the series. To portray an *Avengers* woman being victimised, not in the course of her work, but by her intimate partner, flies in the face of the image of the untouchable action heroine the show had gone to great lengths to cultivate. But rather than undermine Purdey's status as a strong, resilient woman, the scene reinforces it. The fact that Purdey ends her engagement with Doomer, despite being in love with him, speaks to not only her inner strength of character and high self-esteem – many abused women are either unwilling or unable to do the same – but the physical and emotional toughness she subsequently developed that made her a capable agent. By visualising Purdey's adversity onscreen, and how she has changed and grown as a result, the episode adds a new, evolutionary layer to the concept of the *Avengers* woman, exposing how she came to fill that role rather than presenting her to the audience as having always been so impressively formidable, with any adversity only hinted at in the backstory. There is something about the willingness to show Purdey's trials onscreen that makes them more effective, more real, than if they had been confined to a written backstory or throwaway onscreen mention. [3]

The episode then takes things one step further by demonstrating that, though she has learned and grown from her experience with Doomer, Purdey has not done so without difficulty or completely successfully. The easy route for Clemens would have been to make Purdey completely unaffected by Doomer's return to her life, perhaps even scornful. But Clemens was aiming for something more ambitious with Purdey, beyond the now-established trope of the superhuman *Avengers* woman with nothing to prove in the male-dominated action landscape, to someone more complex and multi-faceted. So instead, he portrays Purdey as conflicted: she neither wants Doomer in her life, nor doubts that she made the right choice in leaving him, but still cannot deny that she loved him once, and has difficulty not empathising with his plight; indeed, perhaps she understands his motives better than she would care to admit, having lost her own father in similar circumstances. As a result, her choice of coping mechanism is avoidance, one which has limited effectiveness as Doomer's involvement with her current assignment grows and she continually refuses to enlighten Gambit and Steed about the connection between her, Doomer, and the Emir. Gambit and Steed's well-meaning offers to help, or to at least listen to and understand her plight, are repeatedly rebuffed by Purdey in her usual attempts to keep her emotions, and other people, at bay. The result is ill-formed decisions by all parties and a messy resolution, as Purdey's conflicting emotions and inability to face up to them quite literally jeopardise the safety of the entire country, not to mention the relationships within the team. But Purdey's choices do not weaken her as a character – they humanise her. For all her strengths, the *Avengers* woman is not, and should not, be forever infallible, any more than her male counterparts. In essence, the series allows her to be a human being: sometimes independent, strong, tough, clever, formidable; sometimes vulnerable, lacking in objectivity, and in need of help from good, trusted friends. These are not irreconcilable concepts. Superhumans are never relatable because they can never fail and have nothing to lose, nothing to overcome. Strength is only truly admirable when paired with an acknowledgement of weakness and fault. [4] Purdey's strength and proficiency are not erased because she is allowed to have moments of weakness, and certainly not because she is sometimes forced to rely on those around her – those qualities are instead enhanced by those moments, because there is no longer a need for Purdey to unwaveringly meet a flawless standard in order for her to maintain her exceptional 'action woman' status. This was the final step in the liberation of the *Avengers* woman, and Purdey took it.

© JZ Ferguson

1. While I know a number of French *Avengers* fans who don't like the 'Purdey cut', there is no doubt that it created a buzz and a trend, allowing the new series to echo the original one's influence on contemporary society.
2. I'm sure that I am not alone in finding her schoolgirl-type crush and flirting with Steed uncomfortable in Season 1 and the early episodes of Season 2. Steed/Macnee himself looks embarrassed by it in *Dead Men Are Dangerous*.
3. Here there is no sense of 'thicker cardboard' but of a fully-rounded character.
4. Using Thomas Hardy's words about Tess, Purdey is made perfect by her imperfections.

MIKE GAMBIT

Nothing is ever as it seems in *Avengerland*. Straight-laced nannies tote machine-guns, peaceful rural villages rent themselves out for scheduled murders, and every housecat conceals a 'hidden tiger'. Despite *The New Avengers* adopting a more 'realistic' tone, the juxtaposition between initial surface impressions, and what lies beneath, remains. This is equally true of the series' leads, infamously constructed from 'thicker cardboard', who proved to be infinitely more complex and multi-faceted than they appeared at first glance. Of the three leads, Mike Gambit provides perhaps the greatest rewards for viewers who take the time to delve a little deeper.

Gambit is ostensibly the 'hard man' of the trio, created, according to Brian Clemens, to be Steed's 'legs' and take the burden off the 54-year-old Patrick Macnee in the action sequences. Gambit undoubtedly fulfils that remit in countless fight scenes, with actor Gareth Hunt performing the lion's share of his stunts, most notably dangling off the wing of a taxiing airplane (*Tale of the Big Why*), diving through plate glass windows (*Target!*, *Complex*), and narrowly avoiding being blown up by an exploding police box (*Target!*). Unsurprisingly, this translates into the character taking a fair bit of on-screen damage, including being stabbed (*House of Cards*), shot (*Angels of Death*, *K is for Kill*), and generally beaten up (*Three Handed Game*, *Dirtier by the Dozen*, *Trap*, *Lion and the Unicorn*, *Emily*). This is in keeping with the series' grittier, more realistic feel, one reinforced by tales of Hunt's on-set injuries. The character's written backstory underlines the onscreen 'action man' persona, highlighting his martial arts prowess and past career as a mercenary, service in the Parachute Regiment and Navy, and a crash-happy stint as a race car driver (a skillset he utilises in regular car chases, though he still suffers the odd crash: see *The Eagle's Nest* and *The Lion and the Unicorn*). Like Steed, he can be extremely ruthless when the situation calls for it (see his brutal interrogations of enemies in *The Eagle's Nest* and *House of Cards*), but unlike his partner he does not distinguish between the sexes. Women working for the other side are not afforded special treatment simply because of their sex – such as Sing in *The Midas Touch*, who he has no qualms about intimidating – and are instead judged according to how they behave as individuals. This places him as a modern alternative to Steed's traditionalist in terms of his rules of engagement.

This perception of Gambit as an all-action 'hard man' has resulted in him being dubbed a less 'fantastical' character than his *Avengers* peers, a position not entirely without merit. Where the film-era Steed or his female partner often single-handedly defeats one or more opponents with ease, Gambit's victories can be hard-won, and he occasionally requires assistance from his colleagues. Steed can emerge from a conflict looking immaculate, whereas Gambit's fights often leave him sweaty, bloody, and dishevelled, with dust clinging to his clothes. Hunt was keen to emphasise such fallibility, envisioning Gambit as a man who would save the world but 'at the day's end...shuts his fingers in the car door.' Humour was also important to Hunt, and Gambit cracks his share of jokes, often corny and laced with bad puns that leave his colleagues groaning (see Purdey's reaction to his "undercover" quip in *To Catch a Rat*, and Steed's unimpressed expression in response to his "diving to the bed of the lake" gag in *Forward Base*). The scripts, however, failed to take things as far as Hunt hoped, leavening Gambit's humour with a healthy measure of sobriety, while his physical altercations were often 'super-human' examples of martial arts prowess. [1] This tension between the serious and fantastical aspects of Gambit's character places him in a unique position, allowing him to simultaneously ground the series and inject the realism sought by Clemens, while also engaging with the traditionally fantastical realm of *The Avengers* on film. This affords him a more multi-faceted existence than his action man persona would normally allow, and makes him, in a sense, 'the sane man of *Avengerland*', providing a counterweight to his more eccentric colleagues, Steed and Purdey.

Seemingly in keeping with the stock action man stereotype, Hunt stated that he wanted to keep Gambit's past a mystery, and details about his background are indeed difficult to come by, save for some throwaway references to past careers and family members, including an Irish grandmother and an aunt who faithfully sends him pyjamas every birthday. He also sometimes fits the classic lone wolf template, following his own lines of inquiry separate and apart from Purdey and Steed (*House of Cards, Obsession, Dead Men are Dangerous*). Even when he works collaboratively, he spends many conversations listening to his colleagues, only speaking when he has something to offer, and at times can become so wrapped up in puzzling out a problem that he retreats into himself (*K is for Kill, Tale of the Big Why*). By his own admission, he also spends many a quiet hour poring over the Ministry's files (*The Last of the Cybernauts...??, Dead Men are Dangerous, To Catch a Rat*).

And yet, he is certainly not shy – he confidently confronts those in positions of power who are arrogant and dismissive, such as Brown-Fitch (*The Eagle's Nest*), whom Gambit has no trouble taking down a peg or two. This suggests that Gambit is not a reticent man of mystery, but introverted by nature. This conclusion is supported by his willingness to let his guard down and express the softer, more emotional side of his personality with those he is closest to. He is certainly more open on the topics of love and romance than Purdey, who plays her emotional cards close to her chest. He has a soft spot for animals, feeding Charlie, a little sparrow who visits him every morning, and is saddened when he believes that he has died. He is also visibly upset by the deaths of his friends and fellow agents, whom he cares about and upon whom he often bestows playful nicknames (e.g., "Braddie" for Bradshaw). Even the demises of individuals with whom he does not see eye to eye, such as Turner, leave him sombre, and he takes it upon himself to avenge the death of Marty Brine, despite having been annoyed at the American agent's interest in Purdey. He is particularly close to Spence, the Ministry's martial arts instructor, who claims he taught Gambit everything he knew on the subject (though Gambit claims he has supplemented his lessons by putting "theory into practice"). Given that Gambit's own martial arts proficiency could only be achieved through extensive training, Spence is clearly among Gambit's oldest friends, predating his acquaintance with his Ministry colleagues. This is more than amply supported by their good-natured teasing and playful game of catch with Gambit's squash bag. While Gambit is on good terms with many of his colleagues, he is never as cheerfully extroverted with any of them as he is with Spence. This makes Spence's attempts to kill Gambit all the more effective, as Gambit first attempts to laugh off Spence's attacks, then reluctantly shifts into killer mode when he realises he is embroiled in a fight to the death. Their last scene before the camera cuts away finds them face-to-face, struggling for control of the knife, unable to avoid the intimacy of their friendship even as it comes to an end. There is no sense of triumph in Gambit's victory when he staggers out of the gym, and the next scene finds him seated at David Miller's dining room table, silent and subdued, gloomily pondering the card with his name on it. Later, he points out that David Miller died a good friend to Steed, the unspoken implication being that Spence did not do the same. While Gambit papers over his grief at Spence's loss and betrayal in order to complete the assignment, it has undoubtedly affected him.

Gambit's clothes also reflect his in-between status in *Avengerland*, this time as a working class man in a traditionally elitist profession. [2] Hunt advocated a casual wardrobe for the character, consisting of jeans and bomber jackets, both for personal comfort and to better enable stunt work. (Hunt recalled that the trousers in his three-piece suits were prone to splitting during fight scenes!) Gambit's casual wardrobe did, in fact, stretch to informal trousers paired with leather, velour, and corduroy bomber jackets, or the odd safari coat. However, Clemens predominantly envisioned the character in tailored, custom-made three-piece suits, arguing that these would allow Gambit to blend into the corridors of power he would frequent as part of his work. Hunt's continued lobbying for a dressed down Gambit only garnered the addition of a selection of cardigans to his wardrobe, not quite what the actor had been aiming for, and he promptly gave up on his quest for some comfortable jeans. As a result, Gambit only wore jeans once onscreen, during his stint as a fake glam rocker (*House of Cards*) – though, strangely, his dummy on the target range is wearing a pair! This, coupled with the decision to cover Hunt's forearm tattoo with make-up (a feature that would have been in keeping with Gambit's own ex-Navy background), suggests that Gambit was allowed to be 'rough around the edges' only up to a point – certain standards still had to be met, even in a more realistic *Avengerland*.

Production requirements aside, Gambit's fashion choices reveal something of his character, while also differentiating him from the more conservative Steed. While, as Clemens intended, Gambit dresses partly to blend in – in outwardly conservative colours including navy, black, brown, and tan, sometimes augmented with pinstripes or a subtle check – his suits also feature more playful flourishes that reflect Gambit's boyish sense of humour and love of colour and design. These include green, blue and lemon-yellow shirts; coats with idiosyncratic extra pockets; coloured silk ties; full jacket skirts with deep vents to emphasise movement; a golden silk-backed waistcoat; beautifully-lined jackets; and an array of fashionable (at the time) Cuban-heeled boots that fly in the face of more conventional Oxfords, brogues, or even Steed's classic Chelsea boots. These choices hint at a more playful interest in the art of fashion than his background would seem to suggest. The tailoring of the suits also reflects Gambit's youthful vigour, the suit jackets nipping in at the waist to emphasise the oft-overlooked male figure, the trousers hugging rather than skimming over the hips to create a less boxy silhouette. Like Purdey, he also wears jewellery, with certain pieces – a ring and a small pendant – reappearing throughout the series, suggesting that they hold particular significance for him. The ring – Hunt's own, bequeathed to him by his late father and worn in many other productions – may hold similar sentimental value for Gambit himself. The pendant, also likely Hunt's own, is more of a mystery, difficult to identify onscreen, but given Gambit's Navy background, perhaps it is some sort of sailor's talisman – some fans have suggested a St. Christopher – or other lucky charm, or maybe even a family heirloom, suggesting a certain sentimentality in his character. He also regularly wears a watch, the face turned to the inside of his wrist, adding a subtly quirky flourish to his sometimes-sober office attire.

Despite his tailoring, Gambit is unabashedly working class, and never attempts to hide his background. He prefers a casual mode of address – save for Roland in *House of Cards*, he is always known as 'Mike', never 'Michael' – and readily admits that he never attended prep school (*The Eagle's Nest*) or studied the classics, such as Latin (*Dead Men are Dangerous*). However, while he is not ashamed of his roots, he is not perversely proud of his lack of schooling, either. Instead, he is constantly attempting to close the gap, and has embarked on a course of self-education of sorts, developing an interest in a wide range of subject areas that belies his hard man persona. Indeed, the sheer eclecticism of his topics of interest is reminiscent of Emma Peel's boundless intellectual curiosity and polymath tendencies. A quick survey of his flat reveals a drafting board (suggesting a predilection for either architecture or sketching – or possibly both!); an extensive weapon collection ranging from firearms to crossbows (complimenting his far-reaching knowledge on the topic, as exemplified in *K is for Kill, The Eagle's Nest,* and *Faces*); a peculiar collection of art (some possibly acquired in foreign climes, perhaps during his extensive globe-trotting, and paired with modern Op Art pieces); a telescope; an array of records running the gauntlet from Mozart to Creedence Clearwater Revival (and a stereo system to play them on); and shelves stacked with books. [3] His flat's aesthetic pairs vibrant splashes of green, orange, and yellow with stark blacks, whites, and greys, and couples smooth and industrial metal and glass with richly textured brick and fur, suggesting at least a passing interest in aesthetics and design. He also has a good grasp of mathematics (apparently acquired while doing the football pools), and, like Purdey, has a love of old movies. He is an early adopter and enthusiast of new technology, installing an electronic bed and a number of pushbutton consoles throughout his flat to control everything from the lights to the drapes. He has enough of an interest in photography to have a dedicated darkroom, and dances well enough to keep pace with Purdey, an ex-dancer, at the disco. And, of course, he enjoys his fast cars, as exemplified by his time as a race car driver.

Interestingly, despite, or perhaps because of, his lack of formal education, Gambit is particularly attracted to intelligent, well-educated women. Notable paramours include maths teacher Penny Redfern, pathologist Dr. Jeanine Leparge, German record-keeper Gerda, and artist Helen McKay. Others are savvy about the inner workings of government (Lindsay Duncan's Jane), or somehow involved in the spy business (the mysterious 'Russian Countess'). All are assertive personalities who hold their own in their interactions with Gambit, and also possess a well-developed sense of humour. Given that Gambit has no trouble attracting the opposite sex, the recurrence of these qualities suggests that his choice of dates is motivated by something beyond physical desire (though sex undoubtedly factors into his choices as well!), and that Gambit prefers women who challenge him verbally and intellectually, enjoys learning about their areas of expertise, and is secure enough in himself that he does not need to be the dominant force in the relationship, instead preferring a warm, equal, positive, friendly dynamic. This suggests a man who is infinitely more complex than the generic character tropes of swinging bachelor or womaniser would suggest. It also explains why Purdey, an ex-dancer educated at the Sorbonne with a quick wit, sharp intellect, and dominant personality, has become the object of Gambit's ardour.

Speaking of Purdey, her relationship with Gambit has always been complicated to say the least. While Purdey forever seeks to conceal her feelings for her partner, Gambit very much wears his heart on his sleeve, openly and repeatedly expressing his desire to take his relationship with her to the next level. His sexual interest in her is regularly conveyed through his response to her oft-chorused refrain of, "Mike Gambit, one of these days", namely "I'm looking forward to it", and also through innuendo (see *The Eagle's Nest*: "I tipped you out of bed, not into it."), or by whispering something unintelligible but undoubtedly suggestive in her ear (*Cat Amongst the Pigeons*). He also endeavours to initiate physical contact, whether by covering her hand with his (*The Last of the Cybernauts...??*), or attempting to embrace or put his arm around her (*Faces; K is for Kill, Forward Base*), though these attempts are always respectful, often in response to Purdey's own initiation of physical contact, and never inappropriately intimate. When Purdey rebuffs him and pulls away (as she often does), he does not attempt to force the issue. This stands in sharp contrast to the behaviour of some of Purdey's other potential paramours, such as George Myers, who grabs her thigh, and lacks the possessive overtones of Larry Doomer and Cromwell. Gambit has no such need to 'own' or dominate, only physically crossing the line when professional reasons demand it, such as when he harasses Lolita in order to maintain his cover as Terry Walton and to try to dissuade her from replacing the real Purdey (actions which Purdey, as Lolita, derides as being out-of-character for the real Gambit), or when he needs to extract information from the traitorous Coldstream's secretary, Jane (*Angels of Death*).

However, Gambit's interest in Purdey extends beyond the sexual. On the rare occasions that Purdey senses his attraction to another woman, he looks sheepish and uncomfortable, as if he somehow feels he has been unfaithful (*K is for Kill, Three Handed Game*). These reactions suggest that Gambit's interest in Purdey surpasses lust and has developed into love. Indeed, love is often on Gambit's mind where Purdey is concerned, and he uses the word, not entirely jokingly, when Purdey asks if she's missed anything ("Only that you love me very much", in *The Last of the Cybernauts...??*), and perks up considerably when Purdey mouths the word at him ("But I do [love] you."). An unexpected kiss from her, though chaste, leaves him grinning, while his views on relationships ("No man would ever up and leave a woman, not if he really cared for her.") suggest his belief in ones that are deep, meaningful, and lasting. His devotion is also evidenced by the way he tenderly cradles her as she lies unconscious from curare poisoning, as well as his despair and desperation at the possibility of her demise, and his vow to hunt down those responsible if she dies. This corresponds with his strong desire to protect her from harm, often at his own expense, such as when he tells her to stay hidden while he attempts to capture 'Mad Jack' Miller solo.

When she ignores him and winds up in a minefield for her troubles, he fires desperately at her feet to keep her from moving, and naked fear appears on his face when he believes that he has accidentally blown her up. When Miller offers to trade Gambit's surrender for Purdey's safe passage, Gambit takes the deal without negotiating for his own safety, even though Miller threatens to incite World War Three. And while Steed saves the day and ultimately gets the credit in both that instance, as well as in *Hostage* (when he earns a hug from Purdey), any jealousy at being upstaged on Gambit's part quickly gives way to relief that she is unharmed; *Hostage* ends with him gazing lovingly at her while responding ironically to Steed's comment that Suzy believes him to be "inordinately fond" of Purdey, implying his own fondness in the process.

Interestingly, Gambit often seeks Purdey's assistance by claiming to be "lonely" (*Target!, Dirtier by the Dozen*). Perhaps after twenty years of a mostly-transitory existence, spent criss-crossing the globe with the Navy, Army, and as a race car driver, to the point that, after four years, he has failed to fully unpack his flat, Gambit longs for the stability of a home life. But even if Gambit enjoys the challenge of Purdey's repeated refusals, surely her tart rejoinders and put-downs might wear thin eventually and lead him to search for a less-frustrating potential long-term romance? Given that Gambit has no trouble attracting women, he could surely find other candidates. His enduring pursuit of Purdey (they have known each other for at least two years, perhaps longer), therefore, signifies the strength of his love and commitment, and he endures, taking comfort from Purdey's occasional scraps of encouragement or admissions of affection. The ball remains well and truly in Purdey's court, however, and any romance will be at her instigation, not his. As the series progresses, Gambit sometimes appears to resign himself to the possibility that Purdey will never be more than a close friend, particularly as her interests appear to drift toward Steed in the early episodes of Season 2 (note his deflated expression when Purdey hugs Steed in *Hostage*, and his lack of comment on Purdey's dinner date with Steed in *Dead Men are Dangerous*), a possibility he seems to have accepted, though with a touch of melancholy. [4] Things are made worse by the events of *Obsession*, with Gambit's offers to let Purdey confide in him about her past with Doomer being met with hostility. He is then eventually forced to kill the man, leaving Purdey screaming abuse in his ear while he restrains her from the nearby missile blast (a thankless task that he nonetheless stoically endures). The episode is undoubtedly a turning point in their relationship, and perhaps allows Gambit to more fully understand Purdey's reluctance to engage in a serious romance. By the Canadian episodes, they appear to have reconciled and reached a deeper intimacy and comfort level with one another, one that drifts into the territory normally occupied by married couples – they read the newspaper together, bicker about directions and Gambit's fighting proficiency, and have long conversations about the nature of commitment (*Forward Base, Emily*).

And yet, Gambit's ardour for Purdey is not completely unfettered. She has a particular knack for pushing his buttons, often by gratuitously expressing her interest in other men (*Three Handed Game, Trap, The Lion and the Unicorn*). She also enjoys puncturing his ego and putting a damper on his occasional bouts of cockiness, whether through a witty rejoinder, by delighting in his misfortune, or through simple one-upmanship, mostly when she saves his skin in a fight (*Three Handed Game, Emily, The Lion and the Unicorn*). Sometimes Gambit manages to get his own back and do the same to Purdey, who can be egotistical and cocksure herself on occasion, and so the pair manage to keep each other in check – something they both subconsciously desire, perhaps? There are also Purdey's oft-tangential thought processes to contend with, in which she leaps from point to point without explaining the connection, leaving Gambit struggling to keep up with her logic and earning derision from his partner for his troubles (e.g., her deducing Perov's plans by swallowing the fake poison capsule), though that never stops him from trying. Ironically, Purdey's eccentricities are probably part of what attracts him to her – she quite literally drives him mad, in more than one sense of the word. And the fact that Gambit trusts Purdey with his life, in addition to enjoying a warm friendship with her – consisting of shared jokes and socialising outside working hours, whether for dinner, dancing, a game of Scrabble, or a debate on old movies – allows them to rise above any momentary grievances. [5]

Meanwhile, Gambit's relationship with Steed, while not quite as complex as the one he shares with Purdey, is still more intricate than may be assumed at first glance. On the surface, the pair would appear to be a study in opposites: Steed a well-bred, Eton-educated gentleman of the establishment, Gambit a knockabout-educated working-class London lad from the wrong side of the Thames. Hunt highlighted the contrast between Gambit and Steed's (and Macnee's and his own) backgrounds when encapsulating the characters' differences in both personality and *modus operandi*. And yet, just as Macnee and Hunt were both Webber-Douglas Academy-trained ex-Navy men born in London almost exactly twenty years apart, Steed and Gambit are more similar than perhaps either realise. They often speak in unison ("Are you seeking sanctuary?" in *Cat Amongst the Pigeons*), finish each other's thoughts (*K is for Kill*), develop the same theories (Gambit intuits that Steed is also questioning whether Perov may have faked his suicide in *House of Cards*), and almost obsessively brood over niggling problems (e.g., the up-to-date photo of the Gaspard in *K is for Kill*). Purdey, who often fails to share their brainwaves, dubs this their "telepathy" in *Tale of the Big Why*, after Gambit disarms Turner at Steed's request, despite the man's supposedly-loaded gun; Gambit counters that he simply trusts Steed.

The strength of that trust may be due to Steed and Gambit having previously worked together before Purdey joined the team, or a result of natural chemistry, but regardless of the reason, Gambit's loyalty is particularly strong where Steed is concerned. He defends Steed even when the evidence is stacked against him in *Hostage*, and is devastated when it appears the man has truly turned to the other side. Even after Steed knocks him out, Gambit's loyalty wins out and he checks out Steed's story about Purdey being kidnapped rather than immediately report his actions. Steed reciprocates this trust by making him his right hand man and first point of contact/co-investigator on many assignments (*The Eagle's Nest, Faces, Cat Amongst Pigeons, House of Cards*), sometimes confiding in him alone to the exclusion of Purdey (*Faces*).

Steed and Gambit are also close on a personal level. Steed shares his fears about his friend, Harvey, and his sense of loss after the death of Mark Clifford, with Gambit (not Purdey), and Gambit attempts to console him after other losses by pointing out that Steed still has a friend in him, or that the deceased "died still a good friend". The pair are also not adverse to sharing a matey beer (*Sleeper*), and recreate together, whether it be clay pigeon shooting or horse riding (*Target!, Faces*). On occasion, they even refer to one another by their first names (Gambit calls Steed "John" in *Sleeper*, while Steed calls Gambit "Mike" on several occasions). Gambit, in particular, is unafraid to admit worrying about Steed's well-being, while Steed does the same, albeit more subtly (such as by sending Purdey to assist him in *Gnaws*, knowing that Gambit would not ask for help himself). One particularly meaningful exchange occurs in *Trap*, when Gambit asks Steed if he ever worries about him, to which Steed admits "sometimes". Gambit, in turn, asks why he can't worry about him as well, and the pair bicker about worrying about each other, before an exasperated Purdey brings them back to the problem at hand. There is also a father/son quality to their dynamic, such as when Steed gently – and wordlessly – encourages Gambit to give Purdey space after he kills Larry Doomer (*Obsession*), or casually pulls his magazine rack out from under Gambit's feet to persuade him to keep his shoes off his furniture (*Three Handed Game*). On other occasions, Steed doles out his accumulated wisdom to the younger agent, encouraging Gambit to cultivate his instincts (*Angels of Death*). Perhaps Gambit views Steed as a surrogate father because he lacked a steady father-figure, having left home to join the Navy at 14, suggesting a less-than-idyllic home life, and partly explaining his unswerving loyalty to the man. [6]

That mutual affection does not eliminate all traces of conflict between the pair, however. At times they are more like master and (recalcitrant) pupil, with Gambit butting up against the senior agent's methods – see Steed's disapproval of Gambit's pump-action shotgun (*Faces*), Gambit cringing as Steed sceptically pokes holes in his recounting of events (*Forward Base*), or Steed's lack of enthusiasm for Gambit's chosen method for ferreting out potential double agents: "The trouble with you, Gambit, is that you're a student of modern physics, where the least likely hypothesis is usually the right one" (*Angels of Death*). They also compete, with *Hostage* finding Steed half-jokingly dismissing Gambit's offer of a bout by telling his younger charge that he is "too young to die", and watching Gambit's pummelling at the hands of Marvin and the Unicorn with a measure of schadenfreude, while Gambit allows himself a victorious smile at managing to outwit Steed despite his partner's thorough attempt at disarming him (*The Lion and the Unicorn*). And like Drs. Keel and King before him, Gambit does not let his friendship with Steed cloud his judgment about what the man is capable of, commenting on his ruthless and devious qualities (*Three Handed Game, Hostage*), and shooting the man's clay pigeon out of the sky before he can draw a bead when Steed comments that he cannot "help" his background, explaining that he "can't let [Steed] get away with everything." These comments are often made with wry humour and warmth, however, something Dr. Keel's barbs were normally lacking. He also does not subscribe to Steed's methods himself. Indeed, where Steed zigs and zags, Gambit is more direct and dislikes games, preferring instead to lay all the cards on the table and confront his enemies and friends alike with clear-eyed facts and logic (and sometimes, in keeping with his in-between status, a willingness to accept evidence of the fantastic, such as psychic phenomena in *Medium Rare*). As a result, Steed rarely resorts to subterfuge where Gambit is concerned. Perhaps Gambit's straightforwardness appeals to him as it is a rare quality in his business; it may be one of the reasons he trusts him. He may also appreciate that Gambit, like Keel and King, is unafraid to confront him about his own nature, suggesting that Steed enjoys the challenge of such partners, perhaps realising that they are useful for keeping him in check. His lack of male colleagues post-Dr. King may be a product of him having difficulty locating another, similar individual. If Steed were to manipulate Gambit as he did Keel, he can rely on Gambit's ability to keep his half of the bargain and challenge him.

Gambit's relationships with both Steed and Purdey also reveal his self-sacrificing nature when it comes to people he cares about, as he is more than willing to put his life and well-being on the line in order to protect his partners. (He comes to both of their rescues in *Hostage* and *Angels of Death*, despite being injured in the process.) It is also interesting to note that Gambit's most overtly violent scenes – his manhandling of Ralph in *The Eagle's Nest* as he attempts to pry the cyanide capsule from the man's mouth, and the implied use of the crematorium to interrogate Cartney in *House of Cards* – both occur early in the series, suggesting that Gambit is suffering a hangover of the ruthless, cutthroat mentality he developed for his physical and psychological survival in his previous careers, ones which he likely chose because of a lack of options and people to rely on, other than himself. In Purdey and Steed, Gambit has, perhaps for the first time in his life, capable friends who he can trust and rely on, and, more importantly, who care about him. This has allowed the wall to come down and his gentler personality to emerge. While still a capable, deadly agent, this willingness for Gambit to let his guard down and reveal the man behind the façade contributes to his complexity as a character, a man who is so much more than he seems at first glance, if only one takes the time to look.

© JZ Ferguson

1. I immediately think of his impossible bullet-defying acts in both *K is for Kill* episodes.
2. And a traditionally elitist series.
3. Creedence Clearwater Revival was an American rock band active in the late-1960s and early 1970s.
4. Purdey also seems keen to gain entrance to Steed's St. Dorca guest bedroom in *The Eagle's Nest*, with Gambit literally cut off from proceedings, left behind on the mainland and left out by Steed bringing their radio communication to an abrupt end.
5. I think that Gambit's hopes for a deeper relationship with Purdey are doomed from the very beginning by their class divide. While the triumvirate are close friends, and the more democratic *New Avengerland* allows Gambit in, there are still limits. This theory would fit in with the idea of a degree of melancholy. Despite his key role at the Ministry, there remains a sense that he does not quite belong.
JZF: Interestingly, class does not appear to be at the forefront of Purdey's mind, either generally or in relation to Gambit. Other than assuming he went to prep school (*The Eagle's Nest*), their conversations never touch on issues of class, instead revolving

around their shared interests and other esoteric topics that occur to Purdey's quicksilver mind. Gambit's engagement with her on those topics, their ability to share jokes, and her general enjoyment of his company therefore appear to be more important to her than his background. And Gambit's predilection for educated women (and interest in Purdey) means he has no qualms about dating 'above his station'. Since neither of them appears to be particularly bothered by the class issue, it seems unlikely it would pose an issue to any potential romance. Purdey's reluctance to make herself emotionally vulnerable in a relationship is far more of an impediment to things going any further.

6. The scenes in Gambit's apartment in *Sleeper* subtly evoke their close, caring relationship, in particular Gambit's sensitivity.

ECCENTRICS

Before Monty Python's *Flying Circus*, there was *The Avengers,* in which lots of lovable eccentrics prance around the countryside. They consist of a wide variety of characters, from shopkeepers, to professors, to aristocrats, to the military and beyond. Clearly the English have a love affair with quirkiness. [1] In other countries, eccentricity is often considered embarrassingly odd and can lead to one becoming an outcast. However, the English tend to regard it as a positive thing. Eccentricity is viewed as, at worst, charming and endearing and, at best, a sign of originality or even outstanding ability. As John Stuart Mill, the philosopher and economist of the Victorian age, put it:

'Eccentricity has always abounded when and where strength of character has abounded; and the amount of eccentricity in a society has generally been proportional to the amount of genius, mental vigour, and courage which it contained.' (John Stuart Mill, *On Liberty*) [2]

Professors Poole and Quilby in *The Avengers* are such examples. Their passion and love for their life's work make them extraordinary. Poole is a 'mad' scientist who is in love with birds in flight. We first see him prancing around his estate in a winged costume, as if attempting to take flight. As he tells Emma Peel, "To watch a man walking is to see a clumsy machine. To watch a bird flying is to witness a vision." His passionate aim is to free men from their "shackles" and he has invented a boot that allows him to walk on ceilings.

Dr. Quiby is in love with inventions of all sorts. In fact, he has a new one every week, each of them rejected with regularity by the Ministry. But when he makes a revolutionary, groundbreaking scientific discovery – a formula to create an invisible man – the Ministry similarly sends him another rejection letter, returning the formula to him. It is not only Dr. Quilby who is eccentric here. In *The Avengers*, bureaucracies are often bonkers, and the bigger and more inefficient they are, the more loony they become, as the Ministry is portrayed here. As the brilliant Christopher Hitchens observed:

'There are various forms of English mania and oddity, and they tend to be more notorious among the upper classes, if only because true eccentricity requires some leisure time, and some money, for its cultivation.'

A stunning example of this is portrayed in *The Avengers* episode *The Gravediggers*. Horace Winslip is like a character straight out of *Alice in Wonderland*. As an aristocratic eccentric who lives in an *Avengerland* full of train paraphernalia, he is so busy fantasising that he does not realise that the charity foundation he funded, the Sir Horace Winslip Hospital for Ailing Railwaymen, is being exploited. Sir Horace belongs to a bygone era of the industrial age; his family made their fortune on the railroad and he longs for the 'good old days'. He is deeply troubled by the fact that the train is being replaced by the motor car. In order to deal with the loss of railway lines in the real world, he converts his house into an eccentric contraption: a faux train station. In fact, Steed discovers that in order to even gain entry into Sir Horace's stately home, he has to buy a platform ticket. Inside, the living room is decorated with false tracks, platform awnings, a signal box and a train carriage. His servant in this comedic scene is turning on fans, rocking the train carriage and – the most hilarious part – running a revolving scenery canvas and gramophone while Sir Horace and Steed eat lunch on a parked train carriage. What is most striking about this eccentric is that he steals the scenes with a manic joviality, yet underneath the laughter is something subversive. Here is a man who feels dead inside; the love of his life, the train, is a 'dying species'. The invention of the automobile is killing them both off. Compounding all of this is how deeply he defines himself by his railway. However, he has a solution to his despair that he hopes could resurrect the grandeur of the past. As an extraordinarily wealthy man, he believes he can change his external world with money by plotting with the villains to blow up the motorways. His attempts to change the world are deluded and this wealthy aristocrat discovers that all the wasted money spent on this fantasy was truly a futile attempt to halt progress. Sir Horace is a genuinely unhappy man who feels there is little left for him in this world. The cheerfulness is simply a façade.

The military eccentrics in *The Avengers* are often depicted as officers who long for their former glory days in service of their country. As eccentrics they re-enact battle scenes with unadulterated enthusiasm and pride. Brigadier Whitehead, a retired army officer, tapes his memoirs by playing sound effects of battle on a dozen ancient Victrola. He recreates the moment when invasion is imminent – "You, Major Collins, you will lead the first battalion" – as he instructs what we presume to be junior officers awaiting their orders. Suddenly the camera pans to the 'officers', only for us to discover that he is actually talking to empty chairs. In a bizarre twist of fate, while re-enacting the battle scene, the Brigadier is murdered. The irony of it all is that he survived an entire eventful military career, only to be killed while play-acting a battle; how Avengerish. The elderly eccentrics who long for their youth, who cannot cope with societal 'progress', provide a recurring theme in *The Avengers*. Often the solution to this dilemma is for hired staff to create the illusion that they are frozen in time. Colonel Rawlings believes that he is seeing out his remaining years in the Kalayan jungle, where he served as an officer, and that the British Empire is still flourishing. Unbeknownst to the Colonel, however, the 'jungle' is an artificial habitat located in the Home Counties in his very own garden. Sir Horace Winslip deals with loss in a similar way. Not surprisingly, these characters are easily exploited given the 'blinkers' they wear in life.

Colonel Adams runs a military museum where her ancestors' portraits are proudly displayed. She is the last in line of a family rich in heritage. She talks about their portraits as if they are still alive. Similarly, the elderly Mr. Dickens comes from a long family lineage of solicitors. He keeps memorial wreaths of his deceased ancestors on the empty Victorian desks in his law practice. This veritable family gravesite of sorts leaves little room for him in his office. It is as if the deceased family members are alive and well, ceremoniously in charge. Even if they are all dead, they seem to have more clout than the only surviving member, who honours and obeys family traditions. These eccentrics depict how entrenched in the past some members of the upper echelons of British society are; they simply cannot move on or progress. They are lovers of a vanished Edwardian or Victorian age when their families and businesses thrived. They dislike modern technology and are outsiders in present day England. [3]

Brian Clemens was one of the main master minds behind *The Avengers'* increased eccentricity and he influenced what went into *Avengerland*. It is not surprising that he found the 1998 Hollywood movie simply unAvengerish. He suggests that the quintessential *Avengers* character sits indoors drinking tea while an umbrella shields them from the rain dropping on them, as in *A Surfeit of H2O*. As the television series progressed, Clemens became known for cutting and rewriting scripts, redefining what he felt belonged in *Avengerland*. As an example, the following quirky character was cut from the original treatment in Season 5. Professor Pierson – running a memory-expanding laboratory – is an eccentric described as having virtually no memory at all, created by Roger Marshall. Rodney Marshall describes how his father's episode – *A*

Funny Thing Happened on the Way to the Station – was altered by Brian Clemens as it was not deemed sufficiently "weird". In Season 6, the bar for the bizarre was raised even higher. In its final season, Marcus Rugman, played by John Cleese, has a most obscure occupation:

"You see before you twenty-two years of patient brushwork...every clown's face in Britain, registered and copyrighted, by being painted on an egg...large size."

Every clown's make-up is described as being as individual as their fingerprint. His job is to record that image onto an egg. He warns, "Don't knock. Don't even breathe!" as if echoing the fragility of it all.

The Avengers depicts a 'nation of shopkeepers' where espionage takes place. Sometimes the shopkeepers become innocent victims, while at other times their store front is used willingly as an integral part of a villain's smuggling operation. Either way, they are usually murdered. There is a startling disparity between the happy, carefree, eccentric shopkeeper and his sudden, violent demise. The mood similarly shifts from a manic high to a dark brooding tone. A toy shop owner is shot dead by his own toy gun. An umbrella salesman is murdered in a running shower while wearing a bright yellow raincoat. The murder weapon: an umbrella for sale. The shopkeeper normally has a child-like passion for the product he sells. B. Bumble is a lover of bees and honey. He is dressed in horizontal stripes, patterned after a bumblebee, and is 'buzzing' around his shop, bursting with enthusiasm.

Bumble: Treat my bees like children...Happy bees make bumper honey...One of them has a bad knee at the moment. I may have to operate.

He lives in a fantasy world where his relationship to his bees is that of a father to his sick or injured children. The clothing and the irrational banter are part of what defines the eccentric, and are also what make him so endearing. [4]

Names of characters and the use of acronyms are other ways to add to the eccentricity of the series. Mr. Cheshire in *The Hidden Tiger* is a perfect caricature of the Cheshire Cat, a fictional cat created by Lewis Carroll in *Alice in Wonderland* and remembered for its distinctive, mischievous grin. Mr. Cheshire, who is obsessed with cats, runs an organisation called PURRR. His mannerisms are that of a cat. He offers Steed a drink, but instead of alcohol the cabinet turns out to contain an assortment of milk aperitifs. "Homogenised, pasteurised, full cream, dairy special, or perhaps you'd prefer a short?" As he laps up the milk, like a feline, his assistant notes, "On the bottle again, Cheshire?" Cheshire explains to Steed that:

"It's the food of the Gods and Gods these creatures are. Worshipped by earlier civilizations, such grace, beauty and intelligence. It was said that one day cats would inherit the earth. And one day, Mr. Steed, they shall" (smiling with a mischievous grin.)

Hobbies are embraced with cult-like obsession by the eccentrics. Crewe, a train fanatic, is a poor man's version of the aristocrat, Sir Horace Winslip. He does not have the wealth to create a faux train station in his home, so his solution is to live in a signal box. He is negotiating to buy the *Avengerland* deserted station, with plans to one day purchase a mainline station such as Kings Cross. He can tell the Avengers nothing about the previous night's events as he had been lured into a wild goose chase for an 1892 Jubilee edition water cistern: "When I got there, it was a practical joke. Final insult – I missed the last train. Had to take a bus. A *bus*!" Just as Crewe is offended by the "ignominy" of having to catch a bus home, Hickey (in *The Hour That Never Was*) is, similarly, singularly loyal to Air Force bases. He won't venture anywhere near Army or Navy ones. Crewe's skills come into play as he can identify trains by their sounds. Steed's umbrella – with a Dictaphone audio – records train sounds, and Crewe's expertise is employed. When Emma tells Crewe, "I'd like you to listen to this umbrella", she craftily gets the eccentric to think that she is more absurd than him.

Arkwright, the knitting instructor, is fanatical about the hobby. He appears to almost be singing nursery rhymes in the form of knitting instructions to his students.

"Fingers nimble, fingers spright.
Cast to the left. Cast to the right.
First one pearl, then one plain.
Then two pearl and back again."

A true *Avengers* eccentric, Mr. Arkwright happily chats with Steed, but then gestures angrily with a knitting needle when he learns that his 00 size needles have been stolen.

In *The Avengers*, science is often portrayed as something to be feared. Dr. Sheldon, a brilliant female botanist, explains to the Avengers – in complex terminology – that the gigantic plant they see before them is actually man-eating. In fact, she nearly becomes a victim of the very science she so dearly loves. As art imitates life, veteran actress Athene Seyler was the perfect fit for the brilliant botanist in *Man-Eater of Surrey Green,* as she had been educated at a progressive school in Surrey, where she enrolled in advanced biology classes, including one on Darwin's *On The Origin of Species*, the foundation for evolutionary biology. At other times in *The Avengers*, scientists are misused by the villains, as is the case with Professor Popple, who is forced to construct an atom bomb.

The British have had a love affair with eccentrics for centuries, dating back to Roman times. *The Hermit in the Garden*, by Professor Gordon Campbell of the University of Leicester, describes the intriguing habit of British aristocracy to hire ornamental or garden hermits during the 18th century. It was the must-have accessory for the grand gardens of Georgian England. Hermits would live in follies or caves on the estate. Those who took employment as garden hermits were typically required to refrain from cutting their hair or washing, and some were dressed as druids. In *The Avengers*, Jonah is such a character, who appears to believe he is Noah, building his ark to deal with the "great flood coming".

The Avengers portrayed eccentrics with a brilliantly polished, unique British flair. Often these characters are harmless victims, though sometimes they are used as conduits or informants; they effectively poke fun at British traditions and frequently push the series into the realms of the absurd. However, they all have one thing in common. Put simply, their eccentricity makes them extraordinary. To borrow the words of an English national treasure, Lewis Carroll:

The Mad Hatter: Have I gone mad?
Alice: I'm afraid so. You're entirely bonkers. But I'll tell you a secret. All the best people are. [5]

© Margaret J Gordon (Dedicated to Lucille Gordon)

1. A BBC 'sketch comedy' series broadcast between 1969 and 1974 which contained surreal elements.

2. John Stuart Mill was talking about the 'tyranny of opinion' in an age of 'conformity', and how eccentricity is a way of breaking through this.
3. Could this also apply to John Steed? Or is his eccentricity simply a façade to fool villains?
4. JZF: The likes of Bumble and his ilk are also some of the most sympathetic characters in the whole of the series, and their deaths the most tragic. While the various and myriad spies and secret agents knowingly accept the risks that come with their profession, and the corrupt scientists and other specialists invite their own misfortune by choosing to align themselves with nefarious individuals, eccentrics such as Bumble are guilty of nothing more than loving something passionately, almost childlike in their enthusiasm, and are hurting no one. Steed and his compatriots seem to recognise the tragedy of the deaths of such innocents, and their reactions reflect this. Emma Peel's obvious delight with Bumble's enthusiasm, and refusal to patronise him for it, is contrasted starkly with her dismay and sadness when she discovers he has been killed; his loss is keenly felt by both her and the viewers. In this way, eccentrics are a key source of humanity and childlike innocence in the often consequence-free (and virtually child-free) world of *Avengerland*.
5. As MJG observes, many of the eccentrics examined in this essay – and others such as bird lover Quince (*Silent Dust*) – care passionately about their particular field of expertise or interest, and often die in its pursuit, adding a heroic quality to their characters.

HAND OF THE WIND: FOR QUEEN AND COUNTRY – MARTIAL ARTS IN *THE AVENGERS*

'Should you desire the great tranquillity, prepare to sweat.'
Hakuin Ekaku, Japanese Zen Buddhist teacher and artist (1686-1768)

Opening Titles - A Martial of Arts
Within the opening titles of Season 4, in an artistic collection of just six television still-frames, Mrs. Peel's Martial Arts credentials are spectacularly exhibited and framed. Six action-stills of Emma Peel in black leather, captured on film, cut together at micro-second high-speed, forming a striking virtuoso of combative Karate poses – culminating with the stylish silenced Walther P38 shot.

A Sense of History
The Martial Arts of Jujitsu, Judo, Karate and Kung Fu originated in ancient China, where nomadic Buddhist priests developed their own form of unarmed combat to defend themselves from thieves and bandits in the mountains. In the 1650s, travelling Japanese monks learned from their Chinese counterparts this highly effective style of self-defence. The inhabitants of the island of Okinawa combined the ingenious Chinese fighting style with the unarmed combat perfected by the Japanese aristocratic Samurai warrior, and refined the art of Jujitsu to its present form.

In 1882, Jigoro Kano collated the finest elements of Jujitsu. He developed a sport which he named Judo and established the Kodokan, the first Judo school in Tokyo. Kano developed Judo from Jujitsu, principally as a form of self-defence combat and sport, but which could incorporate elements of more deadly Jujitsu and Karate with lunge punches, knife-edge strikes, with Judo choke-holds and submissions. Karate is a much more lethal and offensive form of unarmed combat, with none of the holds or throws found in Jutjitsu and Judo. Karate uses five striking surfaces of the human body – the fist, the edge of the hand, the finger tips, the ball of the foot and the elbows – to execute blows to the thirty-seven vulnerable parts of the human body, to disable or kill.

The historical Martial Arts connection between three cultural colossus of literature, television and film – Sherlock Holmes, James Bond and *The Avengers* – is one of intriguing providence and serendipity. In 1905, Sir Arthur Conan Doyle ingeniously resurrected Sherlock Holmes from his death plunge with Professor Moriarty over the Reichenbach Falls by arming Holmes with the knowledge of a new self-defence system called bartitsu. Conan Doyle's ideas were gleaned from the writings of English engineer and self-defence enthusiast Edward Barton-Wright. Barton-Wright imported Jujitsu from Japan into Britain in the 1890s and adapted the essential idea into his own particular variation – a new British martial art for the English gentlemen called Bartitsu ('Bart' from Barton and 'itsu' from Jujitsu). In his essay *'The New Art of Self-Defence'*, Barton-Wright described how his new concept of Bartitsu incorporated the finest elements of eastern and western methods of self-defence: Japanese Jujitsu, British boxing and wrestling, French kick boxing (*Savate*) and *Canne de combat* – cane or walking-stick fighting. At the same time, Judo was being introduced into Britain by instructor teacher Gungi Koizumi and demonstrator/performer Yiuko Tani. The development of Bartitsu and Judo provided Conan Doyle with the perfect and credible method for Holmes's escape from the fearful Reichenbach Falls, explained 12 years later in *The Empty House*.

Oddjob meets John Steed

In 1958, as part of his research for his new *James Bond* novel, Ian Fleming visited a women's Judo exhibition and tournament at the Kodokan in Tokyo. Fleming was so intrigued that he was inspired to incorporate the Martial Arts of Judo and Karate into one of his finest *James Bond* novels, *Goldfinger* (1959), later adapted into the classic 1964 film. Fleming thus armed his implacable Korean assassin Oddjob with a profound knowledge of, and the immense expertise in, the lethal unarmed art of Karate, and an iconic steel-rimmed bowler (an idea later developed for John Steed with his Pierre Cardin steel-lined bowler). Fleming was one of the first western authors to describe the discipline of Martial Arts in an espionage thriller.

Martial Arts Maestros

During the years 1962-1968 and 1976-1977, *The Avengers* production team assembled a remarkable group of elite world class Martial Arts experts: exceptionally gifted instructors, fight choreographers, stunt co-ordinators, exponents and masters in the arts of Judo, Karate and Kung Fu. *The Avengers* stunt-team's credentials included six black belts in Judo, three in Karate and two in Kung Fu.

From 1962-64, Joe Robinson (Judo black belt 8th dan, Karate black belt 5th dan), Doug Robinson (Judo black belt 9th dan, the highest dan grade), fight instructors, choreographers, stuntmen, exponents and actors coached Honor Blackman in Judo and Karate. In real-life Blackman attained the grade of brown belt in Judo.

From 1965-1968 and 1976-1977, Ray Austin (Judo black belt, stunt-man, stunt arranger/co-ordinator, fight choreographer and film director) and Chee Soo (Judo, Karate, Kung Fu black belt 9th dan and Grand Master) trained Rigg in the Taoist Art of Feng Shou – Hand of the Wind – a branch of Kung Fu; and Cyd Child (Judo black belt, 2nd dan, the 1975 Women's European Heavyweight Judo Champion), and Joe Dunne (Judo black belt, stuntman and actor) instructed Diana Rigg, Linda Thorson and Joanna Lumley in the arts of Judo, Karate and Kung Fu. [1]

Black Belts and Black Leather
The genesis and legacy of Catherine Gale's on-screen Martial Arts and Blackman's real-life penchant and ability for Judo (assimilating components of Karate) in *The Avengers* developed by glorious happenstance. The producers knew that they didn't want her simply screaming for Steed. Initially, they tried surprise tactics: she was equipped with a tiny .25 calibre Derringer pistol. But how could the weapon be concealed on Blackman's person? Carrying it in her handbag was impractical and slow. An underarm holster, as Macnee observed, constricted her figure. The black lace garter-holstered Derringer pistol impeded her natural walk. The 'firearms-concealment-about-Blackman's-body' concept was eventually rejected. As Blackman said, 'I was left with the purely physical - the noble art of self-defence.' [2]

Macnee introduced Blackman to René Burdet, former head of the French Resistance in Marseille. He had trained English, French and Polish WWII Special Operations Executive (SOE) female spies – secret agents in the arts of Judo and Karate. He referred Blackman to black belt Judo instructor brothers Joe and Doug Robinson at their Robinson Martial Arts Gymnasium. 'Slowly, Judo expertise (and black leather) were worked into my part...I still have the scars on my back from being thrown in a fight before I learned to fall properly.' Martial Arts in *The Avengers* was born.

'Cathy led a very active life and I soon realised that skirts were out of the question. When your legs are flying over your head you don't want to worry about showing your stocking tops. The fact myself, actor Peter Arne and Patrick happened to choose tight black leather trousers with matching jerkin and boots for my fighting kit was almost accidental.'

However, even the uninhibited Blackman had reservations about wearing black leather: 'Oh God, don't you realise what you might be starting?' Nevertheless, after evaluating the options of bizarre fetish fan mail versus revealing stocking tops, Blackman agreed to be measured for her all black leather combat suit. [3]

The Martial Arts/leather costume motif inheritance was significantly advanced by the athletic physique of Diana Rigg as Mrs. Emma Peel, and the progression to the more forceful Martial Arts of Karate and Kung Fu, yet crucially still preserving some the most effective constituents of Gale's Judo. Thus, the Cathy Gale leather combat suit became the Emma Peel leather fighting cat-suit. If the British public had elevated Blackman's Gale to the status of St. Catherine, then Rigg's Peel did the impossible: first equalling, then surpassing, the popularity of her illustrious predecessor.

The Girl with the Hand of the Wind
The irresistible combination of Peel performing spectacular balletic Martial Arts – high-kicking in hard-hitting fight sequences whilst clad in sleek, throat-to-toe leather and jersey cat-suits, designer Crimplene trouser-suits, sweaters or halter-tops and hipster slacks or mini-skirts [4] – took the new black and white *film noir* fourth season to an even higher, more extraordinary level of charismatic chic and accentuated kinkiness. I believe there is a distinct correlation between the most outstanding Martial Arts *Avengers* fight sequences and their concomitant, incomparable designer fashions – a perfect combination that created unique television of thrilling, mysterious enchantment. The

trendy cult of the 'Karate chop' and 'Kung Fu high kick' pervaded 1960s television and film drama/comedy. An advertiser cleverly realised the creative potential; witness statuesque actress Valerie Leon responding to the overwhelming effects of *'Hai Karate'* Aftershave – the lotion that *'drives women wild; careful how you use it'* – in a series of highly successful Karate and Kung Fu orientated television adverts.

The art of stylised, enjoyable Kung Fu combat was pioneered on television by stunt choreographer, Ray Austin. He recalls that when he saw Diana Rigg he was inspired by her athletic figure to train her in the little known Martial Art of Kung Fu, a combat technique rarely seen on European or US television or film. Other contemporary television programmes which demonstrated Kung Fu and Karate moves, and who may have claimed to be the originator, were *The Green Hornet* (Van Williams and Bruce Lee, 1966), *The Man From Uncle* (Robert Vaughn and David McCallum, 1966) and *Honey West* (Anne Francis, 1966), but it was Ray Austin, in *The Avengers* of October 1965, who was first.

'I was the first person to bring Kung Fu to the television screen but I did not have the experience or knowledge to perform it correctly on camera. I should have suggested we do fights partially in slow-motion similar to the techniques used in the David Carradine *Kung Fu* series, because with Diana's magnificent physique this could have looked absolutely phenomenal. No one had heard of Kung Fu until I showcased the art in *The Avengers* – Diana was the first to do it.' [5]

Diana's stunt double, Martial Arts co-trainer and Judo black belt, Cyd Child, endorses Austin's assessment of Rigg's fighting prowess: 'Diana performed Kung Fu which suited her personality because she moved like a cat.' [6] Rigg's elegant fashion-model deportment, posture and effortless flexibility thoroughly impressed Austin when he instructed her how to roll, somersault and fall correctly. Rigg gave Peel a combative, lithe athleticism, an exquisitely poised panther-esque movement and the lissom high kicking grace of a ballet dancer. Barefoot, Emma Peel exquisitely demonstrates her extraordinary athleticism during the harem sword-fight sequence in *Honey for the Prince* with one of the highest Karate kicks ever executed by any *Avengers* screen actress.

The Bond Connection
The Martial Arts combat legacy of both Cathy Gale and Emma Peel was cleverly reflected and transferred to the big screen in *Goldfinger* (1964) and *On Her Majesty's Secret Service* (1969), with specially written customised fights for Blackman's and Rigg's multi-dimensional Bond girl characters: Miss Pussy Galore and Contessa Teresa di Vicenzo. Mrs. Gale's judo expertise was transferred into the character Pussy Galore. During the hay-barn scene, she applies a Judo hold and throws James Bond, even though – as Blackman observes, 'It's me, Pussy, who ends up flat on the mat in submission and surrender to Bond, who then applies a few holds of his own!' [7] The 1969 screenplay for *On Her Majesty's Secret Service* was specially adapted to accommodate elements of Emma Peel's combative character into the persona of Tracy di Vicenzo (Diana Rigg) in a fight specifically created to exhibit Rigg/Peel's athletic fighting ability with the colossal Russian Heavyweight professional wrestler and actor Yuri Borienko. [8]

The Immoveable One versus The Irresistible One
Peel's fabulous flair for Karate, Judo and Kung Fu is admirably demonstrated in the iconic *Cybernauts* Martial Arts episode and is the only occasion in which we see Mrs Peel dressed in the white Karate uniform. Oyuka, the 'Immoveable One', is a 3rd dan at Judo and a 1st dan at Karate. As the Sensei observes, "There are few men who could pass her if she did not wish them to." Peel, in her stocking feet, heels together in the Heisoku-dachi pose, and, in her tight tailored two-piece,

short jacket-skirt wool suit, solemnly bows to Oyuka, who looks at Peel arrogantly and impassively. Both women adopt the classic crouching Front (Zenkutsu Dachi Kihon) and Sparring (Ippon Kumite) stance – in which the opponents flex and push their left leg forward, keeping a straight right back leg, Tiger Claw hands, left arm out-stretched, right arm back and arched in a classic combat pose. Peel steps left, then right, then left again in a move to pass, but is blocked, by Oyuka – both women lunge forward but Oyuka is faster and lashes downwards with a vicious left-handed Ridge hand strike directed at Peel's jaw. Peel uses an Upper block (Jodan uke) to protect her face and deflect the whipping stroke from Oyuka's left hand with her right forearm. She grasps Oyuka's right underarm with her left hand. Oyuka is jerked forward, right arm pulled straight for Peel to execute a downward slicing guillotine Knife-edge hand strike, a right-handed Karate chop move (Shuto uchi) to Oyuka's offered neck. Then, when Oyuka attempts a surprise claw-blow to Peel's right knee, Oyuka is somersaulted flat onto her back.

Mrs. Peel Meets Her Match
Emma Peel meets her match, her Martial Arts *bête noir*, in the form of two formidable 6'6" powerhouse opponents. First, when she is literally blasted across Steed's lounge, catapulted backwards over his sofa by the explosive Karate whiplash of the massive automated Cybernaut beast in *Return of The Cybernauts,* in which the charmingly evil Paul Beresford transforms his 'dear Emma' into a cyber puppet for his own amusement. Second, when she is overwhelmed as her Karate strikes are efficiently blocked and balletic high kicks are deflected and caught, overbalancing her, in the sensational Kung Fu defeat by the indestructible duplicate of Professor Frank N. Stone (Christopher Lee) in *Never, Never Say Die.* [9]

King's Karate *Coup de Grace*

In Season 6's *All Done With Mirrors*, we witness a thundering Martial Arts battle between Tara King and the enormous executioner, Gozzo, that is deserving of, and equal to, the very best combative challenges won and lost by Cathy Gale and Emma Peel. Splendidly co-choreographed, directed and performed by Joe Dunne, Ray Austin, Linda Thorson and Cyd Child, the ninety second encounter is surely Thorson's/King's finest ever fight, and moreover, one of the Martial Arts highlights in the history of *The Avengers*. The match is enhanced by one of Thorson's/King's most suitably stylish fighting outfits. Sidestepping the homicidal Gozzo inside a house, Tara is caught escaping and is contemptuously hurled full length, face down onto gravel outside. She runs for her life onto the grass lawn, somersaults, resists and performs a perfect Judo shoulder throw upon her opponent. She attempts a Karate high kick but Gozzo catches her leg and thumps her down onto the grass. King then executes an impeccable and spectacular crunching Tae Kwon Do style flying front-thrust kick (Ap chaki) into Gozzo's chest, blasting him backwards. She immediately drops onto her back and fires Gozzo high over her head in a thrilling Judo Sacrifice throw. The Martial Arts technique then switches from Judo to Kung Fu and Karate. Tara draws her right arm back and whips in a right handed Karate knife-strike impacting deep into Gozzo's side, then a short-armed chop to the neck. Gozzo doubles up in agony. King drives forward with the full weight of her right shoulder behind the move, hitting Gozzo with a straight, stiff-fingered powerhouse strike directly into the solar plexus. An elegant, flashing high kick into Gozzo's face sends him crashing backwards into and through the wall of a garden shed – a classic King Karate *coup de grace*. [10]

Purdey and the French Art of Savate
La Savate is the classic late 17th century French Martial Art system of kicking, punching, grappling and wrestling, demonstrated by Pierre, the

ballet dancing, side-stepping Master Savateur (Shooter) in *A Touch of Brimstone*. The la Savate theme was continued ten years later by stunt co-ordinator/director Ray Austin, who was at the preparation, planning and rehearsal stage for the fight choreography of *The New Avengers*. He asked his protégé Cyd Child to get Joanna Lumley and Gareth Hunt exceptionally fit for the new series. Child had just won the Women's European Judo Championship and, upon Austin's instructions, designed a strict Olympic standard crash course in physical fitness. Lumley's Purdey was required to convincingly display both the gymnastic athleticism of a former Royal Ballet dancer and proficiency in the French Martial Art of Savate. Lumley remembers her exhausting short sprint, weight-lifting and ballet training. Austin supervised and Child trained Lumley to accomplish an incredible high kick, to the same head height degree achieved by Diana Rigg in 1965.

In *The Eagle's Nest*, Steed and Purdey are confronted by four neo-Nazi fishermen assassins. Purdey, clad in a green leotard, is 'reeled in' by a deadly Nazi fishing rod. She then performs a dazzling succession of balletic pirouettes: a red booted Savate high kick to the throat, a left handed whipping Karate slice to the neck. She leans forward on Steed to execute a classic Mrs. Peel move, a right footed Karate/Savate reverse thrust kick, her left standing leg remaining perfectly straight in an exquisitely balanced balletic pose. Purdey spins, eases back onto Steed and high kicks a thumping right red boot into the face of the fourth and final Nazi adversary. [11]

In Karate Master Spence's private gymnasium in *House of Cards*, Purdey, garbed in her shimmering gold and purple silk Kimono fighting suit, executes a phenomenal Tae Kwon Do two-footed, leaping, spiralling, smacking barefoot kick to her instructor's face. The subsequent ferocious Karate 'competition' combat-bout and ensuing knife-fight between Spence and Gambit is one of the most brutal fight sequences ever seen in *The Avengers*.

Cyd Child's exhilarating choreography of the fight sequences for these *New Avengers* episodes is sublime and she finally receives deserving on-screen credit for her inspired work. She is Ray Austin's Martial Arts protégé, who doubled, trained and choreographed for Diana Rigg, Linda Thorson and Joanna Lumley. I believe that she matches the extraordinary skills of her maestro mentor by performing and planning some of the most thrilling fight sequences in the history of *The Avengers*.

End Credits
In the closing credits of Season 5, we witness Emma Peel in a Crimplene cat-suit, performing a series of silhouetted artistic poses: hand thrusts, flick, whip and high kicks, an erotic exhibition in the art of classical, balletic Karate and Kung Fu. *The Avengers* is synonymous with intelligent, beautiful, athletic, Amazonian women performing gymnastic Judo, Karate and Kung Fu fights in costumes of sensational virtuosity. The continuing legacy of fabulous Martial Arts fighting is absolutely crucial to the international phenomenon that is *The Avengers*.

© James Speirs

1. JS: In real-life, Rigg was trained in Judo and Karate and, according to a *Your Martial Arts Resources* report, in 1966 achieved the grade of Black Belt in Judo. Later, in 2008, the Guinness World Records recognised Diana Rigg as the first western actress to have performed Kung Fu on television, in 1965.
2. Honor Blackman quotes are taken from *Honor Blackman's Book of Self-Defence* (Bell, 1965).

3. JZF: Leather was also chosen for other practical reasons. The issue of Blackman's skirt flying up was easily solved by putting her in trousers, but these failed to hold up to the strain of the stunts and tended to split, which was less-than-ideal when the episodes were being shot 'as live'! Leather proved to be much hardier and withstood the wear and tear of the fight scenes, though it proved inflexible and 'creaked on the soundtrack'. It was for this reason that Rigg was eventually given the stretchy Emmapeeler cat-suits.
4. JS: Or wickedly risqué historical fancy-dress costumes.
5. JS: Austin had been a graduate student of Chinese-British Kung Fu Grand Master and teacher Chee Soo. Quotes taken from 'Master of Mayhem – Ray Austin', *Stay Tuned - The Avengers* Volume 3 Issue 3.
6. Cyd Child quotes taken from 'Perils of Cyd', *Stay Tuned - The Avengers* Volume 2 Issue 6.
7. This is an example of how *James Bond* conformed to gender stereotypes, completely lacking *The Avengers'* revolutionary elements in terms of its sexual politics.
8. JS: Honor Blackman and Diana Rigg featured in the BBC Four documentary on the history of Jujitsu, Judo, Karate and Kung Fu in Britain. Blackman is shown, in rare footage, with instructor/stuntman Joe Robinson, rehearsing in the Robinson gym in her judoka suit; and Rigg is revealed exhibiting her Judo and Karate skills in a scene from *The Cybernauts*. *Timeshift: Everybody was Kung Fu Fighting: The Rise of Martial Arts in Britain* (BBC4 Television, 26th February 2013).
9. JS: Cyd Child injured her back during this sequence - Diana Rigg stepped into the breach to Martial Arts double for Child and complete the scene.
10. It should be pointed out that it is landing on the garden shed rake that finally finishes off the indefatigable Gozzo.
11. JZF: It is a shame that Purdey's first major fight scene of the series is clearly partly performed by a stunt double, rather than Lumley herself, most likely because the twirls were too difficult

and required the skill of a genuine ballerina. Lumley performed several high-kicks, but would have to wait for subsequent episodes to demonstrate the fruits of her rigorous stunt training.

MISS KING, YOU'RE NEEDED! or HEDONISM & LEATHER BOOTS – *THE AVENGERS'* SUCCESS IN FRANCE

In 1969, a girl arrived on French television screens. She was the heroine of a series called *Bowler Hat and Leather Boots* and, with her, the choice of title is easy to understand. Miss King really is the queen of leather boots. She wears boots all the time, with shorts or mini-skirts. Blacks, browns, yellows, reds, greens...even snake-skin boots. Miss King provides us with a veritable parade of boots, alongside her male partner resplendent in his famous bowler hat.

And yes, in France *The Avengers* is called *Bowler Hat and Leather Boots*. One has to say that this title works really well in Season 6, the era with which the series began its popular success story in General de Gaulle's homeland.

It is difficult to explain why, but the success of *Bowler Hat and Leather Boots* has never wavered. It has grown in popularity, always getting stronger, reaching a peak in the 1990s with the release of the first videos and then later the initial DVDs. So much so that today, *Studio Canal* – the copyright holder and also a French company – has released the Blu-Ray versions to the same level of excitement in France as in England, Germany, and other European countries where this cult show still reigns.

Yet things began badly. When Season 4 arrived in France, in April 1967, only thirteen episodes were broadcast, on the second channel and in an uncertain time slot, moving from 10.30 pm to 8.00 pm from the third episode onwards. Very few magazines heralded the arrival of this new series which offered the viewer surprising and avant-garde drama. Only *Télé 7 Jours* and *Télé Poche* – two popular TV magazines in France at the time – covered it, the former offering a double page dedicated to Diana Rigg. This was meagre fare and a long way from the 'Emma Peel Mania' which had hit Germany a year earlier.

Emma Peel returned, this time in colour, in July 1968. Even if the television press now paid more attention to the series, it was a bad time for the series to attempt a gain in popularity. In those days, the French abandoned the cities and towns for their holidays and, unlike today when the media can follow you everywhere, people were cut off from their television sets. [1] Only thirteen colour episodes were broadcast. Extremely positive reviews followed, but the show still did not achieve the same level of popular success it enjoyed in Germany, Italy, Spain or the Netherlands.

It was in October 1969 that everything changed. For the first time, the series was broadcast on Saturday nights at 10 p.m. Season 6 landed with *All Done With Mirrors*, presenting the new heroine as a female action hero, impetuous but also possessing a sense of autonomy. [2] The following weeks continued with some very, very good episodes: *They Keep Killing Steed*, *Game*, and *Super Secret Cypher Snatch*, which established John Steed and Tara King as the star duo of autumn/winter 1969. The seduction was completed by the broadcast of *Look...* on December 27th, the thirteenth and final episode of this first salvo.

A year later, this started all over again in the 1970 autumn/winter schedule with the following ten Season 6 episodes. This time the series was shown on Saturday evenings at 'prime time' (8.30 p.m.) and the heroes regularly featured in magazines. Profiting from the show's success, Amber Records decided to distribute Linda Thorson's single

Here I Am in France, a record which had already made the rounds elsewhere in Europe. The young actress found herself in Paris to publicise it on various television shows which were delighted to host her. At the beginning of 1971, after the broadcast of *Bizarre*, *Paris Match* used it for its cover, something which was the sole privilege of the greatest stars or political figures. The title read, 'Goodbye, Tara King'. There is no doubt that the presence of Linda Thorson in Paris contributed to the success of the show, increasing its popularity. The young actress was everywhere, on television screens, magazines and social gatherings where she mixed with the Parisian jet set. She was even going to make a TV movie with a director, Youri, who was fashionable at the time. For a period she thought about establishing a career in France, but was soon tempted back to London for the play *No Sex Please, We're British*.

From 1973 onwards the repeat transmissions began. French viewers familiarised themselves with Emma Peel; some people were rediscovering her, but others were discovering her for the first time. These repeats continued until one day in 1975, when a producer phoned Albert Fennell. Rodolph Roffi wanted to use Patrick Macnee and Linda Thorson for a champagne advert for Laurent-Pérrier. The advert was made but Roffi was stunned to find out that the series hadn't been in production for many years. [3] Thanks to France's affection for Miss King the series would return. And this time with French money!

This 'marriage', which gave birth to *The New Avengers*, would not be a very happy one. It began well (Season 1) but finished badly (Season 2), forcing Canada to complete the divorce after this short-term relationship. Even if the France/Britain collaboration had not really worked, the French continued to love their British heroes. Thanks to the many repeat broadcasts, Emma Peel – who has ended up being as popular as Tara – Tara King and, of course, John Steed have continued to insinuate themselves into the public's heart. Then came the release in 1993 of the series on video. This was a genuine fireworks display. No television show had enjoyed a similar distribution: whole columns of video boxes in department stores. In Paris, one of the largest Fnac stores [4] displayed a genuine Bentley with its boot containing the complete series. And despite being priced above the normal valuation, it was sold!

Yes, the French love *The Avengers* and the sales of these initial videos prove it. The same year, Paris' most beautiful cinema, Le Grand Rex, organised an *Avengers* evening with four episodes from the monochrome Peel season. It was an absolute triumph; the 2,700 seater venue was full to bursting. Shortly afterwards, the *France 3* television channel decided to broadcast the entire Season 4 in its original version with subtitles, in Alex Taylor's *Continentale* slot. The pretext was that it was an English language course. The ratings, in a nine o'clock in the morning slot, exceeded all the channel's expectations. *France 3* immediately followed this up with Seasons 5 and 6. The popularity of the series had reached a new peak. Diana Rigg had finally got her 'revenge' and was the main feature in three magazines. As for Linda Thorson, she was the cover for the chic *Télérama*. The adventure continued with more repeat broadcasts until the Franco-German channel *ARTE* bought the television rights. As of now, the entire series from Cathy Gale to Purdey has been broadcast three times by a channel whose aim is to provide viewers with the 'best of our culture'.

But why does France love this British series so much? No doubt there is a definitive answer, but this is just a personal viewpoint: it is the hedonism, which clearly governs the lives of Steed and his lovely partners. Serving dinner with champagne in the middle of a field (*All Done With Mirrors*); drawing a sumptuous feast in a comic strip with charcoal and then making it actually appear at night (*The Winged Avenger*); or inventing a champagne fountain (*Who Was That Man I Saw You With?*). This is what our heroes deliver at mission's end, after defeating a dubious ideology or domineering mastermind! They also see shows, dine out in tuxedos and evening dress, drink wine and make love…but all of this is off-camera of course, strongly suggested or hinted by subtle staging. In *Epic*, the couple finally decide to spend the evening at home. Just as in *Invasion of the Earthmen,* Steed invites Tara to 'practise' her 'moves' rather than go out…but you would have to be very naïve not to understand the exact nature of the liaisons which unite John with Emma and, later, Tara.

Elegance, *haute couture*, champagne and fine wines, art and the art of living! The taste for pleasure pushed to its extreme…how could they not enchant us? These British agents with their values which are, finally, so French, and so important to defend, today more than ever before. [5]

© Eric Cazalot (© translation by Rodney Marshall)

1. Eric's observation reminds us how different and inflexible television viewing was in the days before video recorders, never mind 'on demand' options.
2. JZF: This transmission order for the series is perhaps the key to Tara King's popularity in France compared to the rest of the world. A strong opening episode, which portrayed Tara as eminently capable, undoubtedly allowed her to make a favourable first impression, and the follow-up episodes from later in the season's production would have only reinforced it. The inconsistency in the writing of Tara's character that plagued the season's early episodes would have been easier to forgive as a result. The topsy-turvy broadcasting order across the Channel, which had Tara oscillate between inexperienced ingénue and capable agent, was far less forgiving. In addition, the slower

take-up of the Peel episodes meant that France did not subject Tara to the comparisons to her predecessor that plagued her acceptance by other audiences. This fascinating comparison between territories illustrates how the reception of the series' different seasons was affected as much by the order and context in which they were aired as the content of the episodes themselves. Tara King may have always been in for a rough ride in some countries, but the broadcast order often did her no favours.
3. It is wonderfully strange that Roffi was unaware that the series had ended, in view of the fanfare which publications such as *Paris Match* had offered.
4. Fnac is a large French retail chain.
5. This indirect reference to the Paris Attacks in November 2015 offers an elegiac reminder of how important it is to celebrate all the elements of our culture, including *The Avengers*.

MISS KING, YOU'RE NEEDED! ou L'HEDONISME & BOTTES DE CUIR – LE SUCCES DE *CHAPEAU MELON ET BOTTES DE CUIR* EN FRANCE

En 1969, une fille a débarqué sur les écrans français. Elle est l'héroïne d'une série qui s'appelle « *Chapeau Melon et Bottes de Cuir* » ! Et le titre avec elle est facile à comprendre ! Car Mlle King est bien la reine des bottes de cuir ! Des bottes, elle en porte tout le temps avec ses shorts et ses mini jupes ! Des noires, des brunes, des jaunes, des rouges, des vertes... Et même des bottes en serpent ! Bref, Mademoiselle King nous fait un véritable défilé de bottes, devant son partenaire qui porte si bien le fameux chapeau melon !

Et oui, en France « *The Avengers* » s'appelle « *Chapeau Melon et Bottes de Cuir* ». Et ce titre, il faut le dire, va très bien à la saison 6. Saison avec laquelle a démarré le succès de la série au pays du Général de Gaulle.

Il est assez difficile d'expliquer pourquoi, mais le succès de « *Chapeau Melon et Bottes de Cuir* » en France ne s'est jamais démenti. Il n'a fait que croître, toujours plus fort, atteignant des sommets dans les années quatre-vingt-dix, lorsque furent distribués les premières vidéos, puis les premiers DVD. À tel point qu'aujourd'hui, pour STUDIO CANAL, détenteur des droits mais aussi groupe français, il faut le noter, la sortie des Blue Ray est aussi importante en France qu'elle ne l'est en Angleterre ou en Allemagne, autre pays européen où le culte règne toujours...

Pourtant, tout avait plutôt mal commencé ! Lorsque la saison 4 arrive en France, en avril 1967, seuls 13 épisodes sont diffusés sur la deuxième chaîne et sur un créneau horaire incertain, passant de 22 h 30 à 20 h 00 à partir du 3ème épisode. Très peu de magazines se feront l'écho de cette nouvelle série pourtant surprenante et avant-gardiste. Seule une double page est consacrée à Diana Rigg dans « *Télé 7 Jours* » et aussi « *Télé Poche* » [1]. C'est peu et nous sommes très loin de l'*Emma Peel Mania* qui s'est déclenchée un an avant en Allemagne !

Emma Peel revient, cette fois en couleurs, en juillet 1968 ! Même si la presse télé donne plus de visibilité à la série, c'est une mauvaise période pour faire un succès. En ces années-là, les français fuient les villes pour les vacances et sont, contrairement à aujourd'hui où les médias les poursuivent partout, déconnectés des postes de télévision ! 13 épisodes couleurs seulement. De très bonnes critiques, mais toujours pas le même succès qu'en Allemagne, en Italie, en Espagne ou en Hollande...

C'est en octobre 1969 que tout va changer. **Pour la première fois, la série est diffusée le samedi soir, en deuxième partie de soirée (22h00).** La saison 6 débarque avec « *Miroirs* » (*All Done With Mirrors*), présentant la nouvelle héroïne en super femme d'action, impétueuse et autonome ! Les semaines suivantes continuent avec de très, très bons épisodes : « *Mais Qui est Steed ?* » (*They Keep Killing Steed*), « *Jeux* » (*Games*), « *Le Document Disparu* » (*The Super Secret Cypher Snatch*) imposent John Steed et Tara King comme le duo vedette de cet automne / hiver 1969 qui achève de séduire les français le 27 décembre avec « *Clowneries* » (*Look, Stop Me...*), treizième et dernier épisode de cette première salve.

Un an plus tard, cela recommence pour l'automne hiver 1970 et 10 épisodes suivants de la saison six. Cette fois **la série accède désormais**

au prime time - 20h30 - du samedi soir et les héros sont régulièrement à la Une des magazines. Profitant de ce succès, la maison de disques Amber Records, décide de publier en France le single de Linda Thorson « Here I Am », déjà sorti un peu partout en Europe. La jeune actrice se retrouve donc à Paris pour en faire la promotion dans de nombreuses émissions de télévision, enchantées de la recevoir. Début 1971, après la diffusion de « Bizarre » (Bizarre), Paris Match lui offre sa couverture, sachant que seules les plus grandes stars ou hommes politiques ont cet honneur. Le journal titre : « Au revoir Tara King ». Cette présence de Linda Thorson à Paris a sans aucun doute contribué à faire encore davantage monter la côte de popularité de la série. La jeune actrice est partout ! Sur les plateaux télé, mais aussi dans les magazines et les soirées mondaines où elle sympathise avec la jet set parisienne. Elle ira même jusqu'à tourner un téléfilm avec un réalisateur en vogue, Youri. Linda Thorson envisage un temps de faire carrière en France, mais elle est rapidement rappelée à Londres où le succès l'attend avec la pièce « No Sex Please, We're British ».

Dès 1973, commencent les premières rediffusions. Les français se familiarisent alors avec Emma Peel, qu'ils redécouvrent ou, pour certains, découvrent. Les rediffusions continuent jusqu'à ce jour de 1975 où un producteur appelle Albert Fennell. Il souhaite utiliser Patrick Macnee et Linda Thorson pour un spot de publicité sur le champagne Laurent Périer. Le spot se fera, mais le producteur, Rodolph Roffi, est halluciné d'apprendre que la série n'est plus en production depuis longtemps ! Grâce à l'affection que la France a pour Mademoiselle King, la série va revenir ! Et cette fois avec de l'argent... français !

Ce mariage, qui va engendrer *The New Avengers*, ne sera pas forcément très heureux. Il commencera bien (saison 1) mais finira mal (saison 2), obligeant le Canada à consacrer le divorce... De courte durée. Si la collaboration France Angleterre n'a pas vraiment fonctionné, les français continueront pourtant d'aimer leurs héros british ! Grâce aux très nombreuses rediffusions, Emma Peel (qui a fini par devenir aussi populaire que Tara), Tara King et bien sûr John Steed vont continuer de s'insinuer dans le cœur du public. Jusqu'à la sortie, en 1993, de la série en vidéo. Un véritable feu d'artifice. Aucune série télé n'aura eu droit à une telle diffusion. Dans les grands magasins, on peut voir des colonnes de coffrets vidéo ! À Paris, une des plus grandes Fnac présente une authentique Bentley dont le coffre contient l'intégrale de la série ! Et malgré sa mise à prix plus que conséquente, elle sera vendue !

Oui, les français aiment *The Avengers* et les ventes de ces premiers coffrets vidéo vont le prouver. La même année, le plus beau cinéma de Paris, LE GRAND REX, organise une soirée *Avengers* avec 4 épisodes de la saison 4. Triomphe absolu, la salle de 2700 places est pleine à craquer. Peu de temps après, la chaîne de télévision France 3 décide de diffuser la saison 4 intégralement et en version originale sous-titrée dans le cadre de l'émission d'Alex Taylor, « Continentale ». La série est alors prétexte à un cours d'anglais. Le résultat, pour une diffusion à 9 heures du matin, dépasse toutes les espérances de la chaîne. Aussitôt France 3 enchaine avec les saisons 5 et 6 ! La popularité de la série est à son comble. Diana Rigg obtient enfin sa « vengeance » et fait la Une de trois magazines... Linda Thorson, elle, sera en couverture du très chic Télérama... L'aventure continue de rediffusions en rediffusions, jusqu'à ce que la chaîne Franco-Allemande ARTE achète les droits de diffusion. À ce jour, l'intégrale de la série, de Cathy Gale à Purdey, a été proposée 3 fois par cette chaine dont le rôle est de diffuser le meilleur de la culture...

Mais pourquoi la France aime-t-elle tant cette série britannique ? Sans doute la réponse se trouve-t-elle, mais ce n'est qu'un point de vue personnel, dans l'évident hédonisme qui régit les existences de Steed et ses ravissantes partenaires. Servir un dîner au champagne en plein milieu d'un champs (*All Done With Mirrors*), dessiner un somptueux festin au fusain et être capable de le faire apparaître en pleine nuit (*The Winged Avenger*) ou encore inventer la fontaine à champagne (*Who Was That Man I Saw You With ?*), voilà à quoi se livrent nos héros en fin de mission, après avoir vaincu une idéologie douteuse ou un mastermind dominateur ! Ils vont aussi voir des spectacles, dîner en ville en smoking et robe du soir, boivent de bons vins et font l'amour, bien entendu... mais cela bien sûr, est toujours hors caméra ! Même si fortement suggéré par une subtile mise en scène. Dans « *Caméra Meurtre* » (*Epic*), le couple décide finalement de passer la soirée à la maison ! Tout comme dans « *L'invasion des Terriens* » (*Invasion of the Earthmen*) Steed invite Tara à la « pratique » plutôt qu'à sortir... Mais il fallait être bien naïf pour ne pas comprendre la nature exacte des liens qui unissaient John à Emma et plus tard à Tara...

Élégance, voire haute couture, champagne et grands vins, art de la table et art... de vivre ! Le goût du plaisir poussé à l'extrême... Comment n'auraient-ils pu nous enchanter, ces agents britanniques aux valeurs finalement si françaises et si importantes à défendre, aujourd'hui plus que jamais.

1. EC : Deux magazines de télévision très populaires dans l'hexagone.

© Eric Cazalot

Eric Cazalot vit à Paris. Scénariste de télévision, romancier et auteur de biographies, il a publié un livre sur la série en 1994 : « Chapeau Melon & Bottes de Cuir : Irrespectueusement vôtre » aux éditions DLM. Son dernier livre est sorti le 5 novembre 2015, aux éditions de La Martinière, il s'agit de « Le Style Vartan » co écrit avec la célèbre chanteuse française Sylvie Vartan.

ROGER MARSHALL: AN INSIDER'S VIEW

Throughout the long history of *The Avengers*, only three script-writers created more than a dozen episodes: Brian Clemens, Roger Marshall and Philip Levene. Clemens and Marshall crossed the videotape/film divide and, between them, contributed half of the iconic Emma Peel monochrome season. While this final volume of *The Avengers on Film* relies on outsiders' viewpoints, I wanted to take this unique opportunity to interview my father and provide an Insider's View.

What is the 'timeless appeal' of *The Avengers*? After all, there were other well-made 1960s espionage shows such as *The Saint* and *Danger Man*, yet it is *The Avengers* which continues to be shown on television around the world more than fifty years on.
It was more individualistic and 'different'. It had the thrills and excitement of television drama, but also the wit and humour. It was probably the first successful mixture of thriller and comedy. At its peak its quality was unrivalled. You could always pull in a great cast, while the directors and set designers were outstanding. Getting Johnny Dankworth in to write the music was a terrific coup and then Laurie Johnson took the music to another level. Scoring individual episodes could only be done once success had arrived. Early directors such as Peter Hammond and Don Leaver created *The Avengers*' in-house style. Hammond, with his artistic background, had a terrifically visual eye, shooting through mirrors and from quirky angles, while Leaver as an ex-actor got the best possible performances out of the cast. [1]

What did casting a female as the co-lead add to the show?
A woman who was the intellectual and physical equal – if not superior – of her male partner...It was the first series to do so, as simple as that.

(Have there been many series since?) Suddenly it went in a different direction. I'm sure that for female viewers it added something new.

What were the advantages of the videotape era for a writer?
You were *physically* involved. You stayed for the rehearsals, even if the writer has to bow out at this stage. It evolved while you were watching. Sometimes you had a marvellous dress rehearsal followed by a less satisfactory 'live' recording. That is the ephemeral part or nature of television. Lethargy, perhaps? Or over-confidence? Nevertheless, at the recording there was an electric, 'Cup Final' atmosphere.

Film freed the show. How did this transform the writer's job?
It allowed us to go location hunting, something which could lead to story material for future episodes. In the case of *The Hour That Never Was* it was the location which led to the plot, rather than vice versa.

What did Diana Rigg bring to the table?
She was young, fresh. She took the show in a different direction, allowing the evolution to continue.

Why was the end of the videotape era and the beginning of the monochrome filmed one arguably the artistic pinnacle of the show? What went wrong later on?
In the case of Gale and Steed, by practising you get better, in terms of the on-screen rapport; a twosome doesn't bed in overnight. It takes time. Peel and Steed continued to develop the combination of humour and thrills. [2] However, *The Avengers* was always in danger of toppling over, of the wit/drama balance being lost and of camp taking over. Which it did. It also ran out of creative energy.

Were fellow script-writers jealous of those working on *The Avengers*?

It was something that *everyone* wanted to work on – actors, directors, writers. *The Avengers'* jobs tended to be 'nailed on'; not that many people got to work on the show.

You have created your own television dramas such as *Public Eye* and *Travelling Man*, but where does *The Avengers* rank in your television career?
Creating your own series is the ideal scenario. However, *The Avengers* is right at the top. When you've done that on a regular basis, it is a guarantee that you can work. It was tremendous.

Was Alfred Hitchcock a big influence on *The Avengers*, as Brian Clemens has suggested?
Yes. Those films of his which combined humour with thrills were highly influential.

Tell me about the problems of structuring an *Avengers* episode?
The Avengers is a three act play with a 'stinger' required at the end of each act. The teaser is there to whet your appetite and ensure that the viewer doesn't turn the television off or change channel. (With a half hour show such as the original *Danger Man* ones, it is like a three act play where you have to throw away the first act, funny as that might sound.)

***The Avengers* constantly evolved, but on-screen continuity was provided by Patrick Macnee in the role of John Steed. What are your personal memories of him? Why was he a perfect fit for the role?**
Patrick's acting style was more 'fly-by-the-seat' and 'off-the-cuff', rather than great preparation, which suited some directors more than others. After a couple of seasons, the role had evolved into Patrick's version of John Steed. He made it fit his own character and personality. A line frequently heard in the rehearsal room would be, "Steed wouldn't say

that!" and the writer or director would reply, "Well what do *you* think Steed would say, Pat?" Patrick became the number one authority on Steed, the character's co-creator. Steed had steel and a darker side in the videotape era; his relationship with Cathy Gale was more edgy or confrontational, partly because the two actors were similar ages. With his subsequent, younger female partners it became more paternal. His mellowing on film would no doubt have been influenced by American television. As a spy and a secret agent, Steed's attitude was, "The rules are for you, not me." It had to be, if he was to survive.

How would you label *The Avengers*? Why did it survive for the entire 1960s decade?
Tongue-in-cheek drama. It continually evolved, almost by itself.

© Roger Marshall and Rodney Marshall (Telephone interview on October 7th 2015)

1. What a great shame Hammond never directed a filmed episode and that Leaver – who felt unwelcome in Season 4 – soon departed.
2. Macnee and Rigg look so comfortable together in *The Town of No Return,* which launched the first filmed season. However, it had been re-made mid-production and they arguably look less at ease in *The Murder Market*. Even so, I would suggest that their wonderful on-screen chemistry was swiftly established.

AVENGERS REMEMBERED

by Raymond Austin, aka Ray Austin

I remember a time in England when on an *Avengers* night you could not get people to leave their homes. Even the pubs had a noticeable drop in trade on those nights. In the work place next day, fans would talk over the plot and what Steed and Emma Peel had been up to. *The Avengers* was the only British series to have the distinction of being networked at prime time in the United States. It was, without question, one of the most popular television series ever produced and has etched its name indelibly into television history, and with it the names of Brian Clemens, Patrick Macnee, and Diana Rigg.

I was the man behind the fights and the action on the show. 'Stunt Coordinator' they would have called me now. Back in those days I did most of the fights and stunts for ATV and Thames Television. [1] They had the only long running television series showing at that time. I can remember going from one studio to another . . . a fight here, a fall there. At night I would turn a car over, then go home, book two more stunt men, and we would be jumping off a building the next day. With *The Avengers*, it was Patrick Macnee's wife at that time, Katie Woodville, who told Patrick about me and my skills as a stunt man.

The Avengers was the show that put me on the map as a director, that and Roy Rossotti, the director of the episode *The Bird Who Knew Too Much*. Rossotti messed it up and was fired and, as second unit director, Brian Clemens had me take over, finish and repair the episode. I now had my name on my chair. [2] When *The New Avengers* came into being, I was one of the full time directors and eventually went on location to Canada, as Coordinating Producer/Director.

I played parts in many of *The Avengers* episodes, always the second or third baddie, and always with a fight or stunt attached to my part, thanks to Brian Clemens. Brian, the man behind *The Avengers*, was the main writer and producer of the show. Without him, there would not have been an *Avengerland*. Why one of the networks did not get hold of Clemens years later and say, "Come make *The Avengers* for us again!" I will never know. We were before our time, thanks to Brian. We were class, and Patrick Macnee gave the show that class. Brian had to put it on the page week after week with his other writers. It was no small task honing his co-writers to keep the plots fresh and absorbing. Patrick dressed it up with his immaculate characterisation of John Steed Esq. Steed was always so slick and debonair; nothing ever fazed him and he took everything in his stride. So did our Patrick.

He tiptoed around his first leading lady Honor Blackman, tailoring his Steed to fit a niche that would bounce back off her rather sophisticated Cathy Gale. That was the true beginning of *The Avengers*, the live black and white shows. After its initial success, it moved from its live taped form to monochrome film and then glorious colour.

Now Patrick had a new leading lady. He again took his Steed and fashioned him a tad differently for Elizabeth Shepherd. He seemed to keep her at a distance on screen, which worked so well for his performance. Off screen everything was chummy. Sadly, Elizabeth was never seen by the *Avengers* audience. A super lady but not the right one for Brian or the network. Elizabeth was replaced, and went on to do nice things in the theatre.

The search started for Steed's next Emma Peel. I will never forget the young, pretty Diana Rigg walking out on the stage to meet me. You see, as well as testing a dialogue scene with Patrick, she, like all of the other ladies, had to do a fight scene with me. I had had a week of this with different actresses, and was black and blue. Enter Diana. Tall, good figure, legs that seemed to go on forever. That's why the fights looked so good, not thanks to my orchestrating. I was over the moon. From my point of view, she was reliable in her fight test. Meaning that if I told her to hit me with a right she did not surprise me and land a left from out of the blue. The bosses looked at her test and she became the one and only Emma Peel. Patrick again did a clever adaptation with his Steed, and the whole of our viewing audience waited for him to fall for Emma and her for him. There was a strange underlying current between them. This had never happened with the other ladies that came to the show. I think Brian would have admitted, he never tailored any of the scripts this way until he saw the warmth start to generate in certain scenes. From then on, Brian let little things happen. Even the press and television weeklies kept on about it, 'When are they going to kiss?' When Emma was in trouble, Steed was at his best. Patrick and Diana were super together. I am still surprised that they never did a play or something in later years. [3] Diana has become a great talent. I knew she would be, from the first time she threw me down the stairs!

The sad day came, when Diana was ready to move on. She wanted to spread her wings and play something other than Emma Peel and she has. There was a lot of resentment behind the scenes. *The Avengers* had given Diana Rigg her big break and now she was turning her back on it. There was talk of the show folding. However, as Brian Clemens once said, the show was not about Emma Peel, it was about Steed: "Pat carries the show." And he was right. Tara King was born. Enter Linda Thorson. This was a fun and very spirited young lady. Steed lived on, and so did *The Avengers*; not for too long, though.

Later we returned when Brian turned us into *The New Avengers*. This time Purdey came on the scene: Joanna Lumley, though very different from the one we see in *Absolutely Fabulous*. Did I say Diana had long legs? Ha! Although the show had the word *New* in the title, it was basically the same show, as it was intended to be. Steed was still the Kingpin and the series was tailored around him. [4] Joanna was sexy and hardworking; her action scenes were more than the other girls had ever had to cope with. She *was* Purdey. All of England and Paris knew about the 'Purdey haircut' and were copying it. Joanna took us back to stockings and suspender belts. From time to time we would get a glimpse of stocking tops and cami-knickers as she twirled around in a fight, or kicked out at the bad guys. They were fun days. Patrick, Brian, Joanna, Gareth. [5] I will always remember fondly my stops at Patrick's dressing room; the champagne was being poured freely and plentifully after the day's shoot. The best vintage.

When I was making the show, whether as a stunt director or director, I always knew *The Avengers* was a marvellous, humorous adventure, with a satirical view of life. The female was dominant over the criminals, week after week. Clad in kinky boots and leather, or a cat-suit, she annihilated all the bad guys, and was always an equal to Steed. This is the one ingredient that is not in a lot of the current shows. Everyone seems to be worried if the male lead is bigger than the female and vice-versa. Is her part bigger than mine? Is he too dominant? Is she? And so on.

Remember, Patrick as Steed rarely carried a gun. He didn't need one to give him the balls that the show had. He was forever brandishing his umbrella instead. If only we could make it again.

© Raymond Austin

1. Both of these were ITV television franchise holders. ATV provided the service at weekends for the London region between 1955 and 1968, and a seven day a week service for the Midlands region from 1968 until 1982. Thames Television served the London region on week days between 1968 until 1992. Thames was the result of a forced merger between the Associated British Corporation and Rediffusion.
2. In fact, Peter Graham Scott started out as director of the episode according to *Bowler Hats and Kinky Boots*, p. 197. Austin went on to direct episodes for a number of cult British shows, including *The Saint*, *The Baron*, *The Champions*, *Department S*, *Randall and Hopkirk (Deceased)*, and *The Professionals*, before directing episodes for US shows *Hawaii-Five-0*, *Hart to Hart*, *Quincy, M.E.*, and *Magnum, P.I.* (and many other prime time network shows and pilots.)
3. Macnee did appear in an episode of Rigg's 1973 American sitcom, *Diana,* before *The New Avengers*.
4. Austin's comments suggest that he didn't feel that Steed was being marginalised in *The New Avengers* series. His suggestion that the new series was simply an extension or continuation of the original is more controversial, and is at odds with director Robert Fuest, who felt that this was a very different (and inferior) show.
5. RA: May Gareth rest in peace but with lots of laughter. RM: Austin's essay was written before Patrick Macnee passed away.

PATRICK MACNEE: 'THE WORLD'S FAVOURITE ENGLISH GENT'

When the news broke on 25th June 2015 that the actor Patrick Macnee, known the world over as John Steed of *The Avengers*, had died at the grand old age of 93, I really didn't want to believe it. I'm sure I was not alone in hoping that this news was some unpleasant internet hoax, and that Patrick was still alive and well – but of course, this was not to be. We all go in the end, even the marvellous Mr Macnee.

His passing felt particularly poignant as, in the early months of 2015, I had spent a significant amount of time working with fellow *Avengers* fans Christine Stutz and Denis Kirsanov on a website devoted to Patrick. Launched on 6th February to mark the occasion of his 93rd birthday, *The World of Patrick Macnee* (http://www.the-world-of-patrick-macnee.com/) was set up to provide a place at which information and imagery from his long life and career could be collected and shared freely. We hoped maybe to interview Patrick for the website, but it was not to be and our work will now stand as the most complete record of his considerable legacy.

It could be said that Patrick was an actor in the Cary Grant mould, in that when a director hired him, they knew exactly what they would be getting – Patrick Macnee – and that was a positive, not a negative. Patrick was always humble about his acting abilities, even suggesting that in some roles, including that of John Steed, there was no great dividing line between actor and part. When interviewed in September 2003 by IGN UK, he typically downplayed his achievements:

'Most parts that you think you'd do well, most other people don't. So they offer you something; *The Avengers* is a good example… I fitted into that because I came from that sort of background. It's not even acting. But of course I'd like to have been the greatest Hamlet, Macbeth, and everything in between, but I wasn't.'

It is probably fair to say that Patrick was never a character actor, not someone who you'd see in a film or television role underneath layers of make-up and wonder who it was you were watching, because Patrick for the most part played himself twisted this way or that, and he was so distinctive. When asked about his accomplishments in the same 2003 interview, Patrick's response was hardly what the interviewer had expected from an actor with such a wealth of experience:

'Accomplishment is such a patronising, dangerous word, isn't it? I haven't really accomplished anything. The most accomplished thing I've done is to have lived this long.'

Patrick may have truly believed that he had achieved nothing of particular note, but his screenography and list of theatre credits suggest otherwise. There can't, for instance, be a great many actors who have worked with the legendary director Alfred Hitchcock and then been called back for a second production almost immediately (Patrick featured in two 1959 episodes of *Alfred Hitchcock Presents*, both of which were directed by 'Hitch' himself) or who have played Dr. Watson three times on television (alongside Roger Moore in 1976 and Christopher Lee in 1991-2) before graduating to the role of Sherlock Holmes (in *The Hound of London*, 1993). During his television and film career, Patrick worked in many different countries, including the USA,

Canada, Australia and Europe, and of course enjoyed a long-running association with *The Avengers*, a series which was a worldwide smash hit as much through his hard work and star appeal as through that of anyone else.

Patrick was a fine performer, a wonderful interpreter of dialogue and scene, who would imbue each character he played with a magnetism that drew in the camera and audience alike. Despite this, he was always generous and accommodating with co-stars, guest artistes and crew both on screen and off, recognising that he was but a cog in the mechanism of production, albeit a vital one who knew his value.

Had the cards fallen in a different way for him, he could easily have been a major star in feature films, but destiny held for him a different path leading towards international fame. It was one that he clearly did not foresee, thinking in 1961 that his future would place him behind the camera in a production capacity. That his production credits are today viewed as but a footnote in his career, when he was convinced that with his work on *The Valiant Years* he had finally found his niche, shows that one can never tell the twists and turns of life and career.

When Patrick was offered the role of John Steed in *The Avengers*, he could never have guessed that this second-string role alongside lead actor Ian Hendry would lead to his likeness being identifiable the world over, or for people to come to view him fondly as the archetypal Englishman gentleman.

To begin with, though, he struggled to find the character, it being somewhat under-developed within the pages of the scripts. In his '*Avengers* autobiography' *The Avengers and Me* (Titan Books, 1997), he revealed that, 'I hadn't actually thought about Steed in any great detail until, after about two or three episodes, [ABC Drama Supervisor] Sydney Newman called me into his office and forced me to take stock of my position.' Told to think hard about how to bring the character to life, Macnee drew on a variety of sources to concoct a distinctive persona for John Steed, including his father Daniel, his wartime commanding officer Bussy Carr, Sir Percy Blakeney – 'the Scarlet Pimpernel' – and Ralph Richardson's remarkable turn in the 1939 film *Q Planes*.

'I thought of the Regency days – the most flamboyant, sartorially, for men – and I imagined Steed in waisted jackets and embroidered waistcoats. Steed I was stuck with as a name, and it stayed. Underneath he was steel. Outwardly he was charming and vain and representative, I suppose, of the kind of Englishman who is more valued abroad. The point about Steed was that he led a fantasy life – a hero dressed like a junior cabinet minister. An Old Etonian whose most lethal weapon was the hallmark of the English gentleman – a furled umbrella.' (*The Ultimate Avengers*, Boxtree, 1995)

As the sixties decade progressed, Patrick went from being Ian Hendry's sterling support to series lead, becoming one of the top star actors working in Independent Television (ITV). The burgeoning success of *The Avengers*, which by 1965 was a hit in many parts of the world as well as at home in the United Kingdom, turned Patrick from a little-known jobbing actor into a household name just about anywhere that televisions and households were to be found.

Patrick proved to be the perfect choice for John Steed, and from a modern standpoint it is difficult to imagine or accept anyone else in the role, particularly in the visual media, so indelible is the mark that he left on the role. Part of this difficulty is because for more than fifty years Patrick seemed to be playing Steed in real life, even when the show itself was many years in the past as a going concern. When studying his numerous appearances on chat shows and other such programmes, one can be forgiven for seeing Steed's influence in Patrick's own demeanour, though of course the reality is that Steed was an extension of the actor. However, as Patrick himself has suggested, it is sometimes difficult to identify where the dividing line falls between actor and part; audiences often blur those divisions in any case and see the character ahead of the performer, even in situations that are clearly not fictional.

Perhaps Patrick stayed with *The Avengers* for too long, at least from the perspective of his career. Major film roles did come, for instance in *The Sea Wolves* (1980), *This is Spinal Tap* (1984) and the James Bond thriller *A View to a Kill* (1985), but for the most part his work beyond *The Avengers* was confined to television and the stage. He regarded his greatest work as being in the Broadway production of Anthony Shaffer's *Sleuth*, in which from July 1972 he took on the role of mystery writer Andrew Wyke, which had previously been played to great acclaim by Anthony Quayle. The 16-month run met with positive reviews and Patrick's contribution was much fêted. When writing in *TV Times* magazine in 1976 as part of the pre-publicity for *The New Avengers*, Patrick revealed that, 'I believe *Sleuth* was my personal turning point as an actor. I think it made me stronger. For the first time in years, I realised I could do more than lift a bowler and dash about as Steed.'

In later years, with Patrick having set up permanent home in California, his occasional visits home to England became something for his fans there to look forward to. He occasionally featured in British productions, such as *Nancherrow* (1999), in which he was reunited with his co-star from *The New Avengers*, Joanna Lumley. For the most part, however, his returns home seemed to be for promotional reasons, occasionally to tie-in with screenings or home video releases of *The Avengers*, or to embark upon book-signing tours for titles that he had co-written, such as his autobiography *Blind in One Ear* (Harrap, 1988). Patrick would even occasionally revive the role of Steed, either in commercials for appropriate products such as Laurent-Perrier Champagne, or in television programmes such as *The Hardy Boys* (1978). This latter appearance, in which he portrayed a Steed-like character by the name of 'S', is arguably the most brazen of the 'John Steed in all but name' entries in Patrick's screenography. He also featured in a cameo role as Invisible Jones in the ill-starred 1998 Warner Bros feature film *The Avengers*. As the character name implies, the role was heard but not seen, and by providence, of all the actors trying to scrub the film from their list of credits, he was the one in the best position to do so, having supplied only his voice!

Although he rarely stopped working in the years after he had finally left *The Avengers* behind him, enjoying success on the stage, television and the big screen, Patrick Macnee will forever be remembered as John Steed. The actress Julie Walters once said that, 'I can understand why people get annoyed at being remembered for one thing, but a lot of actors aren't remembered for anything,' and the fact is that while Patrick maybe considered himself an also-ran as an actor, that one role, played to perfection week-to-week for a decade and then some, has caused him to be remembered, loved and admired for half a century. He lived to nigh on a century himself, and it is not impossible to imagine that he will remain a recognisable and much-loved figure for at least that time again. As long as *The Avengers* prevails, Patrick Macnee's quintessential Englishman will prevail also, and in the opinion of this author, he will never be eclipsed in the role that he made into a worldwide cultural icon.

© Alan Hayes

AFTERWORD: MONOCHROME VERSUS COLOUR; EMMA VERSUS TARA; *NEW* AVENGERS OR NEW *AVENGERS*: ETERNAL INTERNET DEBATES

With any long-running television drama series there will, inevitably, be comparisons made between the various seasons or vintages. In the case of a show such as *Doctor Who*, every critic and fan has his or her own view of each reinvention and reinterpretation of the Time Lord. With *Blake's 7*, did the post-Blake world 'work' in Terry Nation's space dystopia? Does the final season of *The Sweeney* suggest that the series' shockingly new approach had run out of steam? Were the surreal and playful elements introduced in that final run welcome, innovative aspects or simply out of place in a hard-hitting police drama? Analytical debate sees individuals' highly subjective discourses meet and frequently clash, but critical opinion is healthy. Without it, television producers could simply sit on successful drama formulas and constantly churn them out, allowing once-fresh approaches to stagnate.

Stagnate is not something which *The Avengers* can be accused of. It constantly evolved in terms of its cast/lead characters, style and its recording format: from videotape (multi-camera set-up), to monochrome 35mm film (single camera) and finally 'Glorious Technicolor'; from Keel/Steed, Gale/Steed, Peel/Steed, to the triumvirates of Mother/Tara/Steed and Purdey/Gambit/Steed; from a gritty realism via Op Art, Pop Art, pastiche and surrealism towards something far harder to define.

It seems foolish and unhelpful to compare *The Avengers* pre/post film. The studio stricture of 'live' videotape with its budgetary, time and space constraints and heavy, unwieldy cameras meant that the first three seasons can never look or sound as good as the later era, however talented the actors and writers were, and despite the wonderfully creative innovations of the directors and set designers. As Darren Burch has commented, 'It lacks the film polish on a technical level' despite being 'more creative in other aspects.' [1] The limitations of the Teddington recordings belong to a vanished age, a totally different world from the freedom of film.

Is it controversial to suggest that the single monochrome film run represents the creative pinnacle of the show? Most critics see this crossroads season – caught between videotape and colour – as the artistic high point of *The Avengers*. The narrative complexity and variety, the wit, subtlety and playfulness of *The Town of No Return, The Murder Market, Death at Bargain Prices, The Hour That Never Was, Too Many Christmas Trees* and *The Cybernauts* set a benchmark for the series that would be hard to match. 'Badger hunting' on the Norfolk sand dunes, time standing still in a deserted airbase, disturbing festive dreams, wine glass duels in a bank cellar ... a stylish, unsettling *Avengerland* was firmly established. The season also polished a winning formula and structure, in the best traditions of Greek tragedy: Teaser (*Prologue*); Three Acts (*Episodes*); Commercial Breaks (*Stasimons*); Tag (*Exode*). The simplicity of the delightful tag scenes – as Steed and Emma head off towards another bright horizon – demonstrated that 'less is more'. While the colour Peel run would prove to be more popular in commercial terms, for many critics some of the subtle charm and *film noir* menace was lost.

Diabolical debate comes into play in the candy-coloured world of *Avengerland*. The first potential problem highlighted by many critics is a perceived dumbing down of the series' subtlety as it luxuriated in its new world, creating a self-referential comic strip in which 'style' dominated. While some critics such as Lauren Humphries-Brooks see this as an interesting development towards 'pastiche', others see it as self-serving. Alan Hayes suggests that while the monochrome Peel season represents 'the high water mark', the Peel colour run is 'the absolute nadir of the series. Formulaic, predictable and lacking in the invention and variety of its predecessor.' [2] Jaz Wiseman agrees, describing the colour Peel era as 'the absolute worst of all. Formulaic to the point of boring, silly beyond necessary, style over substance but actually not particularly stylish but very stylised.' [3] Part of the debate is whether John Steed and Emma Peel's wonderful rapport had simply developed to the ultimate degree or whether it had become 'too stylised and knowing'. [4] Wiseman senses that, given both the popularity and critical acclaim of the initial filmed season, the producers should have 'stuck with the ingredients that were working so well.' [5] This opens up an interesting point. Having constantly evolved, should the series have stood still once it reached this artistic peak? (How was the production team to know that things would never be better?) Or should it have continued experimenting and venturing into new territory? Did colour encourage the producers, writers and directors to focus on the 'look' and style of the series, at the cost of plot and 'substance'? Undoubtedly, in my opinion. The initial batch of episodes in Season 5 is disappointingly bland and there seems to be a crisis of identity. Later, a number of episodes are Cathy Gale remakes, while others push the envelope out in a bid to employ a metafictional layer, as in *The Winged Avenger* and *Epic*. Was the reworking of Gale-era episodes a playful way of connecting to the past, and paying homage to the show's roots? Or was it a case of the creative well running dry? Either way, it does not sit comfortably with the idea of 'making it new'. The episodes which threaten to collapse the fourth wall are genuinely experimental, within the show's formula. However, that does not necessarily make them interesting dramatically.

One problem with the Peel colour season which is rarely talked about is the way in which Diana Rigg/Emma Peel tends to dominate. It is her *outré* costumes which dazzle in colour, rather than Steed's more traditional attire. It is no coincidence that three of the episodes which have gained the most acclaim are virtual Emma one-handers – *Epic, The Joker* and *Murdersville* – while Season 5 only offers us a single Steed-dominated outing. Peel's boast in *Epic* that she is "the star of this picture" resonates beyond that particular episode. The season offers us a fair amount of what JZ Ferguson calls 'Emma spotlighting'. [6] (This is hardly surprising, given her talent, screen presence and beauty.) While some critics see the second Steed/Peel season as bringing perfection to their on-screen rapport, I sense that the wonderful balance between the co-leads was being lost. In addition, while Technicolor *Avengerland* dazzles us, there is, I believe, also a sense of loss. The *film noir* feel of the previous run – what webmaster David K Smith describes as its 'dark, stylish imagery and subtle *avant garde* touches' (*The Avengers Forever!*) – had made way for something closer to *Batman* than Hitchcock. Of course this is a generalisation. There are a number of memorable Peel colour adventures which make the most of the rainbow world which *Avengerland* was now being painted in: *Who's Who???, Death's Door, Something Nasty in the Nursery* and *You Have Just Been Murdered* among others. These avoid the need to rework old scripts or journey too far down the navel-gazing of metafiction. PURRR's cat sanctuary corridor set in *The Hidden Tiger* is a glorious example of the set designers' colourful creations. The accusation of the series becoming formulaic or stale was one thrown out at the time and is still used today. This is, no doubt, a result of a decision which Jaz Wiseman regrets:

'All the previous series were building on ideas, getting better in every department, but with the introduction of colour the producers took the decision to basically cut the creative writing team to two people, deciding that sending itself up was the future and that 'style' was everything.' [7]

With Brian Clemens' single-minded vision of *Avengerland* now dominating and dictating, writers like Roger Marshall and Tony Williamson were badly missed, [8] as were innovative directors such as Don Leaver and Roy Ward Baker. Darren Burch goes as far as to suggest that 'I don't think many of the directors that season were good enough for the show.' [9] A greater variety of writers and directors would be employed on the Tara King run and, arguably, it shows.

As Frank Hui notes, the single topic which is most divisive among *Avengers* fans and critics is the Tara King (extended) season. Both Alan Hayes and Jaz Wiseman see it as 'a return to form', while Lauren Humphries-Brooks laments both the characterisation of Steed's new co-lead and the stories themselves as 'reinforcing gender, cultural, and sexual categories with few of the subversive aspects inherent in earlier incarnations.' [10] Sunday Swift agrees, stating that 'the gender inversion that was a cornerstone of the programme...is erased entirely.' [11] Nor was Patrick Macnee happy with the show's new gender dynamics:

'She arrived just as *The Avengers* was losing its appeal. Her character loved Steed but I always thought that was a bad idea. The show was so much better with Steed and his leading lady as sparring equals, without the woman being subservient, but with Linda it leaned that way.' (*Daily Express*, 09/10/2010)

It was Linda Thorson's idea to play the character that way and so, unsurprisingly, her own views on the Season 6 gender debate are the opposite of Macnee's; she recently suggested that the shift freed him up to play an excitingly new role, that of a 'romantic lead' (BBC Radio 4 *Today* programme, 26/06/2015). I'm not convinced that this gear change was a progressive one.

I can understand Humphries-Brooks' argument that both the plots and Tara King's characterisation veer wildly. Subordinate? Pupil? Equal? Lover? Both Humphries-Brooks and Swift sense that Steed had changed, forced into 'a more foppish, action-orientated masculinity that does not suit him.' [12] There is certainly an inconsistency in the portrayal of both lead characters and in terms of the style of the episodes themselves. In part — but only in part — this is explained by the production chaos explored in *Anticlockwise* and elsewhere. Linda Thorson's inexperience also came into play, forcing Clemens to introduce Mother as the sturdy boss for Steed to bounce his banter off. Did this, as some have suggested — including Thorson — undermine the female lead actor/character? Or did it add an intriguing and comically subversive extra layer to the mix? I think it's unhelpful to come down on either side of the Mother debate. At times he and his ever-changing sets are welcome additions; at others — *Wish You Were Here* springs to mind — they are annoying distractions. Mother offered a nod to the bosses of Steed's videotape past but also formed part of the series' continuing evolution. Far better — I would suggest — to have this larger-than-life figure, seen against all his glorious backdrops, than hear a number of Peel-era anonymous bosses snarling and barking unseen down the telephone in infantile cartoon-style.

It is easy to criticise the Tara King era: Linda Thorson lacked Diana Rigg's experience, poise and feline grace; Tara's character is inconsistent; the season began and ran for some time amidst production chaos and unrest which filters on to the small-screen; there are a handful of fairly awful episodes... However, the use of a number of new writers and directors – like Jeremy Burnham and Robert Fuest – breathed new life and genuine style back into the show. As I have suggested elsewhere, when Thorson was given a decent wigless wardrobe and the chance to be set free, such as in *All Done With Mirrors,* her capabilities are amply demonstrated. The criticism of an inconsistency and unevenness in terms of the storylines is a valid one, but it refers to the Peel candy-coloured world as well. Even in the 'perfect' world of Season 4, the writers were occasionally guilty of one-dimensional writing: too straight (*Room Without A View*), too serious (*The House That Jack Built*), or too silly (*How to Succeed ... at Murder*).

I don't think that the Peel colour era is as stylishly clever as some critics believe, nor the Tara King season as 'conservative' as others suggest. Cathy Gale, Emma Peel and Tara King all had cerebral strengths and physical prowess, but all three were manipulated by Steed and coerced into joining his adventures. At its best, the Tara era stories offer a genuine dramatic undercurrent devoid of the 'style-over-substance' of the previous season; at its worst they portray a crisis of identity. The introduction of location filming outside the co-leads' apartments allowed Steed's Stable Mews and Tara's Crescent to become four-dimensional worlds and the latter was, arguably, the best 'permanent' set in the entire series. Tara's continuing popularity in mainland Europe – particularly France – and the colour Peel fascination for many English-speaking fans suggests that there is something for everyone in candy-coloured *Avengerland*.

The emergence of *The New Avengers* in the mid-1970s once again has divided opinion. Does this represent two additional mini-seasons of *The Avengers*? Or a new series entirely? I've always thought of it as belonging to the overall dynasty but also maintaining a certain independence. As I have suggested in previous volumes, it is by its very title both *New* and *Avengers*. Why choose between the two? It takes the triumvirate character structure of the King era a step further. It also allows ordinary people to tiptoe into *Avengerland*. Its music, cars, clothes and locations are decidedly mid-1970s. And yet it recaptures the spirit of the original in so many ways while offering 'thicker cardboard'. Was Steed's character marginalised, turning him into a Mother figure? Not in my opinion, even though – by his own admission – Patrick Macnee was no longer capable of the physical performances of the 1960s. It would have looked silly anyway to have him take on the fighting. What emerges is an older, nurturing Steed, a role which the Tara era had prepared him for. The Purdey/Gambit/Steed rapport is as good as any in the show's history. Filming abroad – a financial/contractual necessity – was always going to take the show away from its geographical and spiritual home, but foreign investment had dictated (to a certain if unknown extent) throughout the filmed era. Mini-season 2 will always – collectively speaking – remain in the first run's shadow in terms of quality control, but fans of the original series who ignore, deny or avoid *The New Avengers* are missing out, in my opinion. Ultimately, what tends to define individual critical opinion on the 1970s remake is whether or not the viewer encountered *The New Avengers* before the original. [13]

Ultimately, the artistic pinnacle of Season 4 left the subsequent seasons with an almost impossible task: to improve on near-perfection. Simply carry on in the same style and vein and you will be accused of standing still, of stagnation. Continue to evolve and people will lament the loss of their favourite vintage. Polish the 'look' and it can become stylised; change the balance and characters and you will upset many of the viewers. We should be thankful for the evolution – both linear and cyclical – because somewhere along the way lies the ideal episode or season for each of us. If the chapters in this book and the four previous volumes have made you want to revisit the 'films' themselves or re-energise online debates then the past eighteen months of researching, writing and editing have been worthwhile.

Ultimately, what makes the series such a delight is its unique blend of ingredients: the fine acting of its lead actors and guests; the mix of the real and the surreal; the light, frothy, witty humour contrasting with and sometimes merging with the darker dramatic undercurrents; the innovative writing and direction; the visual delights of *outré* sets and deserted, atmospheric, brooding locations; the aural pleasure of Laurie Johnson's scores. *The Avengers* goes beyond genre and resists labelling. It is a series of its time and yet somehow out of time. Over fifty years old, its charm lives on.

© Rodney Marshall

1. Darren Burch, *The Avengers: The International Fan Forum: Bowlers, Brollies and Banter*, April 23rd 2015.
2. Alan Hayes, *The Avengers International Fan Forum*, April 18th 2015.
3. Jaz Wiseman, *The Avengers International Fan Forum*, April 17th 2015.
4. Darren Burch, *The Avengers International Fan Forum*, April 15th 2015.
5. Jaz Wiseman, *The Avengers International Fan Forum*, April 17th 2015.

6. JZF: The use of the 'star of this picture' quote is particularly apt. Emma was one of the main draws for me personally when I first discovered the series (with Season 5), and I've met many people who, when reminded of the series, immediately think of Emma, and no wonder - she's a wonderful character. But as much as I love Emma, I now find her single-hander episodes lack something. So much of the joy of the Peel-era *Avengers* comes from the Steed/Peel dynamic, and the solo stories lose that. For that reason, I do not place the solo Emma stories among my favourites, even though they are often well-made (*The House that Jack Built, The Joker*). They lack a critical mass of the Steed/Peel spark. The same goes for solo Steed stories. Ironically, I think a lot of the Tara stories work better when the leads are split, because the Steed/Tara dynamic works less well. This demonstrates the degree to which the characters influence an episode's success, regardless of the plot.
7. Jaz Wiseman, *The Avengers International Fan Forum*, April 17th 2015.
8. Roger Marshall penned two episodes, one which was a remake and one partially rewritten by Brian Clemens; Tony Williamson wrote just one. These were the writers who had brought us a host of 'four bowler films': *Dial A Deadly Number, The Hour That Never Was, Silent Dust, The Danger Makers, The Murder Market,* and *Too Many Christmas Trees*.
9. Darren Burch, *The Avengers International Fan Forum*, April 17th 2015.
10. *Anticlockwise*, p. 415.
11. *Anticlockwise*, p. 317.
12. *Anticlockwise*, p. 317.
13. As a broad generalisation, viewers who encountered *The New Avengers* first seem to have a more 'open mind' about the 1970s series. This is, of course, a potentially dangerous stereotype or generalisation on my part.

APPENDICES

THE AVENGERS & THE COLD WAR

Palmer: If the blackout area increased – or worse still, embraced the whole screen...
Emma: We would be in trouble?
Palmer: A missile attack could be launched on this country without any warning whatsoever until it was too late. (*The Gravediggers*)

As the term implies, the 'Cold War' refers to a period of political and military tension, rather than any direct physical conflict. Expert commentators cannot agree on when it started nor on its duration – 1947-1991? [1] – nor which major super-power was more to blame. Many 'Orthodox' Western historians point the proverbial finger at the Soviet Union; 'Revisionists' tend to focus on the United States' attempts to isolate the USSR after World War 2; 'Post-revisionists' prefer to offer a more nuanced argument. Post-war, the Soviet Union was frequently portrayed in the United States as an autocratic, ever-dangerous Communist 'factory' churning out propaganda and spies in a desire to undermine capitalism through psychological and clandestine, intelligence-gathering 'warfare'. However, even a cursory examination of McCarthyism reveals a United States spying on its own, with the Government attempting to silence dissenting cultural voices. Any playwrights, musicians, film-makers, designers, journalists, etc., whose work appeared to carry a critique of consumerism or capitalism ran the risk of accusations of Communism. It was, as Arthur Miller famously portrayed it in *The Crucible*, a witch hunt. The 'Hollywood Blacklists' threatened people's livelihoods. The film studios' denial that blacklists existed suggests that lies, paranoia and the Government's desire for complete control had created a Big Brother cultural climate not totally dissimilar to that in Communist Russia. It calls into question any simplistic East/West polarities. How can this US state surveillance of the individual fit in with the key, core American notions of personal freedom and freedom of the media? [2]

The interconnected Cold War themes of espionage/invasion and the threat of nuclear warfare fascinated writers of fiction and became major themes in the immediate post-war decades. *Avengers* writers picked up on these, particularly in the monochrome Peel season where a number of episodes draw on Cold War threats in their plots. However, in typical *Avengers* style, the series usually refuses to take the subject seriously. For example, the initial interest in a failing early warning radar system – in *The Gravediggers* – is soon forgotten as the absurd Sir Horace Winslip and his fantasy railway-land dominate. *The Hour That Never Was* is all about creating a puzzlingly disturbing atmosphere in a deserted airfield, not about the risk of military men being brainwashed by the 'other side'. The invasion in *The Town of No Return* – "Wipe out the old population and replace them with your own." – is simply absurd, given the snail speed of its town-by-town take-over plan. The biggest threat in terms of a nuclear disaster comes from a businessman determined to prove that he is not out-of-date. However, Horatio Kane's department store atom bomb is used by Emma Peel as a source of humour:

Steed: What would Pinters want with an atom bomb anyway?
Emma: Perhaps they intend mushrooming out. Expanding.

Clemens' storyline reflects a belief that the *Avengers* viewer wanted thrilling escapism or fantasy, rather than anything which seriously engaged with contemporary politics. Characters with ideological convictions – such as Colonel Rawlings who clings fondly to the concept of a British Empire – are delusional figures to be laughed at. Comrade Olga's loyalty to the Motherland in *The Correct Way to Kill* is seen as out-of-place and dangerously naïve in a cloak-and-dagger world of double and triple agents more interested in power, fame or financial gain than ideals.

There are, of course, an array of Russian or Eastern Bloc characters in *The Avengers*. Some, such as Brodny and Shaffer, are comedy figures of fun. Others, including Ezdorf and Arcos, are darker figures, but they too are admirers of John Steed and share his love of the good things in life. One could argue that Brodny's desire to stay in England and continue to enjoy 'decadent' Western culture is a critique of an unrealistic Communist ideology. The series gently pokes fun, presenting most of its Russian characters as stereotypes: openly critical of capitalism's decadence but secretly loving it. Between Steed and his Russian adversaries there exists a cordiality, despite their mutual mistrust.

In addition, if *The Avengers* takes a gently satirical dig at Russian envy of Western greed, it is equally cynical about British politics. Both Steed and Mrs. Peel admire yet mock Stapley's spin-doctoring in *Death's Door* – "Stapley can't help telling half-truths. He's in constant touch with politicians." – while we find out that Dr. Armstrong was mistrusted at the Ministry of Defence because he sought out peaceful solutions: "Armstrong refused to toe the official line. He felt we should be 'constructive' instead of destructive. Had some crazy idea about building a machine to clear debris from radioactive areas." *The Cybernauts* is a rare episode in that it offers us genuine ideological debate about contemporary society and politics in the new push-button age of Cold War:

Armstrong: If I can prevent the ultimate catastrophe.
Steed: But at what price? A Cybernetic police force? People aren't machines. Of *course* they're fallible. *That's* what makes them human!

Armstrong and Steed's fascinating debate revolves around which extreme we consider to be more acceptable: the (relative) safety of Government by automation, which Steed refers to as "electronic dictatorship", or the danger/freedom of our current society. Armstrong warns him:

"That's the trouble with 'man'. Such an impulsive creature. Cannot cope with crises. Today, one wrong decision, one simple error, could bring complete destruction."

Magnificently acted out by Michael Gough and Patrick Macnee, it is a spellbinding philosophical and political argument broken into two parts, in which Steed seems to be arguing that it is, ultimately, mankind's flaws which make human society interesting. [3]

In the 'thicker cardboard' world of *The New Avengers*, the biggest danger in terms of a warhead hitting London comes from the deranged, obsessive Larry Doomer. KGB agents figure in a number of episodes. *House of Cards* and *K is for Kill* both explore the theme of enemy sleepers, albeit in very different ways. Ironically, it is in the surreal *K is for Kill* that we experience the first ever *Avengers* episode where a real fear is created, in terms of how quickly a Cold War might develop into a global conflict. The massed bodies covered by sheets in a church effectively convey the sense of the casualties of warfare, while there is a fascinating, dramatic tension built up between the blindly patriotic and fatalistic Colonel Stanislav and both the Kremlin's Kerov and Ambassador Toy, who typify a new desire to avoid conflict:

Kerov: Times have changed, and attitudes. We have peace with our Western neighbours now.
Stanislav: Peace? A tenuous peace.
Kerov: *Détente*. It is imperative that we do not disturb the balance.

Stanislav: It was perhaps meant.

Stanislav: World War 3. It has to come, comrade. We all know that. And it is the aggressor who will win it.
Toy: No one will win a third world war. None will survive to be the victors.

If *The Cybernauts* is as near as we ever get to genuine debate about the dangers of nuclear warfare, then this French two-parter is as close as the series comes to creating a genuine atmosphere of what East/West tensions might lead to, albeit framed within an outré plot revolving around literal 'sleepers'. Not for the first time, it is a surrealist storyline which provides a darkly disturbing drama. In contrast, as JZ Ferguson comments, *House of Cards* keeps things friendly between British and Russian agents in typical *Avengers* style:

'This lack of animosity between individuals on both sides of the Iron Curtain is reminiscent of the original series, in which characters such as Brodny and *The Correct Way to Kill*'s Olga cultivated friendly relations with their British counterparts, despite the ideological divide. Steed and *House of Cards'* Olga may officially have opposing objectives, but for the most part they seem to be interested in 'keeping things friendly,' throwing the Cold War conflict into sharp relief.' (*Avengerland Regained*, p. 71)

While foreign agents coming in to England, and secrets making their way out, are at the heart of so many *Avengers* and *New Avengers* plots, far greater dangers lurk within. In addition to the aforementioned Larry Doomer, there is the aristocratic Lord Cartney with his literally explosive plans. The diabolical gang members in *Take-Over* planning to assassinate members of a peace conference are also British, as is the mastermind behind the sabotage of another peace conference in *Death's Door*. In neither case do we find out their motive. Does that matter? Possibly not; in *The Avengers*, the spectacle is the thing.

Social historians, such as Dominic Sandbrook, have suggested that the average man and woman in 1960s Britain was too caught up in the post-war wave of a booming consumer culture to actively concern themselves about Cold War issues. Rather than a 'great public concern about the international scene', evidence suggests that there was a 'great public indifference to it.'

'For all the fuss about...banning the bomb...or nuclear testing, or the madness of modern science, it ultimately turned out that to most ordinary people there were a lot of better things to worry about.' [4]

In *The Avengers*, many of the dangers posed to political/economic stability and democracy emanate from mercenaries or unstable ex-ministry scientists, rather than Russian invaders: Marlowe jamming the early warning radar system, the late Prendergast's deadly pesticide, Armstrong's vision of a Cybernetic police force. Instead of enemy agents, danger often comes in the form of advances in modern science and technology: mind-altering drugs, deadly bleepers, killer robots, or out of control duplicates. Even in the light-hearted tag scenes, the 'science of craft' can pose a threat. [5] Electric razors and toasters – rather than representing easy to use, labour-saving luxury devices – are accidents waiting to happen. A toy airplane is more dangerous than enemy agents in *Legacy of Death*. It is technological progress which we are asked to fear, not Communists. In this way, *The Avengers* seems to mirror the public's paradoxical approach to technology's advances – an obsessive interest in buying new products yet a cautionary attitude to scientific 'progress' in general. If the shadowy threat of the atom bomb is part of this caution, this has just as much to do with vague fears about mad scientists, or the presence of US atomic bombers and complete nuclear warheads in Britain, as it does about Communism.

In closing this chapter, I am going to run the risk of being fanciful with my interpretation. Of pushing the envelope a little too far, perhaps. Western 'decadence' is enjoyed by our heroes: stylish clothes, fashionable apartments, vintage/sports cars, *à la carte* dining and fountains of champagne. As Eric Cazalot comments, this is an enormous part of the show's appeal. Yet a surfeit of this same hedonism – exclusive marriage bureaus, luxury hotels, chauffeur-driven cars and health farms – can be fatal or leave you scarred. Shopping, in particular, can be *deadly* serious throughout the series: a London department store where death lurks behind Yogi bear, in the camping department, or in the basement; an aristocratic toy shop where a Jack-in-the-box can shoot you; a joke shop where hit-men hide among the dolls and dummies. It is not even safe to visit an umbrella dealer, a curio shop, a *perfumier,* a honey shop, or tie stores. What are the writers trying to tell us? That a surfeit of... Western decadence can be deadly? Perhaps *K is for Kill*'s Stanislav offers us the show's mantra, a compromise between capitalist excess and Communist austerity:

> "Excess is not pleasure. Pleasure is one degree below excess."

© Rodney Marshall

1. Some historians view the Cold War as commencing *during* World War 2. The super-powers did fight, using 'client states', the Vietnam conflict being the most infamous example. Some historians view the Cold War as a series of phases. Is it even safe to say that it is definitively over?
2. Dominic Sandbrook suggests that Britain was far less anti-Communist than the United States, partly because British

people associated it with the US, and "there were plenty of examples of cultural anti-Americanism in Britain during the late fifties and early sixties." 'The War Game', *Never Had It So Good: A History of Britain from Suez to The Beatles*, p. 233.
3. Sadly, much of the crackling debate between Armstrong and Steed was cut from the final filmed version.
4. 'The War Game', *Never Had It So Good: A History of Britain from Suez to The Beatles*, p. 275.
5. 'Science of craft' is the literal translation of 'technology' from its original Greek.

AND SOON THE DARKNESS/SEE NO EVIL: BRIAN CLEMENS' POST-*AVENGERLAND*

The 2008 *Network/Granada Ventures* DVD box set containing all six series of *Thriller* describes Brian Clemens as the '*Avengers* creator'. The same factual error has been made frequently, both before and since. In many ways Clemens encouraged the belief that he had created the series, which he began to take artistic control of in the post-videotape era. One could certainly justify the idea that the filmed *Avengerland* was a fictional world increasingly of his making. Both as script writer and editor he excelled in the creation of a genuinely menacing atmosphere. This can be seen in the initial episode *The Town of No Return*, where a disturbing *Avengerland* is created both in the unfriendly, claustrophobic pub and the agoraphobic Norfolk coastline. When much of the series' sparkling champagne humour is taken out, as is the case in *The House That Jack Built*, the result is an effectively chilling, subversive spectacle. Equally unsettling are his colour episodes *The Joker*, *Murdersville*, *Pandora* and *Requiem*. The (surreal) sense of stricture and confinement, which Clemens creates in picture-postcard villages and 'country house traps', would play a significant role in many of his ITC *Thriller* episodes. At times in both series there is a sadistically unpleasant aspect at play, and this would be a prominent feature in his early 1970s films: *And Soon the Darkness* (1970) and *Blind Terror/See No Evil* (1971). In many ways, these two represent a crossroads in Clemens' career as he moved from the tongue-in-cheek, playfully artificial candy-coloured world of *The Avengers* towards a straighter world of drama. One could argue that these two movies represent a post-*Avengerland*.

Dominic Sandbrook and Robert Sellers are just two of the cultural critics to emphasise the general movement away from the escapist adventure series of the 1960s towards the more realist drama of the early to mid-1970s. Sandbrook suggests that 'the popular mood had changed...Gritty authenticity was the order of the day.' [1] Sellers agrees, stating that 'escapist fare...was slowly becoming *passé*, as modern TV audiences demanded greater realism.' [2] Both writers suggest that it was viewers' changing appetites driving the changes, rather than television re-shaping audience expectations. I'm not so sure.

In February and March 1969, the last ever *Avengers* episode, *Bizarre*, was being filmed. Written by Brian Clemens, it brought the final curtain down on the ground-breaking, constantly evolving series in fittingly surreal style. Weeks later, filming began on *And Soon the Darkness*, with the movie being released the following year in the UK. [3] It was made by a production team familiar to *Avengers* fans: writers Brian Clemens and Terry Nation had contributed fourteen of the Tara King season scripts [4]; Robert Fuest – whose set designs helped shape the Keel/Steed season – had directed seven of the Season 6 episodes; Laurie Johnson created music for each *Avengers* filmed season; producers Clemens and Albert Fennell were *Avengers* veterans/legends.

Reviews both at the time and since have been mixed. The London-based *Time Out* described it as an 'unappealing women-in-danger thriller... Predictable, implausible, and not a little nasty.' [5] By contrast, *Brit Movie*'s Drewe Shimon describes it as 'one of the scariest, most suspenseful films of all time...pretty much perfect...a masterclass in British horror and suspense.' [6] Caught between these extremes, *Halliwell's Guide* offers praise for its 'style' but criticises it for being 'slow, overstretched, often risible...and short on humour.' [7] In commercial terms, it was a minor box office success.

I can see why some critics dislike it, yet I also share much of Shimon's admiration. The film draws on Clemens' disturbing, deserted vision of *Avengerland* and Shimon understandably praises the film for its reversal of the usual visual horror clichés of fog and/or darkness. It effectively conveys 'at once a sense of tranquil beauty AND an undercurrent of brooding menace.' [8] The blinding sunlight creates an effective atmosphere – Shimon suggests that Clemens and Fuest were unconsciously creating a new sub-genre for British thriller films: 'sun-kissed horror' – and the flat Loire terrain increases the sense of a deserted, beautifully bleak landscape. The film does, however, ask the viewer to wait a long time for the tension to build, as would be the case in *Blind Terror/ See No Evil*. In both films this turns out to be justified. However, there is an arguably unpleasant, sadistic edge to the spectacle, present in some of Clemens' *Avengers* scripts, including *Murdersville* and the Clemens/Nation offering *Take-Over*. When quirkiness is devoid of humour it can make for difficult viewing. This would sometimes be the case in *Thriller*.

The publicity poster for the film draws ambitious connections with the master of suspense: 'Remember the way Hitchcock kept you on the edge of your seat...?' The images cheat us on a number of levels: a young woman lying on the ground with a foregrounded bicycle wheel; a girl's image reflected in a man's sunglasses. We are tempted to presume that the girl is dead, that the man is a killer. Even the title plays with our expectations: the only darkness in the film is a moral one.

The opening images provide us with an idyllic picture: summertime, with a straight country road bordered by an avenue of trees, the upbeat, guitar-dominated score suggesting a carefree holiday for the two young women seen cycling along. The post-titles scene on the *terrasse* of a busy *auberge* – which is described as "dangling", if not "swinging", by

Cathy – is at odds with the rest of the film, which takes place against the backdrop of a deserted *la France profonde*, the French equivalent of the sparsely populated Outback. An immediate, stereotypical contrast is set up between the two young English nurses: serious, map-reading (virginal) Jane, determined to cycle as far as possible, and the playful (sexually-awake) Cathy who is intent on men-gazing and who stares at a sultry Frenchman (Paul) while pretending to photograph her friend. The contrast between the two women makes us wonder why they have come on holiday together, one mesmerised by the "fantastic" deserted landscape, the other finding it "fantastically boring." Laurie Johnson's score, as they cycle into the back of beyond, suggests an edgy tension, particularly once the scooter-driving Paul has overtaken them. The sight of him standing in front of a cemetery, staring at them, seems more stylishly absurd than sinister, although the cameraman is caught in the sunglasses' lenses which is surely an unfortunate oversight rather than a self-referential touch. The gravestone of a young blonde woman, Jan Hele, offers an early warning that this will not be a bucolic idyll. The French spoken by passing cyclists, villagers and on the radio adds a sense of 'otherness', part of a growing feeling that Jane and Cathy are outside their comfort zone, don't belong here and are at the mercy of voyeuristic, dangerous men.

Twenty minutes in, things take on a more sinister turn once the two women fall out and split up. Jane arrives at the aptly-named *A La Mal Tournée café* – where the bar owner warns her that the road has a bad reputation – while Fuest's camerawork suggests a voyeur in the bushes as Cathy sunbathes. As Shimon suggests, the flat terrain and deserted road offer a wonderfully sinister, brooding atmosphere, the passing of the occasional vehicle or sight of a sole figure in a field providing irrational surges of fear. The spinning bicycle wheel and the sound of silence provide a deeply disturbing visual/aural experience as Fuest centres on Michele Dotrice's frightened eyes. He provides us with a lovely framing shot of Cathy through her vandalised bicycle wheel with a subtly chilling Laurie Johnson score as backdrop. The slow pace of the first twenty-five minutes now seems worthwhile as the tension crackles. We won't see Cathy alive again. Shady Paul and the suspicious behaviour of the husband of Madame Lassal – busy burning something outside their *épicerie*/bar – offer us red herrings in a film which is a twisted, perverse whodunit. Thirty-two minutes in, Sandor Eles (Paul) speaks for the first time, an example of the subtle effectiveness of the slow pace of *And Soon the Darkness*. A veteran of *Danger Man*, *The Baron*, *The Saint* and other ITC series – in addition to *The Avengers* – he was often cast in generic outsider/foreigner roles. Is he simply a charmingly mysterious stranger, or is he a chillingly calm murderer? The story plays with us, those with more than a smattering of French able to understand locals' talk of *another* murder, while others are left in the dark, as Jane is until an Englishwoman living locally explains. Such is our paranoia by this stage that even this eccentric, man-hating schoolteacher (Clare Kelly) seems a possible suspect.

There is something almost inevitable about the identity of Cathy's murderer. The old man/voyeur seen standing in the field, Jules Lassal busy burning fabric, and the evasive, flirtatious Paul all seem too obvious, unless the script is offering us a double bluff. The fact that Jane turns her back on both Madame Lassal's advice (about the policeman representing "trouble") and Paul's offer of help increases our sense of her stumbling into a trap, one which she has – ironically – sought out by going to the local *gendarme* for help. *The Avengers*' country house trap here becomes a countryside one. Paul's visceral description of Jan Hele's murder adds an unpleasant reality check:

"Severe injuries to the upper cranial cavity, extensive lacerations and abrasions to the breasts, the loins and the lower torso. Sexually assaulted. Cause of death asphyxia, through strangulation."

As Jane and Paul stare at each other from opposite sides of the country road, a passing lorry cuts through his speech, just as any lingering sense of a rural idyll in Jane's mind is shattered by his words. Pamela Franklin – who would appear twice in the *Thriller* mini-seasons – plays the part of a naïve, terrified young woman with great skill, wholly convincing in the role. As they search the piece of woodland where Cathy went missing, both Johnson's unsettling score and Fuest's handheld, jerky camerawork add to the disturbing atmosphere.

John Nettleton's *gendarme* has the greedy look of someone who cannot believe his luck when Jane comes calling, the camera focusing in on both his furtive eyes and her bare legs. There is a deeply unpleasant irony that she passes her friend's underwear over to the man who has raped and killed her – even if this is merely our suspicion for the time being. Is the local policeman's elderly, deaf father (John Franklyn) meant to add a welcome dusting of humour to the darkness? His placing of the underwear on his head – like a chef's hat – fails to amuse Jane but neither does it add a sinister note. He seems an unlikely sexual killer.

At the back of the *gendarme*'s property lies an interesting rural wasteland for the viewer: wood, metal sheets, abandoned vehicles and dilapidated outbuildings around which hens peck. It offers any number of perfect hiding places for a body. The tension mounts as we flit between the *gendarme*'s search of the woodland and Jane's exploration of the house and the courtyard. Fuest makes the most of the conventional 'cross-cutting' techniques of suspense films. Clemens and Nation's script teases us, daring us to choose the killer from the *gendarme* and Paul Salmon, yet Jane has already made her mind up about the man's identity. Despite our sense that Paul is innocent – there is charm to his shiftiness and odd explanations – dramatic tension is created in the scenes where she hides from the plain-clothes Parisian detective in the house and then flees to a derelict caravan site beyond the courtyard. This is an excellent set/location: a panorama of rusting cars, doors, tyres, buses and caravans. It is the perfect playground for Fuest's direction, allowing him to experiment: shooting with a dripping tap foregrounded, through a broken caravan window, from the inside of a filthy windscreen, through wooden vents, etc. [9] The camerawork draws on Peter Hammond's in-house *Avengers* techniques. As Paul searches each vehicle, there is a delightful quirkiness about every detail and prop – such as the abandoned Porte d'Orleans-Massy bus timetable sign – rusting remnants from a vanished age and as out of place as the young women are. Johnson's almost Hitchcock-esque violin score adds further layers to the tense finale in this memorable location. Jane's discovery of Cathy's body while hiding from Paul in a caravan wardrobe is the unexpectedly chilling highlight as the script continues to surprise us. This certainly is the case when we first encounter on-screen violence as Jane repeatedly smashes a rock into Paul's face. It is not just the act itself which shocks us but its contrast with the almost static, brooding nature of the first hour and the crackling tension of the thirty minutes which followed. With her only possible ally unconscious and her bloody weapon tossed away, it is the fitting moment for her to run into the arms of the *gendarme*.

It is here that the film arguably becomes unnecessarily nasty, as his reassuring embrace becomes sexual and violent, the hand making its way down her back to her buttock. The frenzied attack is mirrored by Fuest's shooting of it as we are bombarded by a myriad of camera angles, from below, above, zooming in on her bared back and blurring his monstrous expression. There is an animalistic hunger as the *gendarme* unbuckles her belt and an almost voyeuristic, intrusive element to the direction. Far more subtle is the relief of the predicted rain as it patters onto the caravan skylight through which we can see Cathy's body. *And Soon the Darkness* ends with the same straight country road, two young cyclists making their way along it to the same score as the opening, only now the previously sunlit landscape is scarred by heavy rain.

Clemens, Nation, Fuest and Johnson created a brooding, disturbing, highly effective thriller with *And Soon the Darkness*. Unsurprisingly, it draws on the darker edges and aspects of *Avengerland:* odd characters, a deserted landscape, playful direction, and an unsettling score. Clemens and Johnson would join forces again on *Thriller* soon after, and this film represents a halfway point in the former's move away from the champagne sparkle of *The Avengers* towards a straighter subversion.

****

Like *And Soon the Darkness*, critical reaction to *Blind Terror* – titled *See No Evil* in the United States – was mixed. Roger Greenspun of the *New York Times* offers (faint) praise for the film's thriller aspect: 'cheap thrills, to be sure, but thrills none the less', but is highly critical of its class conflict sub-plot, suggesting that the film is at its best when it attempts to 'crank up the terror' rather than attempting 'to mean something.' [10] Jerry Renninger praises the film as offering 'peerless' suspense in the style of Alfred Hitchcock, going as far as to suggest that the old master would struggle to do better. However, he does suggest that the film is uncomfortably sadistic. [11] More recently, Charles Derry has bemoaned the fact that Mia Farrow – the 'archetypal waif/victim' of

Rosemary's Baby – 'becomes from the first moment of *See No Evil*, the obvious victim':

'Before Richard Fleischer even begins his conventional suspense constructions, we just know that before the movie is over, Farrow is going to undergo a horrific ordeal that we shall vicariously share.' [12]

Most critics praised Mia Farrow's performance in the lead role and her box office presence guaranteed the financial backing of Columbia Pictures. While *And Soon the Darkness* lacked a well-known actress in the main role, the two films share plenty of common ground. Undoubtedly effective in terms of suspense, slow burners in terms of action, making ironic use of rural idylls as backdrops, both have something unmistakably unpleasant at their core. The publicity poster hints at the way in which Clemens' story draws on Sarah's blindness in an arguably sadistic and exploitative manner. Underneath a picture of the bottom half of the killer standing over a young woman's bed: 'Keep your eyes on what she cannot see.' Clemens would re-use the blind victim who has to 'see' plot again in *The Eyes Have It*. Both *See No Evil* and the *Thriller* episode draw on *The Avengers*' iconic episode *Take-Over*.

The opening image of the film lacks any subtlety as the camera focuses on a double horror billing at a local cinema:

THE CONVENT MURDERS x
&
RAPIST CULT x

As we zoom in on the cowboy boots of a 'faceless' man – in the first of an unremitting series of low-level shots – one wonders if Clemens is asking us to make an immediate connection between violence in popular culture and in the real world. Can the consumption of these images make 'normal' people 'sick'? Or is an obsession with this type of film simply part of a warped individual's depravity? Alternatively, is it harmless, escapist entertainment? It is a timeless debate with no clear-cut answer. What is certain is that there is a self-referentiality at play here: a horror/suspense film opening with people leaving a similar spectacle; the writer asking us whether the product he has created and which we have bought into is morally acceptable. The Western-style score suits the boots but is at odds with the wet, Home Counties high street along which the man walks. Richard Fleischer offers us further images to digest as the figure passes lit, closed shops. The first is a toy shop with soldiers, tanks and guns:

>TRIGGER ACTION TOMMY GUN
>REALISTIC SOUND
>NO WIND UP
>NO BATTERIES
>PULL THE TRIGGER

A book store displays teenage magazine covers featuring war, armed men and scantily clad female victims, while 'real' newspaper headlines reinforce this culture of violence:

>'MACHINE-GUNS BLAZE IN JAIL RIOT BATTLE'
>'MASSACRE OF THE CHILDREN'

A television shop offers images of angry men and a woman screaming. The message is loud and clear, as is the bombastic score, but Greenspun is correct in suggesting that the film subsequently fails to do anything with the deeper layers it seems to be offering us. *See No Evil* is a thriller/suspense/horror film and there is little mileage to be had from looking for depth, either in terms of a critique of the violence at the heart of our Western society or the later suggestion of class conflict. Clemens' film is there to scare us: a frightening whodunit, rather than something more profound. This is demonstrated by the fact that we are never given a reason for why the man chooses to kill the Rexton family. Jealousy? A feud? Money? It simply isn't crucial to the writer's project. What interests Clemens is taking his *Avengers* fascination with 'thriller stricture' and transporting it on to the big screen.

Our first sight of Sarah – at night-time as she arrives at the railway station – is from the cowboy's viewpoint. There is a nice contrast between the foggy, modest-sized suburban train station and the splendour of the Rexton estate with its formal entrance, drive and quadruple frontage mansion. It seems to offer the perfect safety-net for the recently blinded Sarah, but – in typical Clemens fashion – will soon be transformed into the sort of country house trap he effectively reworked many times on *The Avengers*. If *And Soon the Darkness* disturbs us with its agoraphobic, deserted landscape, then here the Rexton home will become a claustrophobic maze for someone still coming to terms with her loss of sight. The film's DVD publicity made much of this:

'IN A WORLD OF DARKNESS, EVIL CAN HIDE ANYWHERE.'

Mia Farrow is instantly believable as a young woman who has lost her sight but is determined to live as normal and independent a life as possible. Robin Bailey and Dorothy Alison are perfectly cast as the kind, caring and reassuring aunt and uncle, although it seems odd that Sarah's parents are never mentioned. Norman Eshley offers a workman-like performance as a young man whose love for Sarah has not been changed by her circumstances. The slow pace of the opening third of the film suits the mood, offering us a genuine insight into the various characters, including how each is coming to terms with Sarah's new, blind world which she herself describes as "bloody awful" without any hint of self-pity. We need time to invest in these people and Clemens provides us with it, a perfect example of the advantages of feature film as opposed to television episode. Given the (unsubtle) pre-release publicity, both cinema and, later, television audiences knew that the Rexton family would be massacred and the three-dimensional portrayal of the main characters allow us to emotionally connect with these decent people. NBC's 'Monday Night at the Movies' publicity spells out the bloodbath scenario:

> "One of the most frightening
> movies ever made.
> Four people are in the house
> with Sarah. Three are dead.
> One is a homicidal maniac.
> And Sarah is blind."

This is inaccurate [13] but it typifies the fact that viewers are forewarned — by cinema posters, TV advertising and DVD blurb — about the mass murders. This film is a whodunit and 'will she escape?' thriller, with Sarah's blindness at the core of the suspense.

The slow but inevitable build-up to the murders is effectively handled by both Clemens and Fleischer. The cowboy's scratching of George's car not only offers us a chilling pre-echo of the physical and emotional scars he will soon leave but even leads to a welcome lighter touch when Sarah's uncle immediately regrets suggesting that she should *see* the damage: "Life's going to get difficult, Uncle George, if you try to eliminate the verb 'to see' from your vocabulary." Farrow plays these witty moments as well as she does the dramatic ones, offering us a portrait of someone who looks like a tom-boyish teenager but who has an older, wiser head.

Before the murders take place, no obvious suspect is rolled out. While the low-level images of the cowboy boots become irritating some of the time, they are a necessary device for maintaining the mysterious menace and keeping us 'blind' or metaphorically in the dark.

The arrival of the star-patterned boots at the Rexton's front porch is effectively underplayed. The last thing we see each family member do is routinely mundane: Sandy reading a magazine, her father shaving before going out, Betty tidying up some newspapers before answering the door. The brutal murders take place off-camera and we will not encounter any of the bodies until long after Sarah's return from riding. For the time being, we see no evil. (In the immediate aftermath, Jacko, a young traveller, is seen lurking outside the Rexton house but this is clearly a red herring; why go to all the effort of masking the killer's identity only to expose it straight after?)

Fleischer draws our attention to a bracelet on the floor on Sarah's return. It is the first in a series of details which lead/build up to the discovery of the bodies: an open bedroom window, an abandoned lawn mower, shards of broken glass on the kitchen floor, Barker's boots in the stables... It is this attention to detail which makes the atmosphere almost tangible: the sight and sound of an empty gun cartridge rolling across the stable yard amidst the autumnal leaves, further shots of Barker's empty boots and the bracelet in the hallway, a door creaking in the evening wind.

With the house now in semi-darkness, the grim reality is gradually revealed, beginning with Sandy lying dead on her bed, a trail of blood from her mouth leading to the bedcovers. The following morning, Sarah's search for the object (the bracelet) she has kicked across the floor leads to our discovery of Betty's bloodstained corpse in a living room chair; her running of the bath reveals George's body. Sarah's obliviousness to the events which are displayed to us adds a surreal quality to the spectacle as we await the killer's inevitable return. The unexpected arrival of Steve postpones her discovery of the bodies, adding to the playfully macabre spectacle as we see bloody water making its way out of the drainpipe. It is artfully written and cleverly directed but there is something disturbingly dark about its playfulness.

See No Evil mirrors *And Soon the Darkness* in its ironic contrast between the beauty of the landscape and the dreadful events taking place. Here, rather than the sunlit summer of the French countryside, we have the autumnal colours of an *Avengerland* Middle England which – we sense – Sarah enjoys both through her memories and the sensations of her ride: birdsong, the sun on her face... The fact that we know what is already waiting for her back at home and who will undoubtedly come stalking undermines any enjoyment which the seasonal majesty could offer us. With hindsight, it also provides a stark contrast to the nightmare ride she will undertake later on. It is stylishly shot, through trees, branches and with multi-coloured leaves whirling around. The writer might have argued that this love story sub-plot offers us something wholesome and positive amidst the moral darkness.

Forty-eight minutes in, Sarah's discovery of George and Sandy's bodies works on a number of levels: first, it brings her almost up to date with us; secondly, it creates a dramatic, literal layer of blind fear. The objects she has previously so carefully made her way around now become hard edges she crashes into. Fleischer's cross-cutting allows us to see that the killer, too, is panicking: his fevered actions as he scrubs his boots and hides his bloodied shirt offer a fascinating mirror scene to Sarah's, reaching a climax as he washes his hands and realises that his bracelet is missing... It is a clever touch that when Sarah runs into an intruder it is not the killer – as she/we expect – but a dying Barker. This increases the dramatic tension as he warns her about the bracelet and keeps us waiting for the inevitable arrival of the intruder.

It is Sarah's prolonged agony in the final third of the film which is, arguably, overly sadistic on the part of both the writer and director. A character who is still coming to terms with her own blindness, who has just discovered a house full of murdered relatives, is now expected to run a gauntlet of physical, mental and psychological torture. To make matters worse, this is sustained over the entire thirty minutes remaining, broken into various sections and hurdles: the country house trap, her cross-country ride and walk, locked up in a quarry shed and, finally, almost drowned in the bath. It is almost as if – having kept the confrontation on hold for so long – Clemens feels the need to extend her trial. The barriers placed in her way in the Rexton house range from the clichéd – the cut telephone line – through the forewarned – the glass shards – to the unfortunate – the dead body of Barker blocking an exit. The glass stuck in the sole of her bare foot is particularly unpleasant and pushes the film towards a visceral form of punishment for both the character and the viewer. Fleischer's attention to detail – the blooded shard foregrounded as the killer hunts, the low-level shots of his boots in the stable block as Sarah hides – are to be admired but once she is knocked off her horse in the leafy woodland there is a growing sense of the writer and director cranking up the terror for as long as possible. It is, perhaps, the combination of her blindness – making her the ultimate pretty young female victim – the prolongation of the nightmare and the fact that three times she is seemingly freed from danger, only to face further misadventures, which makes the final thirty minutes difficult to watch. Having escaped from the killer, she is knocked off her horse; having been rescued from the labyrinthine wood by the travelers, she is imprisoned by Gypsy Jack; discovered by Steve in the clay pit, she is left to face the bathroom ordeal alone.

This is, for some viewers and critics, at least one too many waves of assault, and I tend to agree that the final attack is overkill on the part of Clemens. The twist of two men sharing the name on the bracelet – JACKO – works well but one has to ask whether it was dramatically necessary to have Farrow's character strip naked (off camera) in front of a lurking, hungry voyeur before suffering her bath ordeal. Perhaps by finding his bracelet, Paul Nicholas' character is hoping to avoid a fifth murder. Beautiful, blind and now bare... it is a step too far. As Fuest had done with the *gendarme*'s attack on Jane, here Fleischer's handheld camerawork offers a myriad of angles from low level, to below the waterline, to looking down from the killer's viewpoint, faces coming in and out of focus just as Sarah's is pushed under the surface repeatedly. It is superbly shot but deeply unpleasant; Steve's arrival just in time – like Paul's in the previous film – fails to lift our spirits. The final images sees the corpses taken away in ambulances while a crowd of onlookers stare through the Rexton gates. Like the viewer, they have a morbid fascination in the macabre.

See No Evil is an effective thriller. Like *And Soon the Darkness* it creates a chilling atmosphere, makes full use of interesting locations, while employing innovative direction. I would argue that both films contain a hollow core and a sadistic flourish which would resurface in *Thriller*. However, despite my personal reservations, both the films contain a host of memorable, effective scenes and images as Hitchcock and *Avengerland* merge. They are part of Brian Clemens' remarkably extensive legacy. For *Avengers* fans, the films offer a fascinating insight into what the 'creator' could achieve when freed from the time and budget restraints which are part and parcel of a television series. For

Avengers fans left disappointed by the loss of their show, Clemens' post-*Avengerland* is a fascinating, disturbing cinematic spectacle.

© Rodney Marshall

1. Dominic Sandbrook, *Seasons in the Sun*, p. 395.
2. Robert Sellers, 'The Ultimate Variety Show', *Cult TV*, p. 233.
3. The film was released on 10th September 1970.
4. Clemens rewrote a number of Nation scripts while Nation wrote some scripts from original Clemens ideas. No writer created as many *Avengers* scripts as Clemens.
5. www.timeout.com/london/film/and-soon-the-darkness
6. www.britmovie.co.uk/2010/10/14/and-soon-the-darkness-1970/
7. *Halliwell's Film Guide* 2007, p. 41.
8. www.britmovie.co.uk
9. He would bring some of this wonderful quirkiness to his filming of *The New Avengers* a few years later.
10. *New York Times/The Calgary Herald*, 11/09/1971.
11. *The Palm Beach Post*, 11/10/1971.
12. Charles Derry, 'The Spectator Takes in a Breath', *The Suspense Thriller: Films in the Shadow of Alfred Hitchcock*, p. 35.
13. By the time the killer returns – to find his bracelet – the gardener has returned to the house and dies in front of Sarah.

CONTRIBUTORS

Raymond Austin, aka Ray Austin, was a stunt performer, stunt co-ordinator and director during his time on *The Avengers*. He went on to direct episodes for a number of cult British shows, including *The Saint, The Baron, The Champions, Department S, Randall and Hopkirk (Deceased)*, and *The Professionals*, before directing episodes for US shows *Hawaii-Five-O, Hart to Hart, Quincy, M.E.*, and *Magnum, P.I.* (and many other prime time network shows and pilots). He has also written a number of television episodes and books. He has contributed the essay ***Avengers* Remembered**.

Darren Burch became a fan of *The Avengers* through the 1980s Channel 4 repeats. "Aside from Laurie Johnson's wonderful music, I was captivated by the show's distinctive aesthetic." He lives in East Sussex. His interests include Cult '60s TV, composing music, photography, graphic design, swimming, cycling and nutrition. He has contributed the chapters on **Set Design and Locations** and **Directing *The Avengers***.

Eric Cazalot lives in Paris. Television scriptwriter, novelist and biographer, he published a book about *The Avengers* in 1994, *Disrespectfully Yours*. His latest book was published in November 2015, written with and about the famous singer Sylvie Vartan. He has written the chapter **Miss King, You're Needed! or Hedonism & Leather Boots: *The Avengers*' success in France**.

J.Z. Ferguson is interested in all aspects of British and Canadian popular culture, but has a particular love for television. She resides in her native Canada, where she pursues her interest in an eclectic array of subjects. She has contributed the **Foreword** on the 'timeless appeal' of *The Avengers*, in addition to the chapters on **Main Titles Sequences**, **Music**, **Purdey** and **Mike Gambit**.

Margaret J Gordon MD is a physician residing in the US. She is a fan of British humour, particularly the witty repartee in *The Avengers*. She enjoys 1960s spy series, her favourite being *The Avengers*, and her favourite role model is Emma Peel. She has contributed the chapter on **Eccentrics**.

Alan Hayes has been a fan of *The Avengers* since 1976 (Steed, Purdey and Gambit variety), but didn't fully realise what that meant until the 1982 Channel 4 repeats of the original series! He lives in St Albans, where *The Morning After* was filmed. His interests include archive television (including *Public Eye*, *The Prisoner* and *Doctor Who*), the films of Alfred Hitchcock and Woody Allen, writing and sports. He has co-written two books with Richard McGinlay about Series 1 of *The Avengers*, now compiled as *Two Against the Underworld*. He and Richard have also collaborated on another book, *Dr. Brent's Casebook*, about *Police Surgeon*. Both books are available from the website www.hiddentigerbooks.co.uk. He has contributed the chapter on **Patrick Macnee**.

Frank Hui is a molecular biologist in Austin, Texas. His interests include comic books and photography. He has been a fan of *The Avengers* since the early 1970s. For six years he curated the film and programming schedule for the Austin Gay and Lesbian International Film Festival, and he is the business manager for the fashion brand *Elrick*. He has contributed chapters on **Tara King** and **Fashions**.

Lauren Humphries-Brooks is a writer and media journalist. She holds a Master's degree in Cinema Studies from New York University, and in Creative Writing from the University of Edinburgh. She regularly contributes to film and pop culture websites, and has written extensively on Classical Hollywood, British horror films, and the sci-fi, fantasy, and horror genres. She has written the chapter **Silk and Steel: The Personalities of John Steed**.

Piers Johnson was born in England but has spent almost his entire life in Australia. He holds degrees in History and Computing Science and lives in Sydney with his wife and three children where he builds websites. His

Mrs Peel, We're Needed! site has been constantly updated since 1993. He has contributed the chapters on **Tag scenes**, **cars** and **Mother**.

Rodney Marshall is a teacher and writer in Suffolk, UK and Poitou-Charentes, France. He has written a number of books about *The Avengers,* as well as editing *The Avengers on film* series. He has also written critical guides to Ian Rankin's *Rebus* novels, *Blake's 7*, *Travelling Man* and *Man in a Suitcase*. He has contributed the **Preface**, in addition to chapters on **Television, *The Avengers*, & Cultural Revolution;** ***The Avengers* & the Cold War; Graveyards; Country House Traps; Subversive Champagne & The Art of Murder; Teasers; Script-writers; *The New Avengers'* Sets and Locations; *And Soon the Darkness/See No Evil*: Brian Clemens' post-*Avengerland*;** and the **Afterword**.

Roger Marshall has enjoyed a long, distinguished career as a television and film scriptwriter. He created the private detective series *Public Eye*, writing twenty-one of the episodes. He created/wrote *Zodiac, Missing From Home, Mitch, Travelling Man* and *Floodtide*. He provided scripts for *Emergency-Ward 10, No Hiding Place, Redcap, Shadows of Fear, Survivors, Van der Valk, The Sweeney, The Gentle Touch, The Professionals, Dempsey and Makepeace* and *Lovejoy*, among many others. His films include the critically-acclaimed science fiction-based *Invasion* (1966), and the horror film *And Now the Screaming Starts* (1973), starring Peter Cushing and directed by Roy Ward Baker. He worked on *The Avengers* from the videotape era until the colour Emma Peel season, penning fifteen episodes, fourteen of which carry his name. His *The Hour That Never Was* remains arguably the series' most iconic 'film'. His favourite *Avengers* vintages are the late-Gale and early-Peel periods; his favourite scripts are *Mandrake, Dial A Deadly Number* and *The Hour That Never Was*. He has contributed an **Insider's View**.

Dan O'Shea, after spending 35 years in the corporate world, has retired along with his wife to live on a ranch in Arkansas, USA, and raises Arabian horses. He first saw an *Avengers* episode (*Murdersville*) when he was in college and has been hooked on *The Avengers* ever since. He has contributed a chapter on **The Avengers and the Cold War**.

James Speirs is a retired researcher and writer, living in the North East of England. His interests include graphic art, theatre and cinema, most notably the films of Alfred Hitchcock. A fan of Newcastle United FC, his passion for *The Avengers* stems from "the show's acting, inspired, thrilling story lines and Diana Rigg's cat-suits!" He has contributed a chapter entitled **Hand of the Wind: For Queen and Country - Martial Arts in *The Avengers***.

Sunday Swift recently completed her doctorate at Lancaster University, UK. Her area of research focused on masculinity and Dandyism in contemporary British and American television. Additional areas of research include: Fashion, Popular culture, Television of Britain and North America from 1960-1990, Irish Gothic literature, Cinema, and Contemporary Gothic television. She has contributed a chapter on **Emma Peel**.

Jaz Wiseman is an *Avengers* stalwart. His work on the Optimum/Canal digitally-restored DVD collection – in particular his moderated commentaries with key *Avengers* writers, directors, cast and crew – has ensured that the series' history has been retrieved, captured, protected and attractively packaged for future generations. He has contributed the **cover design**.

BIBLIOGRAPHY OF WORKS CONSULTED

The Avengers: Digitally Restored Special Edition: The Complete Series 2 (Optimum Classic/Studio Canal, 2010)

The Avengers: Digitally Restored Special Edition: The Complete Series 3 (Optimum Classic/Studio Canal, 2010)

The Avengers: Digitally Restored Special Edition: The Complete Series 4 (Optimum Classic/Studio Canal, 2010)

The Avengers: Digitally Restored Special Edition: The Complete Series 5 (Optimum Classic/Studio Canal, 2010)

The Avengers: Digitally Restored Special Edition: The Complete Series 6 (Optimum Classic/Studio Canal, 2010)

The New Avengers/Chapeau Melon et Bottes de Cuir Season 1 1976 (Studio Canal, 2004)

The New Avengers/Chapeau Melon et Bottes de Cuir Season 2 1977 (Studio Canal, 2004)

The Avengers Dossier: The Definitive Unauthorised Guide (Paul Cornell, Martin Day and Keith Topping, Virgin: 1998)

The Avengers: A Celebration (Marcus Hearn, Titan Books/Studio Canal, 2010)

Subversive Champagne: Beyond Genre in The Avengers: the Emma Peel Era (Rodney Marshall, Amazon, 2013, 2014)

Adventure & Comic Strip: Exploring Tara King's The Avengers (Rodney Marshall, Amazon, 2013)

Making It New? A Reappraisal of The New Avengers (Rodney Marshall, Amazon, 2013)

Bright Horizons: The Monochrome World of Emma Peel: The Avengers on film Volume 1 (Amazon, 2014)

Mrs. Peel, We're Needed: The Technicolor World of Emma Peel: The Avengers on film Volume 2 (Amazon, 2014)

Anticlockwise: The Psychedelic World of Tara King: The Avengers on film Volume 3 (Amazon, 2014)

Avengerland Regained: A Reappraisal of The New Avengers: The Avengers on film Volume 4 (Amazon, 2015)

Avengerland Revisited: A Thematic Guide: The Avengers on film Volume 5 (Amazon, 2015)

The Strange Case of the Missing Episodes: The Lost Stories of The Avengers Series 1 (Richard McGinlay, Alan Hayes & Alys Hayes, Hidden Tiger, 2013)

Two Against the Underworld: the Collected Unauthorised Guide to The Avengers Series 1 (Alan Hayes, Richard McGinlay & Alys Hayes, Hidden Tiger, 2015)

Bowler Hats and Kinky Boots: The Unofficial and Unauthorised Guide to The Avengers (Michael Richardson, Telos, 2014)

Never Had It So Good: A History of Britain from Suez to The Beatles (Dominic Sandbrook, Abacus, 2006)

White Heat: A History of Britain in the Swinging Sixties (Dominic Sandbrook, Abacus, 2007)

The New Look: A Social History of the Forties and Fifties (Harry Hopkins, Houghton Mifflin, 1964)

The Avengers Forever! (David K Smith, copyright 1996-2008) theavengers.tv/forever

Le Monde des Avengers (theavengers.fr)

Mrs. Peel – We're Needed! The Avengers 1961-1977 (Piers Johnson) dissolute.com.au/the-avengers-tv-series/

Critical feedback is always welcome and can be directly addressed to me at:
    rodneymarshall628@btinternet.com

109 REASONS TO BE CHEERFUL

The Town of No Return
The Murder Market
The Master Minds
Dial A Deadly Number
Death at Bargain Prices
Too Many Christmas Trees
The Cybernauts
The Gravediggers
Room Without A View
A Surfeit of H$_2$0
Two's a Crowd
Man-Eater of Surrey Green
Silent Dust
The Hour That Never Was
Castle De'ath
The Thirteenth Hole
Small Game for Big Hunters
The Girl From Auntie
Quick-Quick Slow Death
The Danger Makers
A Touch of Brimstone
What the Butler Saw
The House That Jack Built
A Sense of History
How to Succeed...At Murder
Honey for the Prince

109 REASONS TO BE CHEERFUL

The Fear Merchants
Escape in Time
The Bird Who Knew Too Much
From Venus with Love
The See-Through Man
The Winged Avenger
The Living Dead
The Hidden Tiger
The Correct Way To Kill
Never, Never Say Die
Epic
The Superlative Seven
A Funny Thing Happened on the Way to the Station
Something Nasty in the Nursery
The Joker
Who's Who???
Death's Door
Return of the Cybernauts
Dead Man's Treasure
The £50,000 Breakfast
You Have Just Been Murdered
Murdersville
The Positive-Negative Man
Mission...Highly Improbable

109 REASONS TO BE CHEERFUL

The Invasion of the Earthmen
The Curious Case of the Countless Clues
The Forget-Me-Knot
Split!
Get- A-Way!
Have Guns – Will Haggle
Look – (stop me if you've heard this one) But There Were These Two
My Wildest Dream
Whoever Shot Poor George Oblique Stroke XR40?
All Done With Mirrors
You'll Catch Your Death
Super Secret Cypher Snatch
Game
False Witness
Noon Doomsday
Legacy of Death
They Keep Killing Steed
Wish You Were Here
Killer
The Rotters
The Interrogators
The Morning After
Love All
Take Me To Your Leader
Stay Tuned
Fog
Who Was That Man I Saw You With?
Pandora
Thingumajig
Homicide and Old Lace
Requiem
Take-Over
Bizarre

109 REASONS TO BE CHEERFUL

The Eagle's Nest
The Midas Touch
House of Cards
The Last of the Cybernauts...??
To Catch A Rat
Cat Amongst the Pigeons
Target!
Faces
The Tale of the Big Why
Three Handed Game
Sleeper
Gnaws
Dirtier by the Dozen
Hostage
Trap
Dead Men Are Dangerous
Medium Rare
Angels of Death
Obsession
The Lion and the Unicorn
K is for Kill: The Tiger Awakes
K is for Kill: Tiger by the Tail
Complex
The Gladiators
Forward Base
Emily

THE AVENGERS ON FILM

A FIVE VOLUME SERIES

- **BRIGHT HORIZONS**: THE MONONCHROME WORLD OF EMMA PEEL
- **MRS PEEL, WE'RE NEEDED**: THE TECHNICOLOR WORLD OF EMMA PEEL
- **ANTICLOCKWISE**: THE PSYCHEDELIC WORLD OF TARA KING
- **AVENGERLAND REGAINED**: REASSESSING *THE NEW AVENGERS*
- **AVENGERLAND REVISITED**: A DEFINITIVE GUIDE TO *THE AVENGERS*

"These are the sorts of books about the series that I have been longing for for years, especially for the Tara King and *New Avengers* eras, which have never garnered as much attention. They fill a previously-neglected niche for the show, and to have the opportunity to be involved in them has been quite a treat. They are a wonderful way to celebrate an amazing series." (JZ Ferguson)

Made in United States
North Haven, CT
02 July 2023